A Distant Belonging

A Distant Belonging

Tony Chapelle

A Distant Belonging published by Rangitawa Publishing,
Feilding, New Zealand 2017.

ISBN 978-09941490-3-9
www.rangitawapublishing.com
rangitawa@xtra.co.nz

Text and cover design by Marolyn Krasner

Also by Tony Chapelle, and published by Rangitawa Publishing:

Original Sin and Other Stories, 2015

Merely a Girl, 2016

The Youngest Son, 2016

Reviews and comments on other books by Tony Chapelle:

Original Sin:

Joan Curry on Flaxroots: *What a treat! … This is a fine collection… that can hardly fail to entertain, by a man with a deft way with words.*

John Ross in The Tribune: *These are high quality stories.*

Catherine Robertson in The New Zealand Listener: *Chapelle evokes place very well, the characters and their voices are convincing, and a prickly, ever-present tension keeps the reader on alert.*

Azariah Alfante on NZ Booklovers: *Reading Chapelle's diverse assemblage of captivating short stories was a pleasurable treat. To describe the whole collection with a string of adjectives won't do. Simply read the book yourself, again and again.*

'Vivenne' on Amazon: *This book deserves to be on the reading list for all lovers of the short story genre.*

Merely a Girl:

Novelist Maurice Gee: *"It's a marvellous feat of literary ventriloquism… [The heroine] is tough, energetic, frustrated, vulnerable – and not always admirable. A thoroughly believable young woman. I loved her and loved the book.*

Carolyn McKenzie on Flaxroots: *Like an artist, Chapelle presents a subtle portrait of genteel rural society in the mid 1800's.*

Carolyn McCurdie in Takahe 87: *[S]trong, complex characters… [I] thoroughly recommend Merely a Girl… It begs a sequel.*

Peter Beatson, co-founder of the Dianne and Peter Beatson Fellowship: *[T]he more I steep myself in [Chapelle's] elegant but powerful prose, in [his] emotionally complex characters and… perturbing but understated moral and social themes, the more impressed I become.*

The Youngest Son:

Novelist Maurice Gee: *I read [the book] with a lot of enjoyment. It's a good strong novel full of entertaining things. I like the variety… and the feeling one gets of authenticity… [it goes] into places the poor old Victorian novelist was locked out of.*

Carolyn McCurdie in Takahe 89: *Chapelle skilfully captures the voices and attitudes of the time… this is a world of brutal realities. The novel provides a wonderful contrast between the outward orderliness of respectable society and the underlying economic and social changes.*

Carolyn McKenzie on Flaxroots: *Chapelle's evocative word-painting is pervaded by hardship, violence and sorrow… with deft skill [he] has built a network of characters whose lives collide, shy away from each other and interact again… I'm looking forward to how Chapelle will carry this story forward in his next book.*

Novelist, Scriptwriter and Critic, Sue McCauley: *I think I like it even better than Merely a Girl.*

Acknowledgements:

In the course of writing this book, three people in particular have provided me with vital friendship, belief and advice. They are Sue, Peter, and Marolyn, and I am profoundly grateful for, and humbled by, their unstinting support.

Credit and thanks to Paula Clare King for the photography.

I also give thanks to my two little granddaughters, Rhiannon and Farran, who did their best to distract me but instead, though unwittingly, provided me with ample purpose.

As ever, I am indebted to my publisher, Jill Darragh, for her patience and advice.

Although there is occasional passing reference to actual historical figures, the characters in this novel are otherwise purely imaginary.

The picture of Taranaki on the back cover is from an oil painting entitled New Plymouth as it Was, dated 1884. The artist was Mrs H. T. (Jane) Enever.

PART ONE: 1952

Chapter One – The Ashcotts

I

The place where Jamie's mother has placed their picnic things – rug, basket and bottles – is a mile or so up the valley from their home, which is itself near the coast an hour's journey by bus north from Auckland. They have reached the spot on their bicycles.

As soon as he could after helping with spreading the blanket, Jamie has climbed the steep slope above the river and disappeared from his mother's sight. The sun is high, and it is baking hot. The air is heavy with pollen and the thrumming of cicadas, and the path between the thick tangle of gorse and manuka scrub is cracked and dusty. Only by looking directly up at the intense blue of the sky can Jamie Ashcott see anything beyond the narrow tunnel of vegetation and the hard clay beneath his feet.

He follows the sheep tracks. His mind is not plotting the various changes in direction that this entails. Before very long he feels that he might be lost, but he is not frightened by the discovery. He stops running and stands still, enjoying the novelty of the sensations that flood into him. The heat and the shrill of the insects close over him like a cocoon, isolating him from all else – from his mother and his sister, somewhere below him, and from all the vast world beyond. He is alone, completely and gloriously alone. There is only him. For a moment or two he stands stock still, elated. He is the universe, and there is nothing else.

Then there flits into his mind a picture of the picnic lunch that is waiting for him – of home-made lemonade cooling in the waters of the stream, and of the savoury eggs he had watched his mother prepare that morning.

He can see, too, the look of cunning satisfaction on his sister's face as she reaches out and takes his share of the delicious shortbread, just one piece each, left over from yesterday's baking. Righteous determination seizes him once more, and he turns and resumes running, this time hoping that the direction he is taking is the one that will lead him back.

Everything, though, seems the same. The hard clay beneath his feet, the whipping scrub, the thrumming of the insects, and there is no clue to encourage him to believe that he is indeed retracing his steps. Then, above all the other sounds, he hears that of his mother's voice.

"JayMEE! JayMEE!"

Her voice is clear, not at all far away. It is coming from his left. He stops again and looks at the intervening wall of scrub; then he plunges directly into it, feeling the scrape of thorns and rough bark against his bare shins. Only half aware of the pain, he crashes through the barrier and out into the cleared land beyond – and his mother is there, a little below him, separated from him only by a short, steep slope cut by the rutted sheep tracks.

"I'm here!" Jamie screams, his unbroken voice embarrassingly high-pitched, even to his own ears.

Winifred Ashcott, known all her life as Win, adjusted her no-nonsense scarf, as much a part of her out-of-doors self as were the sturdy and much-mended shoes, and attempted to assume a look of reprimand as her son raced down the slope towards her. She had been genuinely worried by his disappearance. He was the youngest of her living children, just eleven years old and small for his age. Her baby, still. Her boy baby – and nothing in the world came near to being so precious to her. At least… not since…

Jamie was beside her, puffing with the effort he had made. She immediately noticed that both his knees were scratched, the blood making trails across his shins.

"What happened?" she demanded. "Did you fall?"

He looked down in the direction of her gaze and pulled a face.

"I think I did."

"You think? How can you not know if you had fallen? You'll probably get sores there, now, on both of your knees. Look at them!"

Dutifully, he looked again at the damage. "I'll wash them in the river."

"Well, do it now. Straight away, before you eat. And wash your hands."

Winifred watched as Jamie began to run again, this time away from her, towards the river, and she turned to follow his receding figure. He is running away, she thought. He is running away from her – but it is to do her bidding. Yet, it won't be so very long before he leaves her behind for good, and she will be left with nothing, with no one. Time moves so quickly. It is six years since the telegram telling her of Haddon's death. Six years – yet it seems like no time at all. It is nine years since she last held Haddon in her arms, last heard his voice. He would have been in his prime, now, a source of endless pride, she thought. Had the war not killed him, he would have been thirty-one years old.

Jamie gives no thought to disobeying his mother's instructions. He heads straight for the fence, scrambles through it, and races to the river bank. He pulls off his sand-shoes and socks and edges into the flow. This far up, away from the sea, the waters are not tainted with salt. They are cool and refreshing. He cups some and lets it trickle through his hand and over the grazes on his knees. He flinches a little at the sudden stinging, but it lasts only a moment before the waters soothe away both the dust and the pain. With his toes, he can feel mud oozing between the pebbles of the river bed. He looks up. On the opposite bank there is a patch of native bush that comes right down to the water's edge, with branches that extend out over a deep-looking pool. It could even be deep enough to swim in, he thinks.

When he returns to the other side of the fence, he finds his sister, Helen, standing under the tall kahikatea tree that provides shade for their picnic. He can see that she is looking at him as he approaches, though she is pretending not to notice him at all. Then she turns to face him, with a look of feigned surprise.

"Oh! I thought you'd got lost. Sorry, but I ate your eggs. And the last piece of shortbread."

As usual, as always, he is taken in, believing her. His spirits slump, and resentment and self-pity bring heat to his cheeks; but before he can say anything, his mother cuts in.

"She did not, lucky for you. But ants got into some of the things. You should have been here in time."

"Sorry."

"Yes, well… Here are your eggs, and your shortbread. You don't really deserve them."

His mother doesn't mean it, he knows. He can always tell when she really means something. He picks up one of the eggs and bites into it, looking across at his sister as he does so. Her broad, freckled forehead is lowered, her pale eyebrows tense with disapproval. She is nearly three years older than him, her one advantage.

Later, he and Helen try swimming in the water hole, their mother accompanying them anxiously as they paddle out across the shallows. She has tucked her frock into her bloomers and stands watching them as they swim around, self-conscious under her gaze. Jamie is in his underpants, but Helen has her togs on, pale green and frilled. She must have had them on all the time, under her sun frock, he realises.

Although the day is hot, the waters of the pool are chilly, shaded as they are by the overhanging foliage. When they clamber out and find a perch on the far bank, Jamie notices the paleness of Helen's skin, the tinges of blue on her thighs and the pale, raised hairs on her forearms.

"You're cold," he accuses.

"No I'm not." It is an expected, automatic response. "You are."

He shakes his head and points to her arms. "Goose bumps."

"They're not goose bumps. Anyway, they don't mean anything."

A familiar look of sulky withdrawal has shuttered her face, and she plunges from her perch back into the swimming hole. "I'm getting out," she calls back to him. "It's not a proper place for swimming. It's too shallow for me. You can stay, if you like."

For some seconds he doesn't move, but watches Helen step gingerly across the shallows, moving towards their mother, who says something to her as she passes. Then he, too, plunges back into the waters. He stands up in the centre of the pool. It *is* quite shallow, even for him, the water only up to his lowest rib. He splashes out with his arms, but it is no fun, alone. He, too, wades across into the sun to where his mother still waits. She reaches out for him and lays her hand on his shoulder.

"Give your sister time to dry off and change," she says. "She can't put her frock back on over a wet bathing suit."

He shrugs, and stands with her, and they both look back, towards the opposite bank.

"Girls need their privacy," his mother says; but he knows that already. He knows that girls are different. For one thing, they are pretty – or some of them are. Girls like Mary Leigh, for instance. Mary Leigh is the prettiest of them all. And they are easily hurt, and cry quite often, and are not very strong. Even Helen can be hurt easily, though she doesn't cry. Not often, at least.

Anyway, it doesn't matter. He likes standing there with the sun warming the droplets of waters on his skin and his mother's hand on his shoulder and his toes fiddling with the pebbles under his feet.

II

The next day, back in the creaking old house that has been their rented home now for the last few years, Winifred Ashcott leaned over the scrubbed wooden kitchen bench and considered what she would wear on her journey to the city. She sighed. It had to be made, the journey. She would go towards the end of the following week, after the children had settled back into their routines. But what could she wear?

Her jersey wool frock was the only really respectable item in her wardrobe. It had been bought, at frightening expense, for Jenny's wedding, and was therefore not yet even two years old – but surely it would be too warm, given the mugginess of the weather. On the other hand, she certainly did not want to arrive at Irene's looking like a frump. The condescending pity would be altogether too much to bear.

She looked out of the narrow, fly-specked window, past the peeling paint on the sill and the water tank on its sagging stand, to her weed-clogged kitchen garden. At least the silver beet was flourishing, and the runner-bean vines looked heavily productive on their flimsy bamboo frame; and the plum tree was laden with fruit that was now mostly over-ripe. They were far from being in danger of starvation. She raised her gaze to the stained grey timbers of the wash-house, and was further reminded of the work that had to be done – of the washing and ironing as well as the digging and weeding, the fruit-bottling and the jam-making and the wood-chopping and the scrubbing and the cleaning and the mending and… Really she could not afford the time to travel into Auckland at all. Had it not been for the rather odd matter of the promised legacy, she would not have considered it even for a moment.

Win thought then of her Aunt Inez – of she who had been the final connection with her parents' generation. They had not spoken, the two of them, for close to thirty-four years – not since she had ignored her aunt's peremptorily expressed order not to do so and married Ned. "A common seaman is not a fit companion for a Gerold," she had barked at her, in her clipped, mannish voice. "And you are half Gerold. You are threatening dishonour to your mother's memory, and that of your grandfather."

She had taken no notice, of course. Her aunt's snobbery had meant nothing to her. She had long since come to terms with Ned's occupation, and to his relative lack of what her aunt called pedigree; but her failure to take notice of spinster Aunt Inez's instruction had led to a complete break with her, and later had even threatened to strain relations with her two sisters, whose choice of marriage partners had at least met with grudging approval from the same source. It seemed that an accountant and a lawyer, while clearly inferior to the landed gentry, were at least bearable.

Well, now her aunt was dead. She must have been… what? Eighty-five? She was about ten years older than her mother, and her mother, she knew, had been born in 1876. Had her mother lived, she would now be seventy-five. It was strange to think of it. She had been only eleven when her mother died. It was hard to imagine the frail, hollow-cheeked woman of her memory as a septuagenarian. She was herself now much older than her mother had been when she died. She was well into her fifties, much closer to the biblical span than her mother had been. Not that she was thinking of dying. She couldn't afford to die, even if she wanted to; and despite everything, she certainly did not want to. Even at the worst of moments – even at that instant when she had opened the telegram that confirmed the very worst of her nightmares – she had not wished even then that she were dead. Not even then.

III

Jamie is pleased that school is about to start for the new year. He has enjoyed the freedom to do whatever he wished on each of the long summer days – or, more truthfully, whatever his mother had agreed he would be allowed to do – but he is excited by the thought that he will soon see Mary Leigh again. It has been so long since he last saw her that he can't remember exactly what she looks like; but what he can remember very clearly are the feelings he had whenever he saw her.

He has walked the half mile to the main road where he must wait for the school bus. Mary Leigh lives three miles or so to the north, across the other side of the estuary and over the hill in the direction from which the bus will come. He waits alone. Sometimes his sister comes with him, just for something to do, but this morning she hasn't.

He is standing at the point where the road loops and divides, one branch going left towards the sea and the other climbing the hill on the other side of the estuary. He is looking north towards where the bus with Mary Leigh will soon appear. He thinks he can hear its distant whine as it begins its descent down the hill.

'Mary Leigh, Mary Leigh, Mary Leigh, Mary Leigh, life is but a dream,' he sings to himself, only half aloud. He kicks at a stone, and scuffs his shoes. Guilt at having done so threatens his mood of expectation.

Then the bus appears, and his excitement is renewed. He forgets about everything else except her. Mary Leigh. Mary Leigh.

The bus pulls up and the door swings open. He clambers on and is struck by a rush of shyness and doubt. He keeps his eyes firmly downwards, on his scuffed shoes. He can feel his heart beating faster and faster. He knows he must find a seat, and to do that he must look up, but he doesn't want to. Then he sees an empty one, right near where he is standing, and he takes a step sideways and moves into it. His heart is still pounding, and he knows his face must be red. He hopes Mary Leigh can't see him.

"Hello." One word, spoken softly, musically. He looks up then to see who it is in the window seat, who it is he has unknowingly chosen to seat himself next to, and his heart lurches into even faster motion.

Her plaits are pinned like a crown on the top of her head. Fair and silvery they look, and neat beyond perfection – like her spotless frock, white collared, and her white, white socks. Her face is solemn, but it is the prettiest thing in the whole world. Her eyes flicker over his face, then she looks away, with just the faintest hint of a smile.

He is frozen, yet burning. Mary Leigh, sitting right next to him! They are almost touching. And she has spoken to him. Just one word, and a smile. A smile; and a word that is better by far than any pledge he could have dreamt of.

"'Lo," he mumbles.

He tries not to even think about how close she is, even tries for a moment to imagine that she isn't there at all. But he can't stop himself. He glances across at her. It is a quick glance. It is like looking at the sun. She has turned her head to look out the window and he sees two tiny little question marks of fair hair lying in the hollow of her nape. He would like to stare at them, but he feels his cheeks redden again. The back of the seat in front of him has a crudely pencilled picture of a heart with an arrow through it, so he stares at that instead.

Much later in the day, at lunchtime, he is mucking around with his closest school-friend. His name is Matiu Jones. It is really good seeing Matty again. Matty with his ears that stick out, and his big grin.

"You like that Mary Leigh sheila, eh?" Matty asks, with a laugh.

"No," he denies.

"Yes you do. But she's too stuck up, eh. You should pick a Maori girl. Not so stuck up."

"Yeah? Like who?"

"Like Rosie Kingi."

Rosie Kingi? Jamie considers the suggestion. She's pretty, too, Rosie Kingi. Not like Mary Leigh, but just about as pretty.

"Rosie'd prob'ly kiss you, if you wanted," Matty says.

Jamie pulls a face. Kissing hasn't featured in his day dreams. Not even with Mary Leigh.

He punches Matty on the shoulder and races away, down towards the bottom field where a rugby ball is being kicked around. He doesn't like being teased about girls. It spoils things.

After the bell rings and everyone heads back to class again, he runs past a group of girls giggling together. One of them is Rosie Kingi. She catches his eye and smiles at him.

"Hey Jamie," she says. "You wanna kiss me?"

His ears burn as though someone has lifted a lighted candle to them. He can think of nothing to say, except… except… "No!"

"Oh. I thought you might wanna kiss me. Matty said."

And she laughs, her face tilted back and her hands clutching at the girl standing next to her. Together they laugh, and other girls nearby join in, shrieking and laughing. Mary Leigh is one of them.

His face is on fire, and he turns and runs into the classroom.

IV

Win Ashcott was largely done with the business of preparing dinner. She had cycled down earlier in the day to the shop at the mouth of the estuary and picked up her order of what turned out to be a small and scraggy rolled roast. Still… it would be a treat of sorts. Now it was spluttering away satisfactorily in the oven of the old wood stove, and the vegetables were on the stove top, and it was just a matter of waiting.

She popped out of the kitchen and walked down the hall to Helen's bedroom, opened the door, and looked inside. Helen was at her desk, looking industrious. Books were piled up to one side, her exercise books on the other.

"Have you finished that assignment?" she asked.

"I've finished the General Science one. I'm just starting on the Geography."

"Hurry up. They have to be posted tomorrow. School Certificate at the end of this year, remember."

"I know." Her head went down again, giving attention to the open book in front of her; but not before Win noted the sulky look on her face. So like her father.

She went back down the passage and sat down at the kitchen table for a few minutes of rest, and turned her mind again to the question of her Aunt Inez's legacy. It was not that she was expecting very much from it. Her aunt was not a particularly wealthy woman, she knew that much – quite apart from the fact of the thirty years or more of frosty silence between them. Still… they had been close once, whether she had wanted it or not.

She allowed her mind to wander back to that time, to the period of her mother's final illness. Aunt Inez had assumed many of the duties of guidance and instruction that her mother was incapable then of giving her, and although her own eleven-year-old self would much rather she had been left to her own devices, she had had no choice but to spend much time in her aunt's company. She had sat dutifully if reluctantly in the gloomy drawing room, her knees together and slightly angled, in the aunt-approved fashion, and listened half-heartedly to her tales of her Aunt's father, her own grandfather, the reputedly handsome and glorious Tomas Gerold, who had given her mother her maiden name – the name still worn like a high honour by her aunt – all the time wishing and wishing that she could escape outdoors and muddy her skirts on the hockey field or by riding bare back the old pony that was still occasionally hitched up to the dog cart that had once been, she was told, the family's main means of transport.

It all seemed like a lifetime ago; as indeed it was, she reflected. That had been before the Great War, when New Plymouth had still had about it some of the excitement and sense of promise that must have filled the breasts of its earliest settlers – of the breasts of her grandparents, both sets of them, not only the grand and glorious Tomas Gerold, but the somewhat lesser Harboroughs. She could never, then, have foreseen the forces that would shape her life; the Great War which took from her her first, cruelly unconsummated love, and left her with… Well, she was not the only hopeful young woman to suffer as a result of that distant conflict and its horrible aftermath of illness and disappointment.

Then had come her bitterly-disputed rebound of a marriage, and her first child, whose beauty and loving nature had made everything right again. Not even the early suspicion of Ned's philandering, not even the Slump and its awful consequences, could dampen her spirits in those years between the wars. Haddon had been her comfort, her whole reason for existence. Surely there could not have been anywhere, a son so perfect, so rewarding in his loyalty and his love. Haddon had been…

But Haddon was dead. War had once again robbed her, this time even more cruelly. Much more cruelly.

And now, Aunt Inez, too, dead – a last, all but forgotten link with that much earlier, simpler world that had existed before wars and the Slump and other deaths had changed everything, everything. When she was just eleven years old, she and her aunt had been brought close together; but now her aunt was dead – and she herself was fifty-five years old. Now, she herself was nearly elderly, though she couldn't afford to think of that. She had four other children. Dougal was somewhere, probably still in Wellington, though in his last letter he had talked of going south, to Christchurch. She wished he would write more often, but she had no real worries concerning him. He was a good lad. Easily led, true – but not in directions that she need worry about. Not like Jenny; but Jenny was well off her hands now – and what a relief that had been, to see her respectably married and to be no longer exposed to the painful results of her wilful ways. Now… there was still Helen to worry about. And there was still Jamie. Yes, Jamie. There was still some purpose to her life.

Her idle thoughts were abruptly ended by the rattle of footsteps on the verandah. No sooner had she risen guiltily from her chair than Jamie burst into the kitchen.

"Was it good to see all your friends again?" she asked.

"It was good to see Matty. Except…"

"Except what?"

"Except he told Rosie Kingi that I wanted to kiss her."

Jamie's face was highly coloured, so much so that his scattering of freckles had almost disappeared. Despite herself, Win had to supress a grin. Such a bright boy, yet so very sensitive!

"And did you?" she laughed.

"Did I want to kiss Rosie? No Mum. I don't want to kiss any girl."

Helen appeared at the kitchen door. "He'd like to kiss Mary Leigh. Wouldn't you Jamie? I know you would."

"Liar!" he says.

"That's enough silliness, both of you."

"He does like her, though. It's true," Helen muttered, sulky again..

"Now you're just being silly. Why shouldn't he like her? You like everybody, don't you Jamie?"

"Not everybody," he replied, glowering.

"That's quite enough, the two of you. Go and wash your hands, then find something useful to do."

V

After they had clattered off, Win returned to her musings. The very idea of Jamie thinking about girlfriends at his age – and one of them a little

14

Maori girl at that, judging by her name. A Maori girl. How Aunt Inez would have bristled at the very notion. Maori! She remembered how her aunt had had difficulty in even pronouncing the word, her neck stiff and her nose white with tension.

"You must never associate with them unless it is absolutely necessary," she remembered being admonished on one occasion. "Only the very worst of people do."

It was another piece of uncalled for advice that she had always been happy to ignore, and her determination to do so had started quite early. She recalled an incident that had taken place on Devon Street, when she was still in short skirts. She and her aunt had just come out of a shop, and their way had been partially blocked by a group of Maori women who were standing there on the street corner. It had been a common enough sight in those days, the groups of Maori women, mainly in black, standing or crouching at the corners, waiting – though for what, it was never clear to her.

Her aunt had pretended not to even see them, but her own attention had been attracted by one of the figures, standing a little apart from the rest. She was an old woman, with a halo of white hair, who had smiled at her and looked at her aunt as they moved past.

"Good afternoon, Miss Inez," the old woman had said, loud and clear, as if she knew that her Aunt's hearing was not good; and her aunt had had no choice but to pause and nod an acknowledgement. "How do you do, Hannah."

Then the old Maori woman had turned from her aunt and looked directly at her, inviting the information that her aunt had then had to offer. "This… This is Winifred. Ellen's eldest."

"Ah!" the old woman had cooed. "Of course, of course she is. She has the look of her grandmother about her. She has the look of my dear Addie." And she had peered at her even more closely, and fondly. There seemed to be tears in her old, old eyes. "She was my best friend, you see," she said, addressing her personally, in little more than a whisper. "Your grandmother was my best friend."

She had gaped at the old woman, then, hardly able to accept the meaning of her words – but she had returned the smile. There was something about her, something warm and real, and she had offered her comments in a soft and, yes, a genteel voice – a voice such as her aunt might have used. A worn old hand had extended towards her, touched her cheek; but at the same moment she had felt her aunt's fingers close around her elbow.

"We must get on," she said. "An appointment."

A final tiny pat on her cheek, and the hand was lifted away.

"It was nice to talk with you, Miss Inez," the Maori woman said, once again in a loud, clear voice. Then more softly: "And it was lovely to meet you, little lady."

And they had moved away. They were scarcely out of earshot when her aunt had brought her head close to hers and offered, with an impatient mutter: "She was your grandmother's housemaid, trained by the Mission." There followed a small pause, then: "I suppose she was also a friend to her, a friend of sorts. You must remember your grandmother was very young then – not long married and newly arrived from Home. She was very lonely, no doubt."

At that, she had been unable to resist the urge to look back. The old woman had been watching them still, and seeing her turn, she fluttered her hand in a final salute.

The incident had played on her mind for much of that day. Neither her aunt nor her mother had ever spoken much of their mother, her maternal grandmother. About all she knew about her was that she had died quite young. Eventually, she had asked her aunt what she had been like.

"My memories are no longer clear," she had brusquely replied. The question seemed to annoy her. "She was very clever. Always reading. Right to the end." Then, more gently: "I do remember my dear father crying. I remember that."

VI

Win Ashcott returned from her trip into the city exhausted but elated, carrying a variety of packages in two large shopping bags. The bus trip to Devonport, the Ferry crossing of the harbour, and the tram journey up Queen Street and beyond to her sister's comfortable house in the comfortable suburb had proved far more rewarding than she had dared think possible. And how Irene had enjoyed playing fairy godmother! Win had had to bite her tongue several times as her sister, in her role as Aunt Inez's chosen executor, had grandly passed on to her the money and the other items either specified in her Aunt's will, or offered to her as a sisterly gesture of condescending, perhaps even pitying, goodwill.

There was still now in her purse a roll of notes, the bulk of the two hundred and sixty pounds that her Aunt Inez had left her. In one of the shopping bags she carried were the other, less exciting examples of her or Irene's largesse – a carefully wrapped tea-set of Old Foley rose-patterned porcelain (minus the teapot), a cameo brooch, and a jade letter seal threaded on a silver chain. There were also – Irene had suggested she would throw them out, but she asked if she could have them – two heavy volumes of what seemed to be very old account books. She had asked for them, as she knew how much Jamie enjoyed books of any sort, and thought that he might find an interest in looking through them.

In the other bag were items she couldn't resist buying as she walked back along Queen Street to the Ferry Terminal. Having her Aunt's legacy lying in her purse gave her the sort of confidence she had not felt for a very long time. From a Draper's she bought some cotton material she could make into a summer frock for Helen, and a longer length in another pattern so she could do the same for herself. Then she had passed a bookshop, and picked up a nicely bound copy of *David Copperfield* for Jamie. She had bought him *Nicholas Nickleby* for Christmas, a little worried that it might be a bit difficult for him, but he had devoured it, hardly able to put it down until he'd finished. Then she had noticed a little shop that specialised in aeroplane, ship and train modelling, and she couldn't resist indulging Jamie yet again, this time with a balsawood kitset of a Spitfire. She knew he wanted one, but it had given her a lurch of grief, buying it. Nevertheless, she approved of Jamie's wanting to build such a model. She thought of it as his way of paying respect to Haddon, the brother he had never properly known.

Win laid the inherited items out on the battered living-room sideboard, while Helen and Jamie watched on. They didn't make a very impressive display. She didn't like the cups and saucers. They were far too flamboyant for her taste. She seemed to remember them from her father's house, long, long ago. Then, they had been amongst many such items displayed in one of the cabinets. As far as she could remember, she hadn't like them much then, either. Which might explain why her aunt had specified she be left them, she thought, with a touch of her old rancour.

But she was far more interested in the items she had bought for the children. Helen showed satisfactory delight in the choice of fabric she had made for her frock, while Jamie was so excited by the sight of his Spitfire modelling kit that he gave *David Copperfield* no more than a hurried leaf through, and herself a murmured thanks, before picking up the kit again, along with the Dickens and the two old account books, and dashing down to his bedroom.

Then she went into the kitchen and opened the parcels that contained the little mince pies and the lamingtons that she had bought from the cake shop. She would heat the pies, and they would do for dinner. And the lamingtons would make a very nice dessert. It would certainly save her from cooking – and that was a blessing, as she was feeling the effects of a long day in shoes that pinched her and a frock that was made heavy with perspiration.

VII

After her mother left the room, Helen lingered behind so that she could take a proper look at the china cups and saucers that had been brought back from her aunt's place in the city. Hideous, her mother had called them when she had taken them out of the bag, scarcely bothering to unwrap them from the newspaper which had been neatly folded around them. From the little she had seen of them then, Helen did not agree with her mother's assessment. Ghastly pinks and reds together, her mother had said. Absolutely hideous. Helen knew that she didn't like the colour red anywhere, even in nature. There were no red flowers anywhere in the garden.

But Helen's eye had been attracted by the ornate tea set, and she crossed the room to the table where her mother had left all the contents of the bag, and cautiously picked up a cup. Its handle was curled like a snake, and the cup itself was shaped like a flower, with indented swirls. On its outside surface, the reds and pinks of the roses looked so real that she brought the cup to her nose and sniffed. Silly, she thought. Silly, silly, silly to think that they might be scented.

She put the cup down on its saucer and picked up the length of material that was intended for her frock. She knew she would have little choice over the style her mother would make. It would be made with puff sleeves, as though she was still a little girl. Still, it would be nice to have something new. Earlier, she had looked over to where her brother was leafing through the pages of a book he'd been given, and felt a tug of resentment. Jamie had not only been given the new one, but some old ones, too. And the model airplane set. It wasn't fair. He was always getting more things than her. The old books looked tattered and grubby, though. She didn't mind so much that he'd been given them.

She put down the dress material without a further glance, and, with resentment creasing her forehead, went down the passage to her room.

Jamie doesn't even notice Helen's look of envy. He is far too interested in the various items his mother has brought home for him.

He goes through them in reverse order of interest. First he picks up the old books, one after the other, and hefts them in his hands. Both of them have scuffed covers. They are heavy. He runs a finger over the spine of one. It is leather, definitely – and the leather extends around to cover about a quarter of the front. On the heavy green cloth that comprises the

rest of the front board, in faded gold lettering, is the word '*ACCOUNTS*'.
He is not quite sure what that means. He opens the book to find that the
pages inside are covered with rows of dates and words and figures. He
stops at a random page and reads more carefully.

'*To:*

Messrs Hall & Co	*baking provisions*		*17*	*11*
do	*lemonade etc.*		*3*	*6*
do	*garden tools & etc. (spade,*			
	hoe, scythe, seeds)	*1*	*14*	*3*
Carthews	*calico for pinafores*		*4*	*0*
Morrissey	*meats, poultry*	*1*	*11*	*4*'

He stops reading and frowns. Figures are not very interesting. Not really.
Perhaps later, if he is bored, he might take a closer look at them. He does
wonder who had written them, though. The figures are very neatly drawn,
as are the letters. They look as though they must have been written by a
girl, a lady, he decides. Not an old lady, though. There is nothing shaky
about the letters or the figures. They somehow seem to be full of life.
And yet…

… and yet of course they are old, very old. Whoever wrote them must
have died a long time ago. He looks at the top of the page. *November
1863*, is the date recorded there. He tries to calculate the years. Nearly
ninety had gone by since those numbers, those words, had been written
down. He experiences a little shiver of disappointment at the thought.
Ninety years. An unimaginable time ago.

Idly, he hefts the pages of the book again and lets it fall open further
on, well past the middle. For a fraction of a second he is confused. The
same neat, faded handwriting is there, but now he can't read it. It slopes
the wrong way, and it seems to be in an entirely different script. Then he
smiles at his own silliness. It is upside down! He turns the book around.
The back is now the front, and he riffles through the pages to find out

where the densely written pages, proper writing, with no columns and no figures, begins.

It is just a few pages from the front of the book, which is really its back, where he finds the very first words:

'*May 1863. I begin this record not knowing how long I shall continue it, nor with any clear idea of its purpose other than a desire to acknowledge my own mistakes and weaknesses. My name is Adelaide Augusta Gilbard. This is not my married name – but then, I have been a Gilbard for far longer than I have been my husband's wife...*'

He closes the book and puts it down. He is mildly interested, but there are far more significant things to investigate.

He picks up the copy of *Oliver Twist* and flicks through the pages. That will be good. He looks forward to reading it, but again, there is no great excitement at the thought. He lays it down carefully.

For now, the most exciting thing by far is the model aeroplane kit. The Spitfire. It is what he wanted more than anything else in the world, and now he has it. A Spitfire, just like the one his brother used to fly in the war. He has finished the Lancaster Bomber, his very first model, and it now hangs in his room, suspended from the ceiling. But that model is only small, and it is made of solid balsa. It can't fly. He wants his Spitfire to be able to fly. He wants it to be a proper model made of a framework of balsa and covered with the special paper, with a propeller powered by one of the long rubber bands he has seen advertised in the modelling magazine his mother brought him home one day. And a kit for such a model Spitfire is exactly what his mother has brought home for him from her trip to the city

He makes a pile of the books – it is quite a heavy pile – and puts the kitset on top of them. Carefully, he carries everything down to his room and deposits them on his desk.

He takes the kitset and opens the box as carefully as his impatience will allow. He is just checking, making sure that everything will be ready for tomorrow. He will start it then. Tomorrow. His Spitfire. Just like Haddon's. The Pilot Officer, his brother, the hero who smiles, blue of uniform and white of teeth, from the wall in his mother's bedroom, his chest emblazoned with wings.

Then he takes the books, the new one and the old ones, and puts them with his other books and magazines on the shelves of his book case. They can wait.

VIII

On a Saturday little more than a fortnight later, Jamie is putting the finishing touches to his Spitfire when Helen flings open the door to his room and triumphantly announces that their father has come to visit. She is happy and excited. She is always happy and excited when their father makes a visit.

It is unexpected – but then, his father's visits are nearly always unannounced. They are also rare. Without even needing to check to see if he is right, Jamie knows that their mother will now be in a bad mood, frowning and distracted. She is never happy when their father appears. For this reason, Jamie, too, is always nervous when his father visits. Jamie definitely doesn't like it when their mother is unhappy.

But this time, he finds, it is a little different.

"He's come in a car!" Helen breathes.

"A car? Who with?" Jamie asks, interested now – interested in hearing who else might now be in the house. Previously, their father has always come on the bus, then walked up the valley.

"Not with anybody!" Helen continues. "He drove it here. It's his car! It's our car!"

A car! That such an unattainable object should be in the possession of his father is astonishing to him. He rushes outside to see, and there, just beyond the gate, sure enough, is a car!

Admittedly, it isn't much of a car. It isn't big and streamlined, like the Willys Knights or the Buicks that swoosh past on the main road sometimes as he waits for the school bus. It's more like a toy version of the big old Essex that the farmer up the road drives down the valley and past their place every day or two. It's a little square thing.

His mother joins them on the verandah, and looks out.

"Hmpphh! It's a matchbox," she mutters, disparagingly. "You can't call that a car." She disappears back inside to continue the inevitable arguing.

Well yes, Jamie thinks. It is certainly tiny and strange looking. But a car! He races along the path and through the gate and peers through its dusty window. From what he can see, it looks cramped and uncomfortable. Upholstery is hanging down from the ceiling, and the seat in the back has springs poking out. But… it is definitely a car!

He races back inside, and interrupts the argument that is proceeding in the kitchen.

"What make is it, Dad? Is it yours?"

There comes a familiar, wheezing laugh. "It's a Rolls Canardley, son. It rolls down one side of the hill and can 'ardly get up the other. And no, it's not mine. I borrowed it from a friend so I could come and see you. It got me here, too, didn't it? I'll be lucky if it gets me back, though!" Another chuckle.

But Jamie doesn't feel like laughing.

Interlude – from the Journal of Adelaide Gilbard

New Year's Day, 1866.Tom has disappointed me. That much, at least, I must record here. But I suppose, having written that much, I should explain a little.

It was not very long after we first arrived here that he began to drink. Well... more than that. He had never been a teetotaller, and I had never wished him to be. But some months after we came to settle in here, I saw him drunk for the first time. He had been at a gathering of the Volunteers – something to do with celebrating success in putting down a minor fracas of some sort – and he came back in such a state that I was at first worried that he had had some sort of heart attack. It was Hannah who quickly pointed out to me that both he and the two or three of his companions who had carried him to our cottage were all very drunk. None more so than Tomas. Hannah and I took over from his shame-faced friends, and I stayed at his bedside for much of the night.

The next day, he was full of remorse, and that show of remorse continued for many days and even weeks after. The drunken episode seems to have lowered not only his own self-esteem, but also to have adversely affected the good opinion the commanding officer in the Volunteers had hitherto shown towards him. I am not sure exactly what measures were taken to discipline him – he did keep his rank of Captain – but I do know that shortly after the incident, Tomas was given a mission connected with his position as Surveyor, that took him away from New Plymouth for long periods of time, and thus removed him from participation in most of the martial activities of the Volunteers.

...

June 1867: I see that it has been almost eighteen months since I last wrote in this journal. Much has happened in that time, yet when I come to write of those things, I find myself hesitating. How much should I tell?

Well, I can say that George, our first born, has suffered a brush with whooping cough. At its worst, his poor little body seemed almost to tear itself apart. But he survived, and is now back to his normal, trusting self. He is not quick, but nor is he slow. He is not big for his age, nor is he small. He is neither meek, nor bold. He is simply George, and I love him dearly.

And I can say that I now have a daughter, just one month old. We have named her Inez Margaret. She is a sweet little thing, with light brown hair and very pink skin, and a tiny mouth that is often puckered as it seeks for nourishment, probing here and there like a nestling's beak. As with George, I have insisted on feeding her at my own breast, despite Tom's doubts as to the appropriateness of doing so. It would be simple enough to find a wet nurse, he mutters when he sees us – but thankfully, we do not truly argue about it.

There is more about the last eighteen months that I should write in these pages, if I am to hold true to my stated purpose of honesty. I should write of the loneliness I sometimes feel during those frequent times when Tomas is away. I do not often feel that deprivation, for I have my children and the loyal companionship of Hannah. But Hannah has her husband to attend to, and I cannot impose too much on her time. True, her quarters are no more than a few steps away from our house, but I do not like to disturb her own domesticity. When Tomas is away, though, she does bring her dear little niece Rangi (short for Rangimarie, which means Peace) with her when she attends to her duties here. Indeed, Rangi and George are almost of an age, and they have become quite firm friends. While George was ill, though, I insisted that Hannah keep her daughter well away in case he gave her his infection.

I talk more to Hannah about my thoughts for the future than I do with Tomas. Much more. That is not because I do not wish to share such thoughts with him, but rather because his dreams for our future seem to me to be phantasms, and altogether too grand to be believed in. Besides, I truly have no wish for grandeur. My vision of our future is modest. I am happy enough as we are. As our family grows, I would like a little more space in this cottage – enough space for a library, for instance – but I have no wish for a park and a ballroom and a legion of servants to look after it all. In fact, I rather shudder at the thought. But these are all part of Tomas's dreams for our future. When he talks of them, I can do little more than murmur vague words of doubt, which I know wounds him rather.

Tomas wants more, much more. He wants land and a big house – a house to rival his ancestral home in Wales. He wants a stable full of fine horses. In short, he wants to be lord and master, he wants wealth and power. It seems he cannot break free from what he believes once was, or what might have been – from those ancestral glories that are, in his mind, much, much greater, more desirable, than they ever were or could have been in truth. This country gives us a chance to be something very different, something infinitely preferable – but that vision is hidden from *him by his nature. He wants to recreate an imagined past. I would rather help shape a different future, a future in which no one is master and no one is impoverished, and where all, all of us, may become fulfilled – a society without fear and without want. I must believe, I <u>must</u> believe that this is possible. Otherwise, my life has lost whatever purpose it ever had.*

...

16 February 1869: I cannot allow this day to pass without recording here my deep sorrow at learning of the cruel slaughter of Lt. Bamber Gascoigne and his wife and children, and at least two other men, one a church minister, on Saturday last. It seems from what reports we have that they died at the hands of a marauding party of Maori tribesmen from the north, though that is still uncertain. The place they were killed is some thirty miles north-east of here, a redoubt called Pukearuhe, or White Cliffs. The eldest of the Gascoigne children, a girl, can have been no more than five years old, while the youngest, also a girl, was just a babe in arms. And there was a little boy, too. We here in town had thought our troubles of this nature were over – but alas, it would seem they are not.

Lieutenant Gascoigne travelled with us here from Melbourne on the Brilliant, and was a friend of Tom's. They have served together in the Volunteers over the past four years, and although they have had their differences, it will be a bitter shock to Tom when he learns of the sad events. He is at present away again, in difficult country far to the south.

I knew Mrs Gascoigne, of course, though she was not a particular friend; but to think of her dying in such a manner, of first seeing her children die so horribly, in all probability, necessarily fills me with great anguish, fear, and anger. It is impossible not to succumb to it. It is expressed by everyone, everywhere one goes in town. It is understandable. It is inevitable. But it is also deeply, deeply disturbing.

Perhaps forgiveness is not possible. There has indeed been great error, but alas, we are not divine. Hannah and I have talked long about it. What a great comfort that has been to me! I think, to her, as well. Her feelings, at least those of sadness and regret, are equal to mine. Sharing those feelings reduced my anger and my fear, and brought about a little portion of understanding. Those poor innocent children, their lives brutally ended as a result of decisions made by those they had no choice but to trust! What could blame possibly mean to them? What should blame mean to us?

To survive, to prosper, we must live peacably together. We must.

...

Friday 14 August, 1871: We have moved to a larger house. Though not very far from our old place, it is a little further away from the centre of the town, and on higher ground. The house is one of the town's finest, built for a doctor who spent less than a year here before deciding to return to Norfolk. I think Tomas used a generous remittance from Wales to purchase the place, though whether or not he had asked that it be sent for that purpose I do not know. Of course, it is possible that he used funds that he had gained through his own efforts. Certainly he was away for quite long periods last year, mostly going to the north of here to the fringes of what is called the King Country, and from the little he has told me, I gather that he there speculated in land.

The property we now own here has somewhat less land attached to it – a little under three acres. There is a field where we keep a cow, and a large orchard, as well as a small stand of native forest. The house itself is of properly milled weatherboard, and it has a wide verandah on three sides. The garden was quite well established when we moved in, at least in its essentials, and everything is growing apace. The soil is excellent – dark and rich. At the back of the house we have stabling for two horses, though at the moment Tomas is content to have just one animal – a rangy hunter that he has called Kingbolt. Also at the back of the house is a proper laundry, with two further rooms attached. Hannah has moved into these with her husband. We are able to pay Hannah's husband to look after the garden, and everyone seems most comfortable with the arrangement. Hannah's only regret, she tells me in rare moments of sadness, is that although she desperately wishes it were otherwise, she seems unable to have a child of her own. It is indeed a sad, sad thing, and

I feel her grief. Still, her normal cheerful disposition soon brings her out of her gloom. I do love her. I do depend on her, and she on me. We give strength to each other. We are like sisters.

As we are so evidently at present in a state of relative prosperity, I know I should be happy – and I suppose I am. Except that Inez appears to be partially deaf, the children are well and seem to have, like both their parents, remarkably strong constitutions. Little Inez's affliction seems to make her somewhat withdrawn, but she is otherwise physically a normal child and she has just begun to take a more active interest in the world around her. George, too, is slowly becoming more adventurous, though he still looks at the world through watchful eyes.

Yes, I am generally content with my lot, and now we have a larger house and are able to put on an improved show for the world, so, I believe, is Tomas. At least, he seems so, when he is at home. And just lately, he has been at home more and for longer periods. When he is not at home, I have the company not only of Hannah, but that of our new neighbours, the Harboroughs. I believe that the proximity of the Harborough's new town house was one of the chief reasons for Tomas to have bought our place.

Anthony Harborough is a friend of Tomas's, and he has a large property near the settlement of Stratford, some distance south, but members of his family are usually resident next door, one of them permanently, and he frequently joins them himself. Harriet Harborough, his wife, stays in town during the week with her boys, as it is more convenient for their schooling. Anthony's brother, Clement, spends all of his time here in town, as he is not suited to a farmer's life, being of a studious nature and a somewhat delicate constitution. Clement has his own rooms in the house. He is attempting to establish himself as a capitalist, and he has an interest in several of the local businesses, including the town's newspaper. He is an observant, thoughtful man of very few words, but with a quiet intelligence and a cautious yet steely will. I think Tomas does not much like him, but they are least polite to each other. It is Anthony, not Clement, who is Tomas's particular friend.

Now that the troubles seem to be largely over, our little town is growing remarkably quickly. The main street is filled with shops and the port is busy and lined with warehouses full of goods imported or ready for export. There is a tangible feeling of permanency where once existed only a sharp sense of danger and risk. Every day there is talk of new things – of parks and a racecourse, of schools and factories. There is excitement and confidence, at least amongst the settlers. The Maori men and women who are still to be seen about the town – and there seem to be fewer and fewer of them – display much less energy. Those who once opposed the settlers do not seem to be seen as a threat any more, and in their faces it is possible to detect sadness more often than resentment. Hannah agrees with me in this assessment, but when we talk of it, we both seem to be holding back something, one from the other. Our attempts to work out ways in which we can bring Maori and settler closer together through the womenfolk no longer seem to hold such promise as they once did. Something is shifting. Something is changing. The opportunity to bring the two peoples together seems to be passing. There is too much power on one side for the notion of partnership to gain hold. Amongst the Maori population there seems to be a dull acceptance of forever changed circumstance, whilst among the settler, there appears most commonly to be a blind drive towards the triumphant establishment of a little England.

I say that the Maori population appears to be dispirited, but there are rumours...

Chapter Two – Fiona and Tela

I

In the wool-rich province of Hawkes Bay, seaward from Dannevirke but not quite as far as the coast, Fiona Finlay tried on her new jodhpurs and riding jacket, the latter a neatly tailored black, the former an equally well-tailored fawn, and examined herself in the mirror. Both items of clothing, specially ordered from a shop in Hastings, were a little too large for her trim eleven-year-old body, but her mother had assured her that she would grow into them soon enough. And, she thought, with a little pulling back of her shoulders, they certainly made her look like… well, like a real horse person. Like an English horse girl, like the pretty girl in the film they had seen last time they went to town. Yes, in National Velvet. Fliss Crosswell would be quite jealous, she was sure.

Of course, she really needed new boots, as well. She would ask her father to get her a pair next time they were in town. She and Murray seemed to be able to have just about anything they wanted these days. It was something to do with the price of wool. Her father was always going on about it and puffing his chest out. A real windfall, he called it. He was even talking about getting a new car, and he'd already bought a near-new Land Rover to replace the old left-hand-drive jeep. What's more, he'd taken the horse float into town and had it repaired and remodelled, and there were hardly ever any more rows now between him and her mother over the cost of Murray's school and boarding fees at Collegiate – or about the extra fees there would be from next year, when she started at Mapledene.

30

Thoughts about school reminded her that they would all be going over to Wanganui next Sunday to take Murray back for the start of the new term. It would be a long drive, and she didn't much enjoy long drives. Not the first bit, at least, the hour or so of twists and turns over the metalled road into town. It wouldn't be so bad from then on, though – and if they had enough time they might be able to shop in Palmy on the way and get the pair of riding boots she needed.

Then she remembered it would be Sunday, and none of the shops would be open. She pouted into the mirror at that thought, and turned abruptly away. She'd just have to wear her old boots to the Weber gymkhana on Saturday week. At least she'd have her new coat and jodhpurs. She'd jump old Midge better than she ever had, maybe even beat Fliss and her flash new grey. Well… maybe not that. They'd not even be in the same class. Midge was too small. Fliss's new grey was just over fourteen hands.

And that thought suddenly made her resentful. It wouldn't be fair. It *wasn't* fair. Fliss was only a few months older than her, and they were almost the same height. Midge was too small for her. Midge was just a kid's pony, and she'd had her since she was just a baby. She loved Midge still, of course, and she'd never let her father sell her, like Murray let him sell his pony when he got sick of it. But she really needed something bigger, like Fliss's grey. Not grey, though. Maybe a chestnut.

Yes… a chestnut, around fourteen hands, and a good jumper. A better jumper than Fliss's gelding… what had she called him? Sheik or something. It was some silly name like that. She'd find a much better name for hers. Maybe Sabre, or Cutlass. Something sharp and dangerous. Even thinking about it made her more and more determined. She felt sure now that she could persuade her father. It was only fair. He'd bought Murray a new horse, even before the wool windfall. He couldn't really not get her one if she asked, even if her mother objected, as she was sure to. A proper pony, something that could keep up with the hunt.

Yes, she decided, she would definitely ask her father if she could have a new pony.

II

Bob Finlay, Fiona's father, was known to one and all, even to his wife and (in secret, and between themselves) to his son and daughter, as Buttercup. The reason for the lasting nickname was very evident to all, unless he was wearing his broad-rimmed town hat – for even at the age of forty-two, Buttercup Finlay had the sort of curling, gleaming, stand-out corn-coloured hair that many a woman had privately, and even at times publicly, declared was wasted on a man. So gorgeous was his hair, in fact, that he had once, as a teenager, hacked it all off, in an effort to avoid the inevitable taunts. As he had matured, though, he had learned to accept his fate, and even to glory a little in the attention it generated, particularly amongst women. But to counteract that outward suggestion of femininity he had cultivated an exaggeratedly masculine swagger and manner of speech. In time, these things had come to define him in the eyes of the world every bit as much, and eventually more, than the colour of his hair. Bob Finlay was generally considered to be a blunt, no-nonsense man. The more timid even feared his tongue or (incorrectly, for he showed violence only towards his dogs), his fists. Some even hated him.

He had inherited the hill-country sheep station on the death of his father in the Great War. As he had been just ten at the time, the farm had continued to be run by the Manager his father had arranged to look after it while he was away doing his volunteered duty. His mother, whose health was always doubtful after her recovery from the influenza that almost took her life, died when he was seventeen and still at boarding school. He returned to the farm at the end of that year with an undistinguished academic record and a reputation for natural sporting ability, marred by a propensity to avoid the sort of diligent training that major success would have demanded.

At first, his older sister looked after the domestic arrangements at the farm house, the cowman-gardener continued to supply their regular sustenance, and the Manager continued to supervise the shepherds or scrub-cutters or fencers or shearers or whatever other personnel were deemed necessary to the proper functioning of the farm. Their father had been a canny man, determined to make the most of the chance that had been given him by his own equally canny father, who had not only made the trip down from Waipu to cast his eye over the land and approve it, but had provided most of the money for its purchase. So it was that although the lean years of the depression had put some strain on their financial resources, the fact that the banks were owed no money, and that the farm produced almost all that was necessary to the basic welfare of those who gained a living from it, meant those difficult years of the Great Depression were survived easily enough.

In the meantime, though, Bob's sister married an accountant, and the pair moved to Auckland. Then, when Bob was in his mid-twenties, the Manager took his wife and children to a position closer to town and to the facilities they had done without for so long. He had seen the farm through the worst days of the Depression, after all.

And so, at the age of twenty-eight, Bob, or Buttercup, Finlay had come to be the true master of his inheritance. In that same year he had also become a married man, believing that all in all, the way that would prove the least trouble and upset the fewest people would be to take as wife the girl he had impregnated – the daughter of a drover who was widely acknowledged to be a very, very hard man.

And a good wife she had proved to be, exactly the sort of wife a man of inherently wasteful habits who now had control of a difficult enterprise should have taken. Sure, she was looked upon by some of the neighbours (and at times by Bob himself, to his shame) as 'tainted by the tar-brush' (her father being not only a very hard man, but also partly of Maori descent), but she had inherited some of the tough determination, confidence and skill of her father, had a hard-nosed love of horses, was very good at managing people, and quickly learned all that was necessary about keeping accounts and generally ensuring that the farm prospered despite her new husband's dilatory habits.

III

Fiona knew where her father would be found at that time of the morning. She knew he would be with his dogs out by the pine plantation. He would have fed them – though only a few scraps at that time – then let all of them loose to race around him until they were called to heel and lay at his feet, panting and eager. She knew there were few things her father enjoyed as much as being with his dogs, testing their obedience and watching the willing effort they put in to following his orders.

"Dad!" she called as she picked her way over the small holding paddock, taking care to avoid the sheep and other droppings that lay all too thickly on the ground. Normally she would not have been quite so cautious, but she had her riding boots on and her new jodhpurs, and she had no wish to soil either.

Her father grunted something in reply to her call and stood eyeing her as she approached. "What's up?" he asked. His dogs gave her a contemptuous look, then returned their attention to their master.

Fiona briefly studied her father's face, looking for clues to his mood. There would be no use making her request if he was in one of what her mother called his blue fits. Not that he had had many of those since he had first heard news of the prices reached at the wool sales last summer. There had been month after month of cheerfulness ever since. He'd even taken to patting her on the head occasionally, and to praising her for her school reports.

Satisfied with her assessment, she awarded him a smile and the sort of shy look that she knew he liked. "Dad, I was wondering…"

One of the dogs gave a short whine of dissatisfaction, and her father growled his annoyance, then gave his own grunt of satisfaction at the animal's grovelling attitude of submission.

"And what were you wondering, then?" he said, without looking at her. "When you or Murray start wondering, it usually ends up costing me money. So what is it?" His voice was gruff and abrupt. His usual voice.

Fiona was still watching him closely. She could sense the hint of softness behind the words. He wasn't really annoyed, that much was clear to her.

"You're always saying how fast I'm growing," she said. She deliberately kept her head cocked, looking up at him. It was a baby trick, but she saw a grin flicker on his lips.

"So?" he said.

"So I was wondering if I could have a new pony. A real pony, you know. Fourteen hands or so. I'd like a chestnut, though I wouldn't really mind. Whatever you think."

She had remembered to speak her words with a little bit of a plum, the way that she knew he liked to hear her speak. She knew why he liked it, too. It made her different from her mother. She knew that the way her mother spoke, the way that she pronounced things and the words she used, sometimes made his face turn sour. Besides, it wasn't hard for her to speak with a bit of a plum. Her best friend Fliss spoke with a plum all the time, and as she didn't like Fliss to get the better of her in anything at all, she, too, always spoke with a plum when they were together.

"Well now, little madam. I don't know about that. Madam wants a flash new pony, does she? Madam Fiona."

He moved away from her, the dogs following when he gave a word of consent; and she, too, trailed after him. They reached the boundary fence of the holding paddock, at a point where the ground fell away quite steeply then rose again, equally steeply, to an even higher elevation on the other side of the gully. Beyond that point there was a clump of cabbage trees, and more lumpy hills covered with brown-top grass. Almost all that was in view, Fiona well knew, was part of their farm. Two thousand acres of it, as their father often reminded them.Some of the slopes of the far hills were dotted with sheep, not long shorn. The money makers.

"Christ! There's a stray down there by the dam, see?" her father said, suddenly animated. "A big old ram, by the look of it. How the hell did he get there?"

Fiona looked, and she could see the animal, partly obscured by the rushes that fringed the dam. He looked woolly, too. Unshorn.

"Maybe it's not one of ours," she said.

"You could be right," her father responded, almost respectfully. "You could be right. Could be one of Boulton's rams. Would've had to've broken through the ninety acres boundary then crossed over and broken through again. Big brute. I'll have to get Nobby to check the fences."

It didn't seem at all strange to Fiona that her father should suggest he would get one of the shepherds to trace the damage, rather than do it himself. That was just the way things were.

"I'll bring him up," her father continued. "Get a closer look at him. Bruce! Sue!"

Two of the dogs sprang to their feet, and the others whimpered in disappointment.

"Giddar!" He pointed down the slope, and both dogs were away, leaving the fence wire vibrating with the speed of their passage. After watching them for a time, he whistled, and they changed direction, slowing down and peering ahead, skirting the stray animal, one to each side.

Fiona could see a look of satisfaction on her father's face as he leaned on a strainer post working the dogs. He seemed to have forgotten all about her, to be in a world of his own.

The ram had scented the dogs, now, and skittered away. But they closed on him, getting between him and the dam. Another piercing whistle and they stopped and slumped down, bellies on the ground. The ram settled a little, then began to change direction, heading up the slope, getting nearer. A further sharp whistle and both dogs came to their feet and warily followed the animal, keeping the pressure on. Zig-zagging, the woolly beast made steady progress up towards them.

"So, Lady Fiona wants a flash new pony, eh?" her father said unexpectedly. His eyes were still firmly on the dogs and the ram, and the look of contentment on his face was now unmistakeable. "Well, I don't see why not. I don't see why not."

She swallowed to control her surge of excitement, but she couldn't suppress her gasp of surprise completely. A new pony! And probably she would get to choose exactly the one she wanted!

"Thanks, Dad!" She tried to keep her voice calm, not wanting to risk his displeasure. The ram had stopped, looking suspiciously ahead. It was close enough now for them to see the three vee-shaped pieces taken from one of its ears.

The look on her father's face was now one of smug righteousness. "I was right. Bloody Boulton mongrel," he muttered to himself.

Fiona stretched up and kissed her father on his cheek. Her mother would probably say she didn't deserve it, but she knew she would get her new pony now. Her father didn't break his word. Not for anything. "Thank you, thank you," she said.

If he hadn't been so preoccupied, she might even have hugged him.

IV

Three thousand miles to the north of New Zealand, on the western side of the island of Viti Levu in the Fiji Group, sugar cane grows densely and abundantly along the coastal fringes and, in some places, far inland as well. Mostly, this cane is grown by the descendants of migrants from the sub-continent of India, though Fijians frequently join with the Indians in the tasks of collecting and transporting the cane to the mills, while Europeans, and others of mixed European and Fijian ancestry, are also to be found, prominent in the management and the operation of those mills.

Almost all the mill workers are housed in company quarters; some in long lines of barracks-like buildings, and some, the more senior, in detached dwellings. Taken together, these company dwellings form compounds that are in some ways as much, in some ways even more, close-knit as communities than the villages and towns from which they are separated by distance or by choice.

The western side of the island of Viti Levu is dry for much of the year, and the compounds, which are a little inland and close to the mills, as well as the roads that lead to them, are often made dusty by the draught of hot winds that blow relentlessly from the north-west. It is under these sometimes difficult but fundamentally benign conditions that tribes of the children that are to be found within each compound are schooled, form alliances, learn the ways of adults, devise games of greater or lesser danger to life and limb, spy on their elders from the fringes of the frequent *yaqona* or beer drinking sessions that provided the greater part of adult leisure activities, and generally keep themselves amused in a mostly harmless enough fashion.

Among those children, in the years following the Pacific War, is a precocious young girl. At this time of uncertain peace in the world, she is just a child – a light, wiry creature who runs with a gang of boys, mostly older than herself, and who refuses to be treated as anything other than a true and full member of the tribe. Her name is Atelaite, although the jumble of vowels is usually shortened to Tela. Her father is a foreman at the Mill, which means that she lives in a house separate from the lines, a circumstance that gives Tela, along with her parents and all of her siblings, a certain extra status amongst others of their kind – a status that is only a little lowered by their relatively dark skins.

There is much variation in regard to skin colour amongst those called variously half-castes (by those who wish to belittle or offend), or *kailoma* or part-Europeans (by those who do not). In general, lighter skin is highly regarded, though not invariably so. More important as indicators of tribal identity and, therefore, of a distinctiveness that is treasured by them, is the constant use of the English language – even though it is a version that is peppered with Fijian and Hindi words – and (perhaps even more importantly) the possession of a European surname. In the last, young Tela and her siblings are well enough served, for their surname is Gilbard.

Much more than any others of her age, Tela Gilbard is aware of the forces of change that have been at work in Fiji since the end of the Pacific War, and she is by turns excited and mystified by them, and wants, above all, to experience and understand them. For Tela Gilbard is a girl of quite exceptional alertness and curiosity. At the age of eleven, she is generally recognised as such by any who come into regular contact with her. She is not simply the sort of bright girl that any parent would be proud of; she is clearly, almost frighteningly, and certainly insatiably, inquisitive and quick in her understanding, to an extent far beyond any of her peers.

V

Because of her marriage to Ollie Gilbard, Tela's Fijian mother, Kelera Gilbard, had eventually been accepted by the part-Europeans with whom she was largely obliged to interact, as an honorary member of that community. It was not an honour that she herself placed much store by, as she was not at all dissatisfied with her own ancestry. She had, however, fallen in love with a *kailoma* (the term meant one in the middle, neither European nor Fijian, and who therefore had no rights to land, no place to stand), despite her own family's strong disapproval of her weakness, and had married him over all objections. She had been a small, slim, yet determined young woman, then. She is larger, now – as befits a matron, mother of a boy and three girls – but she is no less unyielding in her determination to live her life according to her own principles. She had made her bed all those years ago, and she lies in it still. She had had to adjust to her married life in terms of the people she dealt with in her day to day life, but she remains staunchly Fijian, *taukei*, in most of her habits. She takes her church-going seriously, never missing a Sunday even though her husband usually prefers to drink grog or beer with his friends while she worships. She insists, though, that her children accompany her. Furthermore, she cooks *dalo* and *vudi* at meal times, despite her husband's avowed preference for potatoes – a vegetable that Kelera thinks is largely without substance and distinctly insipid in flavour. It is food fit only for Europeans, the *kaivalagi*, and vastly inferior to the produce grown in the dark and fertile soils of her ancestral lands. Nothing other than that produce is fit for her children, she believes.

And that is another thing about Ollie, her husband. Not only is he *kailoma* in his behaviour, that part of him which is not white, the *taukei* part, is from a different province, and not even from the same island. Ollie Gilbard had been born in Ovalau, a much smaller island off the distant eastern coast of Viti Levu. Perhaps, she thinks, he might have been more Fijian had he been able and willing to keep contact with his roots, with the lands and peoples of his grandmother's ancestors. Then he would have at least had a place to stand. Life would have been simpler, she believes, if Ollie Gilbard had been – well, less of a man without true roots – less European.

But whenever she has such thoughts, Kelera Gilbard feels annoying and unwelcome pangs of guilt. She tries to suppress them, knowing that they are, in truth, an admission that her parents had been right. There is nothing now that she can do about her situation other than accept it. And that is made a little easier by the fact that she still loves Ollie. Mostly, at least. And if she ever stops loving him, well that will make little difference. She has made her bed.

VI

Ollie Gilbard, Tela's father, is a tough, wiry man in his early fifties – a hard drinking man who lives as much by his often addled wits as he does by anything else. In part, this is a matter of necessity, as his lack of gravitas and bulk is made even more obvious by his relatively short stature. But he is also a clever man, and he has long used his cleverness to gain the confidence and goodwill of the Manager and other Europeans who comprise the senior staff at the Mill. The Mill Manager is Australian, and a man who is less interested in any physical or moral deficiencies a man might have than in that man's ability to carry out his duties effectively. And in this respect, Ollie Gilbard makes a very good choice as Foreman. He is cunning in his understanding of the men in his gang, with a quick mental agility that he uses to defuse possible problems and to justify his own actions to his superiors when things do go wrong. But that is seldom, as the men under his supervision all offer him at least a grudging respect. He is even liked – by some, at least. He can speak the rapid-fire, jargon laden English of the majority of part-Europeans, but he can also speak the English of the colonisers. In fact (and this has made him more friends than he will ever know), he can speak a superior English to that of the

Manager himself – that worthy being disadvantaged in the eyes of most by his Australian drawl. But Ollie Gilbard can also speak fluent Fijian, and Hindi. The men he supervises, no matter who they are, cannot plot behind his back, nor escape a justified berating. He can discipline them or joke with them in whatever language is required. Ollie Gilbard, it seems, has every eventuality well and truly covered.

Tela's father has long been very much aware of her special qualities, and has favoured, and continues to favour her in ways that her mother refuses to do. As far as he can, and there is generally enough money to be able to do so, he encourages her reading by buying her books that he thinks she might appreciate, even if it means temporarily forgoing a carton of Australian beer, and by boasting of her cleverness, which he brings to the notice of whoever he thinks might be able to further encourage her to extend her knowledge.

It is her father who, in that same decisive year – it is the year that also sees Tela choose, deliberately and painfully, not to be a Fijian daughter to her mother – takes her to see the wife of the Mill's Chief Chemist in the sprawling house on the seaward side of the compound. It is second in size only to that of the Manager himself, with wide verandahs, ample servants' quarters, and the very best (or at least the second best) of Company-provided furnishings.

Mrs Wallace, has the slightly glazed look of one who frequently has one or two too many afternoon gin-and-tonics. She comes to the door herself, and greets Tela's father warmly enough, after a momentary look of puzzlement.

"You kindly suggested I bring my daughter to meet you, Mrs Wallace," her father says, using his very best English. "You mentioned that she might be able to borrow some books."

Tela looks up at her, and can sense her momentary bewilderment. She is a tall woman who sways slightly as she stands there; but then the vague look becomes a smile of understanding, of remembrance.

"Oh yes, so I did. Of course. Do come in, dear. What age is she, Mr Gilbard? I think you did say, but I've forgotten. And her name?"

"Her name is Tela, Mrs Wallace. She is a great reader."

"Yes, yes. So you said," She looks more closely at her then. "And what age are you Tela? You look rather… small."

"I'm eleven, Mrs Wallace. Almost twelve," Tela replies. She, too, uses her very best English.

"Well… I think, perhaps, most of the books I have would be a little too… Are you a *very* good reader, Tela?"

"She reads everything, Mrs Wallace," her father puts in. "She reads your great novelists when she can find them, and she reads science books, too. She reads everything she can find. I think the school library books are mostly too easy for her."

"Goodness! She must be very special. Well, leave her with me, Mr Gilbard, and we'll see what we can find."

Her father leaves them then, looking rather smugly pleased with himself, Tela thinks. She follows the woman into a comfortable looking room over which a large ceiling fan gently swishes. Beside one of the armchairs Tela notices a table on which stands a bottle, some sort of canister, and a half-filled glass. After taking due note of these things, she turns her gaze again to the woman, just in time to register that she has been observing her, and that she has seen her interest in the table and its contents.

"I was just having my afternoon tipple," she says. She smiles, and her eyes seem to offer Tela an apology and an acceptance – an understanding that her original assessment of her being nothing more than an unknowing little girl was completely wrong. "But you mustn't take me to be an old soak."

Tela blinks, watching her closely. "What's a soak?" she asks.

"I think you've guessed already," Mrs Wallace replies, still with a smile. "It's a New Zealand term for a drunkard. And I'm not a drunkard. At least, I hope I'm not."

"Are you a New Zealander, Mrs Wallace? You sound English."

"Yes, I'm a New Zealander, Tela. Though I spent many of my young adult years in England. I was at University there. It's where I met Mr Wallace. He is English."

"Which University, Mrs Wallace? What did you study?"

The woman doesn't answer immediately, but looks even more closely at her, eyebrows raised. Then: "You *are* an astonishing child, aren't you! A child who is not really a child at all." She sits down on one of the armchairs, and with a gesture, invites Tela to do the same.

There is a further pause as they both settle themselves. "I was at Cambridge, Tela. And I studied English literature. Have you heard of a writer called George Eliot?"

"Yes. Her real name was Mary Ann Evans. I've read *The Mill on the Floss.*"

"Have you indeed! And what did you think of it?"

Tela recalls the book in her mind, and is a little surprised at the strength of the emotion she feels as the scenes came flooding back to her. It is like remembering old friends, discovering that they are still there, in her head. She remembers how real Maggie Tulliver had become to her, how familiar she had seemed. Almost like a twin sister. "I think it is the best book I have ever read," she says.

Tall and thin, Mrs Wallace unfolds herself from her chair and stands up. To Tela, her eyes no longer seem glazed, but full, rather, of kindness, with hidden depths. The woman crosses to her and stoops to take her hands, bringing her, too, to her feet. "We're going to be very good friends, Tela. I believe we are already. And I think we will be able to help each other. Come, let me show you something."

She keeps hold of one of Tela's hands and leads her out of the large room and into a smaller one next door, a room lined with bookshelves. On the far wall stands a glass faced cabinet, and it is in front of this that Mrs Wallace stops. Behind the glass are shelves containing neatly arranged books, many of them leather bound.

"This is my George Eliot shrine," Mrs Wallace says. "There are some first editions here, you know. Altogether, every word of fiction she ever wrote. At least… everything she wrote that was ever published."

She opens the cabinet and reaches forward, selecting one of a group of three quite slim volumes that stand to the end of one of the shelves. Opening it, she traces her finger over the very first sentence, showing it to Tela.

Tela reads: 'A wide plain, where the broadening Floss hurries on between its green banks to the sea, and the loving tide, rushing to meet it, checks its passage with an impetuous embrace.'

As she reads, she remembers the words, and remembers, too, exactly where she had been when she first read them, and the pictures that had then sprung to her mind; and neither she nor the woman feel a need at that moment to say anything further about what it is they share.

Interlude – from the Journal of Adelaide Gilbard

March 1873

Our efforts, Hannah's and mine, at bringing more women into our little group – of bringing Maori and settler women together to learn from each other and share our different ways of dealing with the business of living – continue to have small periods of success, and, alas, rather longer periods of failure. The most difficult problem is not unwillingness, but the intrusion into all of our lives of the more personal, the more seemingly urgent problems that relate to our responsibilities as mothers or wives or simply as house-keepers. Too often, there are reasons, and perfectly good reasons, for people not to come to our gatherings, even after they have expressed a willingness, even an eagerness, to do so. Perhaps a child is ill, or a husband has ordered that she be at home for some reason. Such things affect the attendance of both Maori and settler women.

Some months ago I had a minor triumph in persuading another townswoman to come and see what we were attempting to do. I say a triumph, because this woman, Mrs Hicks, is married to one of the up-and-coming commercial men of the town. Her husband has a steadily expanding business, which includes the largest of the blacksmith shops, and a newly opened hardware store in the best part of Devon Street. She herself is a rather timid creature, but with a good heart. Over the course of her visits with us, I came to know her a little, and to like her. Then there descended upon her certain domestic troubles that occupied her mind so much that she felt obliged to withdraw from our gatherings, at least temporarily – and I fear she is unlikely to resume her interest.

These problems, she confided in me, relate to her eldest son, a young man of thirteen or fourteen years, who is not her own, but the child of her husband's first wife; except that it seems to be now proven that the young man is not even that – that he is, in fact, the son of Mr Hicks' first wife by an unknown man. This revelation, brought to her notice by certain correspondence directed to her husband from a legal office in England and confirmed, much to her surprise, by Mr Hicks himself, was followed by the recent arrival by ship of a law clerk, a man who is acting as agent for the father of Mr Hicks' first wife, who is therefore young Hicks' true grandfather. This agent has persuaded both Mr Hicks, and the young man himself, that he should return with him to Wales, where he is to take the name and become the designated heir of his grandfather, a man of considerable property.

Mrs Hicks is made terribly upset by the decision, as not only has she always treated the lad as her own, she also knew and was friendly with his mother, who died on the ship on the way here when the boy was just a new-born. The now-revealed fact that the little babe had not been fathered by the woman's husband, who had then, of course, just been made a widower, had never before been revealed to her. She herself, Mrs Hicks, had been married to another man at this time, a man who later deserted her. It was only some years later that she was remarried to Mr Hicks, and became mother to his supposed first born.

April 17th, 1876.

I am amazed to see that it has been more than three years since I last wrote in this journal. Life has gone on. There have been little triumphs and little sorrows. The house has been shaped to suit our changing needs. The gardens have grown. We are not rich, but we are comfortable. Or so it seems. I believe that the main source of our comfort is the flow of remittances from Wales, but I do not question Tomas on the matter. I am a good and dutiful wife. As long as money is available to meet the monthly accounts, I see no need to enquire further. There would be no point. Tomas is the provider.

Underneath our apparent tranquillity, though, I, at least, have secrets that are almost too much of a burden for me to bear.

Tomas never takes the least bit of interest in the household accounts, so I know that I am perfectly safe in recording my thoughts and secrets here in this journal. Yet the greatest, the most dangerous of those secrets I have not yet recorded. I suppose I am reluctant to expose myself to the judgement even of those who might come to read these words long, long after I am dead. And even more reluctant to expose Clement. How can I be sure that such a reader of these words in the distant future would understand, would not condemn us both in their mind as being the vilest of creatures? We are not – or at least, Clement is not. Clement has not given his heart to any other.

Yet, yet, yet… What would it matter, after all? We would both be gone, far beyond the reach of censure, if these words are ever discovered. What would it matter? And to declare the secret would at least be honest, even if not harmless. And no one, ever, could ever understand who I, Adelaide Gilbard, really am or was unless they also know my secret.

My conscience is my enemy. Or so it seems, when this mood settles on me. When we speak together, Clement and I, our very minds seem to caress. It is almost too comforting to bear. We both know what is happening, what has happened, yet we continue to talk as if all is innocence. It would be easy, so very easy, to admit it to each other; but my conscience will not allow me, and because he is the gentle man he is, he will not take the lead. So… instead of it being the comfort to both of us that it should be, the word hangs above us, like that sword of old, ready to cleave, or kill. But that is too dramatic. At the very least, though, the word would change everything irrecoverably.

Love. Love. Love. There… to this journal I can admit it.

But not to him. Nor he to me.

Clement Harborough is my lover. And I am his.

There! It is done! It is written! How bald and brazen the statement seems, now that I have committed it to paper and ink! That is because those words do not tell of his gentleness, his thoughtfulness, his patience, his sweet, sweet regard for me – and mine for him. What more can I say? My eyes are made clearer by the sight of him, my thoughts are made more consequential when I share them with him – and yes, my body is excited by his touch. Yet my body, which has now produced two children whom I love with all my heart, for him, for Clement, my body is virginal still. Will it always be so? Will it? Will it?

On another matter, and one that is entirely, entirely unrelated – I am shortly to give birth again. He or she will be a May child, if our calculations are correct. I feel more comfortable about the coming event than I felt with either of the other of my children. Less excited, perhaps, but also less fearful. I suppose it is a matter of familiarity making the prospect of the whole business seem more matter-of-fact. I am hoping for a girl. Why, I do not quite know.

PART TWO: 1955-1957

Chapter One – The Ashcotts

I

Shortly before Helen Ashcott left home for the city and a place as a Junior in a design studio, the family moved to a little house in a town near the south eastern coast of the North Island. The idea for the move had been Win's elder daughter's, and it had been she who had located the property in the town which was nearest to the farm which her husband managed. The cottage, set right at the back of a full quarter acre section, had been intended to serve as the garage for the house that the owner planned to build in front of it. However, his job had taken him away from the town, and he was happy to sell the section and its building cheaply to Win's son-in-law, who in turn rented it to Win for a pittance. Of course, in conception it was no more than a temporary living space, but though it was cramped and had only the most basic amenities, it was perfectly habitable. To Win Ashcott, it was in every respect except size an improvement on the near-derelict old farmhouse in which she had been forced by circumstances to spend the last several years.

The conversion contained two tiny bedrooms, a bathroom-cum-laundry that was so narrow that it was necessary to edge sideways to reach the toilet (though it was an inside toilet, Win rejoiced), and one other space that served as a kitchen, sitting room and dining room all in one. The smoky, old-fashioned coal range provided hot water through its wet back, cooked the food, and heated the room in winter. Cramped it certainly was, and in summer the heat inside was at times exhausting – but in winter it was snug, at least. And in part compensation for the restricted space, the section outside was large, and it was not landscaped – which meant that Win could plan a garden, her own little estate in which she could carefully place her own favourite things. She envisaged the whole thing, as it would be when she had finished and the trees and plants had matured. She immediately began spending long hours each day planting dwarf apple trees, rows of blue hydrangeas along the boundaries, clumps of fuchsias and apothecary's roses around the cottage, a little bush walk of native trees in the middle of the plot, and, at the very end, closest the road, a copse of silver birches as a reminder of her old family home in New Plymouth.

For some reason, and it might well have been because she had been giving thought to the imminent problem of Jamie's senior secondary schooling, Win Ashcott had been thinking of her own High School days.

She hadn't enjoyed the experience exactly. There had been a part of her that rebelled against her aunt's and her father's insistence that she should knuckle down and work hard to achieve the best scholarly results of which she was capable. It had all seemed so pointless. On the other hand, she had enjoyed the sport that the school offered, particularly the hockey. She was good at it; quick on her feet and able to wield her stick with skill despite her rather short stature and her stocky build. Her nickname on the team had been Dodge. It was a name she accepted with smug satisfaction. Even her father seemed mildly amused by her hoydenish tendencies and by the discovery that she had been able to excel at something, even if it was not academically. Her aunt, on the other hand…

The thought of her aunt was accompanied by the usual vague feelings of guilt – but also by an echo of the old defiance which had been her defence against her aunt's seemingly deep-seated disappointment at her failure to behave in a way appropriate for the daughter of a lady. She could not but be aware of the fact that her lack of grace offended her aunt. It was not the way a girl who carried the name of Harborough should behave – and even less the way the daughter of a woman who had been born a Gerold should behave. Oh dear, yes! Grandfather Tomas Gerold, he of only uncertain and childish memory, had ever been held up to her and her sisters as the social exemplar, the one who connected them to the higher ranks of society back 'home'.

But it wasn't her 'home', that distant land she had never visited and probably never would. Nor had her mother ever been there – she, too, had been born in New Zealand, as had her aunt. How silly it had seemed to her then, and still did, that her aunt always referred to Britain as 'home'!

So she had seen out her High School years, remembered now more for her constant feeling that her aunt was disappointed with her. Had she cared? She had pretended that she did not. But of course, she *had* cared. It had affected her. It had driven her into further defiance; and yet it had also, at times, led her to imagine ways of gaining her dead mother's approval. Not just during her school years, but also later, when she had left school and begun to seek a further purpose to her life. And, naturally, that further purpose had centred on…

She gasped with the suddenness and the pain of the memory that now seized on her. Ralph… Ralph… Even her aunt had had to accept that Ralph was an acceptable suitor. Tall, charming – and the son of a man who was not only the part owner of the local newspaper and owner of many hundreds of acres of good Taranaki soil, but, more significantly, one whose grandfather had once been Governor of a British territory in the West Indies.

Ralph had entered her life soon after she had left school. Why he had been attracted to her, she had never been quite sure. She was scarcely one of the town's beauties – though she supposed that in other respects she was at least of sufficient social status to be deemed eligible to become his partner. And she supposed that although she wasn't tall and fair, her reddish curls and her sometimes pert, sometimes pouting features at least made her interesting. Certainly Ralph had made his interest clear; and he had been a frequent caller at their house on the hill. On three separate occasions he had taken an opportunity to kiss her. She still remembered each of those occasions with sweet and girlish fondness. By the time he sailed off to fight the Kaiser, they had a kind of understanding. They were not engaged, exactly – but even her aunt accepted that on his return, they would…

But he hadn't returned. He had been killed within a month of arriving at the Western Front. She had been within two weeks of her nineteenth birthday when the news arrived, and that particular future was forever lost. What she had gained from her contact with Ralph, though, was the knowledge that she needed a man in her life. Before Ralph, she hadn't given much thought at all to boys. To men. But Ralph had awakened something in her that now became a part of her, a part of her fabric of defiance against her aunt's view of her as the irredeemable hoyden. As she recognised the needs of a woman within her, so did she become ever more of a rebel. The world had taken her lover; but she would find another.

And a couple of years later, she had found Ned.

III

It was hard to accept, now, that she had ever thought of Ned as a romantic figure. But she had. She must have. If she searched deep enough, she could probably still find the feeling of rebellious excitement that he had generated in her, a trace, still, of that combination of attraction and apprehension that had held such irresistible appeal.

When she had first set eyes on him, he had been a merchant seaman; yet she quickly discovered that he was also an arrogantly intelligent man who read widely, and one whose artistic skills demonstrated a degree of sensitivity that seemed very much at odds with what she then believed would have been the requirements of a seaman's life. At the time of their first meetings, however, none of those anomalies had even occurred to her. His intelligence (corrupted by a selfishness and a sensuality that she had then only dimly recognised – and that as far as she *had* been able to detect it, had only seemed to add to the attraction she had felt), had been obvious enough; but she had certainly not been overwhelmed by it. She had felt then, and still did, that her own mind, while definitely less bookish, was equal to his in most other respects.

Yes, she had been surprised, then, that a seaman should have had the temerity to approach her, let alone that he should have proved so fluent

53

in his use of words, so persuasive and direct in his wooing. It was only much later that she realised that he must have chosen life as a merchant seaman in order to avoid the pressures that all young men in the country had experienced as the call went out for them to sacrifice themselves in the trenches of the Western Front. And a martyr to that particular cause, she was eventually to learn, was something that Ned would never have allowed himself to become.

It was a charity event held in their own gardens, something to do with raising money to help the returning troops, that had first brought her and Ned together. How strange it now seemed that it should have been such an occasion, so contrary in its aims to a whole range of Ned's beliefs, that should have served that purpose! But she hadn't known that, then. And she never did learn what it was that had brought Ned to the fundraising event in the first place. At the time, she had had no reason to wonder. She had not even known that he was a seaman. At the time, she had simply been at first alarmed, and then charmed by his attentions.

Irene had been the first to tell her of Ned's occupation. In that superior, favoured-sister way of hers, she had relayed the information, which she had received from one of her phalanx of acquaintances who deemed it their prime business to preserve social rectitude against any force that seemed to threaten it. "I should tell you, Win," she had said, not even trying to disguise her censure, or her self-righteousness, "that the young man who was paying you such close attention just now is off one of the ships that docked yesterday – a ship that is picking up animal skins, I believe. The ship's captain is over by the cake stall talking with Mrs Liardet. I was with the group when he made casual mention of your admirer. He is a deck-hand, evidently. Why he has chosen to attend such a gathering as this, I cannot imagine."

By then, Ned had excused himself temporarily from her company, but he had promised to return. Irene's news had surprised her – she certainly hadn't taken him to be a common sailor – but the knowledge hadn't caused her more than a passing disappointment. It hadn't killed the interest he had already aroused in her, as had undoubtedly been her sister's intention. If anything, given the mood she was in, it had piqued that interest.

Yes, they would have been deemed, or would have certainly considered themselves to be, the most respectable of New Plymouth's society, those at the charity that day. Collectively, they represented those who saw themselves as the leaders in taste and fashion – many of them treasuring the ties they still had, or pretended to have, with Britain. Yet even at that time she had harboured a particular resentment, certainly not envy, of such pretension. She considered herself to be a true colonial, a New Zealander first last and always. It was yet another bone of contention between herself and her aunt. It was rebellious thoughts such as these that had been in her head when Ned returned to resume his attempt at seduction.

"I detect something special in you," he'd said. "You're not like most of the crowd here, these snobs, are you?"

"I don't know what you mean," she'd replied. But of course she had known. She had known exactly what he meant; and to be considered *not* to be one of those from whom she was, at least momentarily, quite happy to be divorced, added to her burgeoning rebelliousness.

"You know very well what I mean," he'd continued. "And that's what I find most interesting about you. You in your fashionable skirt, you look as though you're one of them. But there's mud on the hem, and you don't mind. That's what makes you different. That's what interests me."

"And what should I care that you should claim such an interest?" she'd asked.

He'd chuckled; that knowing, oddly wheezing laugh that all too soon had become one of the things she liked least about him. But she had felt then that he could see right into the depths of her soul, that there was no point in denying it. She had felt that he was being thrillingly, daringly impudent, as well as presumptuous.

"And yet you do care, don't you?" he'd continued. The gaze of his cold blue eyes had been steady.

"Suppose I do," she'd said. "Suppose I do care. You are a sailor. Tomorrow, or the next day, you'll be gone."

He showed no surprise that she had learned of his position in life, and certainly no sign of humility. "Not if I have some good reason to sign off," he'd said.

And she had gasped, weak-kneed, at the implication of his words. All she knew about him, really, was his name, and the fact that he was a sailor – and even that last piece of information he had not himself volunteered. Now he was implying that if she were to offer him any sort of encouragement, he would leave the sea behind. For her sake. It was preposterous, of course, yet he made it sound believable.

She had been tongue-tied – an unusual state for her. She had tried to meet his gaze, to be as bold as he, but she had failed. Instead, she had felt the heat rise to her cheeks, and she had looked down, like a simpering fool. And he had laughed again – that knowing wheeze – and in that instant she knew that had they been alone together instead of in the gardens of her father's house, surrounded by those who considered themselves to be the cream of New Plymouth society, she would have gone into his arms, have given herself to him willingly, eagerly.

And that is exactly what she had done, many weeks later, in the little worker's hut in Pukekura Park. He had done what he said he would do. He had signed off from his ship, as he had said he would, and taken a job as a gardener in the Park. He had put himself deliberately in her way, and they had met again and again, always in secret. And then, in that cob-webbed shed in the Park, he had kissed her, and she had allowed his practiced hands to roam over her body, under her skirt, his magic fingers tracing and probing until all the feeble protest she was able to muster had ebbed away and she had simply let what happened happen, all her dregs of modesty and propriety cast aside as the irrelevancy she had always, at some level, known they were, and he had taken her virginity, her equally irrelevant virginity, and the world she had known and that had confined her was gone. Forever.

After that, of course, nothing could have stopped her from marrying him. At least he had promised her that much, gasping that promise in reply to her ridiculous request that he do so before she had made the bodily adjustment necessary to permit him that final incursion. But it hadn't truly mattered what his reply had been. She knew that. She had wanted him every bit as much as he had wanted her.

He would have known that, of course. Then why had he agreed? But she knew the answer to that question, too. He had agreed to marry her at least as much because of his desire for a victory over the snobs, as he called them, and her aunt most of all, as he had because of any overwhelming desire for her. He was driven by lust, that was obvious from the start, but it was certainly not a lust specifically for her. Soon enough, that had become indisputable. She doubted that he had given her as much as a single year's fidelity.

But… he had given her five children, and she was grateful for that, even though the youngest two were now her burden and hers alone. They were the only aspects of her life that gave her any hope or pleasure or meaning. True, Helen's looks, and even certain aspects of her personality – her sulky moodiness in particular – were constant and far from welcome reminders of her father, of Ned. But there was nothing of Ned that she could find in Jamie. Nothing at all, neither in his looks, nor in his habits. Jamie was hers. It was not at all hard to imagine that he was exclusively hers, that Ned had had no part in his genesis. It was a conceit to do so, she knew – yet she clung to it. Best of all, she was completely and blessedly certain that Jamie needed her.

IV

Jamie Ashcott is apprehensive and excited, both, by their move from the valley north of Auckland, deep into the southern parts of the North Island. He is more than a little apprehensive when he considers the inescapable fact that he will now have to go to a proper High School. He knows it will be a big school, too – far bigger than the primary school he had travelled to by bus when he was just a little kid. He knows this, because the town itself is big and bustling. Or so it seems to him. Not nearly as big and unfriendly as Auckland, of course. He is happy about that, at least.

He had never enjoyed his few trips into Auckland, with its screeching tram cars and lorries, and all the other traffic, and its pavements full of jostling people, who seemed to think that a small boy such as he had no right even to be sharing their space. He still remembers a time when he was about six or seven and on a shopping trip there with his mother. They were in Smith and Caughey's and something had attracted his attention. The store was crowded. He had looked around to tell his mother something, and she wasn't there. All he could see were stockinged legs that were not hers under coats that were not hers. His heart had raced and he had felt alone in a way that he had never felt before. He hadn't known what to do. He'd been so small then that people didn't even seem to notice him standing there, immobile and breathing fast. Trying not to cry. Then a large woman had almost knocked him over; but she had looked down and seen him, and stooped down towards him.

"Oh, I'm sorry little man," she'd said. "Where's your Mum, then?"

"I don't know," he'd managed.

But just then his mother's anxious face had appeared beside that of the fat woman.

"So there you are, Jamie!" his mother said. "I told you to stay close to me. You could have got lost."

"Sorry," he'd said. "This lady was very kind."

"Lady!" the large woman had exclaimed, smiling at them both. "What lovely manners!"

And his mother had smiled, too; that smug smile that creased her face whenever anyone praised him.

That incident was one of the very few things he ever could remember happening to him during his younger years.

And although the town they now live in at first seems quite big and bustling, he doesn't feel scared in the way he had felt that time in Auckland. It is not that big; and he soon discovers that it is not really frightening at all. In fact, with its picture theatres (two of them!) and its variety of shops, he thinks it might even turn out to be exciting.

He accompanies his mother when she attends an appointment with the Headmaster of the High School to talk about his enrolment. He stands beside her after she takes the offered chair, awed by the sight of the man who has first risen to greet them, then resumes his seat behind the broad desk. The Headmaster's suit is covered by a gown. His blotchy red face turns towards them, and his severe eyes look at them both closely.

"James is how old, Mrs Ashcott?" he asks.

"Well, he's still only fourteen, but he is quite bright, I think. Though he didn't finish all the School assignments he was supposed to finish last year – his Correspondence School assignments, that is. We had no way of getting him to a proper school, you see. I feel sure he could handle the Fifth Form work, though."

"We'll soon find out, Mrs Ashcott," the voice from behind the desk rumbles. He makes a note in the file he has in front of him. He looks up again. "He's rather a small lad, but he has an intelligent look about him. But we wouldn't want to have him out of his depth. Fourteen. But I see he'll be fifteen before the year is out."

"Yes. November."

"Well, I'll put him into one of the Fifth Form classes, and if he struggles we can always drop him back to the Fourth. Fifth Form means a chance at School Certificate, you know, though he doesn't have to take it this year. I presume he'll grow a little bigger, do you think?"

"Oh yes. He's not a… I mean, he's just a late developer. My other sons were the same."

"Very well, Mrs Ashcott. Shall we say the Fifth Form then? And just hope that he can manage?"

"Thank you, yes. I think he will be able to. He's just a little… a little lazy, perhaps."

"They are all a little lazy, Mrs Ashcott. It is a natural part of a boy's make-up. Their minds wander. But there are ways, tried and true. There are ways of dealing with that. We'll try him out. Five D, I think. A general stream. We, and he, will find his true level quick enough."

"Don't you let me down, Jamie," his mother says, on their way home after. "You were lucky not to be made to do the Fourth Form again, so do try your best. You won't be able to get away with avoiding work here. You won't be able to fool the teachers here the way you thought you fooled me. Sending away envelopes that were mostly empty and pretending you'd done the assignments when you hadn't even tried!"

He feels suitably abashed. It is true. By the time he had finished the Third Form he had learnt many ways of pretending that he had done the things he was supposed to do when he hadn't actually done anything at all – anything other than make his model aeroplanes, that is; or read the books he ordered from the School Library. At least he hadn't tried to fool anyone about the number of books he read. The Librarian had even written him a little note of congratulations, saying he had in that year ordered more books than anyone else in the whole of the Correspondence School. But yes, he really should have spent more time on his Science and Maths. But he had kept up pretty well with Social Studies and Art, and especially English. He'd always managed to put something in the assignment envelopes from those three subjects.

V

At first when he starts at School, Jamie feels lost and confused. These rather unpleasant feelings are tempered, though, by an undercurrent of excitement. It is strange being surrounded by boys, and girls, who greet each other loudly, who jostle together, who split into groups and walk around on mysterious missions, laughing or squealing. And sometimes, from the boys, letting off loudly (though he's told soon enough that the accepted term in this superior place is not 'letting off', but 'farting'.) All of this takes place without any reference to him at all except for an occasional unfriendly or curious glance.

He notices that there are one or two others beside himself who seem not to be part of any group. One of these is a boy with hair even more gingery than his own; a tall, skinny boy with glasses and, he thinks, a kind face. In the afternoon, when all of those who have been placed in the same class as him assemble for the first time in their allocated room, he and the boy find themselves seated side by side.

"Are you new too?" Jamie asks.

"No," the boy replies, but with a friendly smile. "I'm Brian Finney. I've bin here since Third Form."

"Finney! Talking as usual!" the Form teacher's voice booms out, as if in confirmation.

"Sorry, Sir!" Finney replies, with a guileless smile.

After class, when the bell rings for the end of school, Brian catches up with him in the corridor.

"Everyone calls me The Professor," he says. "I think it's because of my glasses. I'm not surprised you thought I was new. I'm not sort of… Well, most of them think I talk too much. Even the teachers do. They don't seem to like it."

Jamie wants to show that he doesn't mind. "That doesn't seem like a good enough reason not to like someone."

"Oh, they like me. It's not that. I think what they don't like is the things I like talking about, and the words I use. Too serious, or something."

"Maybe that's why they call you The Professor."

"Yes, that could be another reason. Either that or the glasses. And I don't swear. I think that's because my mother never let me swear when I was a kid, and she'd be hurt if she knew I'd started. We're a church-going family. My father doesn't swear, either. Not when my Mum's around, anyway."

"Yeah?" Jamie is beginning to wonder just how long the particular line of conversation is going to last, but he doesn't want to be rude. It is good to feel that someone thinks he's worth talking to. "*My* mother wouldn't like to hear me swear, either," he says. He thinks a change of topic might be a good idea. "There was no High School near where I came from. This is the first proper High School I've been to."

"It's not bad here," Brian, alias The Professor says. "That's if you don't mind all the swearing."

Jamie and Brian remain friends all year, despite the fact that Jamie quickly discovers that The Professor is not at all good at his schoolwork, and that he sometimes says things that make him seem… well, pretty stupid. *And* he is totally useless at sport. Those things don't seem to matter all that much, though, when measured against the fact that Brian is always ready, and even eager, to be in Jamie's company. So they become and stay close friends, if only during school hours, and the others in his Class seem to accept them as such.

But it is sport that gradually brings Jamie to the attention of other, more popular boys. He has always been good at sport, though being alone for the past two years has meant he has had little opportunity to take part in organised sport since leaving Primary. Still, he now has the chance to start playing team games again; and once the rugby season starts, he starts to feel very much more a part of things. Not confident, but at least more accepted.

At first he is put in a low-grade team that takes part only in Saturday competitions, and not against schools and colleges in other towns, but his speed and determination quickly earn him the respect and attention of the Music Teacher, who is also a senior rugby coach. Only three weeks into the season, he is elevated to the giddy heights of Left Wing in the School's Third Fifteen.

VI

Win Ashcott was beginning to feel more settled, even mildly optimistic, by the chance she has been given for a fresh start in a new place. Helen was no longer a worry, at least not for the moment, as she had found herself a place in the YWCA hostel in Auckland. She would have to find somewhere else eventually, but for the moment she was happy enough. With her job, too – or so she said in her letters. So now it was Jamie she could concentrate on, almost exclusively. Jamie – her biggest hope, almost since he had been born. Well… except for Haddon, of course. But Haddon was dead, though ever alive in her thoughts. No, no, not dead, never dead. But he was gone from the world. Now there was only Jamie. He could never be quite the comfort to her that Haddon had been, she knew that. Haddon had loved her as a son should, had taken her side at all times, protected her from the worst effects of Ned's carelessness, his philandering, his lack of purpose. Haddon had been a constant source of pride – but more, much more than that. He had been the reason she had looked forward to the future. Haddon – so handsome, so perfectly mannered, so loving towards her that she could scarcely believe she had borne him.

Then the shocking news had changed everything, and she had had to suffer not only her own grief, but also Dougal's. For weeks and months Dougal had refused to accept the reality of his adored brother's death, telling her how he was certain that it was all a mistake, that Haddon must have been taken prisoner by the retreating Germans, that he would come back to them. And later still, when reality could not be denied, curling in on himself, withdrawing from her, from his sisters, his brother. Seeking a place for himself, any place that might help him forget. And she had been no help to him at all, consumed as she had been by her own unrelenting grief.

Jenny, closest in age to Haddon, his beloved, or at least tolerated, companion through much of his childhood – she, too, had loved Haddon, in her own, careless way, but his death had hardly altered the flow of her life. She was married now, with her own children. She had always been far too interested in boys. Even while Haddon had been flying his Spitfire over Italy's and the Balkan's battlefields, she had been out on the town, flouncing around seeking male company. Just seventeen or eighteen she had been then, chasing the boys. American servicemen or local lads, it seemed to be all the same to her. She was uncontrollable, and Ned had just laughed off her worries. Girls will be girls, he said. It was just one more thing driving them apart. Jenny, with her irrepressible high spirits, her stubbornness, her flaming red hair, her jaws working at the chewing gum she cadged off the Americans. A lost cause, she had thought her. But it had all come right in the end. A warm-hearted woman now, loving her children, but still unpredictable, still impulsive.

So here she was, with a chance to start her life anew, in a new town. Yet… what had really changed? She was still Win Ashcott.

And with that last thought, her smile vanished. She had never been an Ashcott in any but name. She could never have been. She only wished that none of her children bore the name. The girls could escape it, of course. Jenny had already escaped the curse, and with luck, Helen would not be far behind. But Jamie… Like Dougal, Jamie would have to carry the name forever.

VII

Jamie is awakened by the gentle shaking of his bunk. He becomes instantly alert, thinking it must be an earthquake, like the one that had struck the town earlier that year; then he remembers that there is someone in the bunk bed above him. It is Dougal. His brother.

He lies still for a time, adjusting to the knowledge. Dougal rarely appears, and when he does, it is a welcome interruption to the normal routines of life. Jamie remembers him calling on them just before they left their place up north and came here. Then, Dougal had seemed to want to talk to him seriously, his brows knitted together and his eyes seeking his. He'd wanted to talk about God, and honouring their mother, and putting others first. He hadn't really understood what he was talking about. He'd felt embarrassed, and had avoided Dougal as much as he could during that visit.

This time, he is a bit different. He had arrived only the day before, and said he couldn't stay long. He was still quiet, and serious, but at least he didn't talk about God; and he'd been quite interested to hear how High School was going. He would have liked to talk more with him last night, but Dougal had wanted to talk about things with their mother, things about the old days. Things that he had no remembrance of. The days when Haddon had been at home. He'd tried to stay up, but in the end he'd gone to bed.

Lying in bed before he went to sleep, he'd thought about things in the past, about how little he himself could remember about it. It was often like that with him. He seemed to be very poor at remembering things that had happened more than two or three years ago; and he had no memory at all of the things that his mother and Dougal had started talking about. Even his mind's-eye view of Dougal is less from any remembered images of him, and more from his mother's ways of talking about him. 'You should be respectful of your elders, like Dougal,' she often says; or 'Dougal never uses bad words. You should take a leaf from his book.'

Now, with the morning light creeping into his bedroom, some of the excitement at Dougal's arrival surges in him again. He remembers especially that Dougal had arrived on a motorcycle, a green and black BSA, beautifully noisy. It had been raining heavily at the time, so Dougal had been soaking wet and cold. After he had had a bath and warmed up, and put on fresh clothes that their mother had found for him, he and his mother had walked around the rain-soaked garden and talked about the shrubs and plants and about how to get rid of the pests.

None of this interested Jamie. Once again, he had felt left out. That feeling had continued into the evening, and he'd left the two of them talking in the kitchen and gone to bed. And now, he is awake, and sensing the waking movements of his brother in the bunk above him.

His brother. His surviving brother. At least he knows him. Not well, it's true; but when he is not here he can at least have a sort of personal picture of him in his mind. And when he is here, infrequent though his visits are, he does feel some curiosity, even if Dougal rarely seems to be willing to talk properly with him. And when they do talk, he always feels that Dougal treats him like one who doesn't know much at all about anything; but at least he has stopped trying to talk to him about God. He thinks he likes Dougal, but he is not quite sure. He knows that he is glad he has a brother, though, even if he hardly ever sees him. Even though he seems mostly to be more like a saint, or at least someone he is told he should try to be like, than a brother.

Later that day, when his brother and mother are once again deep in conversation that doesn't interest him, this time about plants and trees, he goes to his room and looks through the books on his shelves. At his insistence, they had brought everything from his room up north, putting the books and magazines, including the copies of Haddon's *Popular Mechanics*, in cartons that he had unpacked soon after they arrived. It was then that he had taken notice again of the old books labelled 'Accounts' that his mother had given him years earlier. He had forgotten about them, and had never looked again inside their covers.

Now he takes one from the shelf and opens it. Once again, the details he finds there – lists of things that had been bought, and their prices – don't seem very interesting. He puts it back on the shelf and instead picks up one of his new schoolbooks. He lifts it to his nose and snuffles in the scent of ink and gum. Unlike most of the other books he has been issued with, this one is brand new, and all the more exciting for that. It is called *Palgrave's Golden Treasury*. It is a book of poetry, and he has already found a poem in it that he thinks is the best he has ever read. He finds it, and reads aloud to himself his very favourite verse:

'Full many a gem of purest ray serene

The dark unfathom'd caves of ocean bear:

Full many a flower is born to blush unseen,

And waste its sweetness on the desert air.'

He reads it a second time. He does not quite understand why it should make him feel the way it does – a little sad, a little tender, yet wanting to seek out the cave, to find the flower – but he is glad of the feeling. It makes him happy to be alone with the book. With T. Gray, the poet.

Chapter Two – Tela and Fiona

I

In her fifteenth year, Fiona Finlay's enthusiasm for horses began to wane. It was partly the fact that both her father and her mother insisted that she take an ever-increasing responsibility for Sabre's exercise, training and general care whenever she was home for the holidays. While she accepted that it was a reasonable expectation on their part, particularly given that when she was in school her father and Jerry, the cowman-gardener – and mostly Jerry, she could be pretty sure about that – had to do the necessary tasks, she did not appreciate the fact that when she was at home, instead of being just able to relax and maybe listen to music or something after a hard term's work at school, she was faced with the very often unpleasant duties associated with Sabre's well-being. If it had remained simply a matter of saddling up and putting Sabre to a few jumps, then her natural feelings of affection for the gelding might have kept her love of horses going longer. But now it seemed to her that her passion had been a childish one, and totally unsuited to the sophisticated young woman she now believed she was.

The mirrors she gazed into every morning, both the tiny, apologetic one in her shared room at school and the considerably more generous mirror in her bedroom at home, gave her constant affirmation of her assessment of herself. What she saw was a face still a little annoyingly softened by what her mother called puppy fat, but one that seemed every day to be getting prettier and more interesting. There was a scattering of freckles over her nose that she wasn't quite sure about; but apart from them, her features were nearly faultless. Beyond pretty, even. She saw grey-blue eyes under brows that she had once thought too dark and prominent, but which she now thought set off her shield-shaped face to perfection. She saw a broadish mouth, with full, bowed lips. 'Eminently kissable' her school friend Briar called them – and she quite often tried them out against her palm, imagining what it would be like to actually have them against those of a handsome boy. Not that there was any chance of that – neither while she was at school nor at home. The only time any boys were allowed at school, or when they themselves were allowed out, they were supervised so closely that nothing like that was even possible. And it was much the same at home.

Yes, even at home. Her mother and father still treated her as though she were a child.

"You need to get up earlier," were her mother's first words to her that morning, the first day home after the School break-up. She'd poked her head through the bedroom door without so much as a knock. It was no different from school, really. No privacy. No chance to just relax and have a bit more sleep.

In fact, Fiona had been awake for some time when her mother came in, but had deliberately chosen to stay in bed and thus, she hoped, avoid a lecture of the sort that her mother seemed now to be determined to give her. She had hoped her delay in appearing at the breakfast table would have meant by the time she got there, her mother would have gone out to deliver her daily instructional to the cowman-gardener. No such luck.

"Your father and Murray have gone into to town. If you'd not been so keen on your bed, you could've gone with them."

She grumbled a reply, pretending indifference. In fact, she was considerably peeved that her brother should have gone into town without her. A trip into town, alone with their father. A trip into town without the crushing effect of their mother. It would have been an opportunity to press for a new twinset, or a pair of red wedgies, like the ones Briar had sneaked into her school suitcase and paraded around in at school whenever there was a chance to do so without getting caught.

"Oh well," he mother continued, "I suppose the fact that you're stuck here means that you can spend the day giving Sabre the exercise he needs…"

The satisfaction in her mother's voice was unmistakeable. Shee-it and frolicking hell! Now she faces a day with only her mother for company. Even giving Sabre his exercise is preferable to that. Boring, boring. Definitely not amusing.

She wishes school had started again already. At least at school she had her friends. When they weren't more concerned about making themselves seem cleverer or prettier or richer or whatever, they could at least at times be amusing. And the thought of being in the Fifth Form next term was mildly exciting. Some extra privileges, and a new batch of little Form Ones and Twos to lord it over or ignore, as the mood suited.

Amusing. It was a favourite word at school. Things were either amusing, or they were not. The food they were given was definitely not amusing, nor were the rules about lights out or the instructions about the appropriate words to be used when addressing teachers or other adults, or how to behave on those occasions when they were allowed out of the grounds to spend an hour or two in the village. Don't do this. Don't do that. Do nothing to dishonour the school or your family. Do not skylark or make unnecessary noise. You are here to learn not only the subjects you take, but also good citizenship. Good manners are what distinguish you from the less fortunate. Blah, blah, blah. Not amusing.

On the other hand, hearing a story about some romantic adventure that happened while on exeat, from those lucky enough to have parents instead of jailers, or comparing notes on the horrors of mothers – or brothers – that could well be amusing. Yes, she wishes very much for the start of school again.

And then for the end of school forever, and a life without the silly restrictions of either school or home.

In the meantime… Well, she should get out of bed, then decide how she was going to be today. Her life wasn't really so bad, she knew that. Even so… a bit of moping wouldn't hurt. A bit of resentment at Murray being taken into town without her. Come to think of it, her father had probably let him drive. Yet another privilege that Murray had that was denied to her. Yes, a bit of moping was called for. Particularly as she had the feeling the curse was about to descend on her. Resentment could rule for a while.

So decided, she let her feet hit the floor with enough of a thump to signal the decision, should her mother have still been loitering outside her door.

II

At precisely the same time as Fiona Finlay is bewailing her lot, but some thousands of miles to the north of her, Tela Gilbard, now fourteen years old, looks up from the book she is reading – a book entitled *Forever Amber* that has been loaned to her by one of her elder sister's friends – and thinks about her personally very limited experience of the sort of romantic preoccupations that seem to be the main, almost the sole, concern of the heroine. It is not as though she has no recognisable urges of that nature, or that she is unfamiliar with the physical processes involved. In fact, over the past year or two, the boys in her tribe have often boasted of their having done it with this girl or that. They still think of themselves as a sort of tribe, and some even still identify themselves by the name they had agreed upon years before, when they were just kids – the Highbirds. They have her to thank for the name. She had suggested that they call themselves The Hybrids, though she hadn't explained what it meant, and was content to let them mispronounce it as The Highbirds.

One boy, a newcomer to the tribe, whose family had only recently shifted to the compound from Suva, had even suggested, not so long since, that they 'give her one', that that was the only way girls should be allowed into the tribe. "She's a girl, eh? She's just a *toi*, eh? If she's gunna stay, she should give us all one whenever we want."

She hadn't been at all perturbed by the threat. He was an outsider, after all. He might think he was one of them, but it didn't happen easily, not just like that. Only one of the others had reacted to the suggestion with a leer, and a sneaky look at her. That was Johnny Falconer, with his bung leg and his ears that stuck out like they had when he was just a snivelling little boy. She had never really taken to him – but along with the rest, she had allowed herself to tolerate his presence. At that point though – that snigger had made him an enemy for life. Both him and Suva-boy.

"No one touches me," she'd said.

"Yeah, no one touches her," Dan Millar had growled; and after that there was a general muttering of agreement all round. Suva-boy had the sense to look down at his feet, abashed, deflated like a pricked party balloon. Johnny Falconer, too.

Looking back on it now, she recognises that the feelings she had had at that moment for big Dan and his determination to protect her, were probably her initiation into looking at boys differently, into looking at them as a girl rather than just as a fellow member of the tribe. Big Dan – strong, with muscles that flowed like poetry. At that moment she hadn't cared that she thought him slow-witted and clumsy in his speech. Something had churned away inside her. Just as well Dan couldn't have read her thoughts. He probably wouldn't have known how to handle them; or her.

Anyway, here she is, still a virgin, yet having run with boys nearly all her life – having been so completely accepted by them that they had never even hesitated to pull out their *boces* and pee in front of her, or to strip off and swim naked with her (though she never did the same) or to joke and boast about what they imagined they would do or had done with their equipment when or if the chance arose. Even, every now and then, showing off their erections to each other. She is probably more aware than most girls of what boys look like under their shorts and what they talk about and what they think is important about girls. It doesn't do much for her own feelings, by and large. Nor does it cause any ripples of lust to flow through her.

She knows quite a lot about female lust, having read, among other books bearing on the topic, a well-thumbed and poor-quality edition of *Fanny Hill* that an unhappy Australian mechanic had thrown out along with copies of *Men Only* and *Playboy*, and less interesting rubbish, shortly before breaking his contract and leaving Fiji for good. No, by and large she is happy enough to be a virgin, even though there have been times, like that occasion with Dan, when she would have been willing to find out what it is like *not* to be a virgin. But really, boys seem to be pretty stupid, on the whole. Nice enough, most of them, and not so spiteful as girls often were – but pretty stupid.

She knows her problem with other girls springs from two things, neither of which she can, or would want, to do anything about. Firstly, there is no disguising from herself or anyone else that she has a very quick mind. As a little girl, it hadn't taken her long to realise that the length of time others took before they understood something, or the mistakes they made in coming to a decision about something, were not so much because they were incredibly slow as because she was incredibly fast. Ergo (and yes, she has long since absorbed the cogito principle), it was she and not them who was different. The discovery had not pleased her, exactly, as her quickness has never made her popular with other girls, but it is something she has had to come to terms with. It is also something that she rapidly learned to use to her advantage.

The other thing that she is forced to accept about herself is that she has fine features, not at all like many of the other part-European girls. Those fine features, her nose in particular, are a source of great envy on their part. They might sneer at her relatively darker skin, or at her small size and her skinny frame, but the chance possession of a narrow nose, and a finely tapered chin, more than compensates for what is viewed as almost unforgivably dark pigmentation. In fact, she knows that even judged by *kaivalagi* standards, her face is a pretty one; and there is nothing more desirable amongst the part-European female population than a face that can be compared with that of pretty white girls. Like those they see on the screen at the cinema, or in magazines, for instance. For herself, it means little – except that she can hardly ignore the jealousy it invokes. It is a further reason why she has always chosen the company of boys rather than girls. She had surmised from a very young age that boys, by and large, would hardly feel threatened by the way she looked.

Using the envied looks, and her quickness, she had soon enough discovered that there were very few situations that she could not profit from in some way, and she had very early begun to have ambitions that stretched far beyond the confines of the compound, beyond the western reaches of the island, and beyond Fiji as a whole. She has long been certain that she will travel overseas, and especially that she will one day visit, perhaps even live in, the countries that feature most in the books she reads.

One such country she has become increasingly interested in is New Zealand. It is partly her friendship with Mrs Wallace, the wife of the Mill's Chief Chemist, that accounts for this; but it is also the fact that ever since she first read some things about its history, New Zealand has seemed to her to be perhaps a little bit like that other, more distant land, the home of the King – or, now, the Queen – and the home, too, of the interesting and adventurous girls and women in the books that are her very favourite reading matter.

III

For a long time Tela Gilbard has been acutely aware that her existence is increasingly a divided one – one part of her dealing with the realities as they are, another part of her already starting to think in terms of the future and what she must do and become in order for her dreams to truly take tangible form. The reality is that in the meantime, she still has to deal with the difficulties attached to living in a noisy house, often full of her father's grog or beer-drinking friends, with a brother and two sisters, and a mother who does not favour her in any way. Her mother continues to offer her genuine affection, of course, as she has always done, but that does not weaken her determination to have her carry out her family duties, to adhere strictly to her lessons on morality and Christian behaviour, and generally to treat her with no special favour at all.

Her father, on the other hand, takes every opportunity, still, to boast of her cleverness to any who will listen, particularly his drinking companions, and to do whatever he can, in the face of her mother's stubborn resistance to treat her any differently from the other of her offspring, to favour her, encourage her, and use her abilities to boost his own self-worth. This excessive pride in her accomplishments frequently embarrasses Tela. She is aware that her successes are, to her father, a chance for him to vicariously live out some of his own long-since surrendered, or addled, dreams. She understands her father only too well. There is much of him in her – enough, even, for her to pity him.

But that is something she keeps very much to herself. Outwardly, she maintains towards him the demeanour that she knows pleases him most. In the house, she waits on him dutifully, exchanging glances of good-humoured understanding when her mother berates him for arriving home drunk, or when she nags him about his taking the Lord's name in vain. It is like that with other aspects of her life, too. She does not want to give the impression that she sets herself above others, or that she thinks herself too special, now, to share her life with her friends. True, she now believes that much of the activity she and her friends engage in is silly, or utterly without any meaningful purpose, but she continues to run with the Highbirds, or at least to greet the individuals within the gang in the same manner as she always has.

But it is all a pretence. She has metamorphosed into something so totally different from the little girl who had first taken up with the Highbirds that she knows within herself she can never any more be truly one of them. Metamorphosis. She likes that analogy. It is in this very year that she has discovered Kafka, and she immediately found she had no difficulty in identifying with the man who metamorphosed into an insect. She feels herself to be kin with him; to be, like him, out of place.

When she had finished primary school, more than two years since, passing her Fiji Junior exams without even having to take them seriously, she had at first looked forward to High School. She had imagined that attendance at the local High School would be her introduction to a new and exciting phase in her life. Soon enough, though, the large class sizes, the overworked, and sometimes inadequately trained, teachers, the dearth of resources, all combined to leave her bored and restless. It was only the Library that provided her with any satisfaction at all, and in very short time she had read every book it contained that held any interest for her.

Some of those books had inside them the stamp of the school in England, or Australia, or New Zealand, that had donated them. She would look at those stamps, and at the frequently ink-stained or dog-eared pages of the books, and imagine the pupils in those far off places who had used the books. How wonderfully lucky they were!

Meanwhile, she had completed the trivial exercises that the teachers required of her and was consistently at the top of the class in whatever subject was at hand, effortlessly beating even the little group of earnest, timid, and astonishingly well-behaved Indian girls and boys. The majority of the other pupils were Fijian, as the local Hindu and Muslim population had established their own schools that most of them attended. There was, though, a large group of part-Europeans at the School, many of them from the Mill. Although she developed a degree of friendship with some of the better and more serious scholars, mainly from amongst the Indian girls who seemed to admire her for her academic success, generally her time between classes was spent in the company of those of the Highbirds who had made it into the school.

The High School Library was not very well stocked, but it did contain a number of books that had enabled her to develop new skills and knowledge. Her reading has led her to distinguish in her mind between those subjects, such as Physics and Chemistry and Mathematics, that depended mainly on the discoveries of very clever people over the ages, and that help her to understand the physical world, and those subjects that are a reflection of mankind's inner life, and emotions such as love and hate, greed and compassion, fear and pride. History and Literature and Art she places in this category, and these are the books she enjoys most.

Religion is one more thing she has examined with her restless, logical mind. When she was nine, she had experienced the full, trembling horror that is sometimes the result of an inculcated belief in an omniscient and omnipotent God. Her mother had always told her that faith in God was necessary to her well-being, both in this life and in a promised hereafter. Those words of her mother's she had accepted without truly thinking about them. Until that time, midway through her tenth year. And it was in that moment of fear that she had turned her mind to examining the implications of her mother's words, and those of the preacher in the church she was obliged to attend every Sunday.

First, she had examined the notions from the point of view that her mother, and the preacher, were right – that God did exist, and that He was all-powerful and all-knowing. That He was vengeful, and would punish those who did not obey his rules for living. She studied the passages in the bible that dealt with the question of sins, and discovered that she had been guilty over and over of committing certain of them, particularly those relating to the honouring of her parents and of strictly keeping the Sabbath.

Her short-lived, initial responses to these discoveries meant that she had become, for a time, the bane of both her parents' lives. She had got under their feet in her anxiety to please them and thus mitigate the sins she had previously committed. At the same time, she had pointed out to them the occasions when she perceived that they, too, were sinning against the precepts of the scriptures. To her siblings, during this time, she became an insufferable prig. She even attempted to spark the conscience of the Highbirds, though with almost total lack of success.

Then her powers of reasoning had taken her beyond the blind acceptance of her mother's beliefs and into questions concerning the logic of a being in whose image mankind was said to have been made, who lived somewhere beyond the clouds, and who had not only made human beings, the earth, and all else besides, but who on a daily basis directed the affairs of the universe down to the last, minutest detail. It defied logic, she finally decided, after a particularly intense twenty-four hours of chasing thoughts down passageways that led to nothing, or to absurdities. That sort of God, she decided, did not exist, and never had.

And so, in the course of a few weeks during her tenth year, Tela had progressed from being a child who simply accepted her mother's view of religion and its importance in a totally unthinking manner, through a fevered determination to understand what the bible expected of her and to obey those precepts with a blind and fanatical faith (and to try to ensure that all others within her orbit also did so), and into a primitive yet developing form of humanism. At the end of this process, still not yet ten, she had announced to her mother that while she was willing to accept that Jesus had really existed, and even to accept that he was a wise man, she certainly could not accept that he was the Son of God – because if God existed at all it could certainly not be in the form of a man-like creature who was capable of impregnating a woman.

Her mother had thrown up her hands in genuine despair, but she had not attempted to answer the arguments herself. Tela, as time progressed and as she thought and read more deeply about the matter, had come to think that many of the problems that arose from a consideration of the role of religion were associated with semantics. Radically redefine God, she decided, and then it was possible to accept that Jesus was, metaphorically speaking, its son. It might even be useful to do so, especially if Jesus were viewed as being a metaphor himself – a metaphor for all of humanity.

This conclusion Tela had reached before the end of her twelfth year – before, even, she first met up with Mrs Wallace. It had served her well, and she had maintained it with only minor modifications ever since. She continued to attend church with her mother and her siblings, but the liturgies, the hymns, the sermons, the prayers and other routines, and even the bible itself, she henceforth treated as man-made accretions that obscured the truth yet no doubt had once served a purpose – and for some still did. She was willing to go along with the deception for the sake of family harmony – and for the sake of her own smooth progress in the world.

But that state of affairs, that inner denial and outward acceptance, could not continue indefinitely. There had come a time when things came to a head.

It had happened shortly before her thirteenth birthday. It was a Saturday. At breakfast, Tela's mother surprised her with the news that the Church Minister, the *talatala*, was coming to the house that morning. To talk with Tela, she said.

"To talk with me?" she asked, using her mother's habitual Fijian.

"I asked him to," her mother said; and she had guessed the nature of the conversation that had led to that result.

The *talatala* was a large, dignified and somewhat frightening man. To see him in their house, seated on one of their best mats, was very unusual. He was given a place of honour, and her mother sat herself, with due humility, a short distance away. She had then been called into the room.

Seeing the arrangement, sensing the special dignity of the occasion, she sank to her knees, then rose again and shuffled, head down, to the corner that her mother indicated. There had followed a solemn silence.

The reverend gentleman cleared his throat. "Your mother tells me you have been asking questions about our faith," he said. His words were delivered in Bauan, the Fijian of the Church. It was the language in which he preached. It was the language of the Fijian bible. It was not so very different from her mother's dialect, though somehow more formal, more alien. But it was commonly enough used for her to have understood perfectly.

She hadn't answered, and had kept her head bowed.

"What is it you question?" he asked.

She had felt a sudden revulsion at the situation in which she had been placed. Competing emotions raced through her. Respect for her mother's traditions. Respect, too, for her mother. It was not even possible to separate the one from the other. But she had for months, even years, felt an increasing alienation from those traditions, at least from the ones connected with her mother's faith, with the church. With that which, she knew, was at the very base of her Fijian-ness.

Then there was fear. She had felt, she had *known*, that the only honest answer she could give to the preacher's question would send her irrevocably down a path that would determine her future beyond any chance of reversal. It was a severance point. She had known.

She had felt the weight of the two figures seated across the room from her. She had been acutely aware of her own physical puniness, of her youth. Of her status as a child. She had felt alone, and so strong had that feeling been that she could still recall it, still summon it. There, in the house that had always been her home, she had felt like an alien, and utterly alone.

But she had decided that it was what she must do. Whatever the consequences, she had to say what she then said.

Her heart thumping in her chest, she licked her dry lips.

"How can I believe the bible, when I know it is often… not true?" she said. She said it in English. Her choice was deliberate. She used *her* language. The language of her books. The language of her head.

The big man exhaled slowly. The expression on his face was one of disgust, surprise, and perhaps even hatred. She saw him glance at her mother. Accusingly, it seemed to her.

Another breath. Another slow breathing out, as though he was trying to control his anger.

"You say that God is a liar?" he rumbled. It was a broken whisper.

She had screwed up her courage, right to the limit. "The bible was written by men. Anyway, I do not believe in your God. I never will," she'd said; again in English. And it was done. It was done. There could be no return.

The man trembled with the offence he had taken, struggling to control himself. He had risen slowly to his feet, then. So had her mother. She looked frightened, her eyes darting from Tela to the preacher, and back again. And she, too, had come quickly to her feet to stand defiantly, watching both of them.

For the first time since he entered the room, the man moved quickly, very quickly. In two strides he was close to her, and his arm swung in an arc, his hand cuffing her brutally behind the ear.

So hard was the blow, she was lifted off her feet, and tumbled to the floor. She was up again in an instant, tears of surprise and anger blurring her vision; then she was out of the room, out of the house, racing away across the dusty compound, her ears ringing.

She hadn't returned to the house until she was certain the preacher had gone. When she did, her younger sister bolted from the sight of her, as though she was Satan himself, and she had found her mother still seated on her mat, crying quietly.

She had knelt beside her, waiting. After a time, her mother had looked up at her.

"Nana! Vosoti au, noqu va cudruvi i ko ni kua," she had said, using her mother's language. "I am sorry to have hurt you."

"Did you mean it?" her mother had asked. "I want to hear you say you didn't mean it."

"I did mean it, mother. And unless you force me to, I never want to go to that man's Church again. But I am sorry to see you hurt. I am sorry for that. Not for anything else."

Her mother had wiped her eyes, and sighed. "You alone of my children… you are not Fijian at all. Not even a little bit." She had reached out for her hand and held it in both of hers, stroking it hard between her fingers. "You are different. It is as though you are almost a stranger, not my daughter at all. It has always been that way." Then she had raised the hand she was fondling to her lips, and smothered it with kisses. "But you *are* my daughter. You will always be."

She had understood all too well what her mother meant, better than her mother did, she was sure. The tears that filled her eyes at that time were not of anger. They were of sadness, true sadness. But it had to be that way, she knew. It had only been a few minutes, an hour at most, but she had already gone far along a path that could only separate them further.

IV

Soon after Tela's fourteenth birthday, Mrs Wallace suggests that she stop being so formal, and call her Cynthia. It is not something that she had anticipated, nor is she, at first, very comfortable with the suggestion, but she does call her by her first name a few times when she thinks Mrs Wallace might have been offended if she had not done so; and soon enough it becomes easy and habitual. Reflecting on it, Tela is still somewhat surprised. For one thing, in her view their relative ages at first made it seem disrespectful; but far more than that, she knows that she holds Mrs Wallace in too much awe, as a High Priestess of English Literature. It seemed at first like a presumption, even though the request was made by Cynthia herself. It seemed as though she, Tela, was presuming to be on the same level as one who had studied at Cambridge and published articles in learned journals. She never doubted for an instant that she would, one day, attain such heights herself, but in the meantime, Mrs Wallace was not only her sponsor, but a peerless exemplar of all that she wished to become.

Still, that little awkwardness is now over, and their meetings together have returned to as they were before – relaxed though structured a little formally, almost like (it is Mrs Wallace's who draws the resemblance) a Cambridge tutorial. And the most frequent topic of those tutorials, even now, are the works of George Eliot.

Of all the George Eliot novels in Mrs Wallace's collection that Tela has now read, it is *Adam Bede* that affects her most and that leaves the most lasting mark in her memory. It could have been because it was, apart from the already-read *Mill on the Floss*, the first one that Cynthia Wallace had taken down from her shelves and handed to her, with just the smallest of hesitations. That hesitation was something that Tela instinctively understood, and it made her appreciate all the more the special privilege she was being granted. When she returned the book (uncharacteristically,

81

it had taken her six days of intensive bursts of reading to finish, not only because she wanted to savour the language but also because she was reluctant to let the characters in their delicious leather binding pass out of her grasp), Mrs Wallace questioned her closely about her impressions. After, she had insisted that Tela read all the other Eliot novels, in the order they were written.

Then they had sat down in the airy, fan-cooled room and talked about literature generally. Tela had told of her earlier readings of Victorian novels – of Dickens and Thackeray and Trollope and Charlotte Bronte – and Mrs Wallace had pointed out gaps in that reading that she felt should be filled. Together they planned and discussed and met again and again, considering what had been the authors' intentions and relating the events and characters to the major social issues of the times in which they were written. From the shelves came authors Tela had not known – Elizabeth Gaskell, Wilkie Collins, Charles Kingsley, Thomas Hardy and a woman called Geraldine Jewsbury. Tela had the feeling that a world she had previously only had longing glimpses of was now opening up before her in all its promise and glory. "A realm of gold," Mrs Wallace said, laughing, when she tried to tell her how she felt.

It was then Mrs Wallace had first introduced the idea of the Scholarship. That was on an occasion when they had together investigated, in a particularly exhausting manner, the ways in which various Victorian novelists, and especially George Eliot, had viewed such topics as religion, science, domesticity and the distinction between the sexes. It was a brain-exhausting exercise, and at its end, if such an investigation can ever be said to come to an end (as Mrs Wallace put it), they both felt a need to give their minds a rest.

Tela had gratefully accepted a glass of special, fruit-only punch, and a freshly made and heavily jammed scone. Mrs Wallace poured herself a very stiff gin. After a comfortable pause in the relatively desultory talk that followed, Mrs Wallace had looked hard at her, then announced: "I've been in contact with my old School, and they have sent me some material and forms to fill in. I'll just go and get them."

Alone with her punch, Tela wondered idly what it was that Mrs Wallace had to show her, but she found her curiosity was not strong. Rather, she felt pleasantly content and even vaguely sleepy – she was a little like Maggie Tulliver, she thought. Full of jam and idleness.

Then Mrs Wallace returned with the papers she had talked of in her hand.

"These are the various forms we will need to fill in," she said. "Not just the School ones. The High Commission was able to provide me with others that will be necessary. Now…" She smiled. There was an air of excitement about her that Tela couldn't help but wonder about. "Of course, you don't know what I'm talking about, do you!"

Tela returned the smile, shaking her head.

"I've been a little sneaky about it, but I didn't want to say anything until I'd explored it all as best I could. I've been plotting, you see. I've been plotting to get you into my old school. In New Zealand. In my day, it was one of the very best girls' schools in the country, and I believe it still is. What do you think of that? You would enter into the Fifth Form, assuming you get the Scholarship – and I think we can safely assume that you will. There's hardly likely to be a better candidate."

Tela had scarcely heard the words that followed Cynthia Wallace's initial announcement. School in New Zealand! It was as though her very fondest dreams were coming tantalisingly close to becoming reality.

"So… what do you think?"

"Could I really… Do you really think I could…"

"I have no doubt of it. It's called the Bishop Selwyn Scholarship, and it's given once every three years to someone from either Samoa or Fiji. And it's Fiji's turn. The last two times it has evidently gone to Europeans – the daughters of New Zealand men working for the government here or in Samoa – but there has been some criticism of that. It was intended that the Scholarship be for the benefit of Pacific peoples. The excuse was that there were no suitable applicants from the local population. This time… Well, you would get it on your own merits, but I happen to have a good contact on the School Board. An old school friend, Daisy Middleton, or Daisy Winslow, as she is now."

Tela had gone home that day and reflected on how much her hopes and ambitions had changed since she had met with Mrs Wallace. It was not so much that a future that included study in academic establishments overseas now figured very much in her plans for the future – they always had, for as long as she could remember – but now the magnetically attractive yet fantastic schemes that went through her mind were truly beginning to have a reality. And that changed them. That made them all the more attractive, yet somehow a little frightening as well.

Later that year, having been awarded the scholarship to Mapledene Hall, Tela Gilbard inevitably began to think more about the consequences – and also began to realise that some of what she must now face could prove unpleasant, or difficult. There was the thought of travelling by herself to a foreign land, and of boarding in a place with a whole school of girls who would probably look down on her – white girls who would speak English differently, not even like proper English, but with accents of their own, and who would thus laugh at the way she spoke. She would be alone in all the ways that really mattered. On the other hand…the thought of learning new things was exciting. So was the thought of proving to all those strangers, those others who would laugh at her, that she could keep up with them. Or maybe even do better than some of them. Not all white girls were smart, she knew that much. Prissy Barrowford, the daughter of one of the Mill Engineers, was not at all clever. She was nice enough on the occasions during the long holidays when she was home from her school in Brisbane and joined in some of the games and the mucking about, and not snobby, but she was really quite dull and ordinary. And she was only one example.

Still, it was going to be a huge change to the way she lived her life, and not just for the few years she would actually be in New Zealand, either. It would change her life forever, probably. So it was an exciting thought, but a frightening one, too. Scholarship girl. On her way. The decision was made; and accepting the conclusion that her immediate future was now determined, she wanted more than anything else to just get on with it.

What was that poem Miss Naidu had tried to teach them last year? 'Excelsior!' Climb the mountain!

V

The events of the months, then weeks, then days before her departure for New Zealand, Tela goes through in her mind before they even occur, rehearsing them in order to better deal with them. And it turns out to be very much as she had anticipated. People from her mother's village drop in to visit, and there are tears and hugs and comforting or instructive words. Most of the callers are women – her aunties, as they are usually referred to in the language of the Gilbard household. During these encounters, Tela, too, allows herself some tears. There is, after all, a true fondness between them – between her and these familiar figures in their long *sulus* with their impulsive, loving gestures. It is not, though, something she allows herself to dwell on, beyond those few tears.

It is her father who orders the taxi and goes with her to the airport, delivering her into the hands of the grey-haired man in uniform the New Zealand authorities in Suva have arranged to look after her, to see her safely onto the RNZAF plane that waits on the tarmac. And all the way to the airport, and while they wait, her father banters with her in exactly the manner Tela has known he would. "You'll make us proud, girl," he says. "Don't be frightened of anything. They'll be more scared of you than you'll be of them!" And: "Watch out for the boys, eh! Tell them you're going to wait for Prince Charles to grow up!"

Silly banter, a cover for his real caring. She knows that. She has anticipated it all.

Yet just as the Air Force man begins to lead her away, ushering her towards the plane, something occurs that she hasn't anticipated. "Don't you worry about anything, Mr Gilbard," the man says, in his kindly voice. "We'll look after her." By this time Tela has shifted her attention to the waiting plane, the farewells over: but she stops short and turns as she hears a strange moan escape from her father in response to the man's words. She looks back and sees him as she has never seen him before. His face seems to have collapsed, and there are tears streaming from his eyes. "Dad!" she cries.

But he shakes his head and raises a hand. "I'm fine, my girl," he says; though his voice is still broken. "I'm fine. You'll be fine. Make us proud!"

And it is a wrench to leave him there, a wrench much greater and harder to bear than she had expected to experience. The implications of it, the unexpectedness, remain in her mind in the minutes and hours that follow, and she is scarcely aware of the huge force as the plane takes off, as though it is being pulled more and more strongly by a giant hand, until it leaves the ground and is over the sea, and she is made dizzy by the growing height until the plane stops climbing, and all is sky and noise, and there is condensation on the small windows, and there are flickering shadows as they pass through the clouds.

Her first view of the strange new land, twisting her neck to see through the distorting windows of the plane that has droned and bumped its way south for hour after uncomfortable hour, drops of water falling like rain from its ceiling, is of a seemingly endless string of tiny houses and other buildings spread like a rash over lumpy hills, and of inlets where the sea seems on one side sparkling and inviting, and on the other, muddy and dreary. Soon after, they land, the aircraft groaning and whining with, it seems, weary relief. Auckland. New Zealand.

Her anxieties about whether or not she would be met, as promised, and whether or not she would make a fool of herself by not knowing how to properly greet the people if they were there to meet her, or whether or not she was dressed appropriately, and if she would be able to eat the food she hoped she would be given (yes, she realised, she was very hungry) and whether or not the sight and sound of her, with her brown skin and her different English, would cause people to laugh or to recoil from her in disgust, all prove to be mercifully unfounded.

The lady who presents herself to her immediately after she has been guided through the entry formalities, turns out to be very pleasant and matter-of-fact about everything.

"I'm an old girl of Mapledene," she tells her, smiling. "You'll be staying with us overnight, and I'll be putting you on a bus tomorrow. You'll love it there, I'm sure. You'll make good friends. The School takes very good care of its Scholarship girls."

Despite all her apparent friendliness, Tela is unsure about the woman's sincerity. To her, she seems a little… well, tight-lipped. Mind you, all *kaivalagi* seem tight-lipped. It is something to do with the lips themselves – some of them so thin that they almost seem like no lips at all.

It is better when they get to the woman's house, though. The trip through the traffic takes about half an hour, and Tela finds herself only half listening to the woman's conversation as she tries to take in the unexpected details of the city; the broad streets, the houses that mostly looked the same, each set on its own neat piece of lawn; the sudden transition to larger, taller buildings, and the frequent appearance of parks with children's playgrounds, of schools and sports grounds. Everything seems well-kept and orderly.

There is nothing at all in all this that takes her by surprise. She has thought often about the differences that she knew she would find, and there is nothing outrageous about the things she sees from the window. The feelings that it generates in her are much more like a vague but persistent, if reluctant, excitement. Her curiosity makes her impatient to find out more, to ease herself into the new experiences that she knows awaits her; and the next of these arrives as the car (pretty flash it is, too, she thinks – shiny and smooth-running and clean-smelling, like a magic carpet) crunches its way up a short, gravelled driveway, and comes to rest in front of an impressive front door.

"Well, here we are!" the woman says. Tela thinks she detects a small note of resignation beneath the words, although they are delivered heartily enough. She half-expects brown-skinned servants to appear and seek out the baggage, as they would have had it been the Mill Manager's wife pulling up outside the big house at the mill back home. But no… the woman herself takes the smaller suitcase (which looks very grubby and scuffed, she notes, with some embarrassment), leaving her to handle the larger, newer one, especially bought for the adventure.

What she notices most about the room she sleeps in on her first night in New Zealand is the quiet. There are other features of the room that she takes in quickly, and that are close to what she had expected. There is the radio set on the table next to her bed – which she hasn't tried to turn on because she wants to enjoy the quiet, that other, unexpected feature. Here she is, she thinks, lying at night in the middle of a big, modern city. Not a really large city, true. She knows that Auckland is not a huge city like New York or London. Nevertheless, out there, beyond the walls, are hundreds of thousands of people – as many people, her research has long ago told her, as live in the entire islands of Fiji. Yet there is a stillness in the room that she has never before experienced, a sense of aloneness that is thrilling.

She listens carefully for sounds, any sounds. After some minutes she hears a muffled rumble that could have been a toilet flushing in some distant part of the house, and shortly after the high-pitched sound of a wailing siren penetrates faintly through the surrounding walls. Immediately, though, the blessed silence returns. It is as though the room is a cocoon, and she is the insect waiting to be metamorphosed into… into what? She knows with an absolute certainty that a change has already begun, that the experience that she is undergoing will indeed change her – but she is far from certain even as to the *from* what, to have any real notion as to what she might become.

Nor does she much care, she decides. Not at that moment. She will take what comes. In that, she has little choice, anyway.

She can feel a tiredness creep up on her, and she welcomes it. Her last thoughts are of what the woman's, Mrs Humboldt's, husband had said to her over dinner that night. Quite formal, it had been, but nothing that she had not anticipated. She had made certain long before her journey had begun that she would not be taken by surprise when it came to selecting the right table implements, or on how she should respond to any attempts at conversation. She believes she had done very well. She thought she could detect a faint look of surprise and approval on her hosts' faces as dinner proceeded. She even noticed a definite look of appreciation that Mr Humboldt gave her after she had lifted her napkin to her mouth and dabbed lightly at her lips, in imitation of the way she had seen Clair Bloom or some other British actress perform the action. The cinema in Ba had been her teacher in many such ways.

The man had glanced at her and smiled. "You look rather like Audrey Hepburn," he'd said. "Don't you think she does, Mel?"

The woman had looked at her too, then. She'd looked rather long and hard at her, and had finally said: "Well, yes. I suppose she does, a little. That gamine thing. Except for the… you know, the colouring. You're a pretty girl, Tela. Just as well you're going to an all-girls school, I should say. You might be distracted, otherwise."

"Or be a distraction," the man had laughed.

The very first thing she had done on returning to her room after dinner that night was to seek out her dictionary. She never, ever allowed a word she had not heard or read before to escape without carefully checking its meaning. She found it easily enough, even though she was not sure of the way it would be spelt. 'Gamine': she read. 'A girl with mischievous or boyish charm.'

Well, that is acceptable. She doesn't mind that, she decides. In fact, she mentally thanks the woman for introducing her to a word that fitted well with her own notion of how the world should view her. Gamine. Gamine. Yes, it will do very well. She decides then and there that she will need to cultivate her sense of mischief, and her charm. After all, if people believe she looks gamine-like, she might as well play the role.

But it had been something of a surprise, to hear them talking like that. Of course, it had been pleasant enough, too, she supposes. That she is sufficiently attractive even to *kaivalagi* strangers to have them say that she might be a distraction had honestly not before occurred to her. The thought plays on her mind like a gentle flutter of possibility, and is still with her as she slips into sleep.

VI

The next morning she awakens to a further consciousness of the silence in the house. She can detect no signs at all of other human life, or of any life at all, until there is a gentle tap on the door and the woman's head shows in the curtained gloom.

"Are you awake?" the woman whispers.

Tela murmurs an affirmative.

"I know you must be tired, still; but as I said last night, we must make an early start. We'll have to leave in just over an hour to get you to the bus on time. If you get up now, you'll be able to have a shower and a bit of breakfast. Is that alright?"

She crosses to the window and pulls the curtain open before taking herself off again.

Tela reaches out to the bedside table and picks up her father's parting gift – a small gold-plated wrist-watch with a mock turtle-skin strap that must have cost him the equivalent of a quite a few crates of beer. It is just before six o'clock. She feels snug under the crisp sheets and the single blanket. On her cheeks she can feel the crisp morning air, but it is not really cold. Not as cold as she feared it might be. But then, she reminds herself, it is still summer. It is still the hot season – not that it is very hot. The hot season of *four*, she remembers. Summer, autumn, winter, spring. She rather looks forward to autumn, and to spring. Even to winter. She has read of the joys and trials of the different seasons often enough.

It is all rather exciting, lying in bed and thinking of these things. Yet beneath it all, she recognises a little fear – of terror, almost. She has prepared herself well – or at least as best she could – but the reality is bound to be different, is bound to put things in her way that she cannot have anticipated.

But she is able to think quickly, she reminds herself. When the unanticipated happens, she will think things through and come up with the best way of dealing with it. Of that she feels… well, if not certain, exactly, then reasonably confident.

And with that thought she slides out from beneath the bedcovers, and into the ante-room of her new life.

Chapter Three – Friends

I

The bus makes several stops over the last two hours or so of the long journey south, then north again on the other side of the dividing range of hills. At each one Tela is prepared to hear the driver tell her that her destination has been reached. But it is close to two and a half hours before yet another stop is made, and most of the remaining passengers on the bus make their way out. The driver, too, walks to the back of the bus, and she can hear the doors to the baggage compartment open and the occasional murmur of voices. It is dark, and she looks out to see the lights of the terminal like an oasis in the night. Only after the driver comes inside again and resumes his seat does he seem to remember her. He heaves himself up again and takes two or three steps down the corridor towards her.

"You'll be needing to get off here, then," he says. "This is the last stop. The closest stop to Mapledene."

She follows in his weary footsteps, out of the bus and along its side to the back, where he opens the luggage compartment doors again with a sigh. He gropes inside and finds her suitcases, then deposits them next to her feet.

"Sorry, young lady," he says. "It slipped my mind there, but all's well that ends well, as they say. There should be someone here to meet you."

He looks towards the terminal, but no one can be immediately seen there.

"Must be someone there," he repeats. "They knew you were coming?"

"I think so." The woman in Auckland had assured her that the School had been informed.

"It'll be alright, then. Might be running a bit late. You'll be safe enough here till they arrive. Just stay in the building, there. I'm afraid I have to get this bus to bed."

He clambers back up the steps, closes the bus door, and settles into his seat. There is a hiss of released breaks and the bus trundles away into the night.

Tela is now alone. She picks up her suitcases and moves through the doors of the terminal. There is no one else there at all, though she thinks she can hear some sort of movement behind a door marked 'Staff Only.' It doesn't really worry her, this being left alone in a strange place. Across the road she can see a taxi rank, and two cars waiting. She feels sure she has sufficient money in her purse to pay for a taxi to the school if no one comes. But she had been told that someone would be there to pick her up, so she waits.

A car pulls up with a jerk immediately outside the terminal doors, and a woman runs around from the driver's side anxiously peering into the lighted space. The door swings open and a look of relief appears on her face.

"Oh my dear! You are Tela Gilbard, I hope?"

"Yes," Tela replies, surprised at just how much relief she feels at hearing her name pronounced.

"Oh my dear! Thank goodness! I am so sorry. I am Matron, Mrs Millbank. I'm afraid I confused the arrival times, thinking quarter past instead of quarter to. Though that is no excuse at all, really. Oh, I am sorry. Poor girl! You aren't too upset?"

"No, Mrs… Millbank. It's all right. I wasn't worried."

"Good girl. Good girl. We'll get you up to school and get you something to eat. There are no other girls there yet. You are the very first."

And so it is dark when Tela arrives at the school that is to be her home for the next three years; so dark that she can gain very little impression of the place, except that it is on a hill, up a long drive lined with trees whose limbs show up like welcoming arms in the lights of the car, and that at the top there are many buildings, close together, lined up to one side of a wide space that drops away steeply on the other side.

II

She spends the night in a small room which the Matron explains is the sick bay; and in the morning, when she is seated before a lonely breakfast in the large dining hall, the woman apologises, saying that she had herself prepared the food on the previous night as well as the breakfast, as the cooks did not start until the weekend.

"That's tomorrow, of course, so it's not so bad. I hadn't quite expected I would need to cook at all, though. I've just started in this job, you see. So we are both new."

"I'm sorry to be such a trouble," Tela said. She was a little bit embarrassed by the woman's confession, yet quite flattered, too. It was almost as though they had become allies. She liked her. She liked the fact that she was willing to share her uncertainties. In her experience, not many adults were like that.

"Oh, goodness! You're no trouble. Please don't imagine you're any trouble. A little later we'll go downtown and get your uniform and other things. But I'll have to get the authority form first, of course. From the office."

As they talk, a door opens and another woman enters the room. She is wearing an academic gown. Her hair is greying, but she is not old.

"Ah! There you are Matron," she says. She pauses as she registers Tela's presence. "And who have we here?"

"This is Tela Gilbard," Matron tells her.

The woman smiles at Tela then. It is a warm smile, sincere it seems to her. "Of course," she says. "You're the Bishop's Scholarship girl, aren't you! The one from Fiji? Tela… what was your surname again? I have the most frightful memory."

94

"Tela Gilbard, Miss," Tela says.

"And I'm Miss Tillotson, the Headmistress. I'm very pleased to welcome you here. We're expecting nothing but good things from you, you know. We've had only the best of reports. Which house will she be in, Matron? Old Main, I expect."

"Well, no, Headmistress. I've put her in Horrocks, as she's new."

"Oh we can't have that. She's a Bishop Selwyn Scholarship girl, Matron. Not an ordinary scholarship girl. She enters into the Fifth Form. She must go into Old Main. Or into Barings, at a pinch. Surely Miss Strickland told you?"

"Oh dear, perhaps she did and I had forgotten. So many things to learn. And looking at her now… I should have realised. I suppose your height led me astray, Tela. You are quite small, but I should have known you were older by the way you speak." She turns back to the Headmistress. "She is very… adult in the way she speaks, Miss Tillotson."

"Well she is an adult, very nearly, aren't you Tela. How old are you?"

"I'm fifteen, Miss."

"Oh, I thought you were older. I'm glad, though. It means you are much of an age with our other Fifth Formers. I hope you can squeeze her into Old Main, Matron."

A worried frown creased Matron's face; then she says: "I could put her into the corner room, I suppose. There are only two beds in there, but there's plenty of room for a third bed, and another desk. And it still has three wardrobes."

"Perfect! Who would she be with?"

Matron takes a few seconds to consult a sheet of papers on her clipboard. "It would be… Fiona Finlay and Briar Hills-Benson."

Tela does not miss the Headmistress's slightly raised eyebrows as she hears the names read out.

"Hmmm. One particular nose might be put slightly out of joint, but that can't be helped." She smiles at Tela. "All the other rooms in Old Main are doubles, you see. That particular room is the most sought after, as it has more space and the best view. But even with a third girl in there, it will still be the most desirable room, so your two roommates won't really have any cause for complaint. Anyway, none of that is your concern."

"And the extra bed?" Matron asks.

"I'll get one of the gardeners to shift one in from stores – and another desk. Miss Blair is to be House Mistress of Old Main this year, and she'll be arriving this afternoon. Which means, Tela, you can sleep there tonight." She grins, clearly rather pleased at the thought that now enters her mind. "And you'll be able to find the best spot before the others arrive."

"Thank you Miss."

"And the Todmore authority, Headmistress?"

"Yes, Matron. They're no doubt somewhere on the desk in here." She steps into the Secretary's office and flips open one of the manila folders on the desk, then another. "Yes, here they are. The full list of requirements is here, and as Miss Strickland isn't here, I'll sign it myself."

III

Tela had not quite expected to see such a long list of garments required for the fitting out of her school uniform. She had known that there would need to be two sets – one for summer and the other for winter – but it proves to be much more complicated than that. There are two light-grey summer uniforms with white collars, one pair of black sandals and two pairs of black shoes, four pairs of white socks, a straw boater with the school emblem at the front and a light grey band around it, a dark grey blazer with the emblem on the pocket, two tailored white shirts, a grey skirt, a school tie, a black swimming costume, a black umbrella, also with the school emblem, and a long hooded cloak. "In case of showers," Matron tells her.

"Now these are just the summer uniform bits and pieces," Matron says. "We'll come back after Easter and pick up your winter uniform. But there's still a few more things to get here."

They move to another counter, and another very respectful assistant, who produces black rompers, a short pleated skirt of some light-weight material, two pairs of singlets, and a pair of tennis shoes. "These are for gym and athletics," Matron explains. "Later we'll need winter things for winter sports. As you say you don't play tennis, we won't worry about a tennis skirt and blouse."

All the items are placed in a cloth bag, also emblazoned with the school emblem.

"Now, I expect you have your own underwear – or is there anything you think you might need? Miss Tillotson tells me that the Bishop's Scholarship fund can cover other items, if they are needed."

Tela assumes she must mean knickers and bras, and indeed she had thought about that before she left Fiji. Her mother had grumblingly agreed to ask her father for money to buy a plentiful stock of those things. "I have plenty, thank you Matron," she says.

"Well, just let me know if anything changes. Sizes, you know. We don't want you uncomfortable."

On the way back to the school, Matron introduces a topic that does embarrass Tela a little, even though she has been half-expecting it. "You have sufficient of the more personal things to meet your needs? I'm thinking of toothpaste and… and sanitary pads, that sort of thing. Girls are supposed to look after themselves when it comes to some personal things, so I'm told, though the school keeps emergency supplies of sanitary pads. Other little things the girls can buy on their trips into the village, from their weekly allowance. You get an allowance, too. It's part of the scholarship funding. I've checked."

It won't be so bad, then, Tela thinks. Going to the shops with other girls, and all getting the things they needed. It had been worrying her a little; but it won't be so bad after all. "I have everything I'll need for a while," she says.

"Good, good. Any other questions, just ask one of the girls, or your House Mistress, or me. There are other rules you must follow. Lots of rules. I don't know them all myself, yet. You'll learn fast enough. It must be all quite exciting for you, really. Bewildering, too."

But she doesn't feel bewildered at all. The routines of the school are, so far, much as she had expected. She has prepared herself well in that respect. But the other girls – will they be friendly? Will they accept her? These thoughts do, indeed, fill her with apprehension.

IV

On the Sunday afternoon after her third night at Mapledene, Tela has her first contact with other girls. As the day progresses a seemingly endless stream of cars and taxis arrive at the front of the school, parking haphazardly and disgorging girls and luggage and parents and other family members. She can hear occasional shrieks of recognition, groans and laughter, and her heart begins to beat a little faster at the thought of what now lies ahead.

Earlier, she had dressed herself carefully in her new uniform, and made her way self-consciously, uncertainly, down the stairs for breakfast, which once again she had taken alone in the dining hall. Now she comes down again to a school that she knows will be utterly different.

The corridors of Old Main are still mostly quiet. Outside, though, in front of the administration block, confusion seems to reign. Groups of people are clustered around the Matron, who, clipboard in hand, is giving directions and answering questions. There are girls with blonde hair, gingery hair, black hair – pony-tailed, bobbed, plaited. There are fat girls and thin girls, tall and short, many seemingly younger than herself, some who look older. Most are smiling, some look glum. There are fathers and mothers, some looking bored and others animated. There are occasional smaller children, not in uniform and clearly brothers or sisters of the girls, getting under feet or staring in apparent awe at their preoccupied seniors. As she scans the activity, she slowly registers a fact she had expected, but that nonetheless leaves her feeling alone, not part of the scene at all. Every person, every last one, is pale skinned.

98

The feeling of exclusion is irrational, she knows. She is most definitely now a part of the school. She wears the same uniform that all the other girls are wearing. She has already eaten at the table they will all eat at. She has a place in a room in one of the senior houses.

That last thought calms her a little. That is where she should be, she decides – in her room. Her room, which she is to share with two other girls, girls she will soon meet. So decided, she goes back inside, climbs the stairs, and finds her temporary sanctuary.

"See, I told you! It's the corner room!"

Tela hears the voice an instant before the door to her room opens and the speaker appears.

Pretty, Tela thinks. God, how pretty! All blonde and pink.

She stands up, dropping the book she has been reading onto the bed. Behind the girl a man appears – a tall man with hair as blonde as his daughter's. Both now have registered her presence, both are standing stock-still for a moment in surprise. It is as though, Tela thinks, they have been struck dumb by a wizard's wand.

The man is the first to recover. "Hello there!" he says, a little too heartily. Tela can almost feel his eyes and mind adjusting to the unexpected sight of her. He looks her up and down, as if to reassure himself that his first impression was the correct one. "I haven't seen you before," he says; smiling, even appreciative, but still a little bemused. She herself feels a comforting relief at his words and his look. She feels that it is less a confrontation than a sharing of surprise.

"Hello," she says. "I'm new. I'm the Bishop Selwyn Scholar. From Fiji. My name's Tela Gilbard."

"And this is Fiona Finlay," he says, after waiting a moment or two in vain for the girl to reciprocate her introduction. "And I'm her father." He looks down at his daughter. "If she's a Scholarship girl, she must be a brainy one, eh Fi? Good to be rooming with a brainy one, I'd say."

The girl smiles faintly at her and shrugs as if to intimate that he is a burden she has to bear. Again, Tela finds the little gesture reassuring. Comforting, even. She smiles back, and the girl's smile deepens. Then the girl says: "You've bagged the best bed. That's fair enough. First come, and all that. When did you get here?"

A friend, Tela thinks, with the first real thrill of pure excitement she has had since arriving in New Zealand. She, Fiona, is going to be my friend. She is quite certain of it. And it isn't nearly as terrifying as she had thought it might be in her off moments, this first unavoidable intimacy with a *kaivalagi,* a European private school girl.

After several further minutes, her first impressions seem to be confirmed. She isn't anywhere near as remote and superior-seeming as she had occasionally feared such a girl might be, this Fiona Finlay, Tela admits to herself after ten minutes or so of questions asked and answered, of a gradual relaxation in the girl's guard. She seems eager to be friendly, and quite disarming in her willingness to talk about the school and what Tela might expect from various teachers, and which ones of the Upper Sixth girls were likely to be prefects for the year. After depositing his daughter's cases on the bed she has chosen, and with a final curious yet appreciative look in Tela's direction, Mr Finlay leaves them to it.

"Oh God! I've just had a horrible thought!" Fiona says after he has gone. "Gabby Williamson will probably be made Head Girl. I saw her with Matron just now, looking down her nose at everyone. She's really a self-righteous prig, and her father's Chairman of the Board of Governors. Oh God! That's definitely not an amusing thought. She's unbearable. She'll probably report us for even smiling in chapel, and she'll make pets of the choir girls. Maybe I should join the choir this year. Do you have a good voice? It doesn't really matter if you don't. They'll take you anyway. Oh God! Should I join the choir? Maybe I should. What Sports House are you in, do you know yet?"

"Miss Blair said it would probably be Parkins. She said Parkins was short of people."

"Oh God! Poor you! Parkins never wins anything. They're mostly the swots. I'm in Farrell. We won the Cup last year. Not that I did anything to help. About the only thing I'm good at is riding, and they don't have that here. Anyway, I've gone off sport. Even riding. It seems such a waste of time, and it's such a drag going to practice and stuff. I suppose you're a swot, are you? Being a Scholarship girl? I suppose you're really clever?"

Tela thinks about the wisdom of denial, but then decides that honesty will do no harm. Not with this girl. "Yes, I'm a bit clever, I think. I'll soon know if I'm not, won't I? There must be some really clever girls here."

Fiona purses her lips, then: "Well, there's Gretchen Weill. You'd have to be good to beat her. She came top in all her subjects last year. She's quite nice, actually. Then there's Fran Barnsdale, but she's not as clever as she thinks she is. She hates Gretchen, because Gretchen beats her. She thinks Gretchen cheats. But I'm not sure that Fran will be back this year, because her father's a diplomat or something and she was boasting about how they'd probably be in London next year. That's this year."

"I like sport, too, though I'm probably not much good at it," Tela chips in, feeling the need to demonstrate a little modesty. "I like running. I'd like to play hockey, but I don't know how. We didn't have it at home. But I've read about it, and I've looked at the rules."

"Poor old Parkins could do with a good runner. Our athletic sports will be on early this Term. Everybody has to take part." She grimaces. "There's no getting out of it."

"Do you play hockey?"

Fiona pulls another face, then nods. "They make you do a winter sport, and it's either that or basketball, and I hate basketball. At least with hockey you get to throw a bit of mud around. But I don't know why they make us play a winter sport at all. Out in the freezing cold. It's supposed to be good for your soul, or something. I've got a spare hockey stick if you need one. There are plenty of old ones in the dungeon, though. Along with mouldy tennis nets and ancient Lacrosse sticks and the bones of forgotten Third Formers."

"What's the dungeon?" Tela asks. To her it sounds like the sort of place you'd find in one of the English Boarding Schools she's read about in books, though she recognises that the reference to bones is an allowable exaggeration.

"That's what we call the place under the Gym where they store all the sports equipment. It's out of bounds unless you're told to go there for something. Last year two Fifth Formers were caught down there smoking. They'd hidden packs of fags down there. One of them was expelled."

"What about the other?"

"That was Katie Winslow. She grovelled. And her mother's an Old Girl who's on some committees or something. Anyway, she got her off. Not fair on the other one – poor old Sarah Smith. But she was sick of the place, anyway. She probably wanted to get expelled. She used to tell us about all the boys she let do it to her, though that was probably just her trying to get attention. Anyway, she had to go." She puts on an affected voice: "'Not the kind of girl we want at Mapledene,' we were told by Dragonbreath in Hall when Sarah got the boot. Dragonbreath's the Senior House Mistress, Miss Caxton. Katie, the one that stayed, passed her School Cert, and she's back. I saw her downstairs, taking her things into Bligh. That's the Sixth Form house."

For several more minutes Fiona chatters on, and Tela is perfectly willing to have her do so. She likes learning the views and opinions of one who is so familiar with the school, though she mentally reserves for herself the right to make up her own mind about things. Fiona is friendly, and that is the most important thing. She is also bright and cheerful and (she decides, with relief) she doesn't look down her nose at her, not at all. And she is certainly pretty. She seems to Tela to be the prettiest girl she has ever seen. Outside of film stars, that is.

Her thoughts are interrupted by a noise in the corridor and the opening once again of the door to the room. This time it is a woman who first appears, though a uniformed girl follows closely behind her.

Again there is a hiatus, as though time has been suspended – Fiona and Tela on their respective beds, the woman and the new girl frozen like statues just inside the door. A momentary tableau.

"Well!" The woman's voice shatters the moment. Her face is suddenly red, and her muscles are rigid, as though she has been slapped. "This will never do! What on *earth* were they thinking?"

A moment later, Fiona calls out: "Hello Briar!" She either ignores the woman's reaction, or is unaware. "Are we going to be roomies again? How amusing!"

"She most certainly is not!" the woman shrieks. She seems to Tela to be close to having a fit of some kind. "Not if things stay as they are, she is not. Out you go, Briar. Out! Out! If they must allow such girls into the school, they should at least provide for them separately. This is not what we pay good money for. Out!"

The girl's face is red now, too. She backs out through the door, following her mother's command. Moments later, Tela and Fiona are alone again, staring at each other .

"Shee-it!" Fiona hisses, pulling a face. "What the frolic was that all about?"

Tela's first emotion is surprise at hearing Fiona swear; but immediately that surprise is replaced by an acute embarrassment. She understands all too well what it is about. She has seen it before, back home – that look of horror, the inability to be close to or even share the same air and space with one like her. With one whose skin is dark.

She looks again at Fiona, whose face now registers a glimmer of understanding amongst the bewilderment. She grits her teeth, attempting to remain calm. "You don't mind, do you?" she asks. "You don't mind that I'm… part Fijian?"

"You reckon that's what it was? Because you're not… European? "

"I *am* – part-European," Tela answers defensively; and then feels silly at having done so. It is not what she would have said if she'd thought first. It is true, though. "It's not… it's not that part of me she was upset about."

"Yeah, I think you're right. The stupid cow. I wonder what she'd say if she knew my Mum had a Maori grandfather. She'd probably have a heart attack."

"I was … I was sort of expecting there might be something like this. I even wondered… when you first came in, I saw the look you gave me. You were a bit surprised, too. And your Dad."

"Yeah, but… Yes, I suppose I was, too. You're right. But it wasn't because… Well, you know. It wasn't because I hated you or anything. It's because it sort of surprised me. I wasn't expecting it. Brown skins are not exactly common around here, y'know."

"I had noticed."

"I hadn't really thought about it before, but I suppose… I suppose I'm glad I'm not brown. I could be, what with my Maori great-granddad and everything. I mean, it's better to be white, eh? Not better because it's better, but because it's easier. It must be a bit hard, eh?"

None of what the girl said either surprises or upsets Tela. She is much more interested in the fact that talking about something serious, the words she uses and the way she expresses herself, even the frown of concern on her face, makes Fiona seem somehow even more just like an ordinary person. Like someone she knows will be her friend. Not at all pretentious. Honest, rather. "Yes, it's hard at times. Even back home. In Fiji. In some ways it's even worse at home, because a lot of the Europeans are so used to brown-skinned people being nothing more than house-girls or house-boys – that's if they notice us at all, with their noses held so high – they don't even know how to talk to us like… like human beings."

Fiona says nothing in reply for a moment or two, but a frown of sympathetic concern appears on her brow. "Is that right?" she says at last. "That's just stupid. I mean…" she grins, "you *are* a human being, aren't you? Underneath that disgusting brown skin?"

Tela grins back, liking her even more. "I thought that sort of thing might come from another of the girls. I wasn't expecting it from a parent. What do you think will happen now?"

Fiona shrugs. "I don't know. It doesn't worry me if Briar's put somewhere else. She's a bit of a pain in the old derriere. She's always talking about how this place is Hicksville and how Auckland has this and Auckland has that, and how they're going to Melbourne or Hawaii or wherever on their next holiday." She pauses and shrugs again. "I just wonder who it'll be if Briar goes somewhere else. Could be someone even worse."

V

Later that afternoon, Briar returns to join them, alone and shame-faced, struggling with her suitcases.

"Sorry about that," she says. "My mother can be a bit… you know."

As she talks, Tela takes note of her features. She is red-faced, but that could be embarrassment, she realises. Her hair is glossy black and bobbed, her body slim and angular.

"Anyway," Fiona says, cheerfully. "This is Tela. She's bagged the corner bed."

"Hello. I'm Briar."

Tela nods, and offers her a smile. The girl drops her eyes, but she does twitch her lips in response. It is a start, Tela thinks. She actually feels a little sorry for her.

"Your Mum's gone, then?" Fiona asks.

The question provokes a sob, and the girl rubs at her eyes. "God! I hate her sometimes," she says.

Fiona gets up and crosses to her, folds her arms around her. "It's alright, Bri," she says. "Not your fault."

"It's just… we weren't expecting to find… I told her I didn't mind." She looked up at Tela, addressing her next words to her. "I don't mind, honestly."

There are things that Tela feels she would like to say, but she stays silent.

"Anyway, Miss T told her there was no way she could put me into another room. And… I'm glad." She breaks from Fiona's arms, and rubs her eyes again. "I am. I'm glad I'm with you again, Fi. And with… you, umm…"

"Tela," Tela says. "It's short for Atelaite. That's Fijian for Adelaide."

"Adelaide?" Briar says, her voice lifting, her smile brighter. "I've been there – to Adelaide. It's in Australia."

Later, when Briar leaves them to catch up with other friends, Fiona explains further.

"You should have been here before Miss Tillotson came. God! Definitely not amusing. We were only allowed to wash our hair once a week. If you were a junior or even a Third Former, you weren't supposed to talk in the dining hall unless you were spoken to by a senior. We weren't even allowed in our rooms until after Prep, and even then we weren't supposed to talk loudly. And the House Mistress came into the dorms and into every room after lights out and before they went to bed themselves to make sure we weren't, euucchh, you know. It was like a nunnery, but worse. Miss Tillotson changed a lot of things. She's not bad, really, even if some people think she's *leading the school to perdition*."

Fiona squawked the last words, with a not very good (Tela thought) imitation of an English plum. It was quite funny, nevertheless. "Do some people actually say that?" she asked.

"Well… one person actually said that, in front of the whole school, and parents too, at Prize-giving the year before last. Just after Miss Tillotson had taken over. She'd only been there a term, and she'd just given her speech. Somebody, a particular person's mother, we all reckon, said those words in a very loud voice. Everyone heard. *This school is being led to perdition*. Can you guess who?"

"You mean…"

"Yes. Mrs Hills-Benson. Poor old Briar's Mum. You could've heard a pin drop. But then Miss Tillotson carried on as if nothing had happened."

Chapter Four – Two Years On

I

It is Saturday night at the A and P Show. As the dark closes slowly around, the artificial lights take over and the squeals of excitement from the growing crowds of people, most of them young, become more frequent. The blaring music from the competing side-shows becomes ever louder. It is all very different from the normal rhythms of life in the town – so different that it seems the usual rules could not possibly apply. It is as though some sort of magical transformation has taken place, this Saturday night at the A and P.

Jamie Ashcott goes down to the Showgrounds by himself, with sufficient money in his pocket to enjoy a few, at least, of the attractions, and with the casual arrangement to meet up with some of his school friends and collectively find adventure; and maybe even some girls to share it with.

He quickly hooks up with two fellow Upper Sixth friends, and together they patrol the grounds. There are plenty of girls around, some in larger groups, some just in pairs. There are many, many mutual exchanges of hopeful looks; grins or giggles. By some mysterious alchemy, it is not long before the three of them drift into what seems like accidental contact with three girls. Within a further minute or two, the six have become a new group, and after a few minutes more, they begin sorting themselves out into couples.

Two of the girls are Fifth Formers. The other is a Third Former, small and blonde with a slim, boyish figure. Jamie has noticed her at School, been attracted by her timid glances in his direction, and by her pert features. 'Cradle snatcher!' one of his friends mutters to him, with a smirk, when he sees Jamie manoeuvring himself to be at her side.

He doesn't care. The other two girls peel away with his friends. He and the girl he knows is called Annie Carter are left together, by themselves. He is pleased, even elated, that he has ended up with Annie. It doesn't matter to him that she is just a Third Former. She is, he thinks, by far the prettiest of the three they've been hanging out with. There are a few seconds of awkwardness before he says: "Want to go on the Wheel?"

She nods shyly, and they move in the direction of the Ferris Wheel and the queue of customers at its base. As they stand waiting, he takes her hand, and she allows it, squeezing his in return. It is a small hand, slim and girlish.

When it is their turn to clamber into the seats and they are locked in, they wait again, seated, for the remaining seats to be filled. This time it is the girl who seeks out his hand. Once the wheel starts to move properly, she slides close to him, inviting; and he slips his arm behind her. Somehow, it has found its way up inside her cardigan, and with the palm of his hand he can clearly feel her backbone and the quiver of her shoulder blades. Delicate and fragile, they seem. Like a bird's wings. He feels strong, protective.

She snuggles into his neck. Her hair smells of apples. She lifts her face, and, after a moment of heart-thumping doubt and uncertainty, he finds her lips. She tastes of chewing gum. Juicy Fruit. He is enchanted. The wheel comes closer to the ground, and she breaks away from him, shyly peering at the crowds. Then their chariot rises again, and she snuggles into him again, raises her face again. Again they kiss, longer, sweeter, her lips moving slightly under his. Juicy Fruit.

The ground comes closer, the waiting faces nearer, and she breaks away again, but still holds his hand tight. Then the exhilarating upswing, and her lips again; and he slides his hand up under the front of her cardigan to the small, yielding mounds of her breasts. But in an instant, her other hand takes his invading one, firmly removing it. It doesn't matter though. He is not disappointed. He is even a little ashamed at his attempt, delighted that she doesn't seem to blame him. Her lips are still on his. He senses a welling of sheer tenderness for her, even toys with the idea that it could be love. Until the ground looms large again.

It is the only chance they have. She is soon enough whisked away by her older friends. But the whole adventure has been the sweetest of his life. So sweet, indeed, that, for the very first time, when he gets home himself, he feels he must tell his mother about his feelings for her; this lovely little Third Former who had snuggled up to him on the Ferris Wheel.

He doesn't tell her the bit about her being a Third Former, but he does say how much he likes her. He is a little surprised and disappointed by his mother's reaction; all the more so when, for the first (and, as it turns out, for the very last) time she addresses him on the matter of sex.

"Well, I hope she's a nice girl," she begins. "Did you… kiss her?"

He feels the heat of a blush on his cheeks. "Yes."

"Nothing else, I hope?"

He prefers to let the tentative groping of her little bosom slip his mind. "No."

"Good. You must be very careful, son. Most girls are respectable, but there are some… who are not. And the respectable girls deserve *your* respect. The others… you shouldn't have anything to do with them."

"No."

"Now I'm not going to go into this, as I'm sure you talk about such things with your friends. About… going further, I mean."

Well, not really, mother, he thinks. It's well-known that there's first base, second base, third base and 'all the way'. I've reached first base with, ummm, maybe six or seven girls, and second base with precisely two; or maybe three now, if I stretch a point. None underneath the bra. Third base, never tried. I know nothing about it, except for a joking reference every now and then, like: 'Choysa tea, stir it with a teaspoon; Seeyouen tea stir it with your finger. Ha, ha, ha.' But I haven't found such advice either very instructive, or very funny. As for all the way, it is no more than a distant and mysterious prospect. I know there are some boys who have gone all the way, but they're not amongst my friends; though one of my friends reckons he all but got there once, only to find that the girl had her rags on. That's something to do with her monthly periods. It sounds a bit messy, but I'm not going to ask you about that. I couldn't. Ignorance is preferable. "A bit," he says.

"Yes. Just remember this: for a girl, the possible consequences of… going further, can be the ruin of their lives. Even for the ones who go about asking for trouble and probably deserve it. The floozies. But you don't want to have anything to do with them, anyway. Remember that. Always respect the girl you're with, and don't have anything to do with floozies. "

His father liked floozies, he remembers. Possibly still does.

"Annie Carter isn't a floozie," he says, with a surge of indignation and loyalty. He can almost smell the apples, taste the Juicy Fruit.

"I'm sure she isn't. But just remember what I've said."

He doesn't get another chance to do anything with Annie, anyway. She sinks back into the oblivion of the lowly Third Form, and Jamie turns his attention to pressing matters of a sporting and academic nature; though later that year he does reach third base.

It is one of those unexpected eventualities. It is the sort of thing that has only happened to him since he reached the exalted heights of the Upper Sixth, and made it into the reserves for the First XV. He has spent much of the early hours of a cold spring Friday night parading up and down the High Street with a couple of his mates, sports blazer proclaiming his status, and his fashionable Ming Blue socks showing beneath his somewhat less fashionable flannel trousers. They eventually decide to go to the pictures, and there are some girls there, sitting in their row. After the show, he finds himself left alone with one of them – and he remembers her as one of those Fifth Form girls who had joined their group the night of the A and P.

He walks her home, and she invites him into a small shed in their garden. It is cramped standing there amongst the leaf rakes and spades, and there is a strong smell of blood and bone, but he soon forgets that once she proves to him how expert she is at kissing. Then she loosens the buttons on her coat, lifts her jersey and does something which frees her breasts from her brassiere. Silky smooth, they are. It is his first venture into the naked territory, the first time he has been allowed really free access. It proves to be a breath-taking privilege that he can scarcely believe he has been granted.

Then the even more exciting initiative. "You can feel me up if you like," she breathes; and she takes one of his hands and pulls it down past her waist, between her thighs. There is a mound there, and only a thin covering blocking further discoveries. She reaches with her own hand again and pulls the material aside. She is nuzzling into his neck. "Go on," she says. His fingers touch wiry hair, then one finds a sudden space, velvety, slippery, warm. He recalls the advice, and explores further, probing and stroking. Stirring.

She is breathing faster, little whimpers that soon enough reach a gasping crescendo. He is not sure what it is that has happened, and is a touch anxious; then he ceases wondering as he feels her fingers fiddling with his fly buttons, pressing against his stiffy. It is too much. Before she has managed to undo even a single one, a familiar sensation has overcome him, this time stronger than he has ever before experienced, and he feels the resulting release wetting his skin.

She stops her fossicking. "Did you come off?" she asks.

"Yes," he croaks.

"Okay, then," she says. "I've gotta get inside."

And she leaves him to make his solitary way home. The sticky wetness is cold and unpleasant against his stomach, but he has a sense of minor triumph.

Then there creeps up on him more than a little guilt. Indeed, every fresh step he takes increases the awful feeling that the girl might well be a floozie.

II

By Tela Gilbard's last year at Mapledene, she has become fully accepted by almost everyone, and, she feels, respected by many, both fellow-pupils and teachers. Despite protests from certain members of the Board who thought that such a thing would be entirely inappropriate and contrary to the School's historical purpose, she has even been made a Prefect.

Quite early in her first year at Mapledene, she had concluded that the structured nature of life there would mean that, in a sense, she would have to mark time rather than expand her interest in literature. The nature of the English and History curricula in, first, School Certificate, then University Entrance, and then again in Scholarship, were such that she was hardly stretched at all in achieving high marks. To satisfy her innate curiosity and her need to understand, she instead took advantage of nearly every other activity and learning experience that the school offered, including taking, and quickly mastering a new language – French.

She and Fiona have been the closest of friends now for over two years. Right from the start, they have been like sisters. Every long holiday has been spent with Fi and her family. She has at times felt a tug of longing for her own parents, but these longings she has managed to reason away, and she has never felt a strong urge to return to Fiji for the summer holidays. Indeed, she has been ever more grateful that the closeness of the relationship between Fiona and herself has meant that she has been able to avoid even the suggestion that she do so.

From the very first time she sees her – on her first visit to Fi's home, as it is always her father who comes to take her on weekend leave – Tela likes Fi's mother.

She is fair-skinned but dark haired, with a severe and practical bob that makes her look mannish. She is attractive, though, for her age, Tela thinks. Trim of figure, energetic. A no-nonsense, confident woman.

"Fiona's really taken to you," Mrs Finlay says to her one morning after breakfast. They are alone, Tela having stayed behind in the big kitchen after offering to help with the dishes. "A good thing, too. She could quite

112

easily have become an uppity little madam, but you've proved a few things to her."

Tela is not quite sure what she means, but she is pleased to hear the words. "We get on really well," she says.

Mrs Finlay puts the last of the dishes away. "I can see that," she says. "But that's not exactly what I mean. She tells me that you're brainy. Top in everything. And you're brown-skinned. That's what I mean."

"Oh?"

"She's part Maori. On my side. I remind her of it every now and then, for her own good. Some of the girls at that school, they hear their fathers or mothers make comments like 'a touch of the tar-brush' or 'a bit of Italian blood' about someone. Not about her, because I she's so blonde and pink the thought wouldn't enter their stupid heads. But it doesn't matter who they're talking about. What they mean is clear enough. It sort of gets into the minds of some of the girls – you know, that being Maori or part-Maori is something to be ashamed of. Something you should sneer at, or pity others for because it's supposed to make them… dumber, or uglier. Then you come along. I know you're not Maori, but you're not white, are you? And you beat them all."

"I don't think Fiona would ever be like that, like those ones you're thinking of."

"She might have been. She's always been a bit easily led. She had a friend here at primary school from a really stuck-up family. She wanted to be like her, sound like her, behave like her. She's not been so bad since she started at Mapledene, but I bet some of the girls there are not much better, are they?"

Tela can think of a few. "Well… that's true. Some of them."

"Then she starts rooming with you. You're not only brainy, you're also…" She pauses, gives her a slow look, and a smile, "brown… and very, very pretty."

"Thank you, Mrs Finlay, I'll try to believe it." She attempts to make it sound deprecating, disbelieving – but she is secretly thrilled to hear the words. She really likes this blunt, perceptive woman.

"You can't fool me, young lady. You know damn well." A smile and a shake of the head. "Why don't you go out now and help Fiona with the mucking out? There's nothing else to be done here; and even clever brown girls can benefit from heaving a bit of horse shit."

Tela goes, grinning to herself. It is what she intended doing anyway.

Fiona tells her more about her own grandparents, both the part-Maori father of her mother, and her father's Scottish one. "I remember my Mum's Dad," she says. "Not that I saw all that much of him. Mum says I called him Pop. I never went to stay with him or anything, though. He'd call in every now and then. He was still droving in those days. I think Dad was a bit scared of him."

"Did you like him?"

"I think so. I don't really remember all that much. I remember my Dad's aunt, Great Aunty Margaret, better. She came to stay with us for a couple of months when she was getting really old. I was eleven when she came, I think. Yes, I must've been eleven, because it was just after we got Sabre."

"You must've got to know her a bit, then."

"Yes, I suppose. I wasn't all that interested in her stories, though. It was all she seemed to want to talk about. Family. She would go on and on about her Mum and Dad and her older sister, that's my grandmother, who'd come to Waipu when she was just a baby. They'd gone from Scotland to Canada, then followed relations who'd come to New Zealand. Her sister, my grandma, married another Finlay. Weird, eh? Great Aunty Margaret married the son of another of the old Waipu settlers. Not another Finlay, though. Her married name was Margaret MacDonald. Her husband was from the biggest clan in Scotland, she'd say. Much bigger than the Finlays. I remember she said the Finlays were once called the Farquarsons, or something. I'm glad they aren't now. I'm glad I'm not Fiona Farquarson. I wouldn't even know how to spell it."

The only letters Tela ever receives from Fiji are from Cynthia Wallace; although on one occasion, shortly after the start of the second Term in her third and final year at Mapledene, there is a short note from her father included in one of those letters. 'I am very proud that you have been made a Prefect,' he wrote. She looks at the cramped, efficient script. 'And also that you have been made Captain of Hockey. With love from us all. Your father.' She smiles to herself. She can imagine that he has just had a report from Cynthia concerning her latest news, and that she has cornered him into penning the note. It is on a sheet of the same paper that Cynthia has used in her letter, and, it seems, is even written with the same pen.

She is pleased to get the note, as it is confirmation that some of the detail of her letters to Cynthia are being relayed to her family. Although she does send the occasional letter to her father, she never had expected either her father or her mother to write back. It is not truly a part of their personal culture to communicate in such a way. Especially her mother. She had never ever seen her pick up a pen or pencil, except to mark passages in the bible and, very occasionally, write something out, perhaps a verse from a hymn, that appealed to her. Always in Fijian, of course.

Cynthia Wallace, though, writes to her every month, and has done so ever since she started at Mapledene. She rarely writes more than a page in her hard to read scrawl, but what she does write, Tela is delighted to read. There is little about Fiji; a great deal more about the books she is reading, or comments on Tela's own letters to her. Tela always replies at much greater length, describing the teachers and telling her of the friends she has made. Especially Fiona. 'I enjoy very much your descriptions of school life,' Cynthia tells her in one of her letters. 'It reminds me of my own time there. And how wonderful it is that you have found a true friend in Fiona! I can't tell you how happy that makes me!' She tells Cynthia of her visits to Fiona's home, of how she has almost been adopted by her mother, how well they get on together. And she also tells her that she and Fi hope to go to University together in Wellington.

'You will win a Scholarship, of course,' Cynthia writes, in response to that news, 'and that will mean you will be able to attend whatever College you wish. I went to Canterbury, as I'm sure I've told you, but

Victoria is very good, too.' The tiny disappointment is easy to detect; but so is the unqualified support. As always.

She often reflects on Cynthia Wallace's affection for her. It is reciprocal, of course – but how much more it must mean to her than it does to Cynthia! It is, for her, a very special relationship indeed – a relationship that is heavily weighted in her favour, as far as the benefits are concerned. Or so she imagines. She wonders why Cynthia has had no children of her own. It is something she has long wondered, but it is not a topic she ever felt she could broach. And by now, possibly, she is past child-bearing age.

Then, from her latest letter, Tela learns that this one regular contact with Fiji is about to end. 'We are moving to Australia at the end of the year,' she writes. 'To Mackay in Queensland. I am not looking forward to it. I was hoping that we might spend some time in New Zealand on the way there, but it seems that is not going to be possible. I do plan a long holiday in New Zealand next year, though. A friend has invited me to stay with her for a few weeks to help plan her daughter's wedding. She lives in Waikanae, so I will be able to visit you in Wellington. I know I look forward to that even more than I look forward to spending time with my old friend. Dear girl! I do miss you, I do miss you. Your letters are one of the main joys in my life. Practically the only one. Your future is the one I most enjoy contemplating. How pathetic that must sound to you!'

It is the most intense expression of her feelings for her that Tela has ever received from Cynthia Wallace. A small, mean part of her wonders if the intensity is the result of too many afternoon tipples; but that thought induces in her a rush of self-castigation. She almost hates herself for it. There is no way, no way at all, that she could possibly doubt the sincerity of Cynthia's sentiments. The uncharitable thought is routed completely by a humbling gratitude, and some deflating wonder that she, Tela Gilbard, could have attracted the devoted support of such a woman. Her mentor. Her personal priestess and fairy godmother.

Interlude – from the Journal of Adelaide Gilbard

February 1880.

There are, thankfully, still times when I feel that the many little difficulties we all face here are minor in comparison to the freshness of an abiding hope that still seems to prevail. Yes, there are those amongst the settlers whose attitudes fill me with fear for our future – but there are others who seem to share in the notion that we can create here a society in which all are friends, and all are fulfilled. We have schools that are open to all, and there is talk of shortly opening a High School that will also be open to all. We have a well-established round of simple pleasures – of pic-nics where boys and girls join in races against each other and their parents, too, engage in good-humoured contests in such harmless pursuits as cake-baking or target shooting. We have theatrical entertainments. In all of these activities, old prejudices of class are forgotten, and people mingle in a spirit of equality.

I think I am inspired to write of such things because we have not been long returned from a journey to Auckland. We took the same coastal steamer there and back, and we stayed in Auckland for three weeks. It was the only time since I first arrived here seventeen years ago that I had been out of sight of the mountain.

I am still uncertain as to the exact reason for our journey. Tom called it a holiday, but he also made it clear that he had business there. The hotel we stayed at was on the main street, called Queen Street, but up the hill, some distance from the port. Our situation gave us a good view of the harbour and the Gulf.

Hannah had been left behind to take care of the house during our absence, so much of my own time in Auckland was taken up by the children. Tom spent most of his time arranging and attending meetings with various people, which meant that the children and I either stayed within the confines of the hotel, or took little walks in the immediate environs, including exploring the numerous shops further down the street. Tom did arrange an excursion on the harbour for us, though – an expedition that did much to alleviate the boredom of many hours spent in the hotel's lounge.

Nevertheless, at the end of our stay I was very happy to board our little steamer and head back to Taranaki. Auckland is much bigger than New Plymouth. It is splendidly sited on picturesque hills overlooking the largely sheltered waters. It is a rapidly growing town, its general atmosphere being one of restlessness. It seems to be growing faster than its capacity to properly absorb the inevitable changes. My impressions were, of course, gained from only a fleeting contact – yet what I did see affected me in a familiar way. The feelings of unease that arose in me were similar to those I had felt during my time in Melbourne, or those even more distant times in London. Auckland is nowhere near the size of those places, but already the signs are there that it wishes to be.

By the time we left, even Tom appeared to be dissatisfied with the town. I imagine that his dissatisfaction, though, was somehow related to his lack of success in attaining whatever ends he sought to reach there. From the little he confided in me, I take it that he had hoped to enter some sort of partnership involving the purchase and surveying of parcels of land ready for resale to the increasing number of migrants entering the country through the port. He knows how I feel about speculation of that nature, so it is not surprising he kept his intentions to himself. If I am right, then I am glad he failed, as success would have meant, in all probability, that we would not have returned to New Plymouth at all.

When we disembarked on our return, Tom sent us home with our luggage while he stayed to conduct some more of his obscure business in Devon Street. I am not a sentimental person, but when we reached our house and I saw again the garden with its hydrangeas in full bloom nestling happily, joyously it seemed to me, amongst the punga and other native ferns; when I heard the tuis calling from our own little patch of forest, and the wood pigeons fossicking for drupes in our precious puriri tree; and, most of all, when Hannah came running from her quarters to greet us, to lift little Ellen high and to smother me with hugs and kisses – then I could not help myself. I cried tears of relief, and I returned those kisses, feeling more strongly than I ever had before that I was where I belonged. That this was my New Zealand. That this was my home. That this was where I wanted to be for the rest of my life.

Inevitably, especially given our present government and its enthusiasm for railways, the various settlements in New Zealand will become more closely linked. I hope, though, that each will be allowed to continue to develop its own peculiar character. I should not like New Plymouth to become simply an outpost of Wellington – or of Auckland.

Most of all, though, I wish that Hannah's people and my people, wherever they are in this most beautiful, this most promising of lands, can live peaceably together, learning from each other and creating a society that will be an example to the world – a society where difference is celebrated and where true concern and compassion for our neighbours, whoever they are, is our most sacred concern. I do wish...

But oh! What do I say? I call it 'My most sacred concern'. But is it really so, the wish that Maori and settler could live peaceably together? I do wish for that, of course; but I am false to say that it is my most sacred concern. I am much too selfish for that to be true. My most sacred concern is... for my children, of course, but... also for myself. Well... not just for myself, but for Clement, too.

Yes! For Clement, and for me! For us. It is torture to admit it, but I have said I must be honest. It is the thought of what we mean to each other that fills most of my inner thoughts. We have found love, and love is demanding of that part of us which is... most sacred. No one except ourselves knows of it, of course. Not even Hannah. Outwardly, we are good friends, nothing more. Our regard for each other is so apparently innocent that neither Hannah, nor Tom, nor anyone else at all could possibly have any suspicion of what we have become to each other. Only when we are completely sure of secrecy do we touch, hold each other's hands, even... yes, even kiss. It is torment. It is sweet torment.

There will not be – there cannot be – anything further between us. I am not even sure that either of us wish it. We are grateful for what we have. More grateful than I can possibly say.

PART THREE – SALAD DAYS

Chapter One – Freshers

I

In his first year at University in Wellington, Jamie finds himself rooming with two others from his High School, neither of whom had been a particular friend. One of them, in fact, had, at school, long taken a dislike to him for some reason. Still, his enemy and the other had agreed to have a third bed put into their twin rooms and thus allow Jamie to stay at Weir House, a boarding establishment for male students, when he hadn't been granted a place in the first instance; so he had some reason to be grateful to them. Even so, they somehow contrive to make him feel like an intruder. He decides he must make an effort to find new friends.

From Weir House, he gains his introduction to the University, which is within easy walking distance. If his first impressions of High School had been intimidating, this was far worse. There are crowds of students milling around, particularly outside the notice boards and in the student Caf. It is too much for him. He once again feels like an alien in the midst of crowds who seem to know what they are doing, who are in groups to which he has no access.

He withdraws, goes outside to where there are few others, and awaits an opportunity to read the time-tables and to find out which tutorials he is in. At least the orientation programmes he had attended with other Post-Primary Teachers' Bursary people in the previous week have given him some idea of what to look for. He knows which papers he has been enrolled in. English I, History I, Geography I.

Later that week Jamie catches sight of Fiona, a girl who had taken his eye the moment he had first seen her sitting opposite him in their first History tutorial. She has blonde hair tied in a jaunty pony-tail, and a figure like Marilyn Monroe's. She is wearing a plaid skirt and a lavender twinset. It is almost like a uniform, or a statement of origin. A Fresher, but private school educated, it says. This time she has another girl with her, smaller and dark-skinned, someone he has never seen before. Fiona notices him as they approach, and smiles gaily.

"Hello, you! Where are you heading?"

"Nowhere in particular," he replies, with much more vigour than is usual with him. He is delighted that she has noticed him. She's almost certainly out of his reach, but her cheerful smile makes him sense a small thrill of promise. Could he really aspire to one so confident, so well-groomed? Such a… a young sophisticate? (He'd come across the term in one of Jenny's copies of *Country Life*, as part of a caption beneath a photograph of a stunning looking debutante at a London Ball.) Well, you never know. In this place, anything seems possible.

They are standing as a group, now, the three of them; and Fiona, still smiling, addresses her companion. "This is Jamie. He's in my History Tutorial." Then she turns to him. "It *is* Jamie, isn't it? I got that right?"

No embarrassment about asking him, he notes. So easy. "Yep."

"Meet Tela. We were at school together, but she's the clever one. Dux and all that."

He looks again at the smaller girl. She is dark skinned, but not a Maori, he decides. She is almost too dark skinned to be a Maori, and her features are sharp, like a European's. Pretty, too. Very pretty. It startles him, particularly the contrast with Fiona's fairness.

"Hello," she says. A brief smile, and the shocking whiteness of her teeth. It is a skirmishing look that unnerves him further, and he shuffles his feet wondering what he should do next. He toys with the idea of saying something about her announced cleverness, but rather than risk it he simply nods. The girl isn't wearing a twin-set, he notices. Her skirt is plain navy blue, and she has over it a chunky, long cardigan.

"We're thinking of going to the Drama Club meeting this afternoon," Fiona says. "They're going to audition for Pygmalion. You interested in that sort of thing?" Head cocked, squinting a little into the sun that has broken through the clouds behind him.

"I hadn't really thought about it," he replies. "I s'pose I should do something – you know, join something – but I auditioned for the school drama last year and they didn't pick me, so I thought bug… blow having anything to do with plays and stuff." He thinks quickly. If he did go along… well, she had brought it up when she didn't need to. Could be a sign. "I might, though. I might go along."

"Yes, you should. You could even get to be Higgins," she says. "You could be a Higgins, I reckon. Be a bugger to miss out on that, eh?"

Smiling, teasing, moving away. He can feel the heat in his cheeks. He feels inordinately pleased and hopeful. Fiona. Fiona. She is the sort of girl he had hitherto only imagined. And she had stopped and talked to him! It is almost too much to properly take in.

Back at Weir House, Jamie is still coming to terms with the routines, discovering the do's and don'ts. In this, he is aided by Arthur, a rather serious boy who had been a year ahead of him at High School. Together, they push open the swinging doors into the Common Room, and look about them. It seems to be empty; but then Arthur nods towards a figure half-hidden by the old couch in which he is sprawled. "Yeah, that's Cossy", Arthur says. "Ever you want anything, just go to him. It'll cost you, of course."

Just then the figure unfurls himself, stands up and slouches over towards them. Tall, yes, but with a little hunch at the top of his spine that makes him look as though he could have been an old man.

"You're not telling lies about me, young Billington, I hope?" he says. There is a quizzical lift to Cossy's eyebrows as he looks at Arthur, then at him, but there is no menace in his expression. Just a sort of reluctant, perhaps contrived, curiosity. "There's only two things you need to know about me," he says. "First, that's my seat." He points to the old chair from which he has risen. "Second, I don't smoke, but I do like to be offered."

"Yeah, I know, Cossy," Arthur grins, extending the packet towards him. "Sorry!"

Cossy shakes his head gravely. "Filthy habit," he says. "But thanks for asking." He turns his attention back to Jamie. "What's your name, then?"

"Jamie. Jamie Ashcott."

"Jamie? Might be better if you call yourself James. Or Jim. If not… well, I suppose I could put the word about that you were your school's boxing champion or something. That might do the trick."

Confused, Jamie turns to Arthur.

"Cossy reckons your name's a bit…"

"A bit mummy's-boyish, Jamie," Cossy finishes for him. Then he shrugs, and looks at him critically. "Nah, I think you'll be right. Still, I'll put the word out about the boxing. Won't do any harm, eh Jim? Might even help you with the girls, if you're interested in that sort of thing. Not that I'm encouraging it. Most of them being as silly as they are."

"Cossy doesn't have a high regard for girls," Arthur explains. "He doesn't see their inner beauty, you might say."

"All that's romantic crap," Cossy rejoins. "A woman is just ovaries, a womb, and mammary glands. The rest, all those sweet lips and apple-shaped derrieres you go on about is just what's necessary to make sure the essential equipment gets to have its purpose served. And don't think man's much more. He's less, in fact. He's just gonads and a delivery system. That's all that matters, mate. That's all that matters to nature. The rest is just shadows."

He and Arthur and Arthur's room-mate decide they'd like a few beers, but it's late on a Saturday afternoon and a long way to the nearest bottle store. Besides, they're all under age. Not that that is an insuperable barrier, but it's always a bit of a risk.

Jamie is anxious to cement his relationship with his new friends, so he agrees to do as they suggest, and ask Cossy if he has anything in stock.

Cossy's room is a single, of course, and one of the best, right by the main entrance. Jamie taps on the door and waits. He'd been warned he should wait. The door finally opens a sliver. The thin sound of a radio broadcasting what sounds like a racing commentary filters out into the corridor, and Cossy's face appears.

"Oh, it's you, young Ashcott. What's on your mind?" The gap in the door doesn't widen, but Jamie can see a narrow prospect of a table and an opened register of some sort.

"Uh, Arthur sent me to ask if you've got any DB to spare."

"Might have. He told you what it'd cost you?"

"Yeah. I've got the money here. Six if you've got them."

Cossy takes the proffered note and opens the door wider, motioning him inside.

"Shut the door," he instructs. "Give us your bag."

Jamie hands over the empty overnighter he'd been told to take with him, and Cossy roots around behind the bed which has been pulled a little away from the wall. There is a series of glassy clinks, then he returns and hands the now heavier bag back.

"I'm not a bloody pub, you know. Emergencies only."

"Yeah, Arthur told me. Thanks."

"Good man. I do like to be thanked. Now scoot. I've things to do."

He opens the door and ushers him out. In the corridor, Jamie smiles to himself at Cossy's intimation that he was only doing a favour. He'd just made five bob profit, by his calculation. And what, he wonders, was that thick book sitting open on Cossy's table, with columns of names and figures? He reckons he'll ask Arthur about that.

"What's Cossy doing?" he asks Arthur. "What degree, I mean."

"He's doing a double," Arthur explains. He's fourth year Arts and Law. No Scholarship or anything. He's putting himself through."

"Must have rich parents," Jamie observes. He wishes he hadn't had to sign up to a Bursary to get a chance, to tie himself to teaching when he finished.

"Dunno," Arthur says. "Don't think so. He must make a fair amount from the gee-gees. Ever you want to make a bet, go to Cossy."

"That's against the law, isn't it?"

"Course it is. So what? Don't you go saying anything to anybody though. Cossy wouldn't be happy. I prob'ly shouldn't've told you."

"I won't say anything."

"Better not."

He doesn't, but he does ask Cossy about it, says he thinks he might take a bet himself. He tells Cossy that when he was young he used to follow the horses. "I used to follow Mainbrace when I was a kid. I read everything I could about him, all the races he won. I even had a photograph of him winning at Ellerslie pinned up on my bedroom wall."

"Did you now? Hair the same colour as yours, old Mainbrace." Cossy says. "So you think that means you know a thing or two about horse flesh, eh? You'd better come in, then."Cossy ushers him into his room again. He reaches under his bed and pulls out one of the thick books Jamie had seen lying on his desk the last time he'd been there.

He opens it, points to the long columns of names and figures. "All in code, except for the figures," he says. "The names wouldn't make sense to anyone but me. But look at the bottom figures, last line. See?" He points them out. They are just figures separated by dots.

"So?" Jamie asks.

"I haven't put the pounds shillings and pence signs in. That would make it too obvious. But look at this figure for instance." Again he points. Jamie reads '11.4.6'. "That's eleven pounds four shillings and sixpence. That's my profit from last Saturday.'

"Cripes!"

"Yeah, cripes. I'm not boasting here, young Ashcott. I like you, and I'm just pointing out that it's a mug's game. I only take bets from silly beggars with more money than sense. There's a lot of them around. Not just students, either. Get me?"

"Yeah, I see what you mean," Jamie says. He's not all that disappointed that Cossy's reluctant to let him put a bet on. Apart from anything else, he doesn't have any cash to spare – not after funding his share of the beers. "Anyway, it's against the law."

"No kidding? But you're not going to tell anyone, are you? Not a soul. Are you, sonny Jim?"

"Of course not, Cossy."

"Good lad."

Jamie leaves the room more convinced than ever that he's never met anyone like Cossy before; and more convinced than ever that he really likes him. But he is also a little confused. Considering how Cossy is getting the money to stay at Varsity, how come he's doing a Law Degree?

He doesn't get a part in Pygmalion, neither does Fiona. He's really pleased that she turns up to try out, though. She's by herself, too. Her friend Tela can't even be bothered auditioning, she tells him, as there are no parts suited to a brown-skinned girl.

At the audition, Fiona sits next to him, and talks with him. She chatters as though they are already old friends. By the time the auditions are over, and they have commiserated with each other about their lack of success, he has fallen completely under her spell. He is in love. He is quite sure of it. He dares not ask if he can see her again, in case the fragile bubble of his bliss is shattered – but he says a cheerful goodbye to her feeling that the biggest adventure of his life is just beginning.

Although he misses out on a part, Jamie does receive encouraging words about his thespian abilities from the casting committee, and this gives him courage to try instead for a part in the upcoming Capping Show, called Extravaganza. He asks Fiona if she intends trying out for Extrav, too, and is deeply disappointed when she tells him that she's not, that she's heard it takes up too much time.

He asks Cossy about Extrav. If that doesn't lead you astray, nothing will, Cossy tells him. But there's a grin on his face as he says it. He goes on to say that he's heard they've got some really good writers this year. Great songs and witty lyrics. Jamie decides he'll find out for himself.

And so it proves to be. Many of the tunes are from My Fair Lady and West Side Story, so Jamie feels he is getting a bit of literature, too. Pygmalion and Romeo and Juliet, anyway. And, he thinks, it's a chance to learn a bit more about the stage, especially as he is given a minor lead. He won't be seeing Fiona there, but at least he should make a few more new friends. Maybe even earn a bit of respect.

But during rehearsals, it becomes very clear to Jamie that there is an insider group that runs things – not just the rehearsals themselves, but the parties after them – and their domination seems to determine the dynamics of the relationships between other members of the cast. The Producer, the Director, and the two Script Writers are at the top of the pole, and the major leads are the only others allowed access to this inner group. As a minor lead, Jamie has some standing amongst the chorus and other nonspeaking cast, but he is very much on the fringes otherwise.

In his effort to rid himself of the feeling that he is not truly accepted by the major players, and to take his mind off Fiona, he downs his beers quickly and often at the after-rehearsal parties. This at least means he is treated with an amused tolerance by the big shots, and is noticed, and even becomes something of a minor legend, amongst the lesser beings. By the end of the season, he feels he's made a bit of a mark, though he fears he's also made a bit of a fool of himself at times. In fact, he's pretty sure he has. To compensate, he spends the few months after the close of the Extrav season concentrating on his courses.

II

For days and weeks after University begins, Tela Gilbard seethes with a strong and not entirely familiar excitement. She knows it is mostly because she is now able to immerse herself in literature, purposefully and, as far as her intellect is concerned, almost exclusively. She is now, at last, in daily contact with others who either share or who can further her interests.

But there is something else, something unexpected and even, in some ways, upsetting and confusing, that settles into her mind and at times even challenges and usurps her determination to concentrate exclusively on her academic work. That something is a person. That something is a boy. A man. And his name is Jamie Ashcott.

From the very first time she met him, he attracted her interest. She is not at all sure why. She finds him physically attractive – but it is not that. Certainly it could not be purely that, as he is neither heroically proportioned nor devastatingly handsome. But there is something in the way he looks at the world, about the way he seems to expect the world to view him, that immediately appeals to her, and that continues to fascinate her the better she gets to know him. There is a kind of uncertainty about the way he talks, and a thoughtfulness combined with an almost childlike wonder when he listens. And he does listen. He listens more than he talks. She likes that.

But she also quickly becomes aware that Jamie is attracted to Fiona. Strongly attracted. When the three of them are together, he has eyes only for her, even though he tries to disguise it. Fairly soon, in fact, it becomes something of a joke between them, between Fiona and her, his infatuation with her. His devotion. It wounds her in strange ways, just to think of it. So she tries not to think of it, and she certainly doesn't let Fiona know how she feels about him.

But they do spend time together, she and Jamie, just the two of them. They are doing two of the same papers, and in both they share the same tutorials. They often also share a table at the Caf afterwards, talking things over. Talking about nothing in particular, with Jamie insinuating questions about Fi into their conversations. Casually. Obviously. But she doesn't mind that. Not terribly. It is nice just to be with him. With him, and without Fi. At these times she can imagine, even half-believe, that they are together, a proper twosome; and it seems right. Perfectly right.

For most of the time, when they are not together, she does her best to forget about it all; not just about him and her own feelings for him, but also his feelings for Fi. Especially that.

Apart from this unexpected development, though, Tela finds herself reverting to a familiar state – that of living much of her life inside her head. At Mapledene, especially in her last two years, she had taken full part, willy-nilly, in the social, sporting and organisational aspects of the school. She had been first a senior player, then captain, of the Hockey First Eleven. She had been a choir member. Chapel had been an essential part of school life, but it had somehow been acceptable to her in a way that church attendance back home in Fiji had never been. She'd had parts in the House and School drama productions. In her final year, she had even been made a Prefect, much to the astonishment and bitterness of some, particularly of some mothers of girls who had not been awarded the distinction.

But now, with access to the magnificent University Library, and with the stimulation of lectures and tutorials, she finds her life once again dominated by books, and by her intensely personal dreams for her own future.

She reads and reads, both in her rooms at the Hostel in which she and Fi have both found a place, and at the Library itself. She reads mainly literature, discovering new passions – the great French novelists – Balzac, Zola, Flaubert and Stendahl. Russians. too – Dostoevsky, Tolstoy, Turgenev. The French novelists she reads sometimes in translation, and sometimes in their French, for she harbours an admiration for that more logically constructed, and frequently more musical, language. But English remains her true love. The novels, all of them, create whole worlds that she sinks into and is reluctant to leave.

She explores the English language not only through its literature, but also through its grammar and its etymology. When she cannot find, or it is impossible to take, courses that forward her ambitions in this respect, she simply follows book trails in the Library. Over time, such explorations lead her to an ever greater fascination with the eclectic nature of English, and its ability to absorb borrowings, and to at times ignore its own rules of construction in order to do so.

She also, as relaxation, takes a paper in that first year, and in subsequent years, that is unrelated to Literature or History. She had taken Maths at School, and found its problem-solving nature a welcome relief from the open-ended explorations that literature offered her. Because of her exceptional performance at Scholarship level, she is granted permission to take papers over and above the official maximum load in each year. In the first year she takes Maths I. The following year she takes a paper in Formal Logic, which provides much the same sort of relief. She finds it satisfying to be able to chase down solutions that she knows are implicit in the problems themselves – tautologies that require only a disciplined mind and the exercise of formulae. She achieves maximum marks in both courses; which is also satisfying in itself, as perfect marks are unheard of in the opinion-based fields of her major interests.

But she does also emerge occasionally from her private world, sometimes on her own initiative, as in the case of her irregular but always anticipated sharing of coffee with Jamie Ashcott; but also, at times, in response to Fiona's persistent and bantering encouragement that she do so.

Tela thinks about the evening ahead. Fiona has asked her to come with her on a date with two boys who play rugby for the University in the Wellington 3rd Grade Competition. "Alistair actually went to Collegiate," Fiona tells her. "Remember when some of us were especially invited and allowed to go across to their Ball? I met him then."

"And who's his friend?" Tela asks.

"He's from New Plymouth. He wasn't at Collegiate, but he seems okay."

Tela smiles inwardly at the implicit assumptions in Fi's judgement; but she is mildly interested. "Go on. More information."

"Well, I've only seen him a couple of times. He's a big bugger. Quite good looking."

"What's his name?"

"Um. Georgie, I think. Or Geordie. Something like that. Yeah, that's right. Geordie. Geordie Hicks."

She considers things for a bit. "What if this Geordie doesn't like me?" She knows that Fiona would know what she meant.

"I told them that you were part Fijian. Alistair had seen you anyway, of course. And Geordie said he likes dark girls. Looked quite excited at the idea. You might have to watch him!"

She hasn't had much experience with kissing and petting. After she'd arranged, through Cynthia Wallace, not to return to Fiji during the long school breaks, she'd been allowed to spend the Christmas and other holidays with Fiona's family; and the first long holiday there they'd all been playing some silly sort of the hide and seek game, and she and Fiona's brother, Murray, who was in his last year at Collegiate, had ended up in a broom cupboard together. He'd kissed her, and she'd liked it. In fact, she thinks she would have been keen to have experimented some more, as Murray was a good-looking, fair-haired boy – well, *man*. Good natured, too. But that had been all that had happened between them. The next year, he hadn't been there at all, she was disappointed to find. He was somewhere in the South Island, working for a Stock Agent. But that New Year's Eve they'd all – she, Fiona and Mr and Mrs Finlay – gone to a woolshed dance at Akitio, and stayed for the midnight bonfires on the beach. She'd ended up in the sand dunes with a really good-looking Maori boy called Joe. She'd liked that, too – and even let him grope her breasts. Then he'd tried to put his hand up her skirt. She'd told him not to, and he was so polite and apologetic about it that she'd let him resume their kissing, even with tongues, and she'd undone her bra and let him stroke her nipples. She could feel how aroused he was, and pretty soon she was nearly out of control, too. She almost wished he'd try putting his hand up her skirt again, but he hadn't.

And that was truly the limit of her experience. But she knew about it all. She knew more about it than most girls. She was pretty sure she knew more about it than Fiona. Running with the Highbirds had taught her all about boys – what they looked like naked and what they were after. And if the right boy came along…

Geordie isn't the right boy. For one thing, he seems to be drunk even before they get to the pictures. So drunk that Alistair has to be the one to drive his car – a flash new Vauxhall with fins. "Geordie's Dad's got a string of garages and car dealerships," Fiona whispers to her. "Alistair told me."

It is certainly a nice car, with plush upholstery and a really good radio.

The film is a Western. *The Magnificent Seven*. She quite enjoys it, though she feels almost guilty doing so. The boys enjoy it, too; especially Geordie, who makes loud comments of approval throughout. He doesn't try to cuddle up to her, as she notices Fiona and Alistair are doing, and she is grateful for that. She can smell the beer on his breath, even so.

They go back to the Geordie's flat afterwards. She feels uncomfortable about it, but for Fiona's sake, she doesn't say anything. It's a decidedly fancy place, with thick carpets and a view out over the harbour. It's not at all like other student flats she's seen.

Geordie waves an LP in the air and goes to the flash-looking radiogram. "The Old man's just come back from California. Picked this up. The latest Elvis album." He puts it on, then goes to the fridge and brings out a couple of bottles of beer and hands one to Alistair. "Wanna beer?" he asks Fiona,

"Small one," Fiona says. "In a glass, please."

"Got some Pimm's, if you'd rather."

"No. A beer's fine."

He opens another bottle, pours some of it in a glass. Elvis is singing 'Hound Dog.'

"What about you, doll?" he asks Tela, finally seeming to notice her again.

She doesn't like being called doll, nor does she like being an afterthought. "Nothing," she says, coldly.

"Jesus! What's the matter with you?" He says it harshly; then laughs. "S'okay. I like a girl who knows her mind."

They talk about the film, and she begins to relax a little. It all seems quite ordinary, really. Quite harmless. Alistair and Fiona resume their cuddling up on the sofa, but in just a friendly fashion, nothing frantic – and Geordie makes no move to try it on with her.

Then the two on the sofa whisper something to each other, and Fiona says: "We're going to leave you to it for a while. You know." She looks at Tela. "You'll be okay for a bit?"

"Don't worry. I'll look after her," Geordie says. He has hardly touched his beer, and seems to have sobered up somewhat.

Tela doesn't feel too concerned. She almost envies Fiona her chance to have some real petting with Alistair. She likes what she's seen of Alistair. A gentleman. Fiona has certainly got the better of the deal.

After they've disappeared through the door to the bedroom, she looks again at Geordie. Now that he seems a bit more in control of himself, she's able to revise her impressions a bit. They talk of ordinary things. Films. Music. He likes some of the things she likes. Or pretends to. She likes the way his hair falls over his face, and admires his grace, and his buttocks, as he gets up to select a new record. Big, broad-shouldered, rugby-fit. Yes, she decides. She'll allow a bit of kissing, maybe even welcome it, if that's the price she has to pay for the evening. That's if he wants to kiss her. She offers him a smile.

She doesn't much like the beery taste of his saliva, his tongue, but something inside her is willing to accept it as a price she must pay for the heart-thumping excitement of it. She allows her mind to turn off her distaste and concentrates instead on the thrilling sensation of shared intimacy, of the co-mingling of parts. Soon, she feels his hands groping at her breasts, unbuttoning her blouse. Then she has a fleeting debate with herself, tries to pull away a little, but… She senses her nipples swelling, and almost without thinking she twists away a little from the sofa, letting him reach behind her to slip the bra hooks from the eyes, and shrugs her breasts free. Elvis is singing 'Love Me Tender.'

His breathing is harsh, now. He rubs a nipple between his thumb and forefinger, hard, hard. Too hard. It is uncomfortable. The pain submerges her pleasure and she tries to pull away. Then his hand is gone, and the discomfort, too. He moves off her, stands up. There is relief and disappointment, both. Then she sees that his hands are undoing his belt, and his trousers drop to the floor; and in a kind of unaccepting daze she watches as he eases his Y-fronts over an enormous erection. "Be with you soon, Doll," he mutters.

Foolishly, she wonders for a moment what he is doing, what he means; then he comes to his knees on the carpet in front of her, puts the full weight of his chest across her as he bites on her neck and pushes her skirt up. Offended by both the action and the peremptory haste, she tries to stop him, but he pins her with one hand and with the other pulls at the waist of her underpants.

No, no, she thinks. Not like this. "No!" she whispers, trying to seize his hand, push it away. "No!"

"Not a bloody cock-tease, are you," he breathes. "I don't mind. You're gonna get it anyway. All the more fun, eh."

His hands are dragging down, his fingers already probing between her thighs. She feels and hears the fabric of her knickers tear. She feels the weight of him, his chest on hers, suffocating. Both of his hands are now grasping, dragging, lifting her buttocks. She suppresses a scream, and panic threatens. Thoughts flash through her mind. It would be wrong to scream. It might not even stop him – and anyway, he would likely just put his hand over her mouth and smother it. And even if she managed to scream and the others heard and came, wouldn't she just be left feeling foolish? She doesn't want to let him do what he wants to do, though… she must stop him, must. But how? She cannot fight him. There is no hope of winning. None at all. He is strong, far stronger than she.

These thoughts take no more than a split second, then suddenly she is calm and determined, thinking logically. She controls her breathing so that what emerges are what she hopes will be taken for gasps of surrender, of wanting. She manages to release one arm from under him and manoeuvres her hand down to where he is struggling with her underwear, pretending to help him in his intention. "Wait," she breathes. "Let me…"

He lifts a little away from her, allowing it, and she slides out from under him. He is clearly still suspicious, and has both his arms firmly holding her. She doesn't try to pull away further, but stays close. She manoeuvres so that she is on top of him, then lifts her rump as if to allow the impeding clothing to be removed.

She knows what she is seeking. Running with the boys back home means that she knows every detail of the anatomy she must now explore, and her catholic reading tastes have filled in any gaps in her direct experience. She reaches down, her hand brushing the silky, engorged warmth of his *boce* (his cock, his tool, his prick, his Priapus, she reminds herself, in passing) and closes, softly, softly, around his sack.

"Yeah. Yeah," he sighs. Any remaining doubts with regard to her intention have clearly been diverted. He gasps, again, his words scarcely intelligible. "Yeah, doll. Yeah, yeah."

She feels his testes move against each other as she gently kneads them, running her finger nails whisper softly across the underside of his scrotum. His breathing becomes irregular: "Ahhh, yeah, yeah! Like that, doll."

Then she closes her fist hard, jamming the twin stones together, twisting and pulling away at the same time.

There is a bellow of pain, and his body instantly and fiercely tenses, throwing her off the sofa and onto the floor.

"Shit! Fuck!" he gasps. The words are scarcely comprehensible, part of his agonising screeches.

She scrambles to her feet and quickly adjusts her clothing, then heads for the front door. She pauses there for a moment, just long enough to see

Geordie folded up in foetal position on the sofa and to see Alistair appear in the bedroom doorway. Then, icily focussed but with her heart beating a tattoo in her chest, she slips outside. The last words she hears are still in the form of a hardly intelligible shrieking wheeze. "Fucking black bitch. I'll fucking kill her!"

Outside, she assesses her situation. Her instinct is to get far away, but she is not sure, even, where she is. She remembers Alistair saying something about the flat being in Khandallah; but that is really no help. She edges around the corner of the house and crouches behind a shrub. She hears the door open again and sees a shaft of light stab into the night, and shrinks further into the prickling leaves.

Alistair's voice: "She's gone, mate. She's gone. Anyway, you can't go racing around the streets without your bloody pants."

The shaft of light disappears, and the door slams shut. She relaxes a little. Safe for the moment.

For several minutes her busy thoughts are her only company. She knows she is still close to panic, on the edge of hysteria. Her heart is pounding. She doesn't want to think about what she has done, or the reason for it, or Geordie.

But the thoughts intrude, willy-nilly. Maybe it was her fault, the whole thing. She had let him… she had even wanted… maybe she should have just… No. No. No! It would have been like betraying herself. She hadn't wanted him. She hadn't. She hadn't really wanted him at all.

And what now? Will Fiona come looking for her? Yes, yes; of course she will. Fi will know that she must be hanging around the house somewhere. She'll know this place is strange to her, that she won't be wandering around the streets. She'll know. Surely she'll know.

The shaft of light appears again, but with no accompanying sound.

"Tel?"

Fiona's whispered voice is so close that she almost jumps in fright.

"I'm here." She stands up, and the two of them hug, holding each other tight.

"I knew you wouldn't be far," Fiona says. "You okay?"

"My knickers are ripped. No other damage. Still virgo intacta." She finds it remarkably easy to sound light-hearted. In fact, with Fiona by her side she is so relieved that she almost feels like laughing – except that she knows it would likely be hysterical, and that is something she definitely doesn't need.

"I can't say Geordie's undamaged," Fiona says, with a reassuring squeeze of her hand. "I doubt he'll be playing this Saturday. I want to know all the details, but I'll sneak back in and get Alistair to see if he can borrow the car to run us back. If not, he can phone a taxi. Just for me, of course, as far as Geordie's concerned." She gives her another hug. "Sure you're okay? I won't be long."

"I'll be here. Sorry to've… Thanks, Fi. Thanks. Oh, and could you find my shoes?"

Another quick hug and she was gone.

It had to be a taxi. Geordie had been throwing up in the bathroom, and in no mood to be asked if the car could be borrowed. They couldn't say all they wanted to say in case the driver overheard, but once they reached the Hostel, and their shared room, Tela was able to tell Fiona what had happened, sparing no detail. At the end, she gave way to some tears; but they were more tears of relief than anything else. And maybe just a little because of her feelings of foolishness.

"God! I couldn't've done that," Fiona breathed. "I wouldn't have had the frolicking nerve. And how did you know to…" There was no need for Tela to ask which part of the description she was remembering; eyes wide, mouth open. "I must remember that. Fingernails." She hugs her again for the umpteenth time that night. "There's a lot more to you than meets the eye, I reckon. You should go down in history."

Tela grins through her tears. "Which reminds me… have you… ?"

"Oh, frolicking hell! Don't say it. I'll work on that essay tomorrow. Will you help me?"

Tela at that moment feels that she would go to the ends of the earth for her friend. "Of course I will," she says.

In the days and weeks that followed, Tela begins to notice looks from some of the boys – looks that she doesn't welcome. Looks that are sometimes followed by glances shared with others, and sniggers of knowing laughter. She is even approached by one burly rugby type and asked if she'd like to come around to his flat – for a beer and afters, he says, with a look that he must have thought was a James Dean smoulder. All it does for her is make her shudder, and to wonder yet again what is going on.

She talks it over with Fi, who says she'll ask Alistair to see if he knows anything. An hour or two later, an angry and breathless Fi reports back over coffee in the Caf.

"Alistair found out soon enough. Geordie's been passing the word around that you're some sort of nympho. That you'll… you know… with anyone."

"A nymphomaniac?"

"If that's what it's short for. God, I was furious with him. With Ali, I mean. But he was only telling me what Geordie's been saying. Oh, Tel! I'm so sorry!"

"What for? It's not your fault. Nor Alistair's."

"I know, but… If I hadn't suggested you might come out with us that night…"

"At least I know now. What a joke. And me still a virgin. Just."

"God, what a creep! Alistair's really pissed off with him, too. He reckons he's going to tell what really happened to anyone who says anything about you to his face."

"Oh… not a good idea, I think. That's not likely to stop people looking at me like I'm some sort of freak."

"No they wouldn't. They'd look at you with real respect. And they'll be laughing at Geordie, not you. God! He'll soon be getting hell! Anyway.

it's too late to stop Ali. He already told one of his friends who was with him when I saw him. It'll be all around the place in no time."

"Might be the end of a beautiful friendship. Alistair and Geordie, I mean."

"Ali doesn't really like him, anyway. He told me. They just play on the same team."

III

It's their final exam for the year. English I. Tela and Fiona meet outside afterwards.

"I'm pretty confident about that one," Fi says. "That should be one pass I get."

"You'll get more than one."

"If you say so. I might scrape through in Ed, I suppose. It might be enough to keep me here next year."

"You'd better. Alistair won't be happy if you drop out."

"Hah! He won't care. He's thinking about transferring to Massey. He thinks he wants to do Agricultural Science or something next year."

They are joined by Jamie, who is also looking quite happy.

"That's the last one out of the way," he says. His smile is directed more at Fi than Tela, but the comment is for both. "How'd you go, you reckon?"

"Well, you can put an A next to Tela's name already, I'm sure of that. I think I might make a C."

"What're you going to do over the break?"

"We'll probably just be mucking about at home, I think. We'll probably go over to the bach at Taupo for a couple of weeks, though, eh Tel?" Fiona says.

"I hope so." She likes that idea. She'd enjoyed staying at the bach during her other two summers spent with the Finlays. But she is going to miss her conversations with Jamie, being with him. The secret

141

anticipation. The thought of spending months without the chance of seeing him blights the prospect a little.

One thing the first year at Vic hasn't enabled Tela to sort out in her mind as well as she'd like is the matter of sex. Mostly, she has been able to push the question away, and to concentrate on the ever-exciting exploration of literature, and everything else connected with the purely academic. Nevertheless, she is made aware every now and then that she is a girl, a woman. That she is inescapably a sexual being.

The incident with Geordie Hicks in his flat at Khandallah has cemented two things firmly in her mind. First, that she doesn't really place much importance on her virginity. Really, it is more of a nuisance than something she has any strong desire to cling to. It is odd, perhaps, that the actions of the big half-wit should have generated such a conclusion; but what prompted it was a recognition that some part of her had indeed been attracted – strongly attracted – by his physical availability. By his beautiful, fit body. It reminds her of the similar attraction she had felt at times for Big Dan of the Highbirds.

So… it is comforting, in a way, to have it confirmed that she is indeed a fully functioning woman, and not just a brain. But that is the other thing that the incident has reaffirmed – that her brain continues to function, and judge, and generally exercise control even while that other, hormone dominated part of her is telling her of a different sort of need. She simply could not then, would not now or ever, allow herself to be the means by which some arrogant, ignorant, insensitive, selfish male animal gains his purely physical satisfaction. Using her body without a thought for her. Using her. No, no. Never.

Which brings her again to the question of her virginity. To the question of finding a partner, and putting that side of her life in order. She knows that Fi is no longer a virgin. She has told her so. Told her that it's fun, mostly, as long as it's safe. But what sort of partner should she be looking for? And does she need one at all?

She goes through, in her mind, the very small number of encounters she has had that she might, just might, have permitted to end in the desired result. There had been that time with Fi's brother, Murray, in the broom cupboard at the Finlay homestead. She'd liked Murray. They'd got on well in a joking sort of way. He was not dumb, but neither was he an arrogant know-it-all. He was the male equivalent of Fi – quite bright, neither shallow nor deep. And he had a nice body, and a friendly face. Yes, she would have been quite happy to allow things to go further, to reach their natural conclusion, with Murray, despite the complications it might have caused. But nothing permanent could ever have followed from it. For that, she needed another sort of boy, of man, altogether.

Then there had been the near-thing at Akitio beach. She had resisted at first, but the boy had been so polite about things, so essentially *gentlemanly*, that she might well have happily lost her virginity there. The attraction, she now thinks, was not just the fact that he was really good-looking, but also, probably, the demonstration of his selflessness. Of the fact that he was thinking not simply of his own wants, but hers as well. But that chance had slipped by. Anyway, she had no idea whether he would in other ways have been sufficiently… interesting. It had been just one of those unrepeatable chances. Nothing worth dwelling on.

So? What sort of man?

She concludes that for the losing of her virginity, it doesn't really matter – beyond his being willing to share rather than simply plunder – and her being to some degree physically attracted to him, of course. But in the matter of finding someone to share not just a bed, but life itself – well… that could wait longer. Only one person has ever generated in her the sort of deep and still incomprehensible feelings that flirt with that possibility, and that person has entered her life only quite recently. In Jamie Ashcott she recognises something very familiar to her – an almost childish wonder at the world. A sort of innocence. More significantly, even more attractively, he has, she thinks, an erratic but obvious emotional depth to him that is quite different from that of any other man she has yet encountered. What's more, he is also quirkily attractive physically.

Or she finds him to be so. But of her feelings, he has absolutely no idea, and for now, and particularly given his undisguised and apparently never-ending and slavish interest in Fiona, she has no choice but to allow that situation to continue.

She decides that in the meantime, she will concentrate almost exclusively on her academic interests. If the opportunity should arise for her to lose her nagging virginity in some pleasant way, then so be it. The rest can wait.

IV

During the long break, Jamie works as a rousie in a shearing gang. It is a job that his brother-in-law, Jenny's husband, has found for him.

For a small while, he finds the noise and constant feverish activity in the shearing shed totally confusing, but with the help of the older hands, he soon gets things sorted out. After a few days he has developed his skills in handling the fleeces, answering the calls of the shearers to tally out, keeping the board clear of dags and bits of stained fleece, and mostly managing to keep out of the way of the fearsomely concentrated gun shearers to a point at which he is quite proud. He is also, at the end of each day, utterly exhausted. But within the week he has, it seems, earned at least the grudging respect of almost all of the other members of the gang.

There is one other new rousie. He is the son of a local farmer and just out of school, and it is clear from the start that he doesn't really want to be there. At smokos, he keeps to himself, despite Jamie's efforts to talk with him. All he gets in return is monosyllables, and a turning away. The resentment in his features is impossible to miss. There is also something effeminate about his pouting sulkiness. In short order, he has an established nickname by which he is always referred. He is called Baxter. Jamie has no idea why.

Jamie himself earns a nickname, too. He is called Roger. He has no idea why.

There are two gun shearers, one pakeha, the other Maori, who keep themselves a bit aloof from the rest of the gang, and who compete fiercely between themselves. There are three other shearers, one a Maori, who are much more approachable and, usually, good humoured. The two experienced rouseabouts are both women, and are likewise Maori; as are the wool sorter and the cook back in the shearers' quarters. Jamie and Baxter, being new, are the constant butt of jokes. Both are also frequently sworn at for the mistakes they make, or for getting in the way of the shearers – Baxter more often than Jamie, who quickly learns to stay out of trouble.

Each morning, he climbs out of his narrow bed and into his shorts and singlet, both made as stiff as cardboard by the grease from the fleeces. It doesn't matter though. They soften soon enough with the heat from his body. There are at least four runs each day, of two hours each – and occasionally, if they are getting behind schedule, another is fitted in before breakfast. Their main meal is a constant variation on the one theme – mutton and potatoes. But again, he finds that it doesn't matter, as at the beginning of the day, in the middle of the day, and at the end of the day, he is hungry enough to eat anything. Before bed he takes a warm shower, rinsing off the accumulated sweat and grime, then he tumbles onto the thin mattress and sleeps the sleep of the just.

There isn't much chance to talk, beyond the joking banter, or the fierce denunciation of the bosses, or the sheep, that are the usual topics during the smokos. The older hands are very close and don't talk about themselves, at least not to the newcomers. It takes some time for him to learn that the cook and the wool sorter are sisters, and that the cook is the partner of one of the gun shearers. The wool sorter is the most constantly cheerful of all the gang. She keeps up a constant stream of teasing, giving better than she gets. For some reason, she has chosen to be openly provocative towards him, making lewd suggestions and wiggling her rear at him. He doesn't know quite how to take it. She is older than him, slim and hard and sexy.

Then the youngest of the shearers sits down next to him one smoko, gulping his tea and cleaning and oiling the shearing combs and other equipment, and clearly willing to talk.

"You're doing okay, Rog. Better than that Baxter, anyway. He won't fuckin' last long, I reckon."

"He doesn't seem very happy, that's for sure. I've tried to talk to him, but he's not interested."

"Nah. Bit of a Mummy's boy."

"Why d'you call him Baxter?"

"Hah! Just look at him, can't ya see? It's backs to the wall when he's around, boy! Eh? Baxter the wall!"

It takes a while to sink in. Then the cruelty of it jolts him. He starts to feel a bit more sympathetic towards the man. The boy. It must be almost too hard to bear. He still can't bring himself beyond pity though. He still can't like the fellow. He dismisses him from his mind. "Why do you call me Roger, then?"

"Roger the Dodger. That's because you're pretty good at keeping out of our way on the board. And pretty quick at tallying out. And you've got to be not too fuckin' bad at throwing the fleeces, either."

He's not unhappy about that. He's quite pleased, in fact. It's good to get some idea of what the shearers think of him. Until now, they've hardly said anything to him except to joke or curse. He decides to find out more. "Lizzie's a bit of a hard case, eh?" Lizzie is the wool sorter. She's sometimes called Delilah, and he doesn't have to have that one explained.

"Yeah. Don't let her fool you, though. Anyway, she'd eat you up and spit you out, and all before breakfast. And her old man runs this gang and three others, though you'll never see him unless there's trouble to sort out. Jeez, mate, you'd be dog tucker both ways if you fooled around with her."

Well, that's that, he thinks – and he's thankful. He had vaguely wondered what it might be like. She's a very sexy woman, even when she's sweating away in her singlet and shorts. Maybe even especially when she's sweating away in her singlet and shorts, her nipples outlined against the soggy fabric. Waggling her backside at him. Not that he's ever taken the signals seriously. Not really. Certainly he won't now.

After that he steers his mind firmly away from any carnal thoughts, and simply joins in the banter and hones his skills. He is so successful in the latter that when he leaves the gang, he's told that he can have a job with them next season, if he wants. He comes away fit, flush with bank-notes and somehow extraordinarily refreshed and ready for the start of the new University year. He did spare a thought for poor old Baxter, though. He hadn't lasted the distance. He'd simply disappeared one night and was never seen again.

Chapter Two – Older Hands

I

In his second year at University, at Weir House, there are three major changes for Jamie. Firstly, he is given a room to himself. Secondly, for some reason that is obscure to him, but has something to do with the feeling that his elevated status as a second year should be marked in some way, he starts smoking cigarettes. The third major change is a result of being next door in the House to another single room, inhabited by one who becomes a new friend.

From the very start, Tame Pickering reminds him of Matty Jones, his closest friend in the distant years of primary school. He saw very little of Tame during his first year at Weir, as Tame was doing law, and he seemed to him to be a bit of a loner. But what he'd seen of him even then reminded him of Matty – the neatly trimmed hair, the ears that stuck out a bit from his semi-shaved skull. Now he was in the singles room right next to his.

They become good friends. They share a need for occasional company, and they share, too, a largely vicarious interest in both art and sports. Tame is the first Law student he has had anything much to do with; apart from Cossy – but that's different.

"How come you're doing law? Got rich parents?"

"No. I'm not like most of those others, the pakeha ones. We're not rich, but we band together. My *whanau*. I've got another cousin that's been sent down to Med School, in Otago. But Law is what the *whanau* decided for me. You know, my uncles and cousins and that."

148

Jamie thinks about it. "That's a good system, eh? Means that not just the rich ones get to be lawyers and doctors."

"Yeah. It means I've got to work like hell, though. Can't let them down, eh."

And he does work hard, Jamie notices. Head down over his desk. But he usually welcomes a visit, and they sit and have a smoke and talk about things. Sometimes it's Buddy Holly, or the All Blacks. Or maybe Pablo Picasso or Murray Halberg. Or the hair blowing around Brigitte Bardot's face in their favourite scene from 'And God Created Woman.' Oh yes.

They talk, too, of their mutual curiosity and scepticism when they learn that the evangelist, Billy Graham, is going to hold a rally in Wellington. They agree they should take time off and go to Athletic Park and hear him speak.

The Park is packed, as many people there – maybe even more – as for a big match. When, after his impassioned oratory, the evangelist gestures, arms wide, to the massive crowds on the bank and in the grandstands, calling for all believers to come forward and be born again, it seems to Jamie and Tame that they are just about the only ones who stay glued to their seats. A constant stream of people proceed forward, moving past them, some almost stumbling in their eagerness, most with glazed eyes, as though they're looking into the face of God. Jamie and Tame glance at each other uncertainly, then shake their heads in unison. Jamie feels good. He feels close to Tame; he feels adult, and vastly superior in judgement, even in wisdom, to those who are now part of the mass around the stage in the centre of the park. He recognises some other student faces amongst them. It makes him feel better still.

Towards the end of the year he and Tame hitch-hike up to Auckland to see the Fourth Test against the Lions. It takes most of the day to get there, and their second-to-last ride is in a big American car driven by a very large and dignified Maori man, with another who could have been his twin sitting in the passenger seat. The car had pulled up just after they'd sat down by the side of the road to have a smoke. It slowed as it went past them, then stopped and reversed to come up opposite them. Tame had jumped to his feet and thrown his cigarette away, uttering a sotto voce, "Shit!"

His whole demeanour had changed as he approached the car, and the passenger side window was wound down.

"Where you off to?" the voice of the passenger rumbled.

Tame ducked his head respectfully.

"We're going to the Test in Auckland."

The man had nodded his head, and Tame opened the back door, and climbed in, then shifted over so that Jamie could join him.

Now the car is moving and they are all sitting there, maintaining a total silence. Then the man in front says something in Maori that Jamie doesn't understand, and Tame replies in a subdued voice, also in Maori. A few more sentences pass between them. To Jamie, they don't seem like friendly ones.

Then they travel in silence again, mile after mile. Tame seems to be avoiding even looking at him. Jamie pulls out his packet of cigarettes and nods towards the front, wondering if he should offer. Tame glances up at the rear vision mirror, then down again, with a curt shake of his head. Jamie puts the packet away.

Eventually they reach the outskirts of a town, and the car pulls up. Again, a few words are spoken in Maori, and Tame nods to him to get out. They do, both of them, and the car moves off down a side road.

Not until it is out of sight does Tame appear to relax.

"What was all that about?" Jamie asks.

Tame grins. "They saw me smoking. They're… elders. Uncles."

"They don't like you smoking?"

"Nah. They don't even think I should be going to the Test. They think I should be back studying. And they didn't like the look of you, much."

"Me? Why?"

"You were smoking, too. And you're a pakeha. Bad influence."

After the match (a disappointing loss, with only one try, and that being scored by the Lions) they're invited back for fish and chips and beer at the flat of one of the local students they were standing with on the embankment, and they're given space on the floor to sleep that night. The next day, they don't get all the way back to Wellington, and have to sleep in a paddock near Hunterville. They're so tired, they actually do sleep for two or three hours, waking up covered in dew, but they make it back to Weir in plenty of time for lunch.

II

He coasts through his papers that year. English II and History II he quite enjoys, at least as far as the reading requirements go. As for lectures, which he mostly avoids, it is only the ones in the English paper that excite him at all.

He does attend most of the English and History tutorials, however. In English, it is mainly because one of the women lecturers, who he is lucky enough to also have as a tutor, has inspired in him an intense interest in Eighteenth Century literature – an interest that even takes him to the Library to borrow, and avidly read, such heavy tomes as the Journals of James Boswell, and to read all of Congreve's plays, and the novels of Fannie Burney and Maria Edgeworth. It helps, too, that Fiona Finlay's friend, Tela Gilbard, is also once again in the same English tutorial group, and likes talking over a coffee after. At the very least, such sessions give him a chance to find out what Fiona is doing. As for History, it has always been his favourite subject, and although none of the lecturers is particularly inspiring, and he frequently skips attendance, he does keep up with the readings.

He comes across an item on one of the notice boards inviting people to a meeting to start a new society devoted purely to poetry. He goes along, but those who turn up seem to know each other, and to studiously ignore him. As is often the case when he screws up sufficient courage to try something new, he feels excluded and foolish, unwilling to contribute in case he exposes himself to ridicule. Apart from Extrav, it is his only

151

attempt that year to broaden his contacts beyond the boozy, undemanding types who turn up at the flat parties that seem to be on just about every weekend.

By and large, then, it is the social life attached to the University that attracts him most consistently. As in the first year, but even more so, the freedom is heady. He discovers and learns to revel in the gradual attainment of inebriety at party after party. Occasionally he sees Fiona amongst the crush of people, but he rarely has a chance to do more than greet her. He thinks about joining the Drama Club, imagining that there might be more chance of a proper meeting with her there, but in the end decides against it. Anyway, he knows that she has a boyfriend, that there is no immediate hope for him there. She is still, though, the girl of his ultimate ideal, always, always in his dreaming mind, whether he is drunk or sober.

He does audition for, and once again gets, a minor part in Extravaganza – which promises to be even louder, more exciting, and even more offensive to the establishment than the previous year's. Besides, he is now almost an old hand. It doesn't mean he'll be one of the inner circle – he suspects that, and has his suspicions quickly confirmed – but at least he'll know his way around. At least he might get the respect of some of the freshers that are bound to be in the chorus. Maybe even of some of the girls.

But apart from a few beery kisses and inept fumbles at some of the after-rehearsal parties – the sort of thing that doesn't do much to stimulate respect from the girls involved, or for himself – nothing much of significance in that particular part of life happens for him.

At the end of his second year, Jamie is obliged to leave Weir House for good. It is the same year that Cossy also leaves – with the promise of a double degree – and returns to his home city of Christchurch.

"You should get out of Wellington when you finish," Cossy tells him in November, when everyone is packing up and heading out. "I'm assuming you'll finish next year?"

"With any luck. Then Teachers' College." He pulls an unhappy face.

"Tell them you want to do your Teachers' College year in Christchurch. You can have a room at our place – my aunt's place. If you want. It's handy for everything. Right near Hagley Park."

"Chee, thanks Cossy." The offer surprises him. Mind you, he thinks, it might not be a serious offer. Still, it's really good of him. Good old Cossy. "I might do that."

"Just keep it mind. I'm serious. I like you, young Ashcott. Don't know why."

"Me too, Cossy."

"Yeah, well. Take it easy next year, right? There's more to life than boozing and chasing silly girls. And by the way…"

"Yeah?"

"Teaching is probably about the most honourable of all the professions. Damn sight more honourable than Law. Don't put yourself down. Or teaching." He pulls a piece of paper out of his breast pocket and hands it to him. "That's my address. Don't lose it. I hope you use it."

Jamie reads it, then puts it in his own pocket. "Thanks Cossy. And… you know. Good luck and all that." He has a rush of genuine fondness for the man, and extends his hand.

Cossy looks at it for a moment or two, then takes it in his and they shake. Jamie tries to make his strong and firm, but Cossy slips his hand away.

"Let's not get sentimental, now," he says; but he reaches out again and briefly grasps his shoulder. "Good man, good man. Year after next, right? Don't let the bastards grind you down."

"I'll try not to, Cossy. Thanks for everything."

Leaving Weir for good, he thinks back over the time he has spent there and has a vague feeling of disappointment. It's not so much that he regrets the time spent, the time wasted, he realises. It's more the fact that he doesn't really feel very much advanced in life. He's not even sure that the two years – reasonably successful years in some ways, he supposes – were more than simply a passing of time.

The one thing throbbing away there in the depths of his consciousness, reminding him of a future that could, after all, be one of real value, giving him the feeling that there might be some purpose to his life, is his mental picture of Fiona. He knows it will be the thought of Fiona, not any strong desire to finish his degree, that will draw him back to Wellington after the holidays.

III

The next year, after spending the summer rouseying again for the same shearing gang, Jamie finds a flat on The Terrace, with two others – Martin, who was at Weir with him and is also trying to finish off a B.A., and Dave, a committed Catholic from Wanganui with an intimidating determination to get into Otago Med School. He'd applied straight from High School, but had missed out, his Scholarship marks not good enough. Now he is set on completing a B.Sc. and reapplying.

The flat on The Terrace gives all three of them a sense of extra freedom and, for Dave at least, a sense of responsibility as well. Jamie, though, gives rein rather to the feeling that his life now is ordered by no one at all but himself, not even the rather loose rulebook and routines at Weir House. In this, he is joined enthusiastically by Martin, and the two of them always ensure that the fridge is ever full of beer, even if that means going without other, more essential items.

Dave says nothing; but his looks and his actions are more than sufficient to make his disapproval manifest. Not that he makes a big show of it. That is not in his nature; neither is it part of the view he has of the requirements of those who have decided to follow Jesus. So the look on his face when he comes into the sitting room to find Martin and Jamie sprawled on the battered couch listening to Brubeck and sucking on bottles of DB is not one of frowning censure, but rather one of understanding martyrdom. He says nothing. He picks up the greasy newspaper from the coffee table, a mute reminder of the previous night's

154

meal but empty now of all but the smallest pieces of cold chips, and takes it away to the kitchen. Only Jamie is sufficiently attuned to the implicit displeasure.

He looks across to the oblivious Martin. "Your turn for tea," he says. "So what are you doing?"

Martin doesn't scowl. For him, food is a topic that is ever to be taken seriously. As is beer. He sucks a final swig from his bottle and puts it down on the stained table. "Yeah. Bacon and eggs, I reckon. And you could go down for some more chips, eh?"

"Why me? It's your turn for cooking. You'd better go now. It's too late to cook your own, and we haven't got any spuds, anyway. And I'm bloody starving."

"Yeah, me too. Couldn't you just… nip down to the shop and get some? I'll pay. Then we wouldn't have to wait. I'll go and cook the bacon and eggs while you're gone."

"No, you lazy prick. It's your turn to put things on the table. We do nothing. That's the way it works."

"I'll ask Dave. He'll think it's his Christian duty."

"Not fair, Marty. Jesus! He does more than his fair share as it is."

"Yeah, well… fuck it all, you win. You'll just have to starve till I get back."

Once Martin has gone, still muttering, Dave comes back into the room and sits down. The Brubeck record has finished, and Jamie heaves himself to his feet and turns the machine off, then resumes his seat. For a minute or two there is silence in the room.

"Marty's gone down to get some chips to go with tea," Jamie offers finally. Then: "You get that essay finished?"

"Yes."

Jamie reflects on the fact that he has two essays to write, one in English, the other in History, and he hasn't started on either. Still… there's plenty of time. They aren't due in till Thursday, and it's only Monday. "Wish I had your… self-discipline," he says. And for that moment, he means it.

Dave smiles. Is it a little condescendingly? Still, Jamie thinks, he probably has the right to be condescending.

"I have the Man on my shoulder, encouraging me," Dave says.

"Yeah, that must help." He doesn't need to ask. He knows what Dave means. "How does that work, anyway?" He's genuinely interested, he realises. He's never before ventured to ask Dave anything at all about his faith, how it works, what it means to him. And Dave has never been pushy about it. They wouldn't have agreed to have him as a flatmate if he had.

Dave shrugs. "You need to believe to understand. It just gives… meaning to life. Pulls me back when I sort of… have weak moments. I think of Jesus. And of Mary. What they did for us. Saved us."

Give meaning to life. Jeez, that would be good, Jamie thinks. That would be good, but… "Yeah, but… it didn't really work, eh? I mean – you say Jesus saved us… for what? The world hasn't got much better since he was… nailed to the cross. It's got worse, probably." The Cold War and nuclear tests, he reminds himself. The threat of an end to everything. And at a more personal level, unrequited love. All of it. Everything.

"That's not the point. Jesus is a personal saviour. Whoever believes in him is saved. No matter what evil and… and misery there is around."

"Saved? I've never understood that. Saved from what? Saved for what?"

"Saved from sin. From death. Saved for… for the Kingdom of God."

To Jamie, these words of Dave's are no more than a chanting of a formula that he has never understood. Meaningless. Evasive. Don't do things that might hurt people. He doesn't need Jesus to remind him of that. It's just common sense. It's the way the world has to operate. It's the basis of common law. It allows society to function. Without it, chaos. And the idea that there can be life after death makes no sense to him at all. None. It is absurd. And what the hell is 'The Kingdom of God'? Too vague, that purpose.

But the couple of bottles of beer he has downed have left Jamie with a pleasant glow of something that approaches well-being, or at least resignation. Poor old Dave, he thinks. The Kingdom of God, Santa Claus and the Tooth Fairy. Ah well – he can almost hear his mother's voice telling him – each to his own.

That year, mainly to take his mind off the seemingly impossible mission of getting closer to Fiona, he again auditions for Extrav, and yet again he is given a minor lead. This time, one of the girls who had been in the chorus the year before is there again, one he'd had brief carnal fantasies about but nothing more.

He's glad of the diversion her interest promises. He notices her sneaking glances at him at rehearsals. He is surprised by it. She is a confident, sassy girl, always in jeans, and always wearing a black felt beret. She has a bit of reputation. What's more, she is pretty, in a tomboyish way.

One night they leave the rehearsal together and walk up towards The Terrace.

"You got any beer at your place?" she asks.

"Should be some. There was when I left."

Inside the flat, the living room has its usual smell of stale fish and chips, and it is littered with empty bottles. Neither of the others is in, it seems – or if they are, they must be sleeping.

He gets her a beer, the last left in the fridge, and she takes a swig. Then she asks "Which is your room?"

He points, and she moves towards the door, full of purpose. He follows.

Inside, once the light has been switched on, he is again briefly shamed, this time by the tousled sheets, the dirty socks and underpants on the floor, the jumble of books and papers on the rickety card table he uses as a desk. He makes to turn the light off, but she stops him. "Leave it on," she says; and she moves into him, her face tilted, inviting.

Her kisses are urgent, her tongue probing. It is good. It is better than even the best of the kissing he has ever had before. More exciting. More urgent. Her tongue is much more practised than those of any other he has tried it with.

She steps away briefly and pulls her bulky jersey over her head. Her Che Guevara beret also hits the floor. Her bra is all she has on underneath the jersey. "Undo it," she says, turning her back. He does, and she shrugs that off too.

Her breasts are small, but not as small as they had seemed when they were confined. They are joyfully free now, swinging a little with the motions of her body. He is enchanted. He has never before been able to observe such things closely. Certainly not in the flesh, not with such clarity. They are magnetically attractive, angelically designed toys. He reaches out to touch the gently yielding flesh.

She doesn't stop him, resumes her kissing, but soon breaks away and stretches out on his bed, impatiently throwing the tangled sheets to one side. And he lies next to her, his hand reaching for her again. Soft, silky, pliable; the nipples, over-sized, they seem, hardening to his touch. But such preliminaries don't seem to feature in her plans for the immediate future. Quickly she arches her back and eases her jeans over her hips, her underpants coming with them. When they are half way down, she pauses, and tugs at his belt. "Come on," she says.

He kneels on the bed and begins the removal, but has to step onto the floor to finish the procedure. He gets his trousers down, then stands and looks at her. "And the rest," she says. For a moment he is uncertain she could mean what he thinks she means. It all seems so sudden and matter-of-fact.

He has had a bit of experience of exploring beneath girls' underwear, but that is as far as he has ever got. The venues for such adventures – in a garden shed, standing in a subway under the railway tracks, on a coat-strewn bed at flat parties – have never permitted anything further. Or his partners haven't. Now the girl who is with him, a girl with a reputation, has undressed for him – and, more scarily still, is demanding that he do the same.

Lust soon enough overcomes his wonder and his uncertainty. He reveals himself. She glances at him, appears satisfied. She opens her now-naked thighs, inviting his touch, and, heart pounding, he obliges, wondering, only half believing it is happening.

It is far, very far, from the sort of blind groping that has been the limit of his experience so far. She is naked, she is visible – clearly visible in the harsh light of the unshielded globe hanging from the ceiling. He pauses in his actions, fascinated by what he sees. Pouting, opening like a flower, glistening. A woman. A girl. Her parts revealed.

He watches her, takes in the heady perfume of her, watches as his fingers explore her; but once again, she is impatient. "Come on then," she says.

She reaches for him, glances over, then quickly removes her hand. "Shit! Haven't you got anything?"

He is confused; then he understands. "Uh, no."

"Christ! You idiot." She is breathing hard, whether with need or anger he is unsure. Perhaps both. "Never mind. Come on. Bloody idiot."

She lifts her hips, guides him into her. She closes around him, totally encompassing. It is the most arousing, the most consuming sensation he has ever experienced. He thinks his head is going to explode with the intensity of his physical response. It is not just in that one part of him, though that is the source of it; but it seems every nerve in his body is participating, that they are all singing the same imperative chorus.

Then, almost immediately, he does explode, climaxes as never before, shuddering further into her in great waves of release.

"Shit!" she says. "Selfish bastard. Fucking typical." She heaves him out of her, but grabs his hand, thrusts his knuckles between her thighs, pushing and pulling them back and forth, bucking against them. He is not sure what is happening, not sure if he should become more involved. He does move his hand, in a sort of counterpoint, and some of the downward pressure she is placing on it eases; but she continues to heave and circle with her hips, grinding urgently against him. She is breathing faster and faster; then she gasps, gasps again; then her breathing begins to slowly subside.

She shoves his hand away. "You'd better not have got me up the duff, you prick," she says, in a small, exhausted voice; but perhaps, he thinks, there is a hint of a job well done about it, of ego-boosting gratitude. Or more likely, he thinks, with a mental flinch, she is just what she seems. Disappointed.

Then the words she has spoken register properly in his mind, sharp and cold, and a terror seizes him. He can almost hear again his mother's voice. 'Remember, for a girl, the result can be their life is ruined. Always think of the girl, son. Always be a gentleman. Don't ever take advantage.' It was the only advice of the kind she had ever given him, and now, remembering, all the more terrifying for that.

Very few further words pass between them. They dress themselves, and he walks her to her own flat. He wonders if he should kiss her before she goes inside, but she runs up the steps and disappears inside, not giving him the option.

Twenty minutes later he is able to stretch out on his bed again. Half of him, at least half of him, is wishing it had never happened. It seems almost like a betrayal of his true self. Worse, far worse, it is a betrayal… of… He groans, and tries to banish the thought of her, of Fiona, from his mind.

Anyway, there is no disguising that a bit of him is seething with astonished satisfaction. Man of the world. Right here, in this bed. A girl. Yeah!

She never offers him another chance, nor does he seek one. The terror he feels at the possible result of the one encounter means that the thought that either of them might want to repeat it never even enters his head. She does, though, promise to let him know whether or not the unthinkable has happened. And this she eventually does, though he has the strong impression that she delays her news until he has suffered long and deep. 'You're off the hook,' is all she tells him, just before Extrav's opening night.

IV

He doesn't see nearly as much of Fiona as he would like, though she does appear at some of the parties he attends, and he snatches the chance to exchange words with her, if he can. It keeps the flame going, and he is grateful for it. That flame has become part of him. He can't even imagine his life without it. Carrying that flame, he feels, has become his chief justification for living.

He sees a lot more of her friend, Tela, as yet again, they take the same English Paper and are in the same tutorial. Quite frequently, after it's over, they continue their habit of having a coffee together in the Caf. He likes Tela, feels at ease with her in a way quite different from any other girl he has ever had contact with. She makes him relax. For some reason, he doesn't seem to need to be someone he isn't when he's with her. What's more, he accepts readily enough that she is clever and hard-working; much cleverer, or at least harder-working, than him, but he doesn't think of her as a rival. He has no jealousy. No envy. Even more importantly, he can look at her in a way that doesn't seem charged with other sorts of longing. She is pretty, but that is simply something he accepts. She has a nice figure, nice legs, especially, but his response to this is rather more like his response to seeing the aesthetically pleasing yet essentially sexless paintings of the Madonna by artists like Michelangelo or Fra Lippo Lippi. Anyway, he reasons, she is not interested in him. Not in that way. Theirs are meetings of minds – and they always leave him feeling good, if a little intellectually inadequate. And certainly virtuous.

Sometimes, rather than spending his leisure time drinking beer with Marty or other friends who drop in to their flat, he reads literature that is not connected in any way with the papers he is doing. It is another way of forgetting, or at least temporarily ignoring, the things that he has deemed impossibilities. Like escaping from the profession his Bursary has committed him to. Like getting with Fiona.

He reads Lawrence Durrell's Alexandria Quartet, and wishes that he could be so highbrow and learned. He reads Dylan Thomas's poetry, and wishes he could be so intense and thundering. He reads T.S. Eliot and wishes he was half as clever. He reads whatever he thinks will either put him into or deepen a mood, or, more rarely, and less successfully, get him out of one. The most common of his moods is one of a mournfulness that even he recognises is very close to self-pity. At these times, it is often to an old favourite, Swinburne, that he turns.

Pale, beyond porch and portal,
Crowned with calm leaves, she stands
Who gathers all things mortal
With cold immortal hands:
Her languid lips are sweeter
Than love's who fears to greet her
To men that mix and meet her
From many times and lands.

Death defeats love. Death and love. Both, in his mind, bear the features of Fiona. There can be no victory, or – only in death. And perhaps that is to be welcomed. Sweet, languid lips. Untasted. Fiona Finlay. Fiona. Fiona.

But what does it all matter, anyway? Better to just have a few beers.

He knows that Fiona has transferred to the Teachers' College, and is training to be a Primary School teacher. Even so, she occasionally turns up, still, at Vic student parties. Every time he sees her, his heart gives a lurch. His feelings for her are different, totally different, from the feelings any other girl has elicited in him. They are not lustful feelings. They are agonisingly gentle, achingly regretful, like hope forever held to ransom. He can scarcely bear to be within sight of her, yet to find himself in her company and then take himself away is even harder, more wounding.

On this occasion, yet another Saturday night party, she is there. He sees her almost immediately he enters the room. It is as though she alone has the power to attract him. Everyone else in the room is irrelevant, almost invisible.

She greets him warmly enough; but she is with her new boyfriend, yet another rugby type, and with a red-haired girl he has never seen before. And Tela Gilbard is with them, too. They and a couple of others form a distinct group. He hangs around a while, on the fringes; but he is not one of them. He is uncomfortable. They are not unfriendly, these others who make a circle around her, but neither do they allow him an opportunity to properly join them.

He drifts away. He gets a nod of recognition occasionally as he circulates around the room with his glass of beer, but nothing more. The music has been turned up, and some couples are dancing. Smoke is thick in the air.

He plays around with the germ of anger and resentment that is growing in his mind. It is all so bloody familiar, and bloody pointless; especially the dancing. Bodies facing each other making ridiculous gyrations. Pointless. Stupid. Cretinous.

He edges through the French doors and onto the verandah. There are others out here, too, but he moves further, around a corner, and finds a spot out of sight, one where the thump of the bass notes from the sound system is about the only part of the music that can be heard.

He looks out over the lights below. Wellington and its thousands of people. The anger is still there within him. It is largely an anger at the feeling that he is not, never has been, never could be like one of those surrounding Fiona. Confident, accepted – rich. Urbane. Sophisti-cated. Which, he reminds himself, means full of sophistry. Full of deception. Up themselves. With parents who if they are not lawyers or accountants or doctors, are probably hill-country station owners.

He is sick of it all, everything. He thinks about leaving the party, but… Fiona is just the other side of the wall. He doesn't want to leave while she is still here. He decides that he might as well go back inside, find the kitchen where all the booze is sure to be, and set about getting drunk.

He is ready to move when someone appears next to him.

"What's up, Jamie? What are you thinking about?"

It is Tela. His heart lifts a little. Someone has sought him out.

"Ah," he shrugs. "About life, I suppose."

"Right. Well, that's a topic worthy of your concern, I should say. Reached any conclusions?"

"Only that… only that I don't really feel I want to be in it."

"No, I don't think so. I think you're feeling that you don't want to be here, at this party. That's another thing altogether. And if it's any comfort to you, neither do I."

"You? You're one of them. You belong."

"You think?"

"You went to a fancy school. You're one of them."

"I was a Scholarship girl, Jamie. And in case you haven't noticed, there are one or two other things that are different about me, too."

"But, you and Fi…"

"Oh yes. We're friends. The best of friends. I wouldn't be here if it weren't for Fi. But that doesn't mean I'm comfortable with the others, or that they're comfortable with me. I just put my armour on, and pretend. You could, too – if you wanted. But you don't seem to have any armour, do you Jamie. Except for the booze."

"Ouch." She is right, though, he realises, thinking about what he was on the verge of doing when she appeared next to him.

She reaches out with one hand and places it lightly on his chest, tapping it with her fingers. "You need some armour, Jamie. Some proper armour. Get some belief in yourself. I… I know that there must be plenty of people who do believe in you. Or will."

"Yeah? My dear old Mum, I suppose. Who else, do you think?"

"If you stopped feeling sorry for yourself and opened your eyes, you'd find out soon enough. But… first you need to get your armour on." She smiles wryly. "Life is easier for some than it is for others. Get your armour on. Here endeth the lesson."

"Thanks Tel," he says. He tries to make his comment sound sarcastic, but it comes out genuine. He decides he has to make his feeling clearer.

"That's easy enough for you. You've proved you're better than any of them."

"Better? No, I don't think so. Anyway… you could do the same." She sounds a bit exasperated herself, now. "You've got a brain, too. You just need the… the gumption."

Gumption. It is a word his mother uses quite often. It hurts even more coming from Tela's mouth. But after she moves off to go back inside, instead of seeking out the booze, he decides he'll leave them all to it and go back to the flat. Maybe write a poem.

And the next morning, he wakes up with a clear head, and another poem to Fiona on his desk, which he reaches out for and reads through even before he heaves himself out of bed. It's pretty good, he thinks. He even feels modestly pleased with himself, and with life itself. Not euphoric, to be sure – but floating along on a cloud of bearable melancholy.

He mentally tips his hat to Tela. Tela, at ease in her lovely brown skin. He likes Tela.

V

In the early hours of that morning Tela waits for sleep. She sighs to herself. If only she could stop thinking about him. It shouldn't be difficult. It was all so pointless, anyway. And it's not as though she can't see his faults. She'd been quite annoyed with him at the party – with his obvious wallowing in self-pity. She hadn't found that attractive at all. And yet…

Jamie-bloody-Ashcott. Get out of my head. Get out!

She shifts her body down further under the blankets, arching her feet and stretching her toes. She can hear the murmuring voices of Fi and her new boyfriend coming from the living room, and the sound of the record-player turned very low. Soon, she knows, they will vacate the room, probably retiring to Fi's bedroom. She hopes she won't be able to hear them at all from there.

Jamie imagines he's in love with her. With Fiona. Well, why wouldn't he be? Why not? Lovely, blonde Fiona. Her best friend. Honey, honey, honey blonde. She can't blame him. Or her. It's just that…

… Jamie-bloody-Ashcott… she turns over, onto her side, and pulls the pillow over her ear… get out of my head.

Chapter Three – Marking Time

I

Jamie takes Cossy's advice and goes to Christchurch for his Teachers' College year. When he writes to Cossy telling him of his intention, the offer of a room at his place is repeated, in typical Cossy style. 'There's only the two of us here,' he writes. 'My aunt is a bit like a mother hen, but it means you'll be well fed.' He quotes a price for the room and board that seems altogether too good to turn down. Besides, he thinks, it will be good to see Cossy again.

And so, indeed, it proves. Cossy is working for the City Council doing some sort of legal work. He doesn't talk about it, but it seems to pay well enough, if the quality of the food and the furniture in the old house, and its general appearance, is anything to go by. It is one of the older houses close to the central city, quite near Hagley Park, and still has about it an air of colonial grandeur.

Cossy's aunt is as interesting to Jamie in her way as is Cossy. She is a tiny woman, and obviously very proud of her nephew, fussing around after him, ironing his clothes, cooking him up little treats, but she also constantly chides him about certain things, including his apparently unsociable habits. Cossy largely ignores her, but is clearly fond of her. He tells him that the house is the one that his aunt was brought up in; but he tells him nothing else about her, or any other member of his family. Jamie simply assumes that he must have been orphaned, and that his aunt's mothering of him is therefore only natural.

His year at Teachers' College is not one he enjoys much. The times on Section, getting teaching experience, are the most interesting, but even then, although he does well and gets glowing reports concerning his pedagogical abilities and prospects, the praise is far from making him certain that necessity has bulldozed him into a satisfying career. There are too many dull and unwilling pupils, too strong an odour of wet wool, stale lunches, urine and farts as he patrols the corridors and the grounds at lunchtime. The teachers he observes too often seem little more than simply resigned to their tasks.

One of the High Schools he is sent to on Section is in the east of the city – a school not long built. He is allocated as his mentor a cynical man with an unpleasant habit of constantly picking his nose as he converses. His chief task seems to be the teaching of English and Social Studies and History to non-academic streams. Jamie quickly picks up on the nickname the man has been given by his pupils. They don't hide it from him. "Old Sloppyguts has sneaked out to have a puff, eh?" one boy looks up and tells him the first time he is left by himself in the classroom. It is true. His mentor is only too happy to allow Jamie to experience the rigours of teaching on his own while he disappears to the Staff Room to smoke.

On one such occasion, he is left to supervise the writing-up of notes from the classroom blackboard. His responsibility seems to entail nothing more than sitting at the teacher's desk and looking up every now and then to ensure that the class, a group repeating the Fifth Form, is doing as they have been instructed.

One of the girls, someone who has already attracted his attention because of her blonde hair (a cruel reminder of Fiona) and her Bardot-like pout, approaches his desk with her exercise book, which she places in front of him. He has been told that this girl's parents are from Eastern Europe, and that they arrived in New Zealand only a few years earlier, as refugees from a Communist regime. The girl herself speaks English well enough, but still with a heavy accent.

Her finger is indicating a sentence she has written in the book.

"What does this mean?" she asks. "How are they rotten?"

He looks, and reads: 'Many such rotten boroughs were controlled by peers and other wealthy men.'

"I thought I heard Mr Terrence explain that," he says.

"I did not understand," she says. She is leaning across him, a breast pressing against his upper arm. Embarrassed, he shifts a little in his chair, but she leans further towards him, restoring the contact.

Disturbed by his body's response to her nearness, he quickly offers her an explanation, closes the book, and hands it back to her.

"Thank you," she says; then she moves away, slowly, to resume the seat at her desk.

But this is not the only demonstration of her precocity. Later, on more than one occasion, when he is doing as his mentor instructed and circling the room to check on the activities, his eye is attracted by a sudden movement as she opens and closes, opens and closes her thighs. Her skirt has ridden high, and the vee of her sex, snug in its white cotton packaging, seems to wink at him; a blind, white eye.

Each time this happens, he looks up hurriedly to find that she is observing him, her green eyes humourless and knowing.

For Jamie, the most difficult question arising from these incidents is the decidedly sexual nature of his own immediate responses. It should not be thought of, he knows. It is the most sacred of taboos. He decides to raise the girl's name with his mentor, to discover, perhaps, if he has experienced anything similar.

"Ah," he says. "The sulky Bianka. What is it you want to know?"

"Oh, nothing really. Just if you've… had any special problems with her."

"Aha! Yes, any number of special problems, as you call them." His finger and thumb are at his nose; pick, pick, pick. "Don't be fooled by her sultry looks into thinking that they disguise any special talents. She is as she seems – slow witted. A no-hoper. Probably the worst of the whole no-hoper bunch."

"Just… learning problems, then?"

"What else? No, no. She's a harmless enough bit of baggage in her way, I suppose. No behavioural problems, if that's what you mean. Just not likely to succeed in anything. She'll be put out to breed pretty quickly, I imagine. Best thing for her."

It is not the sort of response he was hoping for. But then, he didn't really know what sort of response he was expecting. Something to ease his mind, he supposes. Evidence that the girl is an attention-seeker, perhaps, and that his reaction was more her fault than his. Instead, he is left with an aching pity for her, and a resentful disgust at the man's choice of words.

As far as possible, he avoids any possibility of a renewal of the dangers, or further revelations of his mentor's cynicism, and he is relieved when his time at that school is over.

Cossy is, indeed, basically unsociable, except on a one-to-one level. He deals with people only when he must. He doesn't even talk very much with Jamie, though he clearly likes having him around. They sit and read together. They listen to music together. They eat together. His aunt looks in on them every now and then, and she does all the cooking for them; but otherwise she keeps out of their way. Occasionally Cossy offers him some unsolicited piece of advice. "Leave off trying to write poetry," he says. "The only decent poetry is the stuff written by old men, or even, I hate to say it, by old women – the ones too old to have much foolish passion left in them. Try Dorothy Parker." He does, and spends some days after quoting to himself: 'The rangy lilac pushes upward, upward through my heart.'

Jamie takes even greater note of many of the things that Cossy tells him after that. "Stop looking so sorry for yourself," he tells him, one Saturday evening. "You don't have to stick around here. There's a club just down the road. You must've seen it."

So he goes. The club is in a building that looks like an army pre-fab. The bass thump of the music penetrates into the night long before he reaches it. He pays the entrance fee and goes inside.

There aren't many there, and the ones who are there are mostly girls. A few are dancing with each other, doing the Twist. Their faces look glum, uninterested. They also, most of them, seem very young. He looks around, hoping that he doesn't recognise any of them from the High Schools he's been sent to.

He doesn't, but neither does he see anyone who looks at all friendly. He feels out of place, completely out of place. He leaves, and goes straight back to Cossy's.

Cossy is still reading, and the radiogram is playing Beethoven's Pastoral Symphony.

"Getting a bit of high culture, Cossy?" Jamie asks. His usual choice is Brubeck or Beiderbecke. Maybe Benny Goodman.

He looks up. "You back? Go and make us a coffee, then. Aunt's gone next door to have a natter with her friend. Make yourself useful."

Jamie heads for the kitchen, but more words follow him. "And Beethoven's not high culture, young Ashcott. High culture is Bach or Telemann. Not these romantic bullshitters. Will you never learn?"

II

He ends the year with the right to apply for teaching jobs, and the very strong support of the majority of his College lecturers, who seem convinced that he will be an ornament to the profession. But *he* is not convinced. In every classroom he has been in during the year, he has felt like a charlatan, knowing little more than the pupils who sat so sullen or trusting or bored or eager in front of him.

In the end, he decides that his best course will be to stay in Christchurch and enrol at the University to do a Masters in History. He is told that his Bursary will allow him to do so. It will make him even more sought after as a teacher, he is told. Particularly if he achieves Honours. For him, though, it is little more than a delaying tactic; but one with, perhaps, just a hint of possibility in it. A way of escape from the future that threatens to close in around him, cutting off any alternative. At the very least, it will give him time to think.

The Masters course, he learns, involves both papers and a mini-thesis. There is a choice of papers. and some of them excite in him some genuine enthusiasm. The Late Middle Ages. Politics in the Reign of King George III. The American Civil War. He actually begins to look forward to testing himself academically in a way he has not truly done before.

Once again, he spends the summer break with the shearing gang. He's something of an old hand by now. Some of the others are the same, some are new. He thinks he detects a degree of respect for him, even from the shearers. Even so, it is the hardest season he has spent with them, hot and with very little in the way of breaks. What's more, there is a seriousness about the attitudes of everyone – both in the gang and amongst the farmers they are working for – that makes the experience even less comfortable. Besides, he is twenty-one now, and feels he should be ready to test himself in other fields. He decides he'd like to try something else next summer, if he can find it. Fruit-picking, maybe. Not the Freezing Works, though. He shudders at the very thought.

Back in Christchurch, in the first year of his Masters, Jamie at last begins to feel that he is achieving something worthwhile. He doesn't have to worry about the mini-thesis until the following year, but it doesn't scare him, anyway. Best of all, the Head of Department, who is also his tutor in one of the papers, seems to accept him as one of his better students. The papers he has chosen are ones he finds stimulating, and he enjoys writing the essays. He gets good grades in them all. Not quite Alpha pluses, but near enough.

Rather to his surprise, he becomes good friends with another Masters student, though not one who is doing History. His name is Anders Malmo, and his father is something big in local politics. He is tall, with floppy blonde hair and an almost constant grin. Taken together, they give him the air of an elongated Dennis the Menace. The girls love him. Any girl, it seems; and of any age. He dresses with casual elegance, and is friendly with everyone. He is also, he learns, the darling of the English Department, and great things are expected of him.

Within a very short time of their first meeting, Anders makes it clear that he likes Jamie's company, and the implicit offer of friendship Jamie is delighted to accept. They become, in fact, close companions; though it is Anders who decides what to do, and where to go.

Anders is a hedonist, but a caring one, and he really does seem to value their friendship.. He and Jamie usually start off the evenings with a Martini in the private bar at Anders' favourite hotel. Being a Christchurch man, he knows all the best places to go. On their excursions together, anything can happen, and frequently does. Invariably, though, it is Anders who gets the most glamorous girl, and Jamie who is left empty-handed, or with a runner-up who would, he has little doubt, much rather be spending her time with Anders than with him. Sometimes, though, the runner-up agrees to accompany him back to his room at Cossy's for a coffee.

On one such occasion the girl, who looks, Jamie thinks, not unlike Juliet Prowse, seems as eager as him to at least salvage some physical satisfaction from the evening.

"Have you got something?" she asks, her beautiful and quite large breasts swinging above him.

"Uh, no." He hasn't ever yet summoned the courage to ask at a Chemist. Once he almost did, charging through the door in determined fashion and heading straight for the counter. It was a woman who appeared behind it. He'd asked for a jar of Brylcream instead.

She rummages around in her bag. "I've got some pessaries," she says. "I've never used them before, but they're supposed to do the job."

She gets off the bed and crouches. He has no idea what she is doing; but he is glad she wants to go on with it, and that she has the means to keep it safe.

"They're supposed to kill the little buggers," she says. "I hope it works."

He shares her hope. She clambers back on the bed and offers him access. But there is something not quite right – a hissing sound. A frothing sound. They both look to its source.

It is like sea foam, issuing from between her thighs. They both look down, then back at each other. Then the comic nature of the situation takes over and desire is usurped by giggling and laughter.

"Oh God!" she says. "I'm never going to try pessaries again. Talk about killing it dead!"

He is glad she is sharing the glee. It makes the embarrassment bearable. He likes her all the more for it, but the desire for sex has vanished.

They hold each other, chastely, their shoulders heaving. "Maybe we should try it some other time," she says.

"Yes," he says. But they never do.

But there are other times, with other girls, when a kind of consummation is reached. He finds that afterwards, though, he is most commonly left with a residue of both guilt and disappointment.

The year ends with exams coinciding with the Cuban Missile Crisis. Like the others waiting to go in to take the Eighteenth Century Politics exam, he experiences an eerie feeling that the world they will re-enter when the exam is over will be very different from and much more turbulent than, the one they now must leave for three hours. In the event, the crisis remains just that for days more, but there is general relief when the whole thing peters out quite tamely, with an agreement between Kennedy and Khrushchev that seems to leave the possibility that the world will, in fact, become a rather safer place than it was before the showdown began.

And that year, and the one that follows, he also develops an even more passionate interest in art. Not just any art. He has for a very long time been attracted by Picasso's blue period, and has pinned a print of La Vie on his wall wherever he has gone. Other examples have attracted his attention also – such as a girl painted by some eighteenth century English artist. He'd cut the picture carelessly from a glossy magazine, and had neglected to record the name of the artist, but whoever it was seemed to him to have captured the essence of the girl's innocence and vulnerability. Even more especially, he had discovered in a junk shop a framed print of a painting by Leighton called, 'Flaming June', of a red-haired girl sleeping, curled protectively in a silken cocoon, unaware of the threat her beauty elicits.

Now he seeks more examples of similar art – art that triggers in him an intense emotion that is irresistibly attractive, yet makes his chest ache and his eyes prickle with an intensity of longing, or nostalgia, or for something utterly desirable that is undefined and just, just out of reach. He buys art books as he can afford them, and even when he can't, and builds a little library of prints, black and white and coloured, that he pores over. He also spends some of his savings on an ebonised plaster head of a young African woman with gold earrings whose downcast look and faultless beauty he finds particularly haunting. He calls her Nefertiti. But it is mostly paintings that he studies. Nearly always they are of young women. The creations of Mary Cassatt, of Renoir, of Corot and Bonnard. Renaissance artists, too, particularly their depictions of The Annunciation. Then there is Degas and his little ballerinas. Even some of Toulouse-Lautrec's weary prostitutes, who make him ache, not with lust, but with a sweet, sweet sadness.

III

On his way home after his first year at Canterbury University, Jamie spends a couple of days in Wellington, and phones Tela. His main motive in doing so, he recognises, is to get the latest news about Fiona. They arrange to meet in a coffee shop at the top of Willis Street.

He knows that Tela's academic career is by now well established, that she has just finished her Masters.

"And what will you do next?" he asks.

"They've already offered me a Junior Lectureship," she says. "But Joan and Cynthia both think I should only stick around for a couple of years, then apply for a Commonwealth Scholarship and go to Cambridge to do a doctorate."

He knows without asking who Joan is. She is the same woman who had inspired in him an interest in eighteenth century literature. "All worked out, eh? You'll do it, too," he says. This time, he does sense a little bitterness. All worked out. Everything in place. A future.

"Yes," she says. "I'm very, very lucky, I know. My dream is my reality. Or it looks as though it will be, at least."

"Of course it will be. You've got it made."

"Not quite yet," she says. "There's a lot more I want to find. To do. But what about you, Jamie? Are things going for you the way you want them to go?"

He shrugs. He still doesn't even know what he wants from life, apart from… He wants Fiona, he knows that; and in that regard, there is still a tiny hope left glowing inside him. Tela has told him that she has found her first posting, at a country school in the Rangitikei. She is single. "I'm quite enjoying doing the Masters course," he says. "I might even get a First, if I'm lucky. I have a friend who's definitely going to get one, but he's doing his in English."

Afterwards, they catch a tram back down to Lambton Quay. Most of the seats are taken, and there are none that will enable them to sit together. Tela takes one next to a young woman with fair hair done in a tight bun, and stiff, tense shoulders. As she does so, the woman looks across at her with an unmistakeable look of horror, almost terror. She comes quickly to her feet, and brushes past the seated Tela, holding her skirt, trying to avoid contact, then walks hurrying, lurching, to find a seat at the other end of the tram.

Jamie reddens as he sees, and guesses the reason for, the woman's action. He is instantly hot with anger and shame and embarrassment.

He takes the now vacant seat beside her, leaning in close. He feels he would like to hold her, to show her that… "My God!" he hisses into her ear. "What an absolute… God, Tela. I'm sorry."

She puts her hand on his arm. "Oh Jamie, Jamie! I've had a lot worse than that. Don't get upset about it."

"You mean… you mean you're used to being treated like that? You don't mind?"

"Mind? Of course I mind. And yes, it always hurts. But it doesn't happen all that often. Most people are okay. Some might look a bit startled when they look up and see me standing or sitting there. But most don't react like that." She looks at him, and shakes her head. "Some people can't handle difference, you know. They feel threatened."

He is still angry for her. Then he looks at her again, tries to put himself in her place. Would he be so calm about it? "You shouldn't have to put up with that. Never. Never. You're… well, you're… worth a dozen of any of them."

She laughs. "Thank you, Jamie! Very sweet of you." Her hand is still on his arm, and she squeezes a thank you. "We should get off here, I think."

And they do; and they walk up the hill together, and Jamie thinks he has never before been half so proud to have anyone else at his side as he is to have Tela.

V

Tela has found that meeting up with Jamie has once again upset the tenor of her world. Quite apart from anything else, it is a reminder that there is another part to her life, a part that is not connected necessarily to her academic career. But it is Jamie himself who causes the major upset.

She is both amused and touched by his reaction to the incident on the tram on the way back down from coffee. It is so typically Jamie. He seems to go through life trapped in a little bubble of whimsy and self-doubt, and when reality intrudes, he closes in on himself, like the leaves of sensitive grass touched by experimental fingers. What it confirms in her mind, though, is that he is a man with strong feelings of empathy. A man who instinctively detects and shuns brutality. That, she finds a very, very attractive quality. Yet another one.

They walk up the hill afterwards, to her flat, the one she still shares with Fiona, whenever Fiona wants to visit Wellington.

"I've got to be up at Vic in less than an hour," she says. "But come in for bit. You've got time?"

"Yes. I've got nothing in particular to do. I'm catching a bus north tonight."

"Good." She unlocks the door, and they go in.

He refuses the offer of another coffee, but abruptly takes a sheet of paper from his duffle-coat pocket and hands it to her, diffident and awkward. "It's just… just a poem I wrote a while back. I've been carrying it around."

She looks at it. It is hand-written. The title is given as 'The Bitter Flame'.

Not a promising start, she thinks. But then a small pang creeps up on her. Is it pity? It could be something else altogether.

"And it's written to Fi, I expect," she says. She knows it must be. That knife in her gut.

"Well… yes."

She reads the rest of it. There's no doubting the sincerity of his effort, but it is far too high blown. It is as though he's swallowed a whole volume of Swinburne. Her judgement is accompanied by a welling of wicked satisfaction; but the implicit cruelty is not directed at Jamie. With genuine guilt, she admits to herself that she is glad it is an unsuccessful poem, because it was inspired by Fiona.

"Not bad," she says. "Though I'm not sure I understand it." She knows that Jamie is unlikely to take the true meaning from her words. Of course she does understand it; the intent, that is. The naïve, the *wrong*, sentiment. What she doesn't even want to understand, is why.

Why, why, why Jamie? Well, yes, of course she knows why. She understands very well why any man would want her. Fi is lovely, truly lovely, and not simply physically. She is annoyed with herself for even questioning his… his reasons, his right to want her.

But… But… Jamie; why not me?

She puts aside her impatience, pushes away her ridiculous jealousy, her frustration, and turns their conversation to other things. It is just nice to have him around. To gently probe. To get to know him better; the side of him that he mostly hides. The Jamie that triggers her longing.

At least they are friends.

Early the following year, on a Saturday, Cynthia Wallace comes and spends the day with her. She has come over to New Zealand to spend another long holiday with her friend who lives in Waikanae. She has stayed with the same friend every year since Tela was in her first year in Vic.

By now, Tela has started her Junior Lectureship, her First Class Honours confirmed. Fiona has come down from the Rangitikei for the weekend, too – but for much of the day she finds that she has other things to do, and leaves her and Cynthia to talk.

"You have a wonderful friend there," Cynthia says. "Something special."

"I know. I'm lucky. You and Fi. My twin pillars."

They sit for a time in silence; but it is not an awkward silence. There never has been any awkwardness between them. Never.

"There's something I want to talk to you about," Cynthia says. "Something that is not yet quite clear in my mind. I think you might be able to help me with it."

"If I can…" She would like to able to help Cynthia. A little reciprocity.

"It's to do with Charles. Well… with Charles and me."

Charles? She only remembers him as a shadowy figure who once or twice entered their world – hers and Cynthia's. They had exchanged a few words on occasion, but never conversed. He had always seemed vaguely accepting of her presence rather than interested, Cynthia's husband. "Yes?"

"We… we, neither of us, have ever raised the issue. We both seem to want to avoid it. We pretend that things are rubbing along well enough, but neither of us is sincere in that belief. I'm quite sure of that."

Can it be something to do with me, Tela wonders. She desperately hopes it isn't.

"As you know, Charles transferred from Mackay to Brisbane, to take up a senior management position. It's something he'd wanted for a long time. And he's done very well indeed. It suits him. He likes making investment decisions. Sitting in the boardrooms. Making lots of money for himself and the Company. And I… I suppose I have enjoyed – still enjoy – some of the results of his success. The material comforts and so on. Indulging myself in whatever way takes my fancy. But…"

It's not about her, Tela accepts, with some relief. But?

"But I find my life is essentially empty. I don't enjoy it… socially. The people I'm expected to mix with. I have little in common, little interest in, the wives of the men he spends his life with. Nor do I have the energy – or is it the inclination? – to find alternative ways of muddling along. I suppose I simply don't see Brisbane, maybe not Australia itself, as somewhere I can be comfortable. And the simple fact is, I find no comfort at all any more in Charles' company. Nor he in mine. I find it hard to even remember the times when I did. When surely I must have."

She shifts in her chair, rises abruptly. "I'm going to make another cup of coffee," she says.

"Let me," Tela says.

"No, no. I need to do something while I think of how to put it."

"Well I'll help you."

They go to the kitchen together. Cynthia fills the hot water jug and Tela opens the instant coffee jar, spoons the mixture into the mugs. They stand in silence, waiting for the jug to boil.

'You see…" Cynthia begins. "The choices we made all those years ago. They were… the wrong ones. Probably for both of us, but especially for me. But I can't go back. The choices that were available to me then are not available to me now. For Charles… well, he has always chosen the paths we take. I've simply gone along. It seemed the right thing to do. It seemed to be what was expected of… a woman. A wife."

The jug boils. Cynthia picks it up and pours water into the mugs. Then she puts the jug back down, hurriedly, carelessly, some of the water arcing out of the spout and onto the sink bench. She doesn't seem to even notice, but looks sharply at Tela, holding her gaze.

"God!" she says. "That's it! That's all I needed to do. I just needed to *say* it. But it had to be to you. Tela, my wonderful, wonderful girl. It had to be to you!"

She is smiling now, her face a picture of relief, perhaps even joy. "What is it?" Tela asks; but she can sense the answer. In part, at least.

"You know what it is, I think. It is the only thing that has made me truly glad to… to be in this life over the past God knows how many years? You can guess, can't you! It is you! You have shown me my true self, a part of me, the larger part of me, that I had lost. Right from the first time I saw you, I started my rediscovery."

"Me?"

"Yes, my darling. It is you. And you know exactly what I mean. I know you do. Charles never did understand. I think he thought that you were my surrogate child, my surrogate daughter. That thought of his possibly drove us further apart, but it was his own silly fault. He couldn't understand. What I saw in you, what I *see* in you, is not the daughter I never had. Not that, for God's sake, Charles, you silly man! I see my lost self. You restarted my life. You have rekindled a fire in me. But it needs oxygen. And that is why, that is why, I must leave permanently. I must come back here."

"Leave… Charles?"

"Of course. I turned fifty this year. I've given him ten more years than I should have given him. Anyway, he'll be better off without me. He can buy someone else. He probably won't even notice the difference."

"And you…"

"And I'll stay here. I won't go back. I like Waikanae, and Wellington. I'll… I'll try to make some contacts, explore possibilities. At Vic, perhaps. You might be able to help me with that."

Tela is suddenly excited by the thought, and by everything that Cynthia has told her. And now… a chance to help her. Of course she will! She will do whatever she can. It is probably not very much, but at least she will be able to introduce her to people who might be able to help further.

IV

On a Saturday later that same year, Murray Finlay calls her up; hoping that Fiona is there, so he says. He's on his way from Christchurch to Hawkes Bay for a bit of home time before starting at another Branch of the Stock Agent he works for, this time in Hamilton.

"She's not here," Tela tells him. "She comes down most weekends, but she hasn't this time."

"Oh, bugger," he says. "I was hoping you'd both be able to put me up for the night. I was planning on driving up tomorrow morning."

"Well… You could use her room. I can put some clean sheets on."

"You wouldn't mind? Just for the night?"

"Of course not."

"Thanks. It'll be good to see you. What time?"

"Any time you like. Why don't you come up now? I can cook something for us. At least baked beans on toast. Maybe even something more interesting. I'll take a look, see what I've got."

"Sure it's no trouble? I'll bring some beer up."

"If you like. Not for me, though. I still don't drink."

"Oh yeah. I'd forgotten you're a wowser," he says. She has a sudden picture of his lop-sided grin. It'll be good to see him again, too.

"You coming straight up, then?"

"Yeah. See you soon."

She puts the phone down and decides she won't go back to her books, or her marking. She'll look in the fridge, instead; see if she can make something interesting for him. Murray, tall and fair. Murray, who once

182

kissed her in a broom cupboard. She smiles to herself. She is quite glad, in a way, that Fi couldn't get down.

It's less than half an hour before he knocks on the door and she opens it to him. He hasn't changed much. He must be twenty-seven or twenty-eight, she calculates; but he still looks like an overgrown schoolboy. That lop-sided grin.

"Good to see you, Tel," he says, and gives her a quick hug. Then he picks up his bag and follows her in. "Something smells good."

"I found some mince," she says. "I'm just making some sauce for a lasagne."

"What's that? Sounds exotic." He's looking at her appreciatively, and she's glad she had time to pull a brush through her hair.

"It's easy Italian. I eat it a lot." Still a roast lamb and spuds man, she muses. He probably will be all his life. "Take your stuff through to Fi's room," she says.

He does; then he comes back and sits with her, and they talk about Fi and the farm and his job. He even tries to quiz her on her work, but soon gives up. She doesn't mind that.

"Did you bring any beer?" she asks.

"Nah. I thought you said…"

"That I still don't drink? I don't – but I thought you could have one while I'm finishing off in the kitchen."

"Don't worry about me."

With the pasta al dente, she assembles the lasagne, puts it in the oven, and returns to continue talking. She feels quite light-headed, and happy to have her mind taken off the marking she has to do. She can sense a tension in the air between them, but it is not a threatening tension. He keeps looking at her, even when they're not talking. Even when he doesn't have to. It makes her feel quite deliciously uneasy.

After dinner, which he says he has enjoyed, he helps her wash up. Once they've finished she puts a Francoise Hardy LP on the record player, and turns it down to a comforting murmur. She doesn't know why she chooses it, other than the vague feeling that the sound of French will somehow enhance the mood she is in.

He is looking at her again. Appreciatively. Knowing that she knows. Fi has told her he has had considerable success with girls. She has often joked about it, half critically, half fondly. They fall all over him, she's told her. God knows why. Silly cows.

But she can understand why they do. That boyish, feigned innocence.

Something is happening. Something she decides she wants to happen. She is sitting on the big sofa, and he comes over to her, sits next to her.

"You remember the first time you came home with Fi?" he asks her.

"The broom cupboard?"

He grins. God! That bloody grin! "Yeah," he says. "Fancy you remembering that." He moves closer, puts his arms around her, pulls her into him. "Jesus, Tel," he says. "The broom cupboard. That unfinished business. It's been on my mind for years."

Unlikely, she thinks. But at least we both remember. Unfinished business.

He kisses her, and she responds, wanting it. Wanting all that she knows will follow.

The next morning they both agree that Fi must never know what they have done together. They both agree that she might take it as a betrayal of her friendship, a betrayal of her sisterly fondness. While it was possible, even likely, that Fi would have welcomed the totally ridiculous idea of them getting together permanently, a casual liaison between the two of them would surely seem to her to be utterly wrong. Perfidious, even.

Yet that was all both she and Murray had wanted, of that Tela was totally sure. It was simply the completion of that unfinished business. For Murray, no more than another notch in his belt; for her, the final loss of her irritating virginity to someone she actually likes. A bit. Quite a bit.

And before he gets into his car, he gives her a hug and a cheerful wave, and everything, almost everything, is back to the way it had been.

Chapter Four – Crises

I

Tela is at the end of her two-year term as Junior Lecturer. She has enjoyed it. More than that – she now knows that a career as a University Lecturer is precisely the one she wants. But she is also looking forward immensely to taking up the Commonwealth Scholarship she has been awarded. To Cambridge. In four or five months she will set off. Perfection. When she stops to think about it, she can scarcely believe that her life is steadily unfolding in exactly the way she has dreamed it would. The fantasy continues to become reality. To make everything that little bit more than perfect, she has just learnt that she has been accepted into Girton College, the College that Cynthia had attended. And adding still further to her euphoria, Cynthia has told her that she has been offered a part-time position in the Department she herself will shortly be leaving.

The phone in her narrow cubby-hole of an office rings, and she picks it up, ready to assure the Prof that she has, indeed, finished marking the exam papers and collating the results ready for that afternoon's meetings.

"Tela Gilbard," she says; cheerful, confident; smug.

"Tela?" A hesitant voice. A young man's voice. Distant, crackling.

"Yes."

"It's Junior."

For an instant she is confused. Junior? Her little six-year-old brother Oliver, always known as Junior, shy and solemn. That's the only Junior she knows.

"Junior!" Of course; a young man by now. Fifteen, or sixteen. A young man's voice. A stranger's voice. Her head reels with the thought; then there follows a sudden dread.

"Junior? What is it?"

"It's our Mum. She's… very sick."

She could not have anticipated her reaction – the feeling that a whole world she had been shutting out of her mind has arrived like a shell-burst in her skull. Her mother!

"How… how badly? How sick?"

"Very sick. The hospital sent her home. She wanted to come home. To… die."

"Oh Junior! No!"

"Yes. Will you come home?"

Home? Home?

Her mind adjusts to the thought. Home. Not to her flat in the Kelburn hills. No. Home to Fiji. Home to the hot and dusty compound, to the house with its old peeling timbers and its wide verandahs. To her father. To her dying mother.

She is struck then by a lurch of grief, a feeling of separation, such as she has never felt before, and yet… Had it been there all the time, suppressed?

"Oh Junior. Yes, yes. I'll be home as soon as I can. I'll let you know. I'll send a cable."

"She's dying."

Poor Junior. Her brother. Her mother's only son. "Yes. Yes. As soon as I can I'll be there. How… how's our father?"

"He's… old now. The aunties are here. Looking after her. Looking after everything. Helping Margie."

Her elder sister. Still at home, then, surely. Dutiful in a way she herself never was. And her Fijian aunties. Yes. They would know what to do. It is a relief to know that.

"Thank you, Junior." Junior, a young man. Shouldn't she call him Oliver? "I'll… see you soon."

"Yes. Goodbye."

She is thankful that she had applied for a passport soon after getting the papers that affirmed her New Zealand citizenship. She had done that chiefly because she wanted to carry an affirmation of that citizenship with her, in her bag, at all times. Now it has another use.

She manages to get flights to Auckland, and on to Nadi, for the beginning of the following week. She is able to attend the examiners' meetings. She is able to put everything in order before she leaves. She phones Fi, and she agrees to come down to Wellington and stay in the flat as soon as school is over. She pays for her return flights but does not book a date for them, leaving the departure time for her return open.

Early on Monday morning, shortly before her ordered taxi arrives to take her to the airport for her flight to Auckland, a cable is delivered. She takes it from the hands of the delivery-man and goes to the kitchen, and stands at the bench with the peeling knife she has taken from the drawer to open the envelope. She knows. She doesn't want the confirmation. She thinks she doesn't need it. Yet she must have it.

She slits open the envelope and removes the folded piece of paper with its brief message. She reads: 'Mum passed away last night. Junior.'

She has to stay overnight in Auckland, at a cheap hotel close to the airport. The next morning she goes through the formalities and boards the flight that will take her back to Fiji. For the first time in almost ten years. Home to her mother, who has gone. Dead.

Disembarking at Nadi, the first thing she notices is the heat. It is as though a giant fan is sending waves of air from a furnace across her face. There is no one to meet her. She had said in her cable that she would make her own way from the airport.

The taxi takes her through the busy town. It is mid-afternoon, the hottest part of the day, but there are many people in the main street. Mostly Indians, it seems – though there are Fijians, too. Going about the business of their days. Shades of brown. Not a white face in sight. She had given it no thought. It jolts her, the sight. No white faces. None.

The taxi draws up at the entrance to the Mill compound. It is familiar, of course – but somehow it is more than simply familiar. It is… the inside of her skin; so familiar that she senses the ten years that have intervened could have been imaginary.

A scattering of children. School must be just out. At the furthest edge of the compound she can see the side-by-side houses. Their house and the Millar's house. Drab, unadorned.

She pays the taxi driver and walks across the compound with her bag. Some of the children stop in their play, watching. Two people emerge from the house as she approaches; a young man and a woman. She is dressed in black. Tela pauses as the woman runs towards her, arms outstretched.

"Tela! Tela!" Engulfed by her grief, her welcome. Her older sister's welcome, and her grief.

"Oh, Margie! I'm so sorry." The moan of her own voice in response. Unfamiliar, so strange to her ears that she is shocked by it. Her own voice, moaning in shared grief.

Behind them, waiting, the young man. A young man dressed in a grey *sulu* and a white shirt, dressed as a Fijian would be dressed. But not a Fijian.

"Junior?" Still not her own voice, her familiar voice. A whispered croak. And he too steps forward, hugs her briefly, steps away.

"The aunties," Margie says, nodding towards the house. "They're all here. They've been here ever since she came back from hospital. They've been… Dad's been so hopeless. Useless. Can't blame him, of course. But without the aunties… Well, thank God for the aunties."

They mount the wooden steps, cross the verandah. The doors are wide open, encouraging the breeze. As soon as she enters there is a flurry of rising from the women gathered there. *Sulu*-clad women. Her mother's sisters and cousins. Others from the village. Eight or nine of them.

"Ni vosoti au, ni'u sa bera mai!" she says. Her voice is still unsteady, her words ending in a sob; but the Fijian comes surprisingly easily. I'm so sorry to be late.

The oldest of them replies, coming to her, hugging her, kissing her. "Vinaka vaka levu, ni'o sa yaco mai." You are here now. That is good.

One by one the others offer the same gestures, murmuring their shared grief, their understanding.

The funeral arrangements have already been made, she learns. It is to be the following day. The service is to be taken by the same *talatala*, the same preacher, that she had fallen out with those many years ago. He comes to see them. He is grey-haired, grizzled; not nearly so fearsome. He seems not to even recognise her from that time, and she is glad.

Her mother's casket lies constantly attended as people come and go. As soon as she is able to do so, Tela dresses herself in a black *sulu* and a sober blouse given to her by one of the aunties; and takes her place amongst those who keep vigil. She wants, desperately, to see her father, but he doesn't seem to be around. Margie joins her off and on during the afternoon, but she spends most of her time helping with the preparation of the food for the visitors.

People come and go, leaving tributes – lengths of cloth, woven mats, pieces of *tapa*, tins of cabin bread and bully beef. Supplies of *taro* and cassava and *vudi* appear from the village gardens, or from the local market. For a time, the house, and the compound, more usually the domain of the part-Europeans, becomes the centre for ceremonies that are intrinsically Fijian.

Tela takes her place within these activities with what at first is a strong feeling of guilt and alienation. But that lasts only a very short time. She is accepted easily, totally by the women who share the vigil. She listens to their talk about her mother, and about their own lives. She answers their questions concerning her life and is humbled by their responses. Sometimes they express their admiration for what she has achieved, but without a trace of envy; they are mildly curious, but they accept, with cooing murmurs and apparently without any judgement whatever, the answers she gives. And all the time she wonders, wonders where her father is, why he is not with them.

One visitor to the house is a tall, well-built man she recognises immediately as Dan Millar. She goes outside to talk with him privately.

He seems shy, scarcely daring to look at her. She reaches out and takes his arm.

"Dan. Tell me things," she says. "Tell me about yourself."

Oh," he says, his eyes still surveying his khaki shorts, his sandaled feet. "There's nothing much. I'm married."

"And that's nothing much?" she says. "What's her name? Is it someone I know? That I knew?"

"It's Poppy Jones. Except she's Poppy Millar now!" he grins. Relaxing. Looking at her for her reaction.

Poppy Jones! The acknowledged belle of their years. Light-skinned, quiet, dreamy. A girl who stayed well clear of the Highbirds. A nice girl. A girly girl. She dismisses the flash of jealousy. Good on Dan, she thinks.

"Congratulations," she says.

"We have two kids. A boy and a girl. I'm Deputy Chief Electrician, at the Mill. We have our own house."

She gapes in surprise. Big Dan, slow witted, but nice. Or so she had thought him. Two children and a skilled trade, as well as Poppy! How wrong she had been! "Wow!" she says.

He looks down again, deprecatingly. "Nothing to what you've done, I bet," he says.

"Oh God, Dan! Not true. Not true at all." She moves closer, circles her arms around him, around his big, fit body, lays her head briefly against his chest. "That is not true at all."

She steps back, and the tears that run down her cheeks are for the stultifying stupidity, of wilful uncaring, that has been an unrecognised part of her for so very, very long.

It is almost dusk before she gets a chance to spend some private time with Margie, and this proves to be even more painful and personally disturbing. Catching up. Learning what she should have long known.

"I'm married," Margie tells her; and she brings out of her bag a coloured photograph taken on the day of her wedding. She is in white. Next to her, her husband. "That's my Ant. Anthony. I'm Mrs Hadlow, now."

A Hadlow! They are a large and leading family in the part-European community in Suva. They number among their kind doctors and lawyers and prominent people in the commercial life of Fiji, and they famously marry only those of similar caste – or Europeans. In fact, there had been a Hadlow from Fiji in one of her tutorial groups. She had finished marking her exam paper only days ago. Sophie Hadlow. A lovely young woman, but shy and tentative. Sophie had stayed behind a little after one of the tutorials, and hesitantly asked her if she was from Fiji; and she had acknowledged it, but it hadn't seemed relevant to pursue it further.

She tells Margie.

"Oh yes," she says. "I haven't met her yet, but Ant told me he had a cousin at Victoria, in Wellington. Where you work. I wondered, but…"

Yes. But. Her fault again. She had written the occasional letter home to her father, never expecting or receiving a reply. Those letters had told him briefly what she was doing, what she had done, but never asking questions. Each and every one had been full of… herself. Apart from dutifully asking that her love be passed on to her mother, her sisters, her brother, her aunties. Dutifully. Meaninglessly.

She looks more closely at the wedding photograph. He is a fine looking man, Margie's Anthony; pale skin, reddish hair, a proud yet kindly look. This, the husband of her elder sister, who, on her visits home from Nursing School had seemed very dull, interested in little other than the romance books she constantly read. She has married a Hadlow, and she didn't even know!

"We live in Suva. With his parents. But we're hoping to get our own place soon."

"Mum must have been pleased," Tela says.

"She wasn't, very," Margie says. "I think she was hoping I'd marry a Fijian."

Then, the biggest blow of all, apart from the death that has brought them together. "Where's Chrissy? Why isn't she here?"

Chrissy, their younger sister. Little more than a shadow in Tela's memory. Sly and quiet. A peeping girl. She had been only ten years old when she left for New Zealand.

Margie hesitates; looks at her then looks away.

"Chrissy's in Suva. She… didn't want to come."

"Why not?"

"She's… Of course, you don't know. When she was fifteen, she got pregnant. Had a baby, but it was born dead. Then… she went away. To Suva."

She takes a little time to process the words, to come to terms with what is, by now, old yet, for her, shocking news. Her head is reeling, still, with the information, but she manages to ask: "And… what's she doing there?"

"She… always said she wanted to be like you. To get away from here. To go overseas. She was very… wild. That's when she got pregnant. Now… she goes with men. She goes to nightclubs in Suva and lets men buy her drinks and pick her up. Europeans, mostly. I see her every now and then. I've tried talking to her. It doesn't work. I think she hopes that one of them will get serious, and take her away to Sydney or London or somewhere like that."

Little Chrissy. Living inside her head, just as she herself had done. She had never even bothered to get to know her. Little more than a peeping shadow.

She brings her hands to her eyes to cover her useless tears. Useless. Useless. What a useless sister she had been. So self-absorbed. So unheedingly wrapped up in her own dreams. In herself.

Margie hugs her; and yet again a sob is wrenched out of her, making her chest ache.

"I know you haven't had a chance to talk to Dad yet," Margie whispers to her. "Go and find him. Tell him everything you've been doing. He'd love to hear. He's so proud of you."

Proud of her? For what? For being such a useless sister. Such a useless daughter? Even now. She has been so caught up by the crippling knowledge of her own careless selfishness, she hasn't even yet sat down to talk properly with her father. Her father, who is proud of her!

"I've been thinking about him, wanting to see him. Where is he? Why isn't he here?"

"He's… I think he feels sort of… out of it. He's been drinking. He's not drunk, though. He just feels… pushed aside. By the Fijians. By the Aunties. It's silly. But he's all mixed up. Not thinking properly. He'll be out the back somewhere."

She finds him. He is, in fact, seated on an old crate. He looks up as she approaches.

"Ah, my little Tela!" he says. "You have come! Margie told me, but I didn't want to interrupt."

"Oh Dad, that's just silly. Nobody would think that. Anyway, it's you I want to see. More than anyone."

She kneels to embrace him, and he pulls her into himself, his arms still strong and wiry. "My little Tela."

He points to another crate, close to his, and she sits.

"How are you, Dad? Really?" He has changed little physically. The same meagre body and heavily creased face, but his hair has gone from grey to white and his posture as he sits there is slumped, as though he has lost the vitality that had made him seem so… on top of things. Even when he was drunk.

"Yes, I'm doing well enough," he says. "All the better for you being here." A grin. A tired grin. Tired eyes.

"I can see you're not," she says. "Talk to me, Dad. Please. Tell me how you're feeling. Please."

"I'm doing well enough," he repeats. "I want to hear about you. You're going to England. To Cambridge University. My little Tela is going to Cambridge University."

Oh God! She doesn't even want to think about it! Not now. Not here. "I... Yes, Dad. Probably. But that's not important. That's something else. I want to hear about you. How you feel about... mother. About all this. What you'll be doing now."

He looks down, drawing patterns in the dust at his feet with a stick he holds.

"Tell me, Dad. Tell me about you and mother. Please."

He looks at her, sighs. It is a shaky intake of breath, like a surrender. "My Kelera," he says. "She was a fine looking girl. Her people didn't want me, but she wasn't going to let me go. She told them that if they didn't agree to it, she'd run away with me. Stubborn."

She waits for more. The stick in his hands draws more patterns.

"Now she's gone," he says. "I didn't... I didn't do as well by her as I should have. My Kelera. But I gave her children. Three daughters and a son. A good son. Good daughters."

She thinks of Chrissy. She thinks of herself. But yes, there is Junior. A good son. And there is Margie, a good daughter. A daughter who has already offered him a place in her home, if he needs it. But Chrissy, it seems, has chosen not to be a good daughter. And she... well, she made that same choice years ago.

"You let her be what she wanted to be, Dad. I'm sure that was important to her." They had never seemed to be a very loving couple, not to her. But what did she know, after all?

"She kept a good house for me," he says. "Now she's gone."

He looks up at her, and shakes his head. "I never told her that we would have to move out of this house by the end of the year. That they've told me I have to retire. I'm glad I didn't tell her. She would have worried.

But there's just me and Junior left now. He's a good boy, Junior. I'll have to look after him on my own."

So much left to Junior now, she thinks. It will be Junior who is the carer. Junior and Margie, between them. While she…

She gets up from the crate and kneels beside him once again. "Oh Dad. I have been… I want you to know…" What? What can I tell him that he doesn't already know? He understands her. He always has. Better than anyone. Better than she understands herself.

"Don't you worry about it," he says. He strokes her hair, pats her shoulder. "I know. I know."

"I love you, Dad. Do you know that?"

"I know. I know."

She can't help the tears, though she knows they are at least as much for herself as they are for him, for her mother. She will keep close contact from now on, she promises herself. She will do what she can. She must. It will never make up for her years of inescapable selfishness, but she will do what she can. She will, she will. It is not too late to make some amends.

A few days later she is on the flight back to New Zealand, her head and heart heavy still with grief and guilt. But once she is back in Wellington, another feeling takes hold of her. It is a feeling generated, she knows, by her innate rationality. Grief is, in a way, the most selfish of emotions, she reasons. The sort of grief that has been generated in her is little more than further evidence of her own selfishness. She made her decisions all those years ago. She made them for reasons that are still meaningful. Neither grief nor guilt can alter that. That is what she must accept. Her father has accepted it all along. She must, too.

Yet she knows the experiences of the last couple of weeks have changed her. She is more grateful than ever for what Cynthia has done for her, and for the friendship of Fiona. But she knows more certainly than ever that neither of them can take the place of her family. Nor would she wish for that. She is changed forever by the resurrection of what she must have known all along – that she cares for her family. In her heart she cares. The physical caring… well, there was no choice, really; for she knows, too, that she is on the very brink of achieving what she has always wanted to achieve. That remains unchanged. She cannot change it. She cannot have both what she has and what she left behind all those years ago. Her life is… her life. It will be what she decided that it had to be. Hers. But she has changed. And she is glad.

Not long before she is due to take the train to Auckland to board the ship that will take her to England, Tela spends a last weekend with Fi in Wellington. She has given up the flat, and they have booked a couple of nights in a little hotel to be together. A Wellington wind is blowing fiercely around the bowl of the hills, but they are snug in their double room. They are talking of their futures, and Fi has brought up the question of life partners.

"They don't have to be husbands these days, you know. Shacking up with someone is not the unthinkable it once was," Fi says.

Tela is not particularly interested in even considering the topic, but it is clearly on Fi's mind. "If that's what you decide to do," she says, "you'll be spoiled for choice."

"Humph. Like who?"

"Well, there's always Jamie Ashcott. I bet he's as keen as ever. You know, he once showed me a poem he'd written for you."

"Oh God, no. Not Jamie. He's far too nice. Isn't he? I don't want someone who writes poetry to me. I want someone who'll keep me in the luxury I deserve and provide me with daughters who'll hound me for new ponies. And, of course, will give me lots of frolicking."

"Well, I'm sure Jamie's capable of the last two."

"Hey, how come you're so sure? You haven't…?"

"I wish," she responds quickly; then tries to recover. "I mean, I'm just guessing. In that other respect, though, I agree there could be a few problems. Oh, and it wasn't a very good poem, by the way."

"There you go then. But… Hmmm. Jamie, eh? You never know." She is looking thoughtful, head cocked to one side. "He *is* lovely, isn't he? He always has been, except when he gets a bit shickered, then he does tend to act like a puppy."

"Following you around with his tongue hanging out, you mean?" She wishes now that she hadn't brought his name up.

"We shouldn't be making fun of him," Fi rejoinders. "It's probably just a phase. Like spots and pimples. He'll probably be Prime Minister or something one day. He's certainly got the brains, if you need brains for that sort of thing. Probably not, eh? But he's a brain-box. Much more your type, really."

"What about Alistair, then?" She decides it's best to get off the topic of Jamie altogether. "If you so much as crooked your finger, I'm sure he'd come racing back."

"Ah, Alistair! Well, he's another possibility too, I suppose. Once he's got the ants out of his pants. He's got lots of lovely green acres in Manawatu's ram alley coming to him, too. That would certainly suit me. Materialistic cow that I am."

"And he's a gentleman."

"Yes. Whatever that means."

II

At the end of his time as a student, Jamie leaves Canterbury University with the assurance of a good Honours degree, but with little notion of how he should now be spending his time. He knows that he should, indeed must, at some stage honour his commitment to the government that had provided him with the Bursary, and find a job teaching in a secondary school. But not yet, he decides. Not yet.

At Cossy's request, he hangs around Christchurch for much of another year, helping him out with a project he's been asked to do for the Council. It involves spending much time researching in the archives, putting together a history of the city's cultural heritage. The pay isn't great, but it's adequate.

Early in December he finds himself in the shearing gang again, but this time only while they're doing his brother-in-law's flock. He's sleeping in the shearer's quarters rather than staying at the homestead. His transistor isn't tuned to the usual station of his choice. There are too many complaints from the rest of the gang when he does that. Instead, it is tuned to one that plays continuous pop. It is like wallpaper. He hardly ever notices the tunes. But the one that is being played catches his attention. It's an oldie that he remembers from High School, and always quite liked. Harry Belafonte. About a brown skinned girl and a baby.

He doesn't quite know why it appeals to him. He's only known three or four brown skinned girls beyond just saying hello to. One was in primary school. Rosie Kingi. He'd had quite a thing for her, but she'd spent most of the time laughing at him. Then there was Di Potaka at High School. She went around with the captain of the First XV, so she was way out of his league. She'd let him take her to the pictures once, though, when she was having some trouble with her boyfriend. Even sent another girl as an emissary to ask if he'd like to take her. He'd felt pretty good about that – and pretty scared, too. Hadn't dared to try anything with her. Anyway, she'd been quite shy, as it happened, and had thanked him very politely and gone inside without making him feel like the twerp he'd probably been.

And there was Delilah. She's not with the gang this year. She's pregnant, he's been told. Anyway, he never really talked to Delilah. Not properly. Just suffered her banter.

Then there is Tela Gilbard, of course. He knows her. Much better than any of the others. But it can't be her he's thinking of as he listens to Harry. He can't imagine any girl, brown or white, less likely to take kindly to being told to stay at home and mind the baby.

He is glad to leave the shearing gang to see out the rest of the season without him, although he's grateful to have had the seasons he's had with them. It has certainly been a lucrative experience. Having weeks of no-cost living over those summers has meant that the pay packets have been his, all his. But the noise, the constant need to rub along with the others in the gang, even when their habits and their conversation grated in his mind, means that the chance to earn even bigger money at scrub-cutting, a job that would mean, for much of the time, he had only himself for company, is a very attractive proposition indeed.

Oscar, the fellow rousie in the gang who suggested the possibility, is not one who is ever likely to be a close friend, but he is easy enough to get along with. Anyway, the times they would spend directly in each other's company would not be great – or when they were obliged to be in each other's company, it would likely be at times when they would be so tired that all they would want to do would be to eat their *kai* and get to sleep.

It doesn't prove to be quite like that. At times when rain means it is altogether too dangerous or too ridiculously uncomfortable to work, they are in fact obliged to spend long hours together. To Jamie, these times are made tolerable by the fact that he can get out one of the books he has packed and bury his head in it. He reads as long as the light is good enough. As the day ends, it becomes too dark. They have kerosene lamps, but they're hardly worth lighting.

Oscar is a tough, competitive, proudly unintellectual man a couple of years older than him. Hard working, yes. Competitively so. Always boasting about how much more scrub he is able to cut in a morning, in a day, than Jamie. Always inferring that Jamie is free-loading. At the end of the day they inevitably argue as they compare the area of scrub that each has done, Oscar complaining that he is getting the raw end of the deal.

But Jamie doesn't see it like that at all. True, Oscar has greater energy, maybe more skill. He goes at things harder. But this means that he also quite frequently breaks his slasher handles, which in turn means he has to spend time burning out the broken handle and replacing it with a new one. Jaime is more measured, less frantic in his attacks on the scrub. Slower, true, but much easier on the equipment. He gets into his rhythm and lets his mind free-wheel, thinking or day-dreaming.

Wondering where his life is going. He doesn't really care that Oscar is grunting and swearing just down the gully, that the rhythm of the thud and crack of his slasher is faster than his own. It is enough that he can look up every now and then and see evidence of his own steady progress, see the swathes of fallen manuka lying flat. But he does feel resentment at Oscar's constant harping on the superior effort he claims he is putting in to get the contract finished.

"At least I don't keep taking time off to replace handles," he says defensively.

"Yeah, but look how fucking slack you are," Oscar comes back. "I do as much in half an hour as you doing in a fucking hour."

Their quarrels are serious, but not too serious. Jamie acknowledges his relative slowness, but reckons he makes up for it in steadiness. Oscar needs to believe he is better than Jamie, in this at least. Jamie with his fancy education. Both defend themselves, yet both are oddly content with each other. When they call a halt to have a smoko, they sit down together, chew their food together, hone their slashers together. Exchange banter.

"I c'd take the hind leg off a fly at thirty paces with this,' Oscar says, lifting his slasher, running a finger carefully along the blade, surveying his handiwork with the file and stone.

"Yeah, or your bloody foot off if you swing and miss. What're you trying to prove?"

"Don't have to prove anything. I never miss, book boy. I just cut the fucking scrub. Twice as fast as you."

They get back to the *whare* that day to find that they hadn't properly put the lid on the pot of mutton stew they'd cooked up the night before and left on the old wood stove, intending to heat it up and finish it off for *kai* that night. Blowflies have got into it. It is a seething mass of maggots.

"Jeezuz," Oscar breathes. "I wuz looking forward to that." He pokes around in the mess, skimming the maggots off the top with a spoon.

"We'll have to open a can of baked beans," Jamie suggests. He is tired. They are both tired. They'd made good progress that day. All Jamie wants to do is fill his belly and stretch out on the bunk. But he doesn't want a belly full of maggots.

"Fuck that. I want a real meal," Oscar says. He's lighting the fire under the pot, and skimming off some more of the offending invaders. "I've got most of them out. A few cooked ones won't hurt yez."

"All yours," Jamie says, as he finds the can opener.

They finish up ahead of schedule. Jamie uses some of the contract money to buy a car – a used Ford Anglia in good condition. Owning a car boosts his feeling of self-worth for a while. He takes the opportunity between contracts to cruise around aimlessly, exploring the little towns of the Manawatu and the Rangitikei. Then after he gets home Oscar rings to tell him that he's got another contract, near Hunterville.

It's a good one, a big one, that should keep them going for three or four months, at least, and with a fat wad at the end. They're told to make use of an old *whare* out the back of the station, near to the scrubby hillsides that are to be their workspace. They have to pack everything they need out there, a slog of more than an hour. The *whare*'s way past its best, but it is watertight – which is just as well, for the first two days it rains so heavily they can do nothing but sit and wait. With the long hike out to the homestead and the road, where they've left their cars, his Anglia and Oscar's old Ford Ten, they decide the best thing to do it simply to sit it out. Much of the time they spend honing and re-honing their slashers, anticipating them biting into the manuka, boasting to each other of their coming prowess.

Once the weather clears, they make such good progress that about half way through the contract, they award themselves a couple of days' R and R. Oscar, Jamie knows, will spend his time in the pubs, and looking for some easy tail. He won't be fussy. It's all he's been talking about for days. "I need yards of it," he says. "Nah, I want fuckin' *miles* of it." Fondly patting his crutch.

Down at the homestead, they both make use of the ablution facilities in the shearers' quarters, as they had been told they could. After showering, Jamie stands before the discoloured mirror that hangs above the laundry tub that serves as a sink, and contemplates his heard. He had begun growing it even before they had started on the scrub; now it is well-established, copper-coloured and bristling. Should he take it off?

It is the most special of occasions, he decides. Or it will be, if his plan works out. Yes, he will take it off.

Having decided, he quickly proceeds to edge the safety razor over his skin. It is a painful process, and slow. Much later, he surveys the result in the mirror, and feels his heart sink. He shouldn't have. He definitely shouldn't have. The raw whiteness of his skin where the beard and moustache had been contrasts strongly with the other, sun-darkened parts of his face. Christ! The amazing two-toned man!

His hair is now longer, too, hanging shaggily over his ears and neck. But that's not so bad. It is almost fashionable. But the face! He steels himself to the awareness that nothing can now be done about it. She can only take it or leave it.

Jamie asks to use the phone, and calls the school in the town twenty miles or so away, where he knows Fiona is working. It is the thing he has been thinking about most in the hours of relentless battle against the manuka.

"Well, she's in the classroom, but she's not teaching at the moment. I suppose I could see if she's able to come to the phone." A male voice, suspicious and wary. Officious, even. "Who shall I say?"

"James Ashcott."

"Right."

He doesn't have long to wait. "Jamie?" Happily surprised, she sounds.

"Yes. Hello Fiona." He knows his own voice is showing his anxiety, his uncertainty – maybe even his longing.

"Nothing wrong, I hope?"

"No, no. I'm just – I'm working just up the road for a bit. Scrub-cutting. I… was wondering if we could meet up. Be great to see you."

There's a pause. "Yes. I'd like that. When were you thinking?"

"Maybe tonight. I see in the paper here that Dr Zhivago's on at the theatre in town."

"Well… I've seen it, but I wouldn't mind going again. Look, pick me up at seven, say. We can have a coffee first." She tells him her address in town, gives him directions. "The kids'll be coming in from play soon, I'll have to go. But, Jamie?"

"Yes?"

"I'm glad you rang. See you tonight."

What he feels after putting the receiver back on its hook is an enormous sense of elation, and relief – then apprehension as he remembers the face he had seen minutes before, in the mirror in the shearers' quarters. But the die is cast.

III

The theatre is in need of refurbishment, its red plush seats well-worn. It doesn't matter to Jamie though. Fiona is sitting next to him, blonde and sweet-smelling. She seems to have put on a bit of weight, though her face looks more drawn. She is not exactly as he had expected her to be. She is… more corporeal.

They've done most of the immediate news-swapping; not that he had much to tell her, and her gossip was mostly of people he didn't know well, or not at all. She does tell him, though, that she has accepted a post in Wellington for the following year. "At Karori West," she tells him. "It'll be good to be back in Wellington again. But I'll miss the country kids."

They settle in to watch the movie. She has seen it before, of course; and he is not particularly taken by the events as they unfold. The acting seems, to him, to be a little wooden. But then, he is not in a mood to be appreciative of anything other than the girl in the seat next to him and to explore the rather unexpected feelings her near presence is generating in him.

203

She has leaned her head towards him. With a start of disbelief, he feels her hair suddenly touching his cheek, the scent of her shampoo in his nostrils. He scarcely dares to move. Is it an invitation, he wonders? He feels a strange reluctance to accept it, if it is, but he brings his hand up and over the seat behind him and places it on her shoulder. She doesn't respond, but stays still, her head now quite heavy on his shoulder. He tries to look down, to see her face, but it is turned inward against his chest.

Of course, he realises. She is sleeping.

He is not exactly flattered by the discovery, but he finds he is quite relieved by the explanation. He lifts the hand that is on her shoulder and touches her hair briefly before letting his arm drop behind the seat. If she wakes up, he doesn't want her to think that he has been taking advantage of her vulnerability. Besides…

Besides? He finds it hard to explore the thought further. He is sitting next to the girl who has dominated his thoughts for years, now. The girl he had believed, always, no matter what else had happened in his life, that he loved and wanted. They are together, alone, in a way he used to dream they might be. Yet…

She stirs and lifts her head; then straightens in her seat. "Sorry, Jamie. I think I fell asleep," she whispers.

"You did," he answers. "It's alright. You okay now?"

She nods, and pretends an interest in the events on the screen.

Afterwards, they stay talking in his car for half an hour or so, outside the house where she is boarding. It is easy to talk with her; especially easy now that his silly feelings of wanting her have gone. He doesn't know quite what it is that has happened, but he knows that they have gone, those feelings. They have evaporated like the morning mist rising from the hills, leaving the sharp, true contours exposed. It has been sudden, inexorable. He is stunned by it; for a while, unaccepting.

But… It is a relief, he realises. He likes her no less than he did before. In fact, he likes her more truly. Lovely, blonde, wholesome Fiona. He had screwed up his courage and arranged an evening with her in the hopes of starting something that he has long, long thought about in a hazy, sentimental and impractical way. Now that haze has been swept away by the startling revelation that she is not at all the girl, the woman, he had imagined her to be. The fantasy has gone.

Yet the reality is somehow nicer. She is, in fact, a pleasant, warm-hearted friend – a friend he has known for years, yet not really seen until now. And that was his own stupid fault. Pie in the sky. Idiot.

He feels now a real surge of affection for her. The real her.

"I'd better get in," she says eventually. "School tomorrow." She leans across the seat and kisses his cheek. The scent of her fills his nostrils again, and the streetlight allows him to see her quite clearly. He has a sudden vision of her as a matron, filled out further still, surrounded by children. Not his children, though. And that thought doesn't hurt him a bit. He smiles and kisses her cheek in return.

"Off to bed then teacher," he says. He opens his door and walks around the car to open hers.

"Gentleman!" she says. "One little kiss?"

He can't resist. It is, after all, what he has wanted to do for more years than he cares to remember. And it is sweet and special, her lips against his, for a moment. It is nothing more than that.

"Write," she says. "Let me know where you are."

"I will. And… I'll want to know how you get on. Not just teaching. Everything."

She laughs. "Well… I'll probably do a bit of censoring." She turns to go, then turns back. "You know what, Jamie? You're clever. Remember that. Don't sell yourself short."

"Well, thanks for saying so. Not all that clever, I think."

"That's exactly what I mean. You are. You're right up there with Tela."

"Wow! With Tela! Maybe I should go to Cambridge too, then!" he jokes.

She grins back. "Maybe you should," she says.

He watches as she walks up the path, opens the front door. Just before she closes it behind her she turns again, blows him another kiss.

Interlude – From the Journal of Adelaide Gilbard

December 1882

I have been in this country now for almost twenty years. I am forty–two years old. Have I found a place for myself? I believe I have tried. Perhaps I have not tried hard enough, for though I most certainly now think of Taranaki, of New Zealand as home for myself and my children, I do not feel that I have done as much as I could to make it a home in which all can feel content and happy. There is a clearly discernible sense of excitement, of participation in the building of a land of opportunity, amongst the settlers – but there is too much, far too much, discontent and disillusionment amongst the native population.

We have tried. We are still trying, Hannah and I. But the attitudes of the English settlers seem to be hardening further, and this, in turn, means that Maori women are becoming more and more sceptical of our motives, and we of our chances for success. We still have our meetings, at which we not only talk of ways to further our aims, but we also share our domestic skills – I have been taught simple flax weaving, for example, and Hannah and I have, in return, attempted to improve the skills of the women in needlework. In fact, most of those who come seem to learn very quickly – much more quickly than I learn when it comes to weaving! But the numbers of women coming to these meetings has fallen away as the attitudes of both sides seem to harden. There is a sense that the earlier hope is bleeding away.

On the settler side, the common attitude seems to be one of now looking upon the Maori as being largely an irrelevance. They have been defeated. Their numbers continue to decline. What was their productive land is now, mostly, settler land, and what land remains to them is largely of inferior quality. In response to this, the Maori people, at least around this town, seem to have withdrawn into a kind of passive isolation. Their attitude seems to be: 'we have tried everything – fighting and co-operating, friendliness and hostility – we have even accepted many of your customs, in dress and religion – but our only return seems to be rejection. Is there a place for us any more in this, our ancestral land?' I am saddened by it, and even the ever-optimistic Hannah is beginning to lose faith in the vision we once shared of two peoples living in harmony and drawing strength from each other. Even Tom, who has played his part in causing their misery, refers to the displaced as 'those poor devils.'

A little time ago I met by chance with a woman who came to Taranaki with her husband many years ago – long before the conflicts that were to change everything – and she told me that in those early days, she, along with her husband, and the local Maori were on excellent terms. An elderly Maori woman had become her particular helper about the house, expecting nothing in return except basic instruction in English and English ways. The men of the nearby pa would offer their services as woodcutters or stockmen in return for access to her husband's tools. She herself, this woman, learned the local language, at least in its basics, and she and her children occasionally visited the village to take part in the games and other pastimes. It must have all been so very different then.

The unhappy affair at the large settlement of Parihaka seems to have been a crucial turning point, at least for the sort of co-existence we can expect in Taranaki. It will be, it seems, a co-existence, but not an equality. How very, very sad it was. I am grateful, at least, for the fact that Tomas was not one of the volunteers who accompanied the police in that disgraceful affair. It was led by a man, Mr Bryce, whose reputation for carelessness and (it is not too harsh a word) stupidity was well-established, although he had, and has, many supporters amongst those of the English settlers of his class. I know I am not alone in considering that the actions of this Native Minister and his armed constabulary were inexcusable; but most in this town seem to think that they were not only excusable, but were necessary demonstrations of the uselessness of any opposition to the European notion of 'progress'. Any who have read this journal will by now know well that my view of the steps taken in the name of 'progress' are not at all positive.

There are many sad things about the Parihaka incident, but amongst the saddest is that one of the leaders, Te Whiti, had long ago shown his goodwill towards the white settlers by ensuring the safe passage of those rescued from a shipwreck off the western coast of Taranaki through the territories of his tribe. He is a Christian man, and a great orator. When the constabulary approached Parihaka, he ensured that they, the invaders, were welcomed according to custom. There was dignity. There was no resistance. And the reward for his civilised response? His own arrest and that of many of the leaders, and the destruction of their crops, and the razing of the village to the ground. Te Whiti and certain others were then taken away on a forced 'tour' of the South Island, where they were shown the 'benefits' of English conquest. They were not, we are told, at all impressed; and who can blame them?

When news of what had happened at Parihaka reached us, my first duty was to Hannah. She has close kin in the village, which she calls Repanga, and naturally she was very disturbed by the news. This news had come not long after she had been obliged to accept the fact that Amako, her husband, would not be returning from his tribal home the other side of the distant Ruahine mountain range. That knowledge had not come as a surprise to her – Amako had long shown restlessness at the situation here in Taranaki, as well as being unhappy with the fact that Hannah seemed to be unable to give him the <u>tamariki</u>, the children, that both he and she longed for. Then came Parihaka.

It seems that even the sunny-natured Hannah finds herself in a slough of despair. At the time, we clung together, the two of us – old women (well – I am old, if old means being near death, though Hannah is as hale as ever, and seems likely, to me, to live forever) and offered each other what comfort we could. And it worked, as perhaps it could not have worked for any other. We are almost like one person, Hannah *and I. We understand each other, and we feel for each other. We share our burdens, <u>and</u> our joys.*

Yet my feelings were, as ever, tempered by a kind of reason that quickly ended my tears. Of course I felt pity for the victims of the dreadful actions of the constabulary – but that pity was quickly superseded by anger that such an end had been reached. It was all so unreasonable and unnecessary.

Pity is not useful. Pity can even be damaging, because it obscures the issues that should be faced – issues such as justice and prejudice and the need for change. In this country there is a laudable feeling amongst the settlers that Jack is as good as his Master – indeed, that the idea of 'Jack' and 'Master' does not or should not even apply – but that notion of equality seems to be limited only to fellow settlers, and not to those people who were here before us and who have, many of them, welcomed us into their land. That is not simply unfair, it is also crippling. I believe we are in real danger of failing altogether to maintain and develop that spirit of equality and compromise that held so much promise and that excited the vision of so many of those who came to these shores. 'Equality' is not a thing that should be restricted to only the members of one group within a society. An equal society must surely be one in which all peoples are equal, without distinction, be it differences of religion or sex or class or wealth – or race.

The question of education – the one thing that might be said to give some a natural and merited advantage – is one that can be, and is being, answered by a just society, and I think this country can at least be proud of its efforts to ensure that all its peoples receive an education, though there is much yet to be done.

[This part of the journal is not dated.]

I know I do not have very much longer to live. The doctor has told me so, and I feel death creeping up within me. It frightens me, of course. I suppose that is because there is nothing at all that I can do about it. But while I am still able, I want to transcribe here part of Oliver's last letter to me. I had not heard from him in over six years, and I expect I never shall again. Before this letter, I knew little more than the fact of his having been sent to Fiji by the Colonial Office, and of his there being employed as Secretary to a Stipendiary Magistrate in one of the Provinces. That much he had told me in his last letter, all those years ago.

Now, I know more, though I am far from sure that I wish to have that knowledge. Here, then, is part of his letter. The rest, I shall destroy when I have finished this transcription.

' My dear Addie,

I doubt that I will write to you again, and it occurs to me that you might be relieved to hear it. It cannot be a comfort to you to know that your brother has failed so badly in this world. Yet I would have you know that I am not unhappy. Indeed, apart from those foolishly, unjustifiably carefree days before… before I was forced to become a man, I am happier now than I have ever been.

My wife adores me – heaven knows why – and I adore her. I have a little daughter now, as well as George, my first born. She is beautiful, just as George is handsome. Her name is Atelaite, which is the Fijian rendering of Adelaide. I hope it is a name that will be passed down through the generations, as I have nothing but the highest regard and love for you, my very dear sister.

I rub along well enough with the village chief. He tolerates me, because I am occasionally useful to him, though I do not think he has much real regard for me. I am quite useless as a gardener or a builder or a fisherman, or in any other of the many ways in which men make themselves useful. But I can be a go-between and a scribe, and I have established a little village store which I keep stocked with a few items that are in demand. There is a small but growing awareness of what money can buy, and a few ways of earning through the production of copra or vegetables for sale at the Levuka market. My wife, of course, joins in the womanly activities such as tapa making, and she earns a share of produce from the gardens. We get along quite well, our little family.

George I have brought up to speak English, though he is also fluent in the local Fijian dialect, as you would expect. But it is his English that earns him the little bit of respect that he gains from the others boys of around his age in the village. It hurts me somewhat – the knowledge that they do not truly accept him as one of them. He will always be an outsider, as he can never have any claim to land or other resources shared by the tribe. But his use of English gives him some small status, as it does his father – and he is a beautiful and rather clever little boy.

There are a few others of little George and Tela's kind on the island. Some of them are in a closely neighbouring village, the sons and daughters of an American sailor who left his ship some years ago. He has skills that are much in demand – carpentry and sail-making and such – and is quite a big man in the island. He rather looks down on me, though we do, every now and then, have a drink together and talk of the world we have left behind. He has had children by more than one of the local women, and they, and those other offspring of European men and local women, including George, form a kind of tribe of their own. Their constant use of English binds them together.

You will not hear from me again. Our ways are separate. Dear Addie. You are the best of my younger days, yet how very different we are.'

There is more, but I cannot put it down. What do I think of it all? When I first received and read the letter, my emotions were extraordinarily mixed. I did not want to imagine my nephew, my niece, as little brown-skinned outcasts running barefoot in the tropical sun. Was it because they were without status in their community, or because they were half-castes? Surely not the latter! Not given our own ancestry! Yet… perhaps I was not as devoid of prejudice as I imagined myself to be. But no, I think it was because their father had become a person of little consequence, one without real claim to status even in that primitive place he had chosen for his home. And by writing that, I am, of course, displaying prejudice of another sort. How can my nephew, little George (and I still flinch as I write his name, which can only truly be, for me, my father's or my son's name) ever be considered to be a gentleman? Yet, how narrow my vision, that I can even allow that thought to remain in my head! How unnatural, after all, are the notions we hold of the gentleman and the gentlewoman!

Yet I do, I do hold them. I cannot rid myself of them. I want my children to be of that class. I want them to be recognised as such.

Last July I received word of the death of my Uncle Philip, one of whom I was always fond, and who in some ways was the last living connection to my father. He was my father's younger brother, and after my father's death I became very close to him. We had come to live in the village of my father's ancestors, and Uncle Philip had a medical practice in the nearby town. His house came to be my second home. His wife, my Aunt Mary, I also loved – and still love, as she has survived my uncle. I can see them now, Aunt Mary and her only child, her daughter Laura, living together without their dear father and husband. The simple-minded Laura will at least give Aunt Mary comfort and purpose in her remaining days.

Anyway, Uncle Philip left to me some money, and, more significantly, I feel, he also bequeathed to me his entire library of mainly medical and other scientific texts. These were duly shipped out here. The arrival and delivery of the crates of books was a day of great excitement – for me, at least, and Hannah and the children seemed to share my joy. Those books and journals form, now, the bulk of my library. I am particularly appreciative of Uncle Philip's gift, as it demonstrates what he had always led me to suspect – that he considered me to be a girl, a woman, of exceptional worth. It no doubt proves how vain I am – but I cannot help but feel a boost in my self-esteem that a man so well thought of himself, and of such broad scientific knowledge as my uncle, did always view me as a woman of intellectual merit.

It is from one of the medical texts that I have discovered the true nature of my illness. My doctor was evasive when it came to giving me the details, but from what he did tell me, I was able to consult my library and discover that detail for myself. More than that, I cannot bring myself to say. Not even here, in the privacy of this journal. What I can say, though, is that I do not harbour against Tom any resentment concerning my affliction. At least, I try not to. There would be no point. People are… what they are. When it comes to the ability to control his appetites, he is weak. I think I have always known that, or at least sensed it. We are all lacking in some things. It is just chance, I suppose, that Tomas's weakness has proved so harmful to me. He would not have wished it so. He loves me, I know that. Probably more than I deserve.

February, 1884: The certain knowledge that I am ill beyond recovery has placed in my mind a calm resignation. No… that is not the right word. I am not resigned to dying, at least not in any new way. Death is a certainty for us all, and the knowledge that we are dying, all of us, from the moment we are born, is something to which we all should become resigned. But this is different. This knowing that I have an irrecoverable illness is something like having in my pocket a one-way train ticket that I must use by a certain date. It spurs in me a determination to review my life – that life which I can now see with certainty is largely spent – and to calmly prepare for arrival at my destination.

I am not bitter or resentful. Perhaps I should be, but what good would that be, to me or anyone else? When I let it be known, gently and indirectly, that I had made my own diagnosis of my illness, my doctor still tried to shelter me from the full truth; but he soon recognised that I was not to be diverted from it. He had questioned me closely about earlier signs that I had experienced – signs that had not been sufficiently painful for me to seek medical assistance at the time they occurred. I had had an annoying mouth ulcer during the voyage out to Victoria. It was something that had made me reluctant to appear frequently in company, but it had passed and I had thought little more about it. Then, shortly before we docked at Melbourne, the skin on my chest and certain other parts had developed a rash. But that, too, passed soon enough, and I had had little reason to believe that any severe disease had been indicated by these symptoms.

But my books had informed me that these long-ago incidents were a warning of an infection that has since lain dormant within in me, and that has recently awoken to relentlessly attack my heart. There is no possibility of recovery. What that disease is, I have not the strength to name, but there is no doubting the diagnosis. Having put my knowledge down in these pages, I now dismiss it from my mind. I had a brief surge of self-pity when I first was able to put a name to it, an inward wail of despair and resentment as my reason affirmed it; then my mind adjusted to the facts, and I realised that neither self-pity, nor the ascription of blame, would make my remaining days any more bearable. The contrary, in fact.

I have not told Tom, but I think he knows. The doctor may well have told him, though I begged him not to. He has been particularly attentive of late. So much so that I am rarely able to spend any time at all with Clement these days.

Spending time. How appropriate that way of expressing things now seems! My allotment of time is fast diminishing and I must spend what is left of it wisely, if I can. Perhaps it is right that I spend less of it with Clement. Perhaps it is right that I have told him nothing – not of the nature of my affliction, of course, nor even of my... inevitable decline. He will see it eventually, but we do not need to say goodbye. We have no need of that.

One thing I am glad of beyond anything else – that we have never shared our bodies. My corrupt body has never known his. I would wish it had – oh how much I wish! – but I am very, very relieved it has not. The thought that my corruption might have harmed him in any way, is beyond bearing. I could <u>not</u> have borne it, and that would have made my death a worse one by far.

PART FOUR: THE REAL WORLD

Chapter One – Jamie

I

Autumn is well advanced, and there is too much rain about to think of looking for more scrub-cutting contracts. Jamie takes leave of Oscar in a pub bar in Marton, and heads to his mother's place the other side of the ranges.

There is no one there when he arrives, but he retrieves the key from its hiding place and takes his things to his old bedroom. Shortly after, as he is looking in the fridge for something to eat, there is a knock at the door.

It is the neighbour from beyond the tall hedge.

"Your Mum's been taken to the hospital," she says. "Just this morning. They think it might be a heart problem."

The town's hospital is just around the corner, within sprinting distance. He gets directions to her ward and hurries down the corridors, finds the ward nurse. "She's doing well," she assures him. "She's resting, but she'll be glad to see you."

She looks aged and grey, lying there, but she smiles at the sight of him. "Jamie. Don't worry, now. I'm fine. Just a little turn." Her voice is weak and uncertain. He doesn't feel reassured at all.

There is a tube attached to her arm. Her veins stand out, blue against the fragile white of her skin. He takes her hand, cautiously. The stupid thought slips into his mind that he doesn't really know this old woman. She is his mother, but it is as though he has never seen her before. She is too obviously mortal. She might die, and he has never truly known who she is.

216

Stupid, stupid. She is his mother, the parent who has always been there, who has brought him up, who brushed his hair every morning, who made him hearty meals out of nothing, who… never talked to him of her life, her hopes, not beyond her hopes for him. Not beyond the depth of the loss she felt at the death of his older brother, the brother he himself had never known.

She pulls on his hand, urgently. He lowers his head to hers.

"At the back of my wardrobe," she whispers. "In a shoe box. There's enough money for my funeral. In case I go. Tell Jenny. She can arrange everything."

She can't go. There is too much he needs to know. There is too much he needs to say. He doesn't know what to say. He feels the tears running down his cheeks; but it is himself he is sorry for, he realises. Himself. Himself.

"Don't worry, son," she whispers in his ear.

Back in the cottage, he checks in his mother's wardrobe and finds the wad of notes tucked away in a shoe box right at the back, exactly as she had said. He doesn't count them. He does notice, though, his dead brother's uniform hanging there. It smells of mothballs.

He takes it out, and holds it against himself. He is on the short side of average, and is surprised to see that the uniform is one that would fit him. If anything, it would be slightly too small for him. Somehow, that doesn't seem right. He has always imagined Haddon to be much taller – but there is no getting away from it. The uniform belonged to a man smaller than himself. The thought leaves him feeling bereft. Almost unbelieving.

He puts it back and closes the wardrobe door. On the wall above his mother's bed is the familiar photograph of Haddon that she herself had tinted, not trusting the professionals to get his colouring the way it truly was. But the teeth seem impossibly white, his eyes impossibly blue. It is the image he has always had of him, but for the first time he doubts its authenticity.

What cannot be called into any doubt, though, are the medals displayed in the frame next to his photograph. They are arranged around the certificate that is the official recognition of his services to and his sacrifice for his country. Photographs and medals – together the two items comprise a shrine his mother has slept under for almost twenty years. They are all the War had left her. He feels for her then in a completely different way. It is pity, tinged with a touch of disaffection. He is seeing her for the first time not simply as his mother, but as a woman, vulnerable and imperfect, one he wishes he knew better. He desperately, desperately hopes she doesn't die.

And indeed, she doesn't. Within a few days she is home again, a little more frail seeming, but even that, the doctors tell him, is not likely to be permanent. "She's a tough lady, your mother," one says.

Yes, yes. A tough lady. A tough old lady, this woman. His mother.

II

Both the discovery regarding Fiona and the timely reminder that his mother is mortal, leave a gaping absence in Jamie's life. She, Fiona, has for so long represented a particular view he has of himself as… As what, precisely? That is a question he cannot answer satisfactorily, but he knows it has something to do with what he sees as essential to his well-being, his equanimity. Without the sort of beacon of misty hope that Fiona has been for him for so long, and with his new awareness that his mother will not always be in his life, he feels both without an anchor and without a chart to guide him. He feels adrift.

Gradually, and it is a very gradual awakening, he begins to realise that he has never examined his life seriously at all. He has always and ever been adrift, accepting whatever comes along. Those decisions he had made for himself, such as concluding that his and Fiona's futures should be romantically shared, and wasting God knows how much emotional capital in the pursuit of a chimera, have been made from a total lack of understanding of himself. He doesn't even know who he is. Indeed, until now, that question has never, ever been one that he has thought it necessary to consider.

But now he does, and it is like becoming slowly, slowly aware that various paths must have brought him to where he is, but realising that he knows little about them. Even more slowly, he becomes aware that there are paths in front of him, real choices that must be made. First, though, he decides, he must find out more about who he is, and how he has come to be – and one thing he knows he must do is to talk with those who are better informed than he, to tap into their memories of the father he has never properly known, and the yet older generations, the ancestors that he did not, could not, know at all.

He tries to talk seriously with his mother as a first step; but she is strangely reticent, giving him only vague and attenuated answers to his questions. Yes, his father had once loved her. Yes, she had once loved him. Whatever love means, she adds. That sort of love. No interest in expanding. A faint sense of embarrassment. What had Haddon's death meant to her? Silence. Then the statement of the obvious. You could never understand, she says. You never knew him.

She is much more forthcoming, though no more understanding, when he shares his own uncertainties – when he hints at his longings, tries to tell her of those uncertainties, wonders aloud if he will ever find someone who will bring a sense of purpose to his life. Just be careful, she says. Some girls are only interested in marrying so they can get someone to pay to get their teeth fixed.

Not useful. It is typical of the sort of thing his mother has been saying to him since her stay in hospital. Or maybe it had begun to happen even before that. She seems to be caught up in trivia. She repeats things, makes mistakes. He begins to wonder if he will ever be able, now, to get the information he wants from her. Whatever that information might be. He wishes he knew. He senses that his mother no longer has the energy to be truly interested in his quest. That a part of her has closed down. That it is too late.

While fossicking about rather aimlessly in his room in the cottage, he pulls from the bottom of the bookshelf one of the old books that his mother had given him long ago, books that were part of the legacy from his Great Aunt Inez. He remembers, now, how he had taken them to his room then, promising himself that he would take a proper look at them. But he never had. Not even after he had rediscovered them after the move south from the old house by the estuary.

He opens the book, and glances at a page filled with meticulously recorded items and their costs. For a moment he is again disappointed – then he remembers. There was more. That first time he opened the book, all those years ago, he had discovered more.

He turns the book over, and opens the back cover, and there they are – the compact words in the neat handwriting, covering the pages. The very first sentence: '*May 1863. I begin this record not knowing how long I shall continue it, nor with any clear idea of its purpose other than a desire to acknowledge my own mistakes and weaknesses. My name is Adelaide Augusta Gilbard...* '

Gilbard! For the first time, the writer's name registers in his mind. It doesn't seem at that moment to be anything more than an odd coincidence, but it does bring an image of Tela Gilbard rushing to his consciousness. It makes him just that little bit more interested. He is not sure who she could be, this Adelaide Gilbard, but there must be some connection to him, or surely the books would not have been left in the care of his Great-Aunt. And how odd that her name should be Gilbard! Not such a very common name, surely.

More curious than ever, vaguely hoping that the Journal might give him some understanding of the issues that now dominate his mind, he reads further. And in no time at all, it seems to him, he becomes absorbed, transported back to the time of this mysterious woman, back to a New Zealand he had never even thought about except in terms of rather tedious treaties and obscure battles, and the occasional name that has stuck in his mind. Names like Hobson and Governor Grey. Hongi Hika and Hone Heke. Te Rauparaha and Julius Vogel. Distant names. Virtually meaningless. But this… this is different. It is like being back in those times, but inside the mind of a living person, experiencing directly what she experiences. *Adelaide Gilbard.*

Half an hour or so later, after skimming through several pages, certain names provide him with clues to the true nature of the writer's identity. It comes to him only gradually. The first name that takes his attention is Tom. The writer's husband's name is Tom – and he remembers his mother saying that her grandfather's name was Tomas. Tomas Gerold – not Gilbard. But the writer says at the very beginning of the Journal that she is not using her husband's surname. The possibility firms in his mind. It certainly makes sense. Why else would his Great Aunt Inez have the Journals in her possession if she wasn't related? Then he skims a few more pages and reads that very name. Inez. Inez is the name that Adelaide Gilbard gives to her daughter! An unusual name, Inez.

It is with a flicker of something more than simply excitement that he confirms in his mind that the words he is reading have been put there by his great-grandmother, and as he thinks on the discovery, that flicker blossoms into an awareness of an aching absence, of a gap in his knowledge of himself that must be filled.

He stops reading and thinks, first, of what he knows about his father and his father's family. That knowledge, or, more truthfully, those *impressions*, have come almost entirely from his mother. How accurate are they? Then there is the even more limited knowledge he has of his mother's parents. Both dead before he was born. Though his mother has talked often enough of her father, she herself had not known her mother well, and the only thing she has ever told him about her mother's parents is that her mother's father was called Tomas Gerold, and that he was reputedly a scion of Welsh gentry. About her mother's mother, she has said nothing at all. And this is the woman whose Journal he is now reading!

At this point he puts the book down and tells his mother of his discoveries, and questions her further. She is able to confirm the names, at least – to confirm his conclusions with regard to the relationship with himself. To confirm that much, at least. She is not able to do much more than that, though. She even seems uninterested, almost dismissive.

"Oh goodness," she says, when he asks her to tell him what she knows about Tom Gerold. She has already told him that she knows nothing at all about Adelaide Gilbard. That she never even knew that her grandfather's wife, her own grandmother, was called Adelaide, or that she had ever been a Gilbard. "I might have known once, but I wasn't at all interested in my mother's family," she says. "I scarcely remember mother, and Aunt Inez and I didn't get on. Whenever she talked about her father, my grandfather, I just refused to listen. And all I remember about him myself is that he frightened me."

"Why?"

"Well… I suppose partly because he was, according to Aunt Inez, such an important person. More so, though, because he had a huge moustache and wore a sort of metal plate thing under it to hide his mouth. I think his top lip had been eaten away by cancer or something. And he made funny noises when he breathed. I only have a couple of memories of him, anyway. I was about seven or eight when he died, I think. I remember going to see him once. His room was a sort of sunporch, and he was sitting in an old chair, with a table and a whisky bottle beside him. I could smell the liquor on his breath. That's all I remember about my mother's father."

"But he was Welsh?"

"Oh yes, I think so. That's what we were always told, anyway. Aunt Inez kept on and on about how he was a Gerold, and that the Gerolds were some grand Welsh family – but they might just as well have been sheep thieves for all I knew, or cared."

He doesn't think he would be much disappointed if that were the case. It's not Tomas Gerold who interests him. It's his wife he cares about. "Your grandmother. Adelaide. She… she is… she was amazing, I think. I'd love to know more about her."

"Sorry, son. I just can't help you there."

III

Before he has a chance to dip further into the Journals, out of the blue
he gets a scrawled note from his old Prof at Canterbury. 'I've heard
that you are not currently in a permanent position. If you're able to do
so,' he reads, 'you might consider the enclosed request. I've written
recommending you, and telling the writer she might hear from you. With
all good wishes...' It is an abrupt communication, but adequate. It is
almost like hearing him speak.

The note is accompanied by a letter addressed to the University History
Department signed by a '(Miss) Barbara Tiverton.' The address at the top
is simply 'Emberlea, RD 7, Masterton'. The woman briefly states that
a friend has recommended Canterbury University History Department
as the place most likely to provide her with a satisfactory answer to her
request for the name of 'someone both qualified and capable of assisting
me in the research and writing of a private history of Emberlea, and
of the Tiverton family since their arrival from England in the 1850's. I
anticipate the task will take no longer than ten months, or perhaps a year,
during which time accommodation will be provided free of charge in
separate quarters here at Emberlea, though the appointee will be required
to provide their own meals, using the perfectly adequate kitchen facilities
attached to their quarters. Clearly, a single man (preferably) or woman
would best suit.' A very healthy fee is quoted – more than enough to
tempt him away from any thought of further farm contracting of any sort.
Enough, too, to encourage him to push further away the knowledge that
he must one day seek out a teaching position. He decides he will write
and introduce himself.

Within a few days, he receives a letter inviting him to come to the
Wairarapa and introduce himself. It is not an offer of employment exactly,
but it seems that the recommendation from his Professor has at least put
him in the running.

He finds Emberlea relatively easily from the directions given to him in
Miss Tiverton's letter of reply. That letter is in the same formal style as in

her request to the Canterbury History Department, but at least she seems genuinely interested in meeting him.

The main house is a two storied weatherboard building in the true old colonial style, with broad, covered verandahs on both levels and on the three visible sides. His approach has been noticed, and there is someone at the door to greet him. It is not Mrs Tiverton herself, but a man perhaps ten years older than him who, by his mode of dress, is clearly not a farmer.

"Hello," he says. "I'm Nigel Blake, Miss Tiverton's nephew. You must be James Ashcott."

Jamie affirms his identity, and follows the man inside, where he is ushered into a comfortable room to one side of the rather grand staircase that faces the front door. There he finds Miss Tiverton awaiting him. She turns her head sharply as he enters the room.

"It's James Ashcott, Aunt Babs," the man says.

She stays seated, but her eyes survey him, top to toe. She offers him a tight smile that gives him the impression that he has passed the first test.

"Do come and sit down, Mr Ashcott," she says. "I'm glad to see that you are a punctual person."

He takes the indicated chair, and he listens as she launches into an explanation of what she would expect. Her family established themselves at Emberlea in the middle of the previous century, she explains. "Within weeks after the big earthquake. We have a family archives. Not in good order, but rather extensive." She wants a history of the family, and of Emberlea itself, to be her legacy. If she and he are both agreeable, then he will be expected to organise the material, and also assist her in writing some of the actual book.

After an hour of probing, she seems satisfied; and Nigel arranges for tea to be brought in. The necessary business has been done, or so it appears. And indeed, as he rises to leave, Miss Tiverton asks: "And when will you be able to start, Mr Ashcott? I was rather hoping you could do so immediately."

So the job is his! He is elated. The task now in front of him holds no fears. It is the sort of thing he feels confident about. Even mildly excited. "I can return tomorrow, if you like," he says.

"Splendid! It would be best if you arrived late in the afternoon, so we have time to put things in order here. Your accommodation, especially."

So lady-like is the old woman's speech and manners, he almost feels his should bow his way out.

The next day, he brings only one suitcase and a bag. In the bag, amongst other things, he has his great-grandmother's Journals; for he is determined to spend some time reading and thinking about his own newly-discovered heritage, as well as that of the Tivertons.

He rather enjoys coming again into the company of both the old lady, and her nephew. The two of them are the only people from the big house who pay any attention to him at all. The old lady he discovers to be far less formal than either her letters or their initial meeting had made her appear. "You may call me Babs," she says, after spending some time apparently further assessing him and finding him worthy of the privilege. "I am a good judge of character," she says, nodding her head. "And you're certainly a gentleman, I'll say that for you."

He feels rather pleased that he has passed yet another test. "Thank you," he says.

"Nigel will show you to your quarters," she says. "You'll probably prefer to work from there. And I can arrange for all the relevant papers to be taken to you. And then, perhaps twice a week, we can meet here, and you can ask me whatever you like. You'll probably need at least a month just to get the papers in order."

The rooms he is shown to are a short distance from the main house. Nigel confirms his guess that they were probably once the stables, but they are well kept and comfortably furnished. There is a single bedroom, the bed made up with a smart woollen bedspread covering it, a comfortable sitting room, and a large study with windows that look out onto a pleasant garden. There is also a kitchen, with a refrigerator and an electric stove.

The bathroom is small, but well equipped. All in all, it is, Jamie thinks, the most pleasant living space he has ever been able to call his own. Well… his for a while, anyway. And it won't be costing him a penny.

Nigel, the nephew, is a large and rather shambling yet elegantly dressed figure, including an habitual cravat, who at first offers only his occasional presence, with very little comment. After a time, though, he begins to visit the stables frequently, and to sit and talk. It is clear to Jamie from the outset, from both his camp gestures and exaggerated facial expressions, and from his choice of words, that he is gay. Not that he judges. His mother's favourite in-law, and therefore his own favourite uncle, is what his mother coyly termed a 'homophile'. Very early on she had told both Helen and himself that just because 'they' were not the same as everyone else, that did not mean that 'they' should be laughed at, or looked down on, or called names. Or abused. 'Each to his own,' she would tell them. It was one of her favourite expressions. Not that she ever went any further than to simply hint at difference – the details of the difference were never explained. That, or a version of it, he picked up later from the casually cruel sharing of anecdotes or fevered imaginings. He would snigger at the intimations, because that seemed to be expected – but the images evoked by the babblings he found rather dull, worthy of no more than a mental shrug, and he thus had paid indirect homage to his mother's principle.

"You should come along to our Amateur Dramatic Society," Nigel suggests one morning after Jamie tells him of his stage experience. "We're actually quite good, and our next production has a couple of roles that might suit you. I'll be directing it."

So he does go along, driven to the auditions and the subsequent rehearsals in Nigel's Jaguar. The role he is given, as Sandy Tyrell in Coward's *Hay Fever* is not a major one, but it suits him well enough.

"Beware the Jezebel!" Nigel warns him, early on.

Jamie soon guesses, without needing any further hint, the woman he has in mind. She is a very noticeable young woman, glamorous, even.

Her real name is Teresa, but he can tell by just looking that she is no saint. She is playing the part of Myra Arundel.

"Don't get me wrong. I actually like her," Nigel says. "This place could do with more of her type. Well made up and self-assured. But she's a man-eater, or so I'm told. Could be all hot air, of course. But she *is* deliciously vampish, isn't she?"

Teresa sits down next to him during one rehearsal. "I've been watching you," she says. "Standing there with one hip cocked, like a randy young bull."

A randy young bull? He has at times hoped he looked like Byron viewing Shelley's funeral pyre, moody and romantic. And he has even been content at times to assume that he looked a little like Goethe's Young Werther, lovelorn and pitiful. But a randy young bull? He doesn't know how to respond.

After the rehearsal, she speaks to him again. "I'm going to run you back to Emberlea tonight. I arranged it with Nigel, so you can have a coffee with us. With Rachel and me."

Clearly he is being left with no choice.

In the event, as he climbs into Teresa's car, he is told that Rachel has decided she can't spare the time. "Kids at home," Teresa explains. "No matter, we'll just go somewhere and sit and talk. Then I'll run you back. Alright?"

She finds a place – a picnic spot just off the main highway. As soon as she switches the engine and lights off, she turns to him, slides over to him, puts her hands behind his neck and pulls his face towards her.

"God, I've been looking forward to this," she says, just before he feels her lips brush past his, feels her teeth nip at an earlobe.

Heady, expensive perfume fills his nostrils, and her hair tickles his neck. Her hand dives south, her fingers exploring his crotch. His reaction is immediate and instinctive.

"God, yes," she breathes. "This is what I need."

Her hunger is obvious, disturbing. Her tongue is in his ear, her hand still clutching, kneading.

"Get in the back," she says, pulling away from him and opening her door. "More room."

He opens his door, but immediately knows that something is wrong. His head, or his heart, *something*, is blocking his libido, strangling his lust. Not knowing what else he can do, he opens the back door on his side and looks in. Even in the semi-darkness, he can see that she is ready, her skirt around her waist, her lovely, lovely legs elegantly displayed on the plush upholstery. One part of his mind imagines the smooth feel of her pampered skin, the little hollows of her dimpled knees; but that part of his mind soon withdraws, defeated. All he can do is stand there, holding the door open.

Seconds pass.

"Come on Jamie, for Christ's sake," she says. "What's the matter? Come here."

He can't. He can sense a terror beneath her words. She is like a wounded bird. A bird with a broken wing. Lying there, waiting for… For what he knows now for a certainty he cannot give her. It would be like… like… helping her to die.

A muffled scream of fury escapes her, and she sits up and clambers out of the back and into the driver's seat, starts the engine. He is left standing there, the door still open.

She leans across the front seat, as if to close the passenger door, leave him there to walk the miles back to Emberlea.

"Get in," she orders harshly; and he does.

Not a single word passes between them on the journey. When they near the turn-off to the drive into Emberlea, she brakes harshly, brings the car to a sudden stop and kills the engine.

"What happened back there, Jamie," she says. The anger in her voice is still strong. "I'm not used to turning men off."

He thinks, trying to find the words. He doesn't really understand himself. "You didn't… turn me off," he says. "It was me."

"Well, of course it was you! What do you mean? I know you wanted me, and then… What bloody happened?"

"I saw…" God! he thinks. This is going to sound stupid. But it is the truth, more or less. "I saw a… a fantail with a broken wing. You."

"Me! What the hell do you…" She stops abruptly, brings a hand to her mouth. She draws in a long breath that ends in a shuddering howl. He looks across, but he can't see her very well. The only light is that provided by the car's instruments – but he can see her shoulders are heaving, and she is gouging at her eyes with the palms of her hands. Then all her movement ceases. She is stock still and silent, her hands now clutching the steering wheel.

"Push the knife in a bit further, why don't you, Jamie," she says. Barely audible.

She restarts the car and, slowly this time, eases it forward through the entrance and up the long drive. As he opens the door to get out, he can think of nothing else to say except sorry.

"Me too," she whispers; but she doesn't seem to be angry any more.

The next night, on the way to town, Nigel questions him.

"So… tell all," he says. "Did she get her wicked way with you."

"It wasn't… like that," Jamie says. He doesn't want to share anything concerning the incident with this gossipy man. "I think… I think she's probably not very happy in her marriage."

"Well, yes. You don't need to be clairvoyant to guess that, you know."

Jamie doesn't want to take the topic further, but Nigel is not to be diverted. "Her husband's a big fellow. All muscles and swagger. Quite an Adonis, actually."

The wistful tone in Nigel's voice is unmistakeable.

"I wonder why, then," Jamie says. He realises he *is* curious. "There must be something wrong."

"Yes, well… maybe he hits her. Maybe he can't get it up. Maybe it's just a clash of egos. If you stick around long enough, she might tell you, if you're that curious."

No, that won't be happening, Jamie thinks. At that point, he isn't sure that she'll even want to set on eyes him again. And then there is the humiliating thought of what she might have said to her friend Rachel.

But he need not have been so apprehensive, so fearful. Teresa is her normal self, teasing and provocative. He watches closely for signs of what she must have told to her friend, the young mother who plays Sorel, but he doesn't see any behind-the-hand comments pass between them when they look his way. Indeed, he even thinks he can detect an added admiration in Rachel's eyes when they later exchange a few words – or maybe, he thinks, it is wishful thinking on his part. At the very least, though, they clearly haven't been laughing together at his apparent impotence. He soon relaxes, confident in her discretion, and for the rest of the rehearsals and performances, the rest of the time they are within each other's orbit, nothing further of note occurs between them.

Meanwhile, he makes good progress with assembling and collating the various papers pertaining to the history of Emberlea. He enjoys his twice-weekly meetings with Babs, who also seems pleased with his progress, and who offers her opinions freely. The Tivertons were a family that kept close ties with England, even sending their children, both boys and girls, 'home' for their college education – a tradition that had been kept up only as far as Miss Tiverton herself. "I was four years at school in Surrey," she tells him. "I hated it. They, the other girls, treated me as though I was some sort of freak. 'The Colonial', they called me. Even my own cousins."

At each meeting, Babs would ask him to write a few paragraphs to bring the material together. "Give me a few ideas about how it should be done," she'd say. And he'd oblige, leaving the material with her. "I'll straighten it out," she'd tell him. "Put my own stamp on it. But you have done it well, I must say."

In fact, he found his tasks to be relatively undemanding; so much so that he frequently had small pangs of guilt about the generosity of the fee he was being paid – though he became ever more certain that as a Tiverton, she could afford it. The more he read of the letters and other papers, the more aware he became of just how fortunate the family had been. They had arrived from England well-funded. They had chosen their land well. They had prospered, even in the difficult years. They had put the money that Emberlea generated into complimentary ventures that also prospered – abattoirs and a seed company, a wool-scourers and a farm-supply business. They had been opportunistic – and exploitative.

In the evenings that were not committed to other activities, and at other times as well, he read and re-read his great-grandmother's Journal. It was both a relief and a fascination to do so, so great was the contrast between the vision of success contained in the Emberlea papers, and that depicted in Adelaide's Journal. The one showed little but a conviction that success could be defined solely by the creation of wealth, and there was an arrogant and (he found) irritating assumption that such wealth gave status and the right to leadership and other privileges to all members of the Tiverton family. And apart from that tradition of wealth and status, little else seemed to matter to them. It was the sort of vision for the future that, according to Adelaide, his own great-grandfather had seemed to have had, but had failed to achieve, and it contrasted directly with the broader view of a more equal and caring society that was implicit and explicit in the words of his wife.

Adelaide intrigues him more and more. She is honest, almost brutally so, about herself and her perceived shortcomings – but she is also, clearly, thoughtful and compassionate and energetic in her pursuit of her vision of how New Zealand society should be shaped. She envisages a society free from prejudice of any kind. A society of equals. She has no patience with her husband's vision of a kind of feudal hierarchy, of squires and peasants and artisans – the kind of society that is accepted without question in the Emberlea papers.

These are matters that he has not before given any serious consideration. Yes, he has felt good, even smug, about the fact that New Zealand could claim to have led the world in establishing certain aspects of social justice – votes for women, and the establishment of a system of welfare for all its citizens for instance – but he has never before seen it all so clearly in terms of a deep-seated conflict between two opposing visions of society. He has long known that his father's political views offended his mother, but he has never been at all clear what either of their views have truly been – apart, that is, from the approval his mother always gives to Keith Holyoake for his gentlemanly bearing, and her intense disapproval of Mabel Howard for such actions as waving bloomers around in Parliament. And that his father is, according to his mother, a 'Commie'. Insofar as he has had any political leanings at all, he supposes he has rather gone along with his mother's views. But now, thanks to Adelaide Gilbard, he finds himself thinking much more deeply about these things, and with a completely genuine and increasingly passionate interest.

But these insights, intriguing as they are, immediately take second place in the forefront of his mind when his reading of the Journal leads to the astonishing discovery that he and Tela Gilbard are related.

He reads part of a letter to Adelaide from her brother that she has copied into her Journal. In it, he tells her of having a Fijian wife, and of having children by her – a boy he calls George and a girl called Atelaite, which, he also learns from that letter, is the Fijian version of Adelaide. And he learns from the same source that the little girl's name is shortened to Tela.

It takes a little while for the full significance of these words to register themselves in Jamie's mind – but eventually, with a near-certainty, he recognises the astonishing fact that Tela Gilbard must surely be descended from that brother of his own great-grandmother. Which means that Tela Gilbard and he must be cousins! Distant cousins, it is true – but cousins, nonetheless.

Tela Gilbard. Friend and old schoolmate of Fiona. Pretty, brainy Tela, with her dark skin and her lovely legs. Tela from Fiji. Tela, who is at this very moment studying at Cambridge, is his cousin!

He is not at first at all sure how he should feel about his discovery, but once he has properly absorbed the knowledge, he finds that he is inordinately pleased that there is the connection – particularly in the light of his increasing admiration for Adelaide Gilbard, after whom, he now knows, Tela has surely been named.

He feels strongly that it is something he must share with her, this knowledge. He decides that the best way to achieve this end will be to write to Fiona and ask her to pass on the news to her friend. In fact, he finds he is pleased to think that by passing on the knowledge in this way, Fiona herself will know. Furthermore, he feels like shouting it out to the entire world, so strangely excited is he made by the discovery.

In the meantime, however, the days and weeks continue to roll by, and his tasks in relation to the Emberlea papers are almost done. Then there is also the imminent matter of the public presentation of *Hay Fever.*

The production goes well. Full houses every night, and rave reviews in the local newspaper. A triumph, Nigel calls it. There is even talk of being in with a chance for some national award.

The last night of the season coincides with his last day at Emberlea. At the party after the final curtain, Teresa comes over to him, lips fiery red, as provocative and siren-like as she had been when he first set eyes on her. She reaches up and kisses his cheek. "Goodbye, Jamie." Then, directly into his ear, in a husky whisper: "Remember, you could have had me."

He is stirred, exactly as she intended. "I'll probably regret not doing so for the rest of my life," he says. She really is a beautiful, sexy woman. He thinks he means it.

She smiles, and rubs with her thumb at the mark she must have left on his cheek. "You're a lovely liar, Jamie," she says.

IV

He returns home, to his mother. He finds her subdued somehow; more so, even, than in those first few days after she had returned from hospital. Her conversation is interrupted by little sighs, and she has numerous vague complaints about her aches and pains, about the noisy neighbours over the back fence, about the difficulty of getting down town to do her shopping.

"I find I can't use the bicycle any more," she says. "I get breathless. I have to wait for the bus, and they only come past here twice a day."

"You should sell your bike. You know the doctor has said you shouldn't ride it any more. Not at all."

"He told me I should keep active."

"Keeping active is one thing. Trying to bike into town, then back with your groceries is another."

"You sound just like him. While you're here, you can take me down to the shops in that car of yours. You will, won't you?"

"Anywhere you want to go, Mum. We could even go out to see Jenny any time you want."

"No, no. I don't want to go gallivanting around. I just want to get my groceries and have a look around the shops. Can we go tomorrow?"

"Of course."

He feels oddly restless during those first days at home as he potters about doing mindless tasks, such as lawn-mowing, and sanding down and repainting the window sills. He has time to reflect on some of the many things that now crowd his mind. How he has come to be what he is, and what it is that he is. What he should do to find out more about himself.

Then there is the matter of why he cannot seem to be like others he knows when it comes to women. Not just in the matter of sex, though it is that aspect that perhaps worries him the most.

The incident with Teresa, his failure, still plagues him at times. He turns it over in his mind, wondering how others would have responded to the situation. Oscar, for example. There is no doubt he would have relished the opportunity she had offered. He wouldn't have given it a second thought. Anders Malmo too, he suspects. Cossy… well, Cossy wouldn't have even allowed himself to be part of the scene. He doesn't like girls. Or men, for that matter. He apparently has no urges of that sort at all. Lucky Cossy.

Lucky? Well, that is the trouble. He is not like Cossy. Or maybe Cossy has just learned to suppress the urges. Maybe he could do the same. The thought of becoming a monk crosses his mind briefly. There is a monastery near Waipukurau, he knows. Monastic discipline. Spiritual thoughts. Maybe that is what he is suited for. Maybe that would be the answer.

But no – he allows himself a grin at the absurdity of the thought. Not bloody likely. Besides, it's not as though he hasn't been able to satisfy the urges, after a fashion. A few times, anyway. He thinks back on some of those occasions, and decides that 'satisfy' is perhaps not the right word. There has been momentary physical relief, not much more than that. Yet that, it seems, is what it is all about; for Oscar, definitely – and for Anders, and probably, he decides, for everyone else. Even the girls. They seem to expect nothing more from the act than momentary physical relief. Or so it seems. Why should he expect more? What is it he does expect?

He doesn't really know, though there are possibly some hints. His fixation on Fiona for instance – a thing that turned out to be ridiculous and unreal. What he had created in his mind bore no resemblance to reality. Yet the real Fiona is lovely. A lovely person. Someone he is glad he knows and is truly delighted to be able to call his friend. Had he ever fantasised about sex with her? He can't remember ever having done so. He even shudders at the thought. No. If he had ever thought about it, his conscience, or whatever it was that dictated the rules, would have banished any such image and replaced it with angelic singing or soaring violins. He had imagined he was in love with her, maybe even had been; but it was an ethereal sort of love, one that, in the event, had revealed its absurdity in the face of even the vague possibility of a physical consummation.

He thinks of Anders and his partners, the obvious gleeful anticipation of a physical coupling, of a joyful, mutual climax to an evening of light-hearted fun. Of Oscar, hunting down those women whose desires were, apparently, identical to his own. Why couldn't he be like Oscar? Like Anders? Why hadn't he been able to ignore everything else, and simply give himself, and Teresa, what their respective bodies and hormones had clearly wanted?

These are things he certainly can't speak of with his mother. Instead, he tells her of his discoveries relating to her maternal grandmother. He tells her, too, about the astonishing coincidence concerning Tela Gilbard. It is the first time he has brought Tela's name up in conversations with his mother. He tries to describe her, emphasising her academic successes and her prettiness, but his mother seems only politely interested.

"Fiji?" she says, and frowns. "I must say I never heard of such a thing. But I know nothing about my mother's mother at all. She was never talked about, as far as I can remember. She was from Fiji? That's very odd."

"Not her, Mum. Her brother. And he wasn't from Fiji, but his wife was. He married a Fijian."

"How very odd. Are you sure?"

"Yes. It seems like it."

"Oh well. Fancy that."

And that was about all the reaction he had from her.

He tries to question her further about those members of her family she does remember. It seems really important, now, to do so.

He knows quite a bit about his father's side, though mainly from his mother's point of view. A pack of Commy stirrers, she called them. Most of them, anyway. He personally has no memory of either of his paternal grandparents. Though they were both alive when he was born, they died before he was of an age to remember properly, even if he had been taken to meet them – as he had been, when he was a toddler, he was informed. His grandmother outlasted his grandfather by a few years, but he had no memory of her, either. Nor of anyone else in his father's family, apart from the gay uncle, who came to visit a couple of times. He was one of the very few of his father's family his mother had had any time for.

He has only limited success in finding out more about his mother's parents. It seems to be a topic that pains her, as though she does not want to remember a life that could have been hers, but that she turned her back on.

"Your grandfather – my father – was a businessman." she says. "He had lots of shares in various things, and he managed a big firm in town."

"Did you like him?"

"He was… a kind man. He was well liked."

"And your mother?"

"I can't remember her very well. Her name was Ellen. I remember once opening the door and going to see her in her bedroom. It smelt of lavender, and her lying there. Smiling. Then not smiling. Whenever I smell lavender, I think of sickness, because she was very ill, by that time. Lying there. It was my aunt who brought me up. Aunt Inez."

"Yes, I know. What was *she* like."

"She was a terrible snob. We… we had a big falling out."

"Why?" He knew the reason. She had told him. He just wanted to hear her say it again.

"It was… over your father."

"And what about your father's parents? Your mother's parents?"

"I don't remember anything about my father's parents. I think they were both dead by the time I was born. They were farmers, from near Stratford, though they had a house in town. But I do remember my mother's father, though only as an old man with a big moustache and that funny tin thing he had to wear. Under his nose."

"So you said."

"He frightened me. I think it was the tin thing."

That, of course, was Adelaide's husband, he thinks. Tom. He has developed a strong dislike of Tom Gerold, and all, or most, of what he must have stood for. The man responsible for Adelaide's illness. He's not sure, but it seems likely it was syphilis. "What was wrong with him?"

"Oh goodness! I don't know. Something had eaten away his top lip."

"You told me that, Mum."

"Did I tell you that? I think it might have been cancer. I remember the room he used to lie in. It was like a sunporch. There was a little table by his bed with a bottle on it. He always smelt of liquor. Whisky. Horrible."

"And… you know nothing at all of his wife? Of Adelaide, your mother's mother?"

"She died quite young. I know nothing else about her. No one talked of her much. I didn't even know her name, until you told me. Unless I'd forgotten." Then she seems to dismiss the ghostly people from her mind from her mind altogether. "When I was a child, we always had plenty of lemonade in the pantry, in long bottles with glass stoppers. Round, they were, the stoppers. Like little glass balls. I used to sneak in and help myself. I remember that. Then I'd break the bottles and take the stoppers out. They made good marbles."

That seemed to be about as much as he would get from his mother; but he decides that he must find out more. He wants most of all to find out more about Adelaide, yet he knows that unless some miracle happens, he is unlikely to do so. Unless… he wonders if he can get at some knowledge of her by finding out more about her husband – about the despicable Tom, and his family.

In looking through his mother's collection of photographs, he comes across one of an old house – more of a mansion. It is two-storied, with a row of dormer windows above the second story. It appears to be built of stone, but most of it is covered in ivy. On the back, someone had written in ink that was now faded: "Tan-y-bwlch. Merionethshire." He asks his mother about it.

"I think it's my grandfather Tomas Gerold's family home in Wales. Oh goodness, Jamie, I really don't know. I think that's what Aunt Inez said. I really wasn't very interested. She was such a snob. It might have been something she just dreamed up."

"The house looks real to me."

"Yes. But who's to say it has anything to do with us? She might have just… found the photo lying about somewhere. It could be anywhere, that house."

"It says 'Tan-y-bwlch' on the back." He spells the letters out, having no idea how the name should be pronounced. "And 'Merionethshire'. That's in the north of Wales, I think. I'll look it up in the atlas."

"Well… maybe you could find something out about it. Aunt Inez was always going on about how important her father's family was. Not that that means anything. They might just as likely have been sheep thieves, for all I know. They *were* Welsh. I know that much."

"I wish I knew more. I'm going to try to find out more."

"Yes. I'm sorry, son. I should have taken more interest. I loved my father, but I didn't really care much about the rest of them. I was a bit of a rebel, you know."

He smiles. Yes, he's heard that often enough from her, too. And he could imagine it was no exaggeration. Stubborn old woman, and undoubtedly she had been a stubborn young woman. His mother. And now a woman whose memory seems to be failing. He will have to go on a bit of an odyssey, he decides.

IV

Shortly before he sets out on the next part of his quest for self-discovery, Jamie receives from Babs Tiverton a copy of the book that is the result of his time spent at Emberlea. It has been privately published. It looks quite good. He is rather proud of himself. His name is not mentioned as part-author, but it is to be found under the list of acknowledgements. 'James Ashcott, for assistance in organising the historical material.' *And* the rest,

Jamie thinks. But he is not terribly upset. It is really no more than he had expected. His skills were generously bought and paid for, after all.

He travels north, and the first visit he makes is to his father, on the island in the Gulf where he has been living now for ten years or more. It is only the second trip he has made there, and the first, with Helen, was when he was still at High School. Then, he and Helen had come up by train, and their father had met them at the station before taking them on the Ferry across to the island. This time, Jamie leaves his car at a motel and takes a bus to the Ferry terminal.

He has to wait half an hour before one of the island's few taxis is able to take him to the other side, to the broad sweep of beach above which his father's simple, bach-like house is perched. From the road it can hardly be noticed at all, as it is down a steep path, and it faces in the other direction, towards the sea. Before he has managed to even get through the narrow gate, his father appears from around the corner of the building, emerging like a garden gnome from under a clematis-laden pergola.

He is changed, yet unchanged. The same barrel-chest, but it now hangs a little under a back that is no longer straight. He is thinner. He wears a straw hat that covers his baldness – perhaps, Jamie think, the same straw that he habitually wore on the only other occasion he has visited him in his island sanctuary.

"Hello Dad." He covers the last of the downward slope, and joins him under the clematis.

"Good to see you, son."

Half handshake, half hug.

"Come through to the verandah," his father says. "We can sit and talk out there. Dot will bring us some cocoa."

Jamie knows he has a new woman. Helen told him. She seems nice, she said.

They move inside the bach, then straight through the living room and out onto the long verandah that overlooks the scrub covered gully below. There is a glimpse of the beach, and a wide vista of the Hauraki Gulf beyond.

His father takes his seat cautiously, a little painfully it seems, on an old Morris chair. Jamie chooses a rustic bench close by. The deck is cluttered with sculptures, some of stone, many others of wood, a few carved out of punga. They are much as he remembers, though he hadn't then taken much notice of them.

A woman comes out carrying a tray with two mugs, and a plate of buttered scones. Jamie rises to his feet.

"This is James," his father says.

The woman looks at him, offers a smile that is almost coquettish. She is fiftyish, with traces, still, of a once-pretty face. "I'm Dorothy," she says. "We expected you a little earlier."

"I had to wait for a taxi," he explains.

"Well it's nice to meet you at last. I hope you like scones."

"I do."

"Good." She places the tray on a small, unsteady table next to his father's chair. "I'll leave you to talk," she says; and disappears back inside.

Her disappearance is followed by an awkward silence. Thoughts race through Jamie's head, questions as to why he is even here. He scarcely knows this man. What is he seeking? What can he learn about himself from him? What has this man ever done for him?

Well, he thinks, twice in his life he has written to ask him for money, and both times he has provided, though it must have been difficult for him. The first time, he remembers, it was at the suggestion of his mother. At the age of fourteen he had arrived in town from the backblocks with shorts the only items capable of covering his backside, and most of them were patched. In those early days and weeks of living in a town, every time he had ventured out to the High Street he had felt the scarcely disguised ridicule from any of his school mates he happened to see. Shorts had to be worn at school, but they were not the costume for visits downtown. Maybe for Third Formers, but definitely not for Fifth Formers. But his mother didn't then have the funds to buy him long trousers. Write and ask your father, she'd told him. So he had, and within a week a five pound note had arrived with a short letter. The letter he hadn't been much interested in. The fiver he'd handed over to his mother; and the next time he went into town, the entire length of his lower limbs was clad in acceptable grey flannel.

The second time was also a long time ago, while he was at Weir House. He'd run up a considerable bill at the canteen – mostly for cigarettes – and was told he'd not get any more credit till it was paid. Remembering the trousers, he'd written again to his father, and again the money had been forthcoming.

"How is Win?" his father asks. "How is your mother? Helen tells me she had a bad turn."

"She did. But she's recovered quite well."

Jamie waits for his father to respond to the news. He wants some reaction. Anything. It seems important that he hear some reaction.

"Do you care?" he asks.

His father responds with a wheezing chuckle. Nothing else. The question loses whatever meaning it had. He knew the answer before he even asked the question. It no longer matters.

"I'm glad you came," his father says. "It's been a very long time. Helen tells me you've been doing pretty well. I'm glad. Though…"

"Though?"

"Though I know my approval probably means very little to you. I know that if you've done what you've done for anyone other than yourself, then it's not for me. It's for your mother."

Jamie feels both anger and guilt. Of course he should have come to see his father more often. It is entirely his fault. His mother may not ever have encouraged him to see him, but she never actively discouraged him, either. He just… could never be bothered. Not even to write, more than a card at Christmas; except for those two letters asking for money. But… but he doesn't appreciate the implied criticism. If that is what it is.

He can think of no appropriate response, and another awkward silence ensues. Once again, it is his father who breaks it.

"You said in your letter that you were wanting to find out things. About me, about the past. Is there anything in particular you want to know?"

He does; but he doesn't quite know what it is. Since reading Adelaide Gilbard's Journal he has certainly become much more interested in thinking about the forces and attitudes that have shaped him. They have been his mother's attitudes especially, he knows that – but what of her judgements about this man, his father? Was he, is he really little more than a weak-willed womaniser and a would-be artist?

"Did you and Mum argue about politics?" he asks.

"Arguments. Oh yes, arguments. There were plenty of those. But they were mostly about… other things. Sometimes they started about politics," he says, after apparently giving the question some thought, "but I don't think either of us thought very deeply about our… political positions. We took them just because we came from very different places. We were both products of our background. My father, your grandfather, was a deeply committed pacifist and socialist, who viewed wealth and privilege as the enemies of the common man. When I was growing up, and whenever I went back as an adult to see my parents, the house was always steeped in such ideas. I absorbed his views. They became part of me. They still are. But your mother… was from a different background. She thought differently."

"But she always says, still says, that she hates snobbery."

"Well… yes. They were the words she often used. But when it came to things like… Like what she considered to be coarse behaviour. About rabble-rousing, as she called it. She was instinctively always on the side of what she called 'proper' behaviour. King and country. Law and order. What she called respectability."

"She is certainly against what she calls commie stirrers."

He smiles, nods his head. "That's what she called us, we Ashcotts. And it's true that my father, and even my mother, though in her case it was probably because she always agreed with my father, they both would have chosen communism – or at least socialism – over capitalism, any day. And I'm the same, son. You must know that. I find it hard to imagine that anyone who went through the Depression years as a family man without either job or wealth, or who personally witnessed Sid Holland's police using their batons to break the heads of the waterfront strikers, could feel any different."

Jamie vaguely remembers the waterfront strike, and his mother saying that Sid Holland only did what he had to do. He thinks, then, of another issue that surely must have divided them. "And – Haddon joining up. Going to war. Did you argue about that?"

"I… I didn't even try to argue that one," he says. "Haddon was… your mother's son. I lost him to her very early on."

Lost? The word has a finality that surprises him. Twice lost. "And then… the war killed him."

"Yes." He seems to be on the point of saying something else. His features show an agitation that seems somehow incongruous, given the matter-of-fact, dismissive way he initially responded to the question.

"Yes?" Jamie asks.

"No. Nothing son. Nothing."

"What…" He is uncertain how to frame the question he now wants to ask. It seems too personal. The old man sitting next to him is really little more than a stranger. His father. "What… made you and Mum… get together? To marry, I mean. To… have us all."

His father wheezes a laugh; but it dies quickly. He seems to reflect on the question, then he heaves himself to his feet. "I'm going to show you something. It's a fair question you've asked me, son. I'm going to show you something that might answer it."

He disappears for a minute or two, but then he is back through the door, carrying a large canvas covered with an old sheet that he removes with a sweeping gesture that is oddly like a formal unveiling.

"Here's your answer, son," he says.

It is an oil painting. A young woman lies on a narrow bed. She is naked. Surrounding the bed are lush tropical flowers, and on the bedside table to one side is a plate with a cut paw-paw sitting on it, its seeds and its yellow flesh lewdly displayed.

The angle of view is from the foot of the bed, so that the woman's splayed body is like an offering. The style is post-impressionist, and her face is not clear – but there is enough detail to suggest that she is pouting, and that though she might have been physically satisfied, she is not happy.

With the knowledge he has given himself over the past few years, Jamie is able to source the various influences. The tropical fruit and the sinuous vegetation is a combination of Henri Rousseau and Paul Gauguin. The woman, her abandoned pose and her hint of truculence, is Pierre Bonnard. But it is not simply that Bonnard has inspired the work. It is a copy, at least as far as the woman on the bed is concerned. He knows it well. It is one of those paintings that has particularly appealed to him, one that he has frequently pored over in his art books, allowing himself to imagine the woman's feelings, to feel for himself how the sexual act has left a large part of her unfulfilled.

"That's one of my very early pieces," his father tells him. His intention in doing so is obvious. He wants Jamie to reach a particular conclusion about it. Jamie knows what that conclusion is. He cannot make it.

"That's not my mother," he says. "That's Pierre Bonnard's mistress."

A period of silence follows his words. He looks at his father and sees in his face the guilt of a schoolboy caught with a copy of Playboy. Then he looks down, and up again, to catch his eye. This time his expression is one of respect. Adult to adult.

"Yes, you are right," he says. "But it is also the wishful thinking of a young man. You would understand that, I think."

"But it is not my mother," Jamie repeats. "I… quite like the painting. I really like the original. But why did you show it to me? I mean, I'm glad you did. But why?"

"No, it is not your mother. I shouldn't have allowed you to think… But it is, in part, what I found in your mother. Not the pose – she would never have allowed me that – but the shutting-out, the unwillingness to be… as I hoped she would be. Yet at the same time, the… the desirability.

She is… she was… what I wanted. More than anything else. But what in one sense I was never allowed to have."

He begins to understand, then. But it is probably not the sort of understanding that his father might have expected. No, his mother would not have allowed the sort of Bacchanal that his father has hinted he hoped for. A Bohemian she certainly was not, is not, and never could have been. His mother, some sort of Pre-Raphaelite shop girl, gratefully giving herself up to the fantasies of a would-be Rabelaisian dauber? Hah!

Next morning, while he is packing away his shaving gear, his father appears behind him.

"Do me a favour son? Your beard is softer than mine. Would you swap a packet of your blades for this?" He holds out what's left of a packet of cheap blades, the sort that Jamie deliberately avoids. He can hardly refuse, though.

"Yes. Okay." He takes them and hands over an unopened packet of his Wilkinsons.

"Thanks, son." His father takes them and raises a hand to his cheek, stroking. "Like wire. Takes a bit of taming."

Jamie feels oddly happy about the exchange. It seems something like reciprocity. A restoration of balance. The rubbing out of that distant sense of obligation and gratitude.

On the boat back he reflects on the experience. There is no great disappointment with his discoveries regarding his father as an artist, as he had had no particular expectations. Perhaps there had been a vague hope that he might find in him a man of incipient genius. Or perhaps he was just hoping that he would prove to be a man he would be proud to have as his father. Someone whose connection to him would make him feel better about himself. And in some ways, that has been the case. In somewhat unexpected ways. He finds he is rather proud of the fact that his father has remained a committed opponent of the alliance of wealth and privilege and power. A little like Adelaide Gilbard.

As for the other… His father as an artist, or, more significantly, as a father… He is a man of certain talent, yes; but of little originality. And the other image of him that his mother had implanted in his mind – probably unintentionally, possibly not – that of a weak-willed satyr, has proved to be, through the eyes of his adult self, in part true. A rather sad satyr with inevitably diminished powers.

In sum, he thinks, a mildly interesting old man who has surrounded himself, not with family, but with the relics of his personal failures. But in that other respect. Yes, yes, he decides … He can't do anything about it even if he wanted to. He is his father, of course. But now, for the first time, he is more than a little content to accept the fact. Perhaps even happy to do so.

V

On the way back south, he makes a detour into the Thames Valley to see Dougal. It is the first time he has visited him there, on the plot of land he knows he bought some time ago. It is the first time he has seen Dougal, in fact, in something like five years. The last time was when they had both come home to see their mother one Christmas.

The saintly Dougal, Jamie thinks, as he negotiates the metalled track that leads to the house and sheds. Yes, saintly – even though he hasn't heard him talk religion at all since those early years, he still thinks of him as a saintly being. Morally far superior to him. A man without fault, almost; gentle and kind.

He is quite surprised by what he finds. Dougal has established what appears to be a thriving business. The core of it is a native plant nursery. He shows an interest, but it is not Dougal's commercial venture that he has come to discover.

They talk of family, but Dougal seems uncomfortable with the topic. His answers to Jamie's questions are brief, and usually preceded by long pauses and a look of pained concern. It is as though he is hiding something, that he has knowledge that he simply doesn't want to impart.

The afternoon shadows are lengthening. "I'm going to have a glass of port," Dougal says. "Join me?"

Jamie is more than a little surprised. He has never put alcohol and Dougal together in his thoughts. And port! What a strange choice! "Yes, I'll have one," he says.

Dougal fetches a flagon from under the bench. A flagon! Another surprise. To Jamie, it seems entirely excessive and un-Dougal like. Dougal pours their drinks and hands him a tumbler, half full of the sticky liquid.

"I like a port or two after a day's work," Dougal says. He raises his glass. "To life, little brother."

"Cheers."

They have several more than just the one, and as the evening progresses, Jamie learns of a Dougal that he had never dreamed existed.

The port loosens his tongue. It loosens both their tongues. As night closes around them there, in the old cottage that Dougal has shaped into a cosy home, Jamie discovers his brother. He learns that he is not a saint, though he doesn't swear. He learns that he has left God far behind him, though he does indeed still broadly, very broadly, follow the precepts of Jesus. He learns that Dougal has spent many months in hippy communes, that he has been, but is no longer, a pot-smoker. He learns that he has loved and left, or been left by, many a woman. And he learns, gradually, that the single most shattering event in Dougal's life, the thing that brought his world crashing down around him when he was fifteen years old and that he has taken years to come to terms with, that he still has not completely come to terms with, was the death of their brother. The death of Haddon.

But he tells him little about Haddon himself. It is as though the subject is too painful, still, for him to share. Instead, he tells of the fracturing of his own world when he was told that their brother had been killed, his dreams for his future that had ended in that moment; and Jamie doesn't press Dougal to share his memories of Haddon. He has his own half-baked yet sufficient impressions. They are a combination of his mother's sentimental, worshipful descriptions and his own shocking discovery when he lifted his brother's uniform from his mother's wardrobe and found that he had not been the larger-than-life demi-god that had been so long lodged in his mind. Yes, those impressions are sufficient.

The next morning, they both have dry mouths and throbbing temples. They look at each other half-embarrassed, yet now with at least a rudimentary knowledge of each other. And perhaps, Jamie thinks, he has just a little bit more understanding of himself.

Chapter Two – Tela at Girton

I

Tela Gilbard has settled in easily enough to life in Cambridge, at Girton. Most importantly, she likes her Supervisor, and the liking seems to be mutual. Certainly, the sessions of discussion that she has with her are comfortable and stimulating. Very early on, she had been instructed to call her Muriel. Sometimes they talk on for hours, she and this oddly ordinary looking woman of indeterminate age and a rather squeaky voice, who likes to let her mind wander where it will, and is delighted by Tela's ability and willingness to follow her.

But it is one of the Fellows, assigned to help her ease into Girton life, who brings up the topic of sex.

"Is there anything else you'd like to talk about," she says, after going through and explaining the facilities and the people she can go to should she need help of any kind. "Doesn't need to be about the things I've been bringing up. I mean, it might be difficult for you to talk about other things, given you don't know anybody well enough yet."

Tela doesn't quite know how to respond.

"Sex, for instance," the woman continues. She is middle-aged, bespectacled and with donnish features. The topic seems incongruous in her mouth. "You're a pretty young woman, and I've no doubt you'll get lots of male attention. And good on you. But don't go getting pregnant. Or am I talking out of turn?"

Again, Tela can do little more than mumble a negative, so blunt and unexpected has been the turn in conversation.

"So I'm just saying, be careful. Do you take this pill thing?"

Tela knows exactly what she means. Before she left New Zealand, Fi had told her that she'd put a sham wedding ring on her finger and gone to a doctor she'd heard about who didn't enquire too closely, and got a prescription for the pill. It's freedom, she'd told her. It doesn't mean I'm going to offer my services to every man I meet, but it'll mean I can if I want to, and no danger of babies. You should too, she'd said.

Thinking of the disaster it would have been if, the time with Murray, she had been caught, made pregnant, she had hurriedly agreed and gone to the same doctor. She had practised the same subterfuge and been given the same prescription. She hadn't started on it yet, though. She had them with her, but she hadn't started on them.

She is glad the colour of her skin is hiding the heat she feels in her cheeks. "Yes, I have some," she says.

"Well good. You mustn't feel awkward about it."

"I'll start taking them if I…"

"Good. That's out of the way, then. We can stick to the other stuff from now on, unless there's anything else about it you'd like to discuss. It's really a matter of being sensible. Avoiding risks of any kind. Not just the pregnancy thing. I'm sure you understand?"

Tela nods, and smiles uncertainly. She hadn't invited the discussion they'd just had – but she is quite pleased they've had it.

She is soon familiar with the excellent Girton Library as well as the even vaster University Library, and is learning of other places where her supervisor has suggested she might find material of interest and value. But life is not all serious study, although she thinks she wouldn't mind too much if it were. But no… she socialises a little with other post-grads at Girton, and even occasionally joins in friendly activities with the undergrads. Some of them are remarkably mature. Most, however, are not. But that, she reminds herself, is only to be expected.

The most significant part of her hours that are not spent in working on her thesis are spent in town or at one of the Colleges with other post-grads from New Zealand. She finds it particularly relaxing to occasionally be in company with those whose accents are familiar, and whose experiences are similar, with whom she can share information from home.

Amongst those she has become friendly with is an Adonis-like young man who appears to have thrown himself so uninhibitedly into Cambridge life that he sometimes seems to her to be surely in danger of failing his purpose in being there. He has come to Cambridge from Canterbury University, and has, like her, won a Commonwealth Scholarship. His name is Anders, and he, too, is doing his doctorate in literature, and even has the same supervisor as her. But from her very first meeting with him, she has discovered he isn't inclined to discuss his work when he is in a socialising mood. He drinks, he smokes, and, she suspects, he experiments with other of the drugs that she soon learns are quite freely available through College networks.

But he is extraordinarily attractive – tall and fair-haired, his eager, indeed avid, intelligence obvious even when he is high. There is about him an air of delighted enthusiasm for life, and an unmistakeable confidence in his right, and his ability, to enjoy it to the full. He seems to her at first meeting to be bordering on arrogance, and she even decides that she doesn't want to know him; but soon enough she sees that beneath the apparent brashness and self-confidence there is a genuine interest in others, and a boyish tendency to self-deprecation. He is, she thinks, unmistakeably a New Zealander. She likes it, she finds. And she likes him.

Anders has digs in a house in Portugal Place, not far past a landmark house with a golden spiral on an Inn-like sign hanging outside the door, in which, she is told, a Nobel-prize winning scientist lives. Anders' rooms become an occasional meeting place for both postgrads and undergrads from New Zealand and Australia, and other girls from just about everywhere.

She and Anders have bumped into each other in the University Library.

"Come and tell me when you feel like a coffee," he says. "We can get one together." She can see that he is quite confident she will want to; and, of course she does. He is definitely one in whose company she is happy to be seen.

When that time comes, they both decide they've had enough for the day, and Anders invites her around to his digs.

They haven't been long there, the hot water jug not even boiling, when there is a knocking at his door, followed almost immediately by the noisy entry of two girl undergrads, giggling and shrieking. They breathlessly explain that they have just been mentally undressed in the lane outside by a distinguished-looking old guy standing in one of the doorways.

They have clearly found entry through the door before. Tela surveys them critically. They seem unbelievably young, babbling away there like… like highly intelligent heifer giraffes in their tiny mini-skirts. So tiny are the scraps of denim that they barely cover their backsides. It wouldn't have taken the old guy long to complete his mental undressing, she thinks. Not long at all.

She glances at Anders and sees him grinning, mesmerised by the same sight; possibly by the same thought, probably doing what the girls claim the man in the street had been doing. His look is one of totally gleeful anticipation. She looks back in the girls' direction. So young they look more like schoolgirls; and obviously revelling in their cheeky sexiness.

It hits her then that what she is feeling is not some need to censure them. It is jealousy, pure and simple. Such a display of careless sensuality! Jealousy is what she is feeling – and envy. A glimpse into a way of seeing the world, and of the world seeing her, that she has been shutting out for too long.

She makes a mental note to do some shopping. To find something shorter in the way of a skirt. She would like a man to look at her the way that Anders is looking at the girls. She would like that very much. And she knows that her legs are every bit as sensational as theirs. Probably more so.

II

And so her life goes on. She enjoys her research. More than that – she is deeply excited by it, drawn into it. She identifies closely with Geraldine Jewsbury, the energetic, driven woman who is the subject of her studies. At times she feels (stupidly, she knows) that she is in the same circle, that she actually knows her and her wonderful friends and acquaintances; people like Charlotte Bronte, Mary Ann Evans and Elizabeth Gaskell. She comes to share Geraldine's frustrations at her failed attempts to find love, and her exuberance when she finds those closest of friendships – with Jane Carlyle, and with Charlotte Cushman, the American actress who was the talk of the theatre world at the time. Surrounded in her mind and imagination by such luminaries, she is happy to let most of the lighter side of her outside life pass her by.

Yet… now, especially after that incident in Anders' digs, there are more and more times when she wishes she had someone with whom she could forget about the purpose she is here, and just be a girl, a woman. Those feelings are not entirely divorced from the excitement she feels at getting to know Geraldine Jewsbury through her books and her letters. Indeed, it is another point of likeness she senses between the two of them. Like Geraldine, it is clear (and she has long since admitted it to herself) that she cannot altogether ignore the strong urges that come upon her at unexpected moments, prompted, perhaps, by a glance of frankly sexual appreciation on the face of a passing man, or, more personal, more private, her own appreciative reaction when she in turn glances back and sees the casual grace of his body as he moves away from her. She has a habit of recalling such detail just before she goes to sleep at night, of trying to comfort herself, to rid herself of the accumulated tension, in a way that still causes her spasms of guilt. It rarely works to her satisfaction, but it does help her to sleep.

She makes female friends at Girton, though none of them can, could ever, take the place of Fi. There are others of around her age from many different parts of the world,, mostly doing post-grad work of one sort or another. Some seem to have little interest in doing more than offering a brief nod or smile. A few, both amongst the English and the foreign students, do not offer even that.

She comes closest to true friendship in her first year, with a girl who is in the last year of her doctorate when she arrives. She is English, and her smile when they are first introduced Tela can tell is one of genuine warmth and interest. Within minutes of their first conversation she recognises in Antonia Bassett another who is seriously moved by the excitement of research, one to whom whatever social life she might participate in is clearly subsidiary to her main purpose.

They spend some of their free time together, going to Footlights or to talks or lectures at one or other of the Colleges in town, or simply sharing ideas in their rooms; and in early Spring of the new year, Antonia invites her to her family home in the village of Penn in Buckinghamshire. The greetings from her parents and her younger brother, who is at Sandhurst Military Academy, are restrained but relaxed. She believes she is genuinely welcome. The house is large and beautifully, tastefully, furnished. Antonia's father is a banker – a sleek, confident, urbane man whose natural manner appears to be one of condescension. Certainly it is with her. Her mother seems a little more genuine, yet the feeling she gets is that she is there, as far as the parents are concerned, as proof of their daughter's catholic tastes, and of their own liberality. Nevertheless, she enjoys the break, and the journey to London that is part of the experience. They see a West End show, and she shares a room with Antonia in a posh hotel afterwards.

But after finishing her thesis, Antonia leaves to spend a year in Massachusetts, at Tufts, arranged through one of her father's American contacts. They exchange a few letters in the subsequent years, but they do not meet up again while Tela is at Cambridge.

So it is ever her increasing knowledge of the subject of her studies that is the ruling enthusiasm of her life. She is delighted whenever she discovers something new about the nature of the tiny, wispy woman, who was so full of passion and uncertainty. She begins to feel more than an empathy with her – she feels a deep, sisterly connection. She admits, with a pang of guilt, that it is a connection different from yet far, far deeper than that she has ever felt with her real sisters. Not that that is their fault, she reminds herself. For any deficiencies in the depth of her sense of sisterhood with her own sisters, she has no one to blame but herself. Geraldine Jewsbury, though, she has long known and now reaffirms in a multitude of ways, has a mind that resonates with her own.

But Tela's views of Jewsbury's literary abilities are more reasoned. She is no George Eliot. There are none in her gallery of characters who come near to being a Hetty Sorrel or a Maggie Tulliver, a Dorothea Brooke or a Gwendolen Harleth.

She travels to Manchester seeking to read in manuscript the letters that Geraldine wrote to her sister, Maria Jane, and in doing so, in reading the detail of her frustrations and her fervent cogitations on the place of women, begins to understand the close, almost mother-daughter relationship, that the two shared. There are similar themes in the voluminous printed correspondence Geraldine had with Jane Carlyle, a woman who became her intimate friend. She learns of Jane's sexually bleak marriage, and she cannot help but become more and more aware of the passionate, febrile nature of the relationship between the two women. She also sees Geraldine's ideas and her life experience reflected in, not just *The Half Sisters,* but also in the other, less well-known novels she wrote. She sees and feels the anguish that descended upon Geraldine as she wrote about her characters' struggles with religion. She is frustrated, though, by her ambiguous assessment of the prevailing notions concerning a woman's mental and physical strength as compared to a man's – the view that women were incapable of sustained physical effort, and that their brains were smaller, less developed. At times, Geraldine seems to agree with this ridiculous assessment; and here she again sees the continuing extraordinary influence of her elder sister in the attitudes that fashioned her outlook on life, even long after that sister had died.

She sees, too, parallels between the discrimination and prejudice that women then faced every day, and the petty, embedded prejudices that still exist, if not in law, then surely in the minds of many. More intensely, more personally, she also identifies with the frustrations caused by such prejudice when she considers how her own skin colour elicits similar, instinctive reactions and judgements. Every day. Everywhere.

III

Before the end of her first year at Girton, Tela receives a letter from Fiona that tells her that she and Jamie Ashcott have got together. She doesn't say much. The reference is brief, almost as though she wants it to be taken as inconsequential, but Tela experiences a sharp lurch of jealousy and a sense of loss. 'We went to Dr Zhivago,' she writes, 'and afterwards, we talked for ages. It was lovely to see him.' Just that. Only that. The rest is left to her imagination.

She shakes her head, telling herself that the wound is imaginary, that it might all be nothing, anyway. Yet… it goes deep, surprisingly deep. She can feel it inside her, twisting like a live thing.

When she replies to Fiona's letter, she says nothing at all about her meeting with Jamie, nor does she ask if she has seen him again. She doesn't want to know, she decides. She doesn't want to know. She will just get on with things. Turn her mind away.

And later that month she meets a man who becomes someone other than merely an acquaintance, or one who is simply part of a group she finds herself hanging out with at a meeting, or who carries out harmless flirtation with her at an antipodean gathering in someone's digs.

He is Italian, mid-thirties, classically handsome and sensuous. He is a cliché, as is everything about the relationship that develops between them; and that is a thing she recognises immediately, and it is something she welcomes. He tells her he is half way through a two year assignment at the Cavendish Laboratories. He is also married, with three children; a family who are with his wife's parents in Milan. He tells her so on their first meeting, even before he asks her out. There can be no illusions, even had she wanted to entertain any. But she does not want more than he is clearly offering.

He has rooms in town, and it is there they have their assignations.

At first, she still suffers from a reluctance to give herself over completely to his amatory skill. But it is a conscious decision she has to make, and she decides that to do so will be little different from her running with the boys as she did when she was a child. It is a game, and just as the boys of her childhood were more familiar with the territory, so that she had, at first, to follow their lead, so it is with Marco. As with most of what else she does in Cambridge, it is a decision she comes to using her intellect alone, though the consequences of her decision bear purely on the physical. Yes, purely, purely, and in a way far more exciting than she had ever imagined possible.

He is gentle but imperious. He undresses her slowly, and orders her to do the same to him. He feasts on her body. He brushes the back of his hand softly against her nipples, watching, watching the effect, then breathing words into her ear. "You are beautiful," he says. "Your body is beautiful. I want it all; and mine is yours."

He is a musician as well as a scientist. "Think of your body as a violin," he tells her. "Think of it as a Stradivarius, fresh from the maker's hand. And I am Paganini." Stroking her with his fingers, his tongue, every part of her. Every part of her.

Doing to him what he instructs her to do. "Think of *my* body as a Guarneri del Gesu," he tells her, "and you, too, you are a virtuoso violinist. My Teresa Milanollo." (The next morning she remembers to ask the Music Historian in the room next to hers about both the violin and the woman; and of the Guarneri, she tells her: 'It's not quite as highly thought of as a Stradivarius', and she is pleased). "Yes! Yes!" he says, "Like that; and here, and now here. Softly, softly. Your sweet breath, your eyelashes. Now, now… Hurt me a little. First your tongue, then your teeth. Yes! Nip, nip, nip. Ah yes! Yes!"

They meet no more than a dozen times in the course of that year. Each time he brings her near to climax, holds her there, deliciously teasing. He is a maestro.

But he is better at controlling her than he is at controlling himself. "No! No!" he says. "Stop now, stop before… Oh yes, yes!" He is apologetic then, diligent in his determination to repay the compliment. Tongue, fingers, teeth. Folds and crevices so secret she never before even knew her body had them. Every part of her, open, open to his skill. He is gentle and not-so-gentle by turn, until her body arches with the ecstasy of release.

But it is best, best by far, on those occasions when they reach the physical heights together, when he enters her, inching slowly deeper, and deeper; then she feels him resting, nuzzling against the wall of her cervix, until she can herself be passive no longer, but bucks her hips against him. Now, now, you bastard! Now! And it is she who brings them both to their mutually desired end.

Afterwards, they clean up, dress themselves. "Our performance is over for now. You see? Our instruments are snugly stowed away," he says, feigning sadness, when they are ready to go. Putting his lips to her cheek. "Your beautiful Stradivarius with its rich patina, my handsome Guarneri."

The word love is never spoken between them, never thought of, not even as a euphemism. What they do is deliciously enjoyable. It is indeed like making music together. There is no guilt. There is no real attachment. There is not even the slightest twinge of conscience. She is not even sure that she likes him a jot more than simply sufficiently well.

He goes back to Italy. She is glad of the experience; but a part of her, a large part of her, remains unaffected, unappeased, unfulfilled. It is the part of her that Jamie Ashcott unwittingly awakened eight or nine years previously. It is unaffected by the games she and Marco have played. Yet it is the part of her that she knows must, must be satisfied if ever she is to feel complete, whole. She feels, she *knows*, that it is the part of her, the only part of her, that can bring head and body and heart together. It is, she feels, the essential woman in her, but it is more than that. Being a woman is not sufficient. To be whole, she must love. Be loved. And she knows, with certainty yet in a painfully abstract way, what love is. For her, at this moment, it is detached and bereft of comfort. It is an emptiness, an unrealised promise; one that is not accompanied by a guarantee of redemption.

Meantime, not knowing is better than knowing.

Meantime, meantime, (and it is all she can do), she is where she was before Marco. Better prepared, true, but body and heart idling, idling. Back to the familiar. Back to where her head rules.

IV

As she enters her third year in Cambridge, she receives another letter from Fi, one that sets her mind reeling. At first she can hardly take in the words, but as their evident truth takes hold in her mind, disbelief is replaced by a jumble of emotions that she cannot immediately come to terms with. She absorbs the information the letter contains quickly, in a single gulp. She does not doubt it. It is as if she already knew. There can hardly be any doubt. She and Jamie Ashcott are cousins!

Distant cousins, true – she tries to put a name to the relationship. Is it fourth cousins? Anyway, it is clear that they have in common two great-great-grandparents. The things that settle the matter beyond doubt are the information that Jamie's great-grandmother's brother settled in Fiji and had children by a Fijian woman, and that his name was Oliver Gilbard. The one thing she can remember her father ever saying about his English forebear was that his name was Oliver, the same as her father's. And – for her the most telling of all, the piece of information he gives her that seems to click everything into place – the writer of the Journal that Jamie tells her of is called Adelaide. Atelaite. Tela. Adelaide Gilbard. Her own name!

A little later, when she has better absorbed the implications, she writes Fiona a quick reply, telling her how pleasantly astonished she is by the news, and asking her to tell Jamie so. She would have liked to tell him herself, to have written a letter and asked Fi to forward it, but she is still uncertain as to the nature of their current relationship. Apart from the news of the discovery regarding their mutual ancestor, Fi had made no other mention of Jamie in her letter. What is clear, though, is that they are still in contact. 'Please tell Jamie that I can't offer him any other information about our common ancestors, but that it seems absolutely certain that we *do* have some shared heritage. I do know that my great-grandfather was English, and that his name was Oliver. And if Jamie does come over to England, as he told you he was thinking of doing, then it would be great to see him.'

That last bit surely would not offend her, even if they are now together, she reasons. After all, it is only natural that she should want to share the full detail of whatever information he has. She has no idea what part of England her great-grandfather was from. She wishes she did. It is only natural that she, too, should want to know. That she should want to see Jamie, if he comes. Yes, yes. To see Jamie.

The extraordinary information contained in Fi's letter somehow justifies further the topic for her research. Right from the time of her first arrival in Cambridge, she had met those who showed surprise at her choice of subject. There has even been an occasional look of disbelief, even of resentment, that she should have chosen the life and works of a Victorian Englishwoman to study. It is perfectly clear to her why there should be such a reaction, but it doesn't generally bother her.

Her father had been able, or willing, to tell her only the barest minimum about the ancestral ties that she herself had to England. She remembers asking him why their name was Gilbard, and getting a brief response that it was because his father's father's name was Gilbard, and that he was an Englishman – that he, too, had the given name of Oliver. More information than that he never offered or was able to give her, but even that tiny bit seemed important to her. She had by that time already begun to read anything she could lay her hands on, and it so happened that much of what she read was fiction set in Victorian England. She was able herself to readily calculate that many of the books she read were set in the England that must have been familiar to that Gilbard – to her great-grandfather.

Now she has information that makes her ancestral connections with England that little bit stronger and more undeniable. And not only with England, of course; for her forebear had a sister who came to live, and who died, in New Zealand. It has long been of importance to her that she does have those ties with England; and now, even though only laterally, she knows she has an ancestral tie to New Zealand as well – to the land where she has for years now felt that she truly belongs.

Yes. It is to New Zealand, not England nor Fiji, that she feels she belongs. When she was a child, knowing that her great-grandfather was English was important to her. This was mainly because it gave extra meaning to the literature she devoured. But did she, does she, feel 'English'?

No, she decides. She most certainly does not. For one thing, the England she is now living in is not the England of her favourite literature. There are strong traces of that England, certainly – and many traces of an earlier England still – but it is clearly much changed. And although many of the traces of what Victorian England must have been like do appeal to her, many of them do not. She does not like what she sees and experiences of the class system, for instance. It is still to be seen around the Colleges at times – the little groups of braying toffs and their hangers-on who stride across the quads without even a glimmer of awareness of anyone else, clearly expecting lesser beings to keep out of their way. Not that all those with connections to the aristocracy are like that. At Girton, just a few doors from her, there is a girl who is deferential to the point of timidity; yet she, she is told, is a 'Hon.'.

She does feel comfortable with her field of study, though. She is appropriately critical of some aspects of the England of the Nineteenth Century, but she is perfectly comfortable in that England. It is largely a middle-class England, with only glimpses of the life of the majority. It is now an England she knows well – better than almost any of those around her, even though, in most cases, contemporary England is their home. So she can understand the resentment that some of them have that a colonial, and a brown-skinned colonial at that, should be an expert on the literature and one period of the history of 'their' country – but she knows within herself, and with an absolutely certainty, more so now than ever, that their claim to Victorian England and its culture is really not a jot stronger than her own.

And now, in that England of her mind, Geraldine Jewsbury is her intimate companion, and her guide. And Geraldine, sadly, had spent much of her real life in a doomed quest to find the ideal man of her imagination. She feels, she hopes, that she herself won't be so unlucky. In that regard, she has moments of expectation, and moments of despair. The most bitter moments come when she admits that the man she wants is not an ideal, but is flesh and blood, and that she is trapped by circumstance into a sort of helplessness whenever she considers the question. Meantime, she can only try to forget, and to put all her energies into those aspects of her life that she *can* control.

Chapter Three – Cambridge and Wales

I

Jamie Ashcott decides that he must take advantage of his relatively healthy bank account and go to the United Kingdom, to Wales. His desire to find out something, anything, about his Gerold ancestors, and through them, he fervently hopes, some definite leads to discover more about Adelaide Gilbard, has rapidly become an obsession. But he doesn't have the urge that many seem to have to actually spend months, perhaps even a year or more, on his overseas experience. Nor, in truth, would his conscience allow him to do so, considering the Bursary obligations he still believes that he should, in all conscience, fulfil. Rather, he decides to restrict himself to just two or three weeks or so – long enough to meet up with his friend Anders in Cambridge, and to see Tela Gilbard there as well, then to head west into Wales.

He travels by air – a long and tedious experience he does not enjoy. By the time he has reached England and made his way through customs, he is numbed by weariness and by a sense of alienation. Everything he encounters seems impersonal and uncaring. Few people other than those whose job it is to deal with him even seem to acknowledge his existence, and even those who must exchange a few words with him do so without any apparent interest, their faces registering either boredom or a dull suspicion.

He is not seeking a London experience. One day, perhaps, he tells himself, but not now. For the moment, all he wants is to get through the forbidding metropolis and make his way to Cambridge. The anonymous hotel he has booked is exactly as he would have wished – a place to sleep with no demands. When he sets off the next morning to find King's Cross Station (evocative name, he must admit to himself), the one impression of his overnight stay is of the old church directly opposite the hotel. It is grey and austere, with iron railings on either side. He can imagine Hablot's depictions of Dickens' characters shuffling along past those railings, intent on their nefarious or merciful purposes. All else in the London he passes through is a confusion of unfamiliar noises, and footpaths and concourses crowded with people who pass by each other without even appearing to notice either his or each other's presence.

Once settled in the Cambridge train, he begins to look forward to his own purpose – of seeing Anders again, and Tela, yes, but it is Adelaide Gilbard who draws him on, who continues to steel his determination.

Anders is at the Cambridge Station, beaming his remembered smile, apparently pleased to see him – and Jamie is delighted and relieved to look upon a familiar face.

The house in the village where Anders now has rooms looks to Jamie to be quaintly Elizabethan – half-timbered and two-storied. The village itself has two parts. There is the old part where the house is situated, and opposite which is a huge old chestnut tree that hides another house, a bigger house, also old, but built of stone. This part harbours the village church as well, just a few yards further down the narrow street. The larger, newer part of the village is further on, at least a quarter of a mile separated from the old.

"The house is actually seventeenth century," Anders tells him. "And bloody cold. We only just survived winter. Had to spend most of the time in bed," he grins.

His girlfriend is English. She smiles briefly when they are introduced, but otherwise seems to pretend that he is not there. She is bespectacled, dark-haired, tall and willowy. Her name is Kate. Anders shows him to his room upstairs. The doorway is low, very low. He has to duck to get inside. It is a narrow room with a narrow bed. He deposits his suitcase on it. "Coldest room in the house," Anders says cheerfully. "Kate reckons it's haunted."

"By a beautiful maiden, I hope," Jamie says.

"You'd be lucky. Maidens are pretty thin on the ground."

"I can believe that. With you around."

They go to the village pub, where Anders gets a nod or two, and curious eyes follow him for a few seconds. From then on they are ignored. The beer is strong, and it's not long before he feels light-headed – and hungry. Anders relates some of the funnier, more extreme episodes in his life at Cambridge. He falls into the role of listener, just as he has always done with Anders. Apart from the setting, it is all very familiar. Comforting, even; if, in some way, vaguely disappointing.

Kate doesn't look happy when they return, but she does place a couple of plates of food on the kitchen table before disappearing upstairs and leaving them to it.

He stays only two nights with Anders, going to bed drunk on that first of them, before hiring a car and heading west into Wales. But before he does that, he phones Tela at Girton College.

II

The call from Jamie after breakfast affects Tela deeply.

She knew he was coming, of course. Only days before, Fiona had told her so in another letter. And in that letter she had told her something else, too – something that had sent her heart racing and her spirits soaring so high that she had had to rein them in, to calm them with reason. Just because the possibility of a union between Fi and Jamie had now been banished from the realms of the possible, didn't mean that Jamie would now look at her as anything more than a friend. Though even that… surely now, considering their family connection, surely their friendship will become, has become more… intimate. And to hear his voice brings everything she left behind two years previously, the emotions of the past decade, back with a rush that makes her giddy.

"God! It'll be good to see you, Jamie! There are so many things…" She tails off; reining in, reining in.

266

"I'm staying with a friend, in a little village just outside the town," he says. "Can we arrange something?"

"I'm planning to come into town today, anyway. Look, let's meet somewhere central and easy to find. Say… Eaden Lilly on Market Street. It's a big department store. Your friend will tell you how get there. What's his name, by the way? I might know him."

"Anders Malmo. He says he knows you."

"Oh God, yes. I know Anders. Anyway, Eaden Lilly. You can't miss it; and there's a place right there we can go for a coffee. Better there than outside King's or one of the other Colleges, because you'll be able to shelter if there's a shower."

"Yes, good idea. It's raining at the moment, I see. Eaden Lilly on Market Street. I'll find it."

"Eleven?"

"Right."

The dizzy feeling stays with her after he has rung off. She cannot suppress it. It is as though the fabric of her current, resignedly comfortable and familiar cocoon has been ripped open. But it is a welcome feeling. It is an exciting feeling. Soon she will see Jamie Ashcott again. A different Jamie Ashcott from the one who has hitherto, haphazardly and not always happily, occupied a significant portion of her mind, because this Jamie Ashcott and she are connected by blood. Only distantly, true – but the knowledge adds a whole new dimension of disturbance.

She must be patient, she decides. She will wait, choose the moment. It would be so very easy to make herself look foolish.

As they walk along Market Street, they lean comfortably in to each other, talking.

"Who is it you're doing your thesis on again?"

"Geraldine Jewsbury. She's a Victorian novelist and critic, quite advanced in her views on the role of women, though she's not very well-known. I doubt you've heard of her. It's not just her books I'm writing about. It's also about the particular view society had of middle-class women at the time, and the views they themselves had of the society they moved in."

"And it keeps you busy, I bet." he asks. "Do you get much time for socialising? I suppose most of the undergrads do their own thing. From the look of the ones around here, they seem more like kids. But you wouldn't have much to do with them, anyway. Are there many other New Zealanders around?"

"Yes, a few. And there are Australians all over the place. They seem to be particularly popular just now. We New Zealanders are sort of riding on their coat-tails. And Strine is a language that's now heard quite a bit here. Just about everyone seems to know that you should ask Emma Chizzit if you want to know the price of something."

"Oh, God. Painful. Do we want to be riding their coat-tails?"

"We do it cynically. Okay? The silly Brits may be fooled, but we aren't."

"We've been laughing at them for years. The Aussie's I mean."

"Quite right," she grins. "We're vastly superior, of course. Goes without saying. And getting back to the Kiwis, Muriel's supervising Anders as well. That's why I see quite a bit of him. He's doing something on Patrick White. Did you know?"

He didn't. They'd not discussed his thesis at all. "Patrick White?"

"Yes, I know," she says. "Another bloody Australian! But to return to the right side of the Tasman – I come into contact with some of the younger ones occasionally, undergrads, at Soc. meetings and the University Library and at public talks and that sort of thing. I haven't been to many student parties in the two years I've been here, though. You're right about the undergrads. They do seem awfully young, most of them. A lot of them smoke pot, even some of the girls at Girton. I've never been tempted. You didn't smoke pot, did you? Do you?"

"I tried it once. Decided I'd stick to alcohol. But you don't even drink, do you?"

"No. But if others drink, or smoke for that matter, well… that's up to them."

They enter the tearooms that Tela has directed them towards, and take their seat, give their orders.

"Now, Jamie. Tell me about Adelaide Gilbard and her Journal. I want to know all about it."

Jamie looks across, notices how eagerly she is focussed on him; not just alert and waiting, but seemingly ready to pounce and devour. Over their cups of coffee, he tells her everything he can remember, answering her questions as best he can and trying to convey just how anxious he is to find out more about her, this intriguing woman who connects them. And at the end of it all, the eagerness is still there, in her eyes – the hunger and the determination.

"I'll do what I can, Jamie," she says. "I'm surrounded by historians who'll be able to help me. It's a pity we don't know what part of England she's from. That's sort of crucial, isn't it. But that mention of her uncle who's a doctor – that might be a lead in. Or her brother, *my* forebear – as he was in the Colonial Office there are bound to be some records. It has to be the first step, doesn't it? To find out where the family lived."

"Yes. And I might learn something if I can trace the Gerold house. If I can find out more about them, the Gerolds. There must be marriage records. Surely they must have been married from the place where she lived."

"Well… not necessarily, I think. But they might have been. Oh God! So difficult! Yes, find that house, if you can. And dates are important. Get exact dates if you can. You never know what might follow. At the very least, you should find out a bit more about him – the man Adelaide married."

"Yes. And if I do, I hope it's not all bad. I have a pretty jaundiced view of him. I hope his whole family weren't like that. I hope he just turns out to have been the black sheep."

"Generations ago, Jamie," she says. "You're not thinking 'sins of the fathers' are you?"

"He harmed her, that's all I know. He harmed our Adelaide."

"Well, yes. So it seems. But it was surely not his intention if he did. He may very well have loved her, wanted the best for her. You say that Adelaide admits that he loved her. And she forgave him."

They leave the tea shop and resume their walking. The rain has stopped and they stroll along King's Parade, stopping every now and then as Tela points out some architectural feature. For the moment, their talk turns again to her experiences as a student.

"There must be plenty of other things to do in Cambridge, when you want to have a break from research, or writing up, or whatever."

"Plenty of things, yes. Girton's a couple of miles out of town," she tells him. "Most of the girls cycle in when they have to go to lectures or meet up with someone. I even have a squeaky old thing myself, but it's a bit of a struggle getting it up Castle Hill, especially when it's wet. There's a joke amongst the boys that they can recognise Girton girls by their muscly thighs."

He can't help himself. He glances down at her legs, runs his eyes over the shapely curve of her thighs. Very trim, her legs are, under her shortish plaid skirt, sexily encased in black stockings. Lovely really. He's always liked Tela's legs. "Yours don't look like Girton thighs, then," he says.

She laughs. She seems quite pleased, and he congratulates himself on making her feel good about herself. "I actually don't use my bike very often," she says. He wonders if, beneath her flawless brown skin, she is blushing. Probably not, he concludes. Not Tela. Her mind is probably on much higher things.

"What's she like, this Supervisor of yours," he asks.

"She's… wonderful. She's human."

"I should hope so."

"Oh, shut up, Jamie! You know what I mean. She treats me like an equal. We explore ideas. She's always willing to listen. She even brought coffee and cakes to my room one evening. That was probably our longest conversation ever."

"Pretty special, then."

"Yes. She certainly now has a place in my private pantheon of goddesses."

"Who with?"

"'With whom!'" she says, severely, shaking her head at him. "Well, with Cynthia Wallace, of course. She's the one who arranged for me to attend Mapledene. Much more than just that, though. She's been a sort of Fairy Godmother. Then there's my mother. Naturally. She was special, too – though for very different reasons. And Joan at Vic."

"Yeah. I guess she'd be in mine, too."

"Of course. And then there's Fi. Yes, Fi, definitely."

"Fiona? She can't have been much real help to you."

"Oh Jamie, don't you have a dear friend? Friends? Ones that are with you, even when they aren't?"

Jamie thinks. Does he have anyone like that in his life? Maybe Cossy comes closest. He smiles at the thought. Maybe Anders, too – although they don't need each other, he's pretty sure they'll always be friends.

Tela is watching him closely. She, too, smiles. "I see you do, and I'm glad."

"Any gods in your pantheon?" he asks.

"There might be. Any other goddesses in yours?"

"They come and go," he says, feeling suddenly bereft. Then he brightens. "But now there's Adelaide Gilbard, of course!"

III

The next day she arranges to meet him at the entrance to the Fitzwilliam Museum. "You might as well get a bit of high culture while you're here," she chides. They wander around the exhibits. Not having expected it, he is especially taken by the art in some of the galleries. He had thought a museum would be… well, a museum. He tells her, and she laughs.

"They call the Louvre a museum, too, you know. *Arti*-facts."

"And that's another arty fact, I suppose?'

She groans. "Right, Jamie. You win. I couldn't stand much more of that." But she's smiling. She seems very happy, he thinks.

When they emerge from the Fitzwilliam, she directs him across the street to another tea-rooms. Once they're seated, she turns and waves to a couple at a table some distance away, and they wave back – a bearded man who looks tall even while sitting down, and an oriental-featured woman.

Yet again, Jamie finds he is surprised at just how relaxed and comfortable he feels in her company – at ease in a way that he has not felt with anyone else for a very long time. Certainly not with any other woman.

He makes a start on one of the eclairs he has bought them, and she does the same. The cream leaves a trace at a corner of her lips, but she coaxes it in to her mouth with a brief sortie of tongue.

"You seem pretty much at home here," he says.

"At home? No, I'm a guest," she says.

"But you must be getting pleasure from it all. Isn't it something like a dream come true? All these beautiful old buildings and things? Becoming familiar with it all. Belonging."

"Pleasure – yes, definitely. But no, Jamie. I don't feel I belong in the sense you mean. For me, it's like being invited into an interesting stranger's living room. Admiring the furniture – sitting on the Chippendale chairs and sipping out of the Royal Worcester – being granted that privilege for a while. But none of it feels like mine. I don't really belong in that sense. It could never be my home. I don't even wish it was."

"Where is home for you, then, Tela? Is Fiji your place?"

She doesn't answer for a moment, seeming to contemplate what she should say. Then: "Fiji is where I was born and where I spent most of my childhood. It's where my father is, and my brother and sisters. But I think I've always felt that my life would not be lived out in Fiji. Very early on I knew that." She smiles; not so much for him, but at a thought. "I spent a lot of my childhood inside my head. Most of it, probably. It's about the only place I did feel at home, then. It's different now."

"But…"

"I know. It must sound strange to you. Maybe even heartless. But since I first left Fiji I've only been back that once, when my mother died. It took that… that terrible thing to get me back to Fiji. Before that, I had thought Fiji meant very little to me. I'd even thought that… that I didn't need my family. For anything. Or maybe I just didn't think at all."

He looks up sharply when she pauses, but finds she is still clear-eyed. He had thought…

She smiles faintly back at him. "Yes, it was a painful experience, Jamie. And I deserved every bit of the pain. It didn't change much, admittedly. I still accept that they have their own lives, and I have mine. I made that decision years ago. But I learned that I care about them all. That I really care about them. That I love them – my father, my sisters, my brother. That I loved my mother. Fiji was my birth country, and if the chance arises, I want to go back there and… pay my respects. I would like to give something back – to do something in exchange for what it has given me."

"I hear there's a University starting up there soon. That could be a way…"

"Yes. I've already thought of that. But I doubt they'll be looking for a specialist in obscure nineteenth century English literature."

"What about New Zealand. Is New Zealand your true home now? "

"Of course it is. I'm legally a New Zealander now. New Zealand is my home."

"But… you have… no one. I mean…"

"You're wrong, Jamie. Very wrong. I have Fiona, for one – the best friend I have ever had, or ever will have. I have Cynthia Wallace – she's divorced and living permanently in New Zealand now. But most of all I have the experience of… of being welcomed there, of being given a chance I would otherwise have never had. The chance to be what I want to be. To get out of my head and into the real world. Of course, not all my experiences in New Zealand have been happy ones, but underneath it all it's been pretty much as I expected and hoped it would be. More than I expected it would be, thanks to Cynthia and Fi and… and others. It is where I became… grounded. That's the exact word. I can see my future there. I am happy to think about my future there. Besides," she says, with the sort of unexpectedly shy and girlish smile he has always found appealing, "being a New Zealander also means I'm still a Pacific Islander."

She has never spoken so freely of personal matters with him before. He has never heard her talk so freely about such things to anyone. It flatters him that she feels able to open up to him; but it is more than that. He is seeing her in a way he has never done before. She seems somehow more vulnerable, her intellect less intimidating.

"So you're a Kiwi now."

"Yes, I'm a Kiwi."

"And talking of Fiona Finlay…"

She smiles. It has come, the moment when she will learn one of the things she needs to know. She makes her words as casual as she can. "Poor old Jamie. You're not still carrying a torch for her, are you?"

He feels himself blush. "No, no. That's… I know now I never really had any chance. In fact… I know now that I never even wanted to be more than a friend, anyway. No, I'm not carrying a torch. I'm well over that."

"I don't blame you for having been keen," she says, after a pause. Her heart is singing. Singing. "Fi's a honey. And that's not just the colour of her hair."

There is something in the way she says it that causes him to look at her closely. She has her lower lip tucked slightly under her teeth, and is grinning. Or is it a grin? He has always found it hard to read her properly. Anyway, there is something faintly cheeky about both her tone and her look. He grins back in response.

"But I'm glad she's out of your system," she continues. "I had a letter from her a couple of days ago. She's just got engaged."

"Alistair?"

"Good guess. They got together again. It was always on the cards. I'm happy for her. He's a gentleman, in the true sense of the word."

"A jellyman, eh?"

"A what?" she asks.

"A jellyman. Sorry. It comes to my mind whenever I hear someone referred to as a gentleman. I read somewhere that some New Zealand politician, I think it might have been Micky Savage, used to begin all his speeches with 'Lazies and Jellymen.' "

She looks at him, bemused. "Well, Alistair is a jellyman, then."

"You'll be going back for the wedding? When is it?"

"Fiona's planning it for after I finish here. Late next year. She says there's no way she's getting married without me there."

"True friends, eh?"

"True friends."

The couple she had waved to when they entered have risen from their table and now look their way. Tela nods an acknowledgement, and pushes her chair back.

"*Benedictus benedicatur*," she says, with mock solemnity; then explains, with another smirk: "That's giving thanks for what we have eaten, in case you're wondering. We're always thankful, we Girtonians. Now I've got to leave you to finish your coffee by yourself. There's someone giving a talk at Newnham – yet another Australian, as it happens – and I've promised to go along."

He rises with her, suddenly conscious that his mother would have been pleased to see him do so. But he hadn't thought about it. It just came naturally. He supposes that he must be a jellyman too. In some things, at least. He wonders if Tela thinks of him as being one. He hopes she does.

"Call me when you get back from Wales, Jamie," she says. "Promise?"

"Of course I will," he says. "It's been great. I wouldn't pass up another chance." It is true, he realises. He has hugely enjoyed being with her. "Besides, I might have news for both of us."

"I hope you do," she says. "I really hope you do."

Chapter Four – Connections

I

It is autumn in New Zealand, and most of the hydrangeas have finished blooming, their summery heads discoloured and fading. Win Ashcott wandered down the line of the hedge that separated her from her neighbour. It was tall and rank, even more in need of attention than her hydrangeas.

In two months I'll be seventy, she mused. Old and alone. But not really alone, she remembered. Jenny was quite close, and she called in with her youngest at least every month or so. And soon Helen, too, would be coming down for a visit with her kiddies – though she didn't know where she'd put them all. She hoped they'd bring a tent. And Dougal checked on her as often as he could. No, no. Not alone. Old, yes – but not alone.

And then there was Jamie. He was overseas at the moment, but he had written to her just before he left, and he promised to write to her from England. She couldn't quite understand why he had wanted to go to England. So far away. But he was always good at writing letters, even when she would have liked it better if he had come to see her. His room was always ready for him. At least he knew that. He was quite a clever boy, but restless. Not content to settle down to… now what was it he had trained for? Was it teaching? She had always hoped he would go into medicine. Such a respectable profession.

What Jamie needed, of course, was a girl. Not that he hadn't had plenty of girlfriends, she was sure. He'd even told her about some of them. Sometimes he talked or wrote of them in such glowing terms that she remembered she had been quite jealous of the affection he clearly felt, or quite hopeful that something more permanent would come of it. But it never had. He wouldn't have mistreated them, she is sure of that – but he hadn't found the one he could stay with, be happy with. She had told him he should be careful, that there were girls out there who would do anything to catch a man. Anything. It worried her. She wouldn't want him to end up with someone like that. Well, there was plenty of time. He was still young.

There was one girl he had seemed to be especially fond of. Someone from nearby, from a farm out east, near the coast. Jenny had pointed her out to her one day, when they were in town together – a rather pretty blonde girl in a fashionable twin-set and a tartan skirt. "That's Fiona Finlay," Jenny had said. "The girl you say Jamie's keen on? She's lovely, isn't she! He'd be doing pretty well there. But they'll be wanting her to marry into land. You know these East Coast farmers."

And nothing had come of it, although she seemed to remember that he kept mentioning her at times. A nice girl, clearly. Not one of those ones who were just looking for a meal ticket or a set of false teeth. A pity, but Jenny was probably right; though that didn't prevent her from resenting the implied criticism of her son as being somehow unworthy. She doubted the girl's family could have come from better stock than Jamie, on her side, anyway, no matter how big their farm was.

But that was getting close to snobbery, she reminded herself. And she had long ago forsworn snobbery, leaving all that to her aunt.

No, no. She was not alone. At the very least, she had her memories, the happy as well as the sad. But these days, she tried not to remember the sad ones; and she'd found that it was quite easy to forget them. Or at least not to remember them. The little ones, at least. But the biggest and saddest one of all by far – well, that was part of her. It *was* her. That could not be changed, nor would she wish it to be changed.

II

A hemisphere away, Jamie Ashcott has no particular plan for his sojourn into Wales, not beyond attempting to find the old house in the photograph he carries. He buys a tourist map of Great Britain, and uses this to locate the boundaries of Merionethshire. He then decides that he will start in the south of the county and explore there first in the hope of locating it. He knows he is likely to fail in his mission. Indeed, that the house may no longer even exist. But he must try.

He drives west from Cambridge across England, avoiding the major motorways and towns. The amount of traffic on some of the roads is daunting, even so, to one whose motoring experience has mostly been on the country roads of New Zealand. He is too intent on negotiating the hazards to pay much attention to the scenery on the way, and is relieved to find that the further west he travels, the lighter the traffic becomes.

He enters Wales through the little town of Knighton. From there, the road takes him up into the hills. It is an odd feeling that fills him then – as though the hills are enfolding him, welcoming him. Everywhere he looks, he sees what borders on the familiar, but is not quite familiar. Is it because the landscape reminds him of New Zealand? He thinks that is a possible explanation, but… it is not really a New Zealand landscape. The hills seem older somehow, certainly as far as the marks that man has left on them is concerned. Stone walls criss-cross the hillsides, and stone cottages snuggle into the folds or stand out, bleak and exposed, on the heights.

The deeper he gets into the hills, the stronger the feeling of comfortable welcome he gets. It is like reaching a sanctuary after having crossed what had seemed to him to be an essentially hostile, or at least unwelcoming, England.

Eventually the route he has chosen takes him over a divide and into a broad glacial valley. By now, it is late afternoon, and the sun shining through gaps in the shower clouds presents a vista of mauves and light greens. A lake glistens just below. The fields here are divided by fences of slate. It is like nothing he has ever seen before, yet the feeling of familiarity, of safety, is still strong in him. Stronger than ever. It is breath-taking.

Tired, now, but still buzzing with excitement, he finds his way down the valley to the seaside town on the coast where he has booked into a small hotel.

The next morning, the hotel Manager proves to be interested in his quest, and eager to help. "Tan-y-Bwlch," he says, as he reads from the back of the photograph. It is the first time Jamie has heard the name pronounced. He asks the man to say it again, committing the sound to memory.

The Manager examines the photograph of the old house closely again, though, then shakes his head. "It's not a place I know," he says. "But a place that big should be named on an Ordnance Survey Map. And you know you're in the right County. There's a book shop down near the seafront that keeps a good supply of maps. You should go down there and get one for this part of the county, and maybe another for further north, around Dolgellau, then check them carefully. Look for the name."

He buys the maps and brings them back to his room. There, he unfolds them and lays them on the bed. He scans the first one methodically, grid by grid. He can find nothing in this one, though, the one depicting the more southerly parts of the county; but within twenty minutes or so of eye-straining concentration on the second one, and with a thrill of discovery, he finds the name he is looking for. *Tan-y-Bwlch.* It is given in tiny letters, and clearly refers to nothing more than a single dwelling. It seems likely, then, that the house still exists, and that this is its location. He checks the surrounding area, and finds that it is not far beyond the castle and town of Harlech. He feels his heartbeat increase with the excitement of it, the hope.

He calculates it would take him the better part of an hour to drive to Harlech, and rather than heading off straight away, he decides he will spend the rest of the day exploring his immediate environs, and leave Tan-y-Bwlch to the following day. He also phones to book a room in a Bed and Breakfast for the next two nights, in a town much closer to his objective.

On the afternoon of the next day, Jamie drives up the hill and under the walls of Harlech castle, looking for a place to park; but the road and the narrow streets that run off it provide no obvious stopping place. In the end, instead of stopping he drives on, right through the little town and out into the hills beyond. There is no need for him to stop. He is certain that he is on the right road.

Here, quite suddenly, there is no hint of other traffic. He slows to a crawl, looking about him in all directions. It is as though he has stumbled into a hidden Wales. There is something about the closed-in hills, the total lack of human movement, that attracts him, as though there is a special connection between him and the landscape. It is almost as though he has discovered a gateway into a charmed realm of his own. To his left he can still see a prospect of the sea, but the highway below is hidden from his sight. To his right, there are scatterings of oaks behind dry stone walls, and a tiny lane that leads up over a stone bridge. The narrow road he is following leads gently upwards, veering a little towards the hills.

He comes to a fork. The branch that is clearly the most used begins to slope down, veering westward towards the estuary. The other, tighter way, angles a little further east still, and climbs quite steeply upwards, finding a way through overhanging foliage.

For a few seconds he is uncertain as to which route he should follow. There is no sign to help him, and the only sound is the gentle ticking of the engine. The road down would take him to the highway again. It surely must. And the other… it could be a private road, he thinks. Yet it is like a beckoning finger. This way. This way. It must be this way.

He takes the old photograph from his pocket and gives it a final look. He picks up the map, folded to make it easy for him to check his position, and sees that he must indeed be very close, and that the narrow road up must surely be the correct one. Soon, soon, he will see the real thing. Tan-y-bwlch. Tan-y-bwlch.

With a shiver of uncertainty and daring, he moves the car again – slowly, upwards and into the shade of the trees that line the lane. To the right is a tall, moss covered dry-stone wall. He edges the car further, up and up. Then he is at the opened gates, and he can see the house.

The sight of it – the bluish-grey of its stone walls, the looming escarpment behind it – triggers a kind of dizziness. He doesn't need to get the picture of it out of his pocket. There is no ivy covering it, as it is in the faded photograph, but it is Tan-y-bwlch. He knows. He *knows.* It is as though every cell in his body is singing its recognition of the fact.

There are trades vehicles parked in the gravelled area directly outside the house – two vans and a small truck. As he watches, he sees two men come out of the house and fetch a ladder that is secured to the top of one of the vans.

There is too much activity, he decides. The sight of it, and some deeper instinct within, tells him that a visitor would not be welcomed. He would like to see inside, but… He contents himself instead with getting out of the car with his camera, and taking some shots of his own. As he is doing so, another vehicle comes up the lane. A Land Rover. It slows down to a crawl as it passes him, the driver watching him suspiciously. He raises his hand to him, but receives no acknowledgement in return. The Land Rover turns into the driveway.

He decides he has seen all he is going to see. Reluctantly, self-consciously recognising that there is no alternative, he gets behind the wheel again and eases the car further up the hill, looking for a place to turn.

The lane continues up past a little cottage almost hidden by greenery, then winds further, taking first one direction then another, until it reaches the top of the spur. Here there is a tiny church, as well as space to turn around. Although the lane continues, dropping down the other side, it seems to be even narrower and less used, little more than a farm track.

He stops the car again and gets out with his camera. From the height he can see down to the estuary far below. It is a bleak spot. The stonework of the church is dark; darker than the stonework on Tan-y-bwlch, and more weather-beaten. It is surrounded by old grave stones, some of which lie in the grass, while others seem better cared for. He takes some more photos, and turns his attention back, looking down the hill. But the big house cannot be seen.

III

He turns the car and retraces his route, taking another lingering look at Tan-y-bwlch as he passes the gate. At the bottom of the lane he turns right, taking the road down from the heights, and within a few short minutes finds himself in a straggling village near the estuary. On the final corner before the narrow high street reverts again to countryside, he finds a parking area next to an old grey-stone building outside which is a sign advertising it as a restaurant.

As he enters through the door, a bell tinkles a warning. The room is quite a large one, but he seems to be its only inhabitant. He finds a seat at one of the tables, taking it uncertainly. All is quiet. There is no one behind the cashier's desk tucked away in one corner. He is beginning to think he might have missed seeing a closed sign somewhere outside.

Then an interior door opens and a woman bustles in. She is fiftyish, matronly and smiling cheerfully.

"Sorry to keep you waiting, sir," she says. "It's a little late in the day, but I can find something simple for you if it's lunch you're wanting."

"No, no. Just a cup of coffee and a… maybe a piece of cake if you have it."

"Of course we do, sir. And we do an excellent coffee, if I say so myself. Though me, I prefer tea." She crosses to the door through which she entered, says something to someone unseen, and returns to stand next him.

"Just passing through, are you?" she asks.

"Yes, in a way," he says. "Well, not exactly. I'm staying a couple of nights at a B and B in Llanfair." He is a little flattered by her interest, and

282

charmed by the Welsh sing-song in her voice. "I've just been up to have a look at the place where some of my ancestors lived."

"Oh yes?" she says, with what seems like genuine interest. "Where would that be, then?"

He waves towards the hills. "A place called Tan-y-bwlch." He is pleased he is able to pronounce the name, and sends a mental thankyou to the Manager of the hotel in Towyn. "It's maybe a mile or two up the hill, there."

"Tan-y-bwlch, is it? Well now. Your ancestors had something to do with the big house itself, then? It used to belong to a family called the Gerolds, that house and all the land about. My father used to work for them, and my grandfather before him. Now isn't that something? Are you a Gerold, then? But you're not Welsh, or even English. I can tell."

"You're right. I'm from New Zealand. And no, I'm not a Gerold. But my mother's mother was."

"Ach now! That so! And you've just come from Tan-y-bwlch? It's no longer owned by the Gerolds, you'd know."

"Yes, I'd sort of guessed that before I came, so I didn't go right up. I thought I might ask to see inside, but there seems to be some... some work going on up there. I didn't like to bother them."

"Oh yes, there's a lot of traffic been heading up there." She looks out towards the street, and gives a little cry of surprise. "And here's the daughter of the house right outside our door. Now there's magic for you! You could maybe ask her about it."

He looks up then and sees a young woman standing by a low-slung sports car that is parked outside the garage just across the way. She is talking to a man who is wiping his hands with a rag. She is tall, about his age she seems, with fine gingery hair cascading from under her scarf and falling almost to her waist. Even from the distance of the thirty yards or so that separate them, he can tell that she is conscious of her beauty. Her gestures as she talks are graceful and confident.

"She usually comes over here for a cuppa while her car's being seen to. You'll likely have a chance to ask her."

But she doesn't come in, at least not then. The woman disappears out the back again, but shortly returns carrying a tray with his pot of coffee and a piece of cake.

"Baked that myself," she says. "Lemon cake, it is. I hope you like it."

"I'm sure I will."

After unloading the tray she stays standing next to his chair. "Shall I pour for you, then?"

"No, no, I can manage, thanks."

"We don't get many people from New Zealand, here. We know about the All Blacks, though. Very good, the All Blacks are."

"So are the Welsh," he says diplomatically. It was the same at the hotel in Towyn, and at the bookshop where he had bought the map. New Zealand equals Rugby equals the All Blacks.

"That's true, they are real stars, some of them, aren't they. I don't follow rugby all that closely. More of a football girl, myself. The Reds, you know. Liverpool, isn't it."

"Ah."

"But I expect as a New Zealander, you wouldn't be all that interested in Football, would you? Not your game, really. Not ours, either, of course. People are always telling me I'm a bit of traitor."

He nods, and smiles his understanding.

"But fancy some of your old people being from around here! And up at Tan-y-bwlch! Real toffs, the Gerolds were, by all accounts. Good people, though, my grandfather always used to say. Good Welsh people. Not like some I could mention."

He is pleased to hear her description of the Gerolds. Even relieved. They can't all have been drunken pursuers of diseased women, then. He wonders if her final dismissive comment can be a reference to the present owners of Tan-y-bwlch, but decides not to risk asking. He glances outside to see if the girl is still there, but there is no sign of her.

"Well, I'll leave you to your coffee. Let me know if you'd like a refill, or some more cake."

"I will," Jamie says. He has been delaying tasting the cake, or even taking a sip of the coffee, in case it would seem rude, but he is eager to sample both.

For a while after she has gone he relaxes into an enjoyment of the offerings. The coffee is good and strong, and the cake has a powerful lemon scent and a taste that fills his mouth, sharp yet pleasant. Like the village itself, and its surroundings, the hummocky hills and farm gates and the narrow lanes, they seem somehow to be very… *Welsh.* Or is he only assigning a Welshness to those things that appeal most to him? Is it all just silly sentimentality? It is undoubtedly true that he feels more comfortable here than he had in England – except maybe in Cambridge, with Anders, and Tela. But here, the hills, the village, even the tearooms in which he sits, seem much better suited to his nature. Certainly better suited to his mood.

It is a shame, he thinks, that he will miss seeing inside the old house; but at least he has had a good look at the outside, and taken a few snaps of the place. At least he knows for sure that it is still there, and that there is some connection. He is even more pleased to have the family described as being good Welsh people. It was odd, the powerful sense of belonging that had crept up on him when he first saw it. It was unexpected, surprising. It had almost been like a home-coming. Yet that… well, it is a ridiculous thought.

But what should he do now, he wonders. What he has discovered so far, satisfying though it is in its own way, seems of little use to the furthering of his quest for knowledge of Adelaide Gilbard.

His musings are interrupted by the jangle of the bell. He looks up to see the young woman with the long auburn hair enter quickly and take a seat at a table on the other side of the room. She does not appear even to have noticed him. Within moments, the interior door opens.

"Just a coffee, Nel, if you would," the seated girl calls out.

No other word is spoken, and from his seat Jamie looks cautiously again at the occupied table. The young woman has taken a magazine of some sort from the bag she is carrying, and is reading. He is able to risk a longer look at her. She is too far away for him to be certain, but he thinks the skin over her pale features is scattered with freckles.

The door opens again, and the woman he now knows is Nel brings a tray in and deposits its contents at the girl's table. There is a low exchange of words between them, but he cannot make out any of it. As he watches, as surreptitiously as possible, the girl lifts her head and glances towards him, then quickly away again. He can see no hint of interest in her features.

More words pass between the two, and he thinks he hears the woman, Nel, speak the words 'New Zealand'. The younger woman looks across at him again, this time giving him rather longer attention, and there seems to be more animation in her face.

The empty tray in hand, the woman crosses to him, smiling. "Come over and have a word," she says. "May I know your name, Mr…"

"Ashcott," he says. "Jamie Ashcott." He rises and follows her to the table where the girl remains seated. She gives him a brief smile.

"This is Mr Ashcott, Miss Withey. Now you just call out if you want anything else."

As the woman moves towards the back, the girl indicates a chair, and he sits down.

"Jamie," he says as he seats himself.

"And my name is Rowena, Mr Ashcott, Rowena Withey. Nel is nothing if not formal, and that is not a bad thing, perhaps," she says. "So you're from New Zealand. We have a distant connection with New Zealand, though I've never been there."

"Oh yes? And I have a sort of connection with your home." He is made more nervous still by the sound of her voice. Clipped vowels, not a trace of Welsh accent. Very English. Very posh.

"So Nel tells me. Some connection with the family that once lived there."

She seems more reluctantly polite than interested. Almost dismissive. "Yes, my maternal grandmother was born a Gerold. I was hoping…"

"I'm afraid I can't invite you to look around Tan-y-bwlch. We're in the middle of major renovations inside the house." To his ears, it sounds as though she has said 'hise' rather than 'house'. "But I was interested to hear you are from New Zealand. I recall my father telling me that his grand-father spent some time in New Zealand when he was young. I can't remember the details. Something about living under a volcano. I think I was rather excited by that description."

Her skin is very pale, but healthy-looking and without make-up. Her fingers are long, the nails well-manicured. There is indeed a scattering of freckles over both her face and her hands. He is strangely glad of them. Without them, she would have been altogether too formidable.

"Then it's likely to have been in the North Island. Taranaki, perhaps." He knows he is doing what he has found himself quite frequently doing since he arrived in Britain – speaking with greater care, rounding his vowels in a semi-conscious effort to seem less… colonial.

"That sounds vaguely familiar. Are you from there?"

"My mother was."

"And are you here for long? In Wales, I mean."

"No, unfortunately." He is distracted by her eyes. Their predominant colour seems to be a turquoise green, with flecks of gold. "I'm glad I got to see the old place, at least. I've been carrying around a very old and faded photograph of it. It was covered in ivy, then, whenever it was taken."

"Was it? May I see it?"

He takes the photograph from his jacket pocket and hands it to her. She examines it closely. "Yes, it's certainly Tan-y-bwlch. It looks rather gloomy, doesn't it? Mind you, it's not all that light and airy now. That's why my father has ordered the renovations. I liked it well enough as it was, though. It's where I grew up."

"That must have been… I don't know. Rather special? To run around as a child in a place that size. What was it like?"

As he looks, waiting for a response, he sees a subtle alteration in her features, like the drawing of a blind. She hands him back the photograph, not even looking at him.

"Well of course, I didn't think of it as being anything special," she says, more than a touch of frost in her voice. He has presumed too much, he realises. He has become too personal. It is a mistake he has made before, with one or two others he has talked with. With Anders' Kate, for instance. But that was in England.

She doesn't offer any further comment, or ask any further questions. Her attention is removed from him. It is no more than a tiny change in her demeanour, but it is enough. He attempts another line of conversation, but to no avail. Her answers are abrupt, offhand. Whatever little interest she had in conversing has evaporated. He takes one last look at her face, noting the inner arrogance, the knowledge and acceptance of her superior position. She would be younger than him by a few years, he now realises. Around twenty or twenty-one. Twenty-one, going on forty-one.

He thanks her and rises; and as he does so he senses a kind of bereavement, a tug of yearning. She is certainly beautiful, and he has no further chance of ever knowing her. It is not possible, yet how fascinating it would be to be in a position to do so. To have her respect. To have her confidence. To be one of her kind.

Yet… no, no. Not that. Never that. Even to have the thought momentarily in his mind seems like a betrayal of the better side of him. The Adelaide Gilbard side of him.

He pays his bill, and as he does so the woman, Nel, slips a piece of paper into his hand. She comes to the door with him, showing him out. "You didn't have much luck with Miss Withey, then?" she asks him, in a voice so low almost to have been a whisper. "They are like that, the Witheys. Her father's even worse, surly beggar. But the name and phone number of someone who might be able to tell you something about the house is on that piece of paper I gave you. I'm very interested in local history, you see, and I went to a talk he gave once. Very knowledgeable about the old families all around here, he is. I found his number in the book easily enough, and he's not so very far away. Near Criccieth. You're staying in Llanfair, you said? You give him a call."

He nods, truly touched by her concern. "Thank you very much, Mrs…"

"Just call me Nel. Everyone knows me as Nel."

"Thank you, Nel. You've been very kind."

"Well, I'm a true Welshwoman, aren't I?" She laughs, gently. "Not like some I could mention."

IV

The next afternoon Jamie makes his way to the house near Criccieth, following the directions he had been given over the phone. It is a small way out of the built up area, on a road that leads inland from the town centre. The man's description of the entrance to the house, which included the information that he would see a coat of arms and a brass plaque reading 'Hafod Penrhyn' attached to the gate that would be left open for him, means that he has no doubt as to his having reached the right place.

"Hello!" The greeting comes as soon as the door is opened to him. "You must be James Ashcott. How very nice to meet you! I'm Maurice. Maurice Wynne. Please do come in."

The balding, slim and elegantly groomed man pronounces his name in the French fashion, and Jamie remembers with a tremor of embarrassment that he had mispronounced it when he had made his call the previous evening. Still, he hadn't then been corrected. No doubt it is something that happens quite often.

He follows him into the house, through a short hallway and into a sitting room furnished with four armchairs upholstered in leather, and a scattering of small side tables. He notices also a large cabinet filled with display objects, and ceiling-high bookcases against the far wall. On the near walls are hung various framed documents, and over the fireplace is a large portrait in oils of a prosperous looking gentleman in a powdered wig and a many-buttoned coat.

"Please," the man says. "Do take a seat. How wonderful that you should come here to learn about your ancestors. Your mother's ancestors, I think you said?"

"Yes. Well, rather my mother's maternal grandfather, whose name was Tomas Gerold."

"Yes, yes. The Gerolds. I was quite thrilled to hear you say the name, because it means that we are connected, you and I. Not directly, alas, but through marriage. I can explain it all. After you rang last night, I consulted some of my books and papers. Sit! Please, do sit!"

Jamie does so, and the man continues: "I don't drink tea, or I would offer you one. Would you like a sherry? Or is it perhaps a little too early in the day?"

"Nothing for me, thank you," Jamie says.

"Well now, if you're sure."

"Thank you."

"Then let me explain the connection. The sister, the twin sister, as it happens, of my paternal great-grandfather – whose name was Wynne, of course, Harold Wynne – married a Gerold of Tan-y-bwlch."

"I see." He is a little bewildered. Apart from the last reference, the names mean nothing to him.

"So tell me... are you able to tell me? How are you connected to that Gerold of Tan-y-Bwlch? You must, of course, be connected in some way."

"All I know for certain is that my mother's mother was a Gerold, and that her father's name was Tomas. It seems likely that he was connected in some way to... whoever lived at Tan-y-Bwlch."

"That would seem very likely. It should be easy enough to verify. The necessary detail is probably in a rather rare old printed genealogy I happen to have." He crosses to one of the bookcases and selects a very slim volume. He quickly finds a particular place, and brings the book over to Jamie. "Here," he says. "Three sons are listed here, with their birth dates. We have here David William, now he was the husband of my own ancestor's sister. And he is listed as the second son. Born in 1831. The eldest is named as Osborn Fitzroy, born in 1827. Then there is Tomas Llewelyn, born 1836."

"That must be him," Jamie says. "My ancestor." To see his name on the printed paper, to see him confirmed as connected with the house, is strangely comforting.

"Indeed it must. And you'll see next to their names, the names of their spouses. Osborn's is given simply as Francesca Bodell. No marriage date listed. That's odd. Then we can see the name of Marion Wynne as the woman David married in… 1859. And Tomas – it appears his wife's name was Adelaide Augusta Gilbard. Married in 1860. Does that name ring a bell?"

"It certainly does," he says. He is both excited and relieved. That much, at least, is verified. "Though I've only quite recently learned of her. I have a kind of diary that she kept. But… apart from that, there is no family tradition concerning her at all. I would really like to know more about her. Where she was from, and so on. I'm fairly sure she was English."

"I see. Well, Gilbard is certainly not a Welsh name. Rather more Norman English, I should say. Now, let me see. This genealogy was printed in…" He turns to the front of the book. "Yes, 1861. There's no further information concerning her here. But she and Tomas must have had at least that one child, or you wouldn't be here talking with me now, would you!"

"Very true," he smiles. "You wouldn't have any suggestions as to how I might find out where she was from? Where they might have been married?"

"Well, there would be records, of course. Somewhere. A professional could well find them for you, but it would take time, and… money, of course. But I can tell you a little more about the Gerolds."

He is disappointed, but at least it might be possible to discover something eventually. "Yes, anything you can tell me. I'd be very grateful."

"Your connection to the Gerolds is through the distaff line, of course. Not that that weakens anything, except possibly in a legal sense – and not even that these days. Though I must say that I have deep pride in carrying the name of Wynne. Descent through the male line carries that privilege. And it means I have the right to the Wynne crest – you may have noticed it at the entrance?"

"I did."

"I have another copy on the wall there. The colours are truer on that one," he indicates; then he shakes his head. "But I mustn't go on about it. It is the Gerolds of Tan-y-bwlch you wish to learn about."

Jamie is intrigued by the way the man uses his hands to emphasise his speech – very expressively – and they are delicate-seeming and very white. "Yes."

"Well now – the house itself – you have seen it, you tell me. A fine old pile – rather older and grander than the Wynne house of Penrhyn, I must say. Though that has a certain Georgian charm. We are fortunate that both houses still stand, though neither is now home to any of the original family. In fact, by strange chance, both houses are now owned by branches of the same family – one that is not connected in any way with either the Wynnes or the Gerolds."

"Withey?" Jamie ventures.

"Ah! So you have discovered that."

"By chance, I briefly met a young Miss Withey who lives at Tan-y-bwlch. Of course I didn't know…"

"That the Witheys are the owners of *my* own ancestral house, too? Of course you wouldn't have known. But yes. My father's father was a… a speculating man, and not a successful one, unfortunately, and lost most of his estate through his debts. The house and much of the land was sold late last century to a man called Withey. New money. A nobody, really – at least, not in terms of a family. Very probably not even Welsh."

"And Tan-y-bwlch as well?"

"Oh, that was much later. Just after the late War. I remember when it happened. The Gerolds of Tan-y-bwlch had no male heir, just two daughters, I think, who had married and made their lives in England. Their father, the last of that line to bear the name of Gerold – though there is another line further south, somewhere near Machynlleth, I believe – their father was left alone and ill. I remember reading his obituary. It can't have been very long after he sold the house."

"To the Witheys."

"Yes. The older of the two Withey brothers moved his family into Tan-y-bwlch. The other stayed at Penrhyn. Where they still are, eighty years on. And since the War, Tan-y-bwlch has been theirs as well."

The bitterness in his voice is unmistakeable.

"And the Witheys themselves?" A picture of the rather beautiful, if remote, Rowena comes unbidden to his mind. "You know nothing about them?"

"Well, no. They don't interest me as I have no blood connection at all. But they are a very… a very *obvious* family around this part of North Wales. Everything and anything to do with the business of agriculture. Some sort of corporation. Not just land, but contracting and carrying. Their lorries are everywhere."

He is shaking his head again, his lips pursed; then he resumes: "I hear they are ripping the insides out of Tan-y-bwlch in the name of what is called modernisation. They have no respect, these people. They don't even think about the history that is being lost. It is as though they want to destroy any last link with the families who built those magnificent structures. They did the same with Penrhyn."

Jamie is surprised further by the intensity of the man's words and the way they are delivered. There is no doubting the fervour of his feelings. At the end of nearly every sentence he leans back again in his chair, as if inviting a response, but almost immediately begins with another, as though he is unable to contain the pent-up thoughts inside.

"All we can do is salvage what we can from the philistinism of such people. We must cling to those relics that are left to us. Those things that prove our connections. Our private, our personal heritage, you might call it." His hands indicate the walls around them. "As you can see, I have surrounded myself with all the evidence I can muster. I am the last of the Wynnes of Penrhyn. These things are my comfort, my sole comfort. I *am* what you see here."

"It's impressive, all this material," Jamie says. He is more than a little embarrassed by the man's confessions. "These… mementos."

"Yes, yes, but they are much more than mementos. They are *evidence*, are they not? They are defining. They are the sort of proofs that have brought you from the other side of the world. Proofs of the… the *meaningfulness* of the past. Proofs of the connections that distinguish me, that distinguish you, from the ordinary run of mortals. From the Witheys of this world."

The flow of words does stop this time; and in the silence, Maurice Wynne rises to his feet and crosses the room to touch a large photograph that hangs on the wall. It is clearly an enlargement of an old print, brownish and slightly faded. "Take this, for example," he says.

Jamie rises too, and stands beside his host. He is happy to have the diatribe end, especially as he finds he has little sympathy with the sentiments expressed.

Together they look at the figures depicted. There is an amply proportioned man with a look of smug satisfaction on his kindly and somehow child-like face. Beside him is a tiny and very pretty woman, her head no higher than his shoulder. She is leaning towards him, coquettishly. Between them there stands a small child, a boy, who is smiling at the camera placidly. All three are dressed in a fashion that Jamie recognises as mid-Victorian.

"That little boy there is my grandfather," Maurice Wynne murmurs. "I have no personal recollection of him. Though I was alive when he died, I was little more than a baby. He is, of course, the man who lost our estate. But my father always talked of him in positive terms. It was a weakness in him, he would tell me, but his intentions were always for the best. Yes," he continues reflectively, "my grandfather and my great-grandfather. So much alike, are they not? The older, a most impressive man, the younger promising the same. Harold Wynne and his son Harold Junior. I sometimes wish that I had been named Harold."

Jamie has not been listening very attentively. Instead, his eye and mind have been attracted to the woman in the photograph. "She was an extraordinarily pretty woman, your great-grandmother," he says. "It's astonishing how even a posed photograph like this can bring some subjects almost… back to life." He would have liked to say how her sensuality and her femininity made it seem to him almost as if she was in the room with them; how he rather wished she was. But he thinks such an observation might well offend. Instead he contents himself with asking: "What was her Christian name, do you know?"

"Oh yes, indeed I do. She is Jane. Her maiden name was Butterworth. She was English, but with Welsh connections. Her sister also married a Welshman, though not one so well connected as Harold Wynne of Penrhyn. Not one with any connections worth tracing."

V

The journey into Wales has not answered many of Jamie's questions, and has advanced him little towards finding out more about Adelaide; other, that is, than the discovery of the year of her marriage. That could well prove to be decisively useful, he hopes. At least it will be something to pass on to Tela.

He is glad he has made the journey, despite its limited usefulness. It has given him a sense of other parts of his personal history that he feels has made it all worthwhile. He has seen his great-grandfather's ancestral home. The connection, he now knows, is real. And the little he has learned about the family at least makes him feel somewhat less poorly of them. Not less poorly of Tomas Gerold himself, but of the Gerolds. They might even have been relatively well thought of. But none of this alters his distaste for the youngest brother. For Tomas. Adelaide's husband.

Maurice Wynne's ranting against the Witheys also stays in his mind. It both repels and amuses him, the manifest fury that the name of Withey clearly evoked in the man. It is the explicit elitist judgement that he finds hardest to forgive. But his clinging to the supposed glories of the past had also made the man seem laughable. He supposes it is rather cruel of him to have found it amusing, especially when he, like Maurice, is also repelled by the reputed actions of 'The Witheys of this world' as he'd called them. The grasping newcomers. The hungry capitalists. But he certainly cannot help reflecting that the Gerolds, and probably the Wynnes, too, in their turn, would in all probability have once been precisely the same kind of aggrandizing upstarts. Ever since reading Adelaide's Journal, he has discovered that he has little sympathy with either new wealth or old – though he has himself been guilty of envy, he remembers. But that is behind him. That was the product of self-pity, before he had started to really think about such things.

It all, all of it, makes him even more determined to discover as much as he can about Adelaide Gilbard. He clings to the idea of her. He wants to fully acknowledge his connection to her, to know as much as he can about her. She alone, it seems to him, is an ancestor he can unreservedly admire.

Back in Cambridge, he stays one more night with Anders, but it is Tela he most wants to see again; and he senses an undercurrent, a hum of excitement at the thought of doing so that arises not simply because of their shared interest in Adelaide Gilbard, or because they are, by now, old friends. Proper friends. This is something else. Something he cannot yet quite comprehend.

The following morning he phones her, and they arrange to meet for a final time before he returns to London, and thence to New Zealand. The thought of her has been dominant in his mind now for days. He is not at all sure why it should be so, but he knows it has little if anything to do with his recent discoveries; about his meetings with Maurice Wynne and Rowena Withey. Yet it must surely, he thinks, be attributable in some way to her connection to those old Gilbards – to Adelaide, and her as yet unknown family.

But it also, he now realises, has to do with Tela herself; with her manifest joy for life, her appealing combination of enthusiasm and calm confidence. Possibly, also, with the combination of comfortable familiarity and exotic difference. With, he supposes, Tela Gilbard, the flesh and blood girl. The flesh and blood woman.

So eager is he to see her again that he arrives early at their agreed meeting place, and waits impatiently, gazing in the direction he knows she will come. Then he sees her, jacketed, stockinged, carrying a bag over her shoulder; and she sees him seeking her out, and waves, increasing her pace towards him. And he moves, too, not willing to wait further.

It is a cool Cambridgeshire day, with a chilling wind from the east. It is straight off the Russian steppes, Tela tells him. They are much more comfortable after they have taken their seats in the tea rooms. Their talk is easy, and enjoyable, too. He tells her all of the limited successes he has had. She agrees with him that the date of Adelaide's marriage could prove to be very useful, and seems quite confident that, given time, she will be able to find out where she was from. And from that point, she says… well, there could be all kinds of other sources of information available.

He wants to tell her more, especially about how his discoveries have made him feel about her, about Tela herself; but he finds himself stupidly tongue-tied, unable to express what it is he feels. Still unsure *himself* what he feels. Instead, he relates some of his recent experiences in greater detail. She listens intently, questioning him at times, clearly as intrigued yet as frustrated as he is himself at his lack of real progress in finding information about the Gilbards. About Adelaide.

Afterwards, having exhausted their speculations and their immediate hopes regarding that topic, they wander along King's Parade and through the Senate House passage to the Backs. Dull and grey the day might be, Jamie thinks, but there is something in the air that still makes him tingle with a kind of excitement, a kind of anticipation.

They stop in the middle of Clare Bridge, and stand side by side looking up river. The wind from the east is not so intrusive here, but there are few people about apart from a small group walking away from them across the Backs, and another group, further away, by the bank outside King's.

Tela's attention has been taken by something on the waters slipping beneath them, and Jamie takes the opportunity to look at her profile; and it is as though he is noticing her, truly noticing her, for the first time. He sees her lowered lashes against the warm brown of her cheeks; the delicate, perfectly shaped chin and the ever-so-slight pout of her lips; the unruly waves of dark walnut hair that lie on her shoulders. Her beauty, her physical appeal, becomes so obvious that it almost takes his breath away. Why has he not seen it before?

She seems to sense his attention and turns her face towards him, looks at him, looks into his eyes. Hers are, to him, full of intelligence and humour, brown and gold, impossibly deep. He feels drawn to them; feels, even that he is being drawn *in* to them.

Something is happening he does not understand, as though his physical balance, even the balance of his mind, has been disturbed; but it is not an unwelcome feeling. His heart is beating faster with the wonder of it. It is as though she has cast a spell on him, that he is being held in thrall; then her lips curve into a smile, a smile of such affection and gentleness and humour that all the slight unease vanishes.

"So… you're waking up, Jamie." Her eyes are still locked with his.

He knows what she means, he thinks he knows; then it doesn't matter at all if he does or not, because she leans into him, raises her face to him, and her lips are on his and he can feel her tongue, scent and taste the coffee of it as she tickles inside his mouth. Then she brings both her hands up, tracing his cheeks, his ears, his neck, gently, gently passing her fingers over his closed eyelids. He is aware in the most astonishing way that they have never touched before, not properly. Not skin to skin. Never. So much time wasted, so much time without the thrill of it, the rightness of it!

He puts both arms around her, drawing her close, then closer, crushing her against him. He can feel tears sting his eyes and a welling of inexpressible yearning again disorientates him. Holding her, holding her to steady himself, exhilarating in her, he has no intention other than to be as one with her. As one.

She pulls away slightly and takes his willing hand, drawing it to her chest. "I know," she murmurs. "Me, too."

Beneath the softness of the wool he feels the thump of her heart, the gentle swell of her breast. He can feel, too, the harder nub of a nipple tickling his palm. "Can't you tell?" she says.

Then she separates herself from him, matter-of-fact. "But we both have things we must do first," she says. "I have an unfinished thesis, and tomorrow you must return to New Zealand and decide what it is you want to do with the rest of your life. And right now, I must spend some time in the University Library. Banal, but true."

He doesn't want her to go. It is the very last thing he wishes, and she knows it. It is why she sets off in the direction of the Library immediately, leaving him standing there. After a few paces, though, she gives a little skip, then turns to face him. Her voice full of elation, she calls out to him:

"I *will* be back, Jamie Ashcott. You can wait for me… if you want."

If he wants? He watches as she moves further away, watches her black-stockinged legs beneath her slightly swaying, plaid-covered hips, one arm shielding the bag that is slung over her shoulder. No, she is not a witch. There is no artifice in her. None at all. There is just her, her, her. There is nothing else. She is everything.

Does he want? There is nothing in the world he has ever, ever wanted so much.

Epilogue – From the Journal of Adelaide Gilbard

3 May 1884

It is time for an accounting. No, I cannot truly accept that God is forcing me to this. I am not even certain of His existence. What I do find, however, is that arising within me is an undeniable urge to examine closely my own prejudices.

Hannah has frequently reminded me that she is, according to the Maori system of reckoning these matters, a person of low birth. Her mother was, to use the Maori term, a <u>taurekareka</u> – a serf, or slave. Because her father was a free man, a <u>ware</u>, she was herself born free, but of low status. She is, I suppose, the equivalent in Maori society to those of the lowest sort in English society – the sort of person I have always, despite my intellectual attempts to do otherwise, instinctively held in low regard.

It is true that Hannah is sometimes coarse in her manner of speaking, yet I very quickly came to accept this in her, and even to enjoy – it is not too strong a word – the colourful earthiness of her words. Yet if I experience the same sort of speech amongst people of my own kind, I still flinch from it. I judge them harshly. I set myself above, and apart. Is it a matter of expectations? Is it that I am shamed by association – that I can tolerate, and even enjoy, behaviour in certain people and not in others, because of the expectations I have that are based on their race? If so, then I am indeed shamed. Yet I fear I will go to my grave with my prejudice, my instinctive abhorrence, of the vulgar, unthinking and ill-mannered habits of many of the commonalty among my own kind. Yet… not only amongst the commonalty, and far from always even there. I know that. I have experienced many instances where the so-called low-born have shown me, and others, a nobility that has very often been entirely absent from their presumed betters.

What, then, makes a person 'gentle' – a gentlewoman, or a gentleman? I know I would call Hannah a 'gentlewoman', without hesitation. She is honourable, she is loyal, she is thoughtful of others – all of those things that I place within my definition of 'gentle' behaviour. She is also unselfish – much more so than I. I know, also, that I could never accept that the basest of our white settlers could aspire to the term. Yet there have been those instances of nobility of action and thought amongst others of them that I have myself seen and experienced. So, with them, and with Hannah, in mind, I know that it is not simply because of their way of talking or the fortune or misfortune of their birth. It is much, much more. Yet in writing that I must, in honesty, also say that I still recoil when I do hear coarse speech, and in doing so, I know that I am displaying a lack of tolerance – and surely toleration should be another feature of 'gentle' behaviour.

What I am completely sure of is that the actions of those in charge of the troops and others who descended on the people of Parihaka were the very opposite of noble. They were shameful. They were coarse and ignoble. They are guilty of actions spurred entirely by greed and arrogance. I hope the rampant spirit of privilege and selfishness there displayed gives way to that which is surely also present here, amongst the gentler people of this land, whatever their origin – to compassion and caring, to a spirit of cooperation and equality. I know it is here. I have seen it myself, amongst both Maori and settler. I hope their time will come. I hope there is still time for the appropriate choices to be made.

But I should not preach. Especially as I have never myself taken much notice of preachers!

21 June 1884

I have not many more weeks left. I believe I have said most of what I would wish to say and that I have done, or recognise that I am now unable to do, all that I can do. I am not going to attempt a summary of my life – not beyond what is already in these many pages. There are signs that there will be more fierce struggles ahead for all the peoples of this land, but there are also happier possibilities. For instance, there is a woman in Christchurch, quite a young woman, whose efforts to get votes for women is gathering support from all quarters. She is also a leader in the Women's Christian Temperance Union – a cause that I believe is a worthy one, but one that I think is fated not to succeed. But I do believe that the women of New Zealand will quite soon have the right to vote; and surely, surely the world will be a better place for it!

But what does all of this mean? It cannot be any longer of any consequence to me, though it will be of consequence to my children. And after all, it is no longer being part of their world that is the hardest thing for me to accept.

Who are they, my children? Or – more consequential, surely – who will they become?

My son, my George – though his nature is not likely to ever lead him to greatness or leadership, he is a kind boy. He is good with his hands. He is shy and withdrawn in his manner. Awkward. Backward, even. It is rather a sad thing to see in a young man who should by now be taking a greater interest in people, especially in young women. Alas, I doubt he will ever marry.

And my daughters. Inez, like George, is a difficult one socially, though that is possibly owing to her partial deafness. She is a stubborn creature who worships her father. They make a pair, with their pride in themselves and their inability to accept – their determination not to accept – their own weaknesses. It is an odd thing to admit, but I sense that my elder daughter does not much like me. I hope that she loves me, as I love her – but that is not quite the same thing. She almost seems, at times, to resent that we are who we are to each other.

Then there is my youngest. Ellen. She is still just a little girl, only eight years old, but it is apparent already that although she is a bright and pretty little thing, she is not particularly clever. Not as clever as Inez, though she has a much sweeter nature. Will my blood continue? If it does, it will be through Ellen, I feel quite sure of that. Someone, some man, will love her. I hope it is someone worthy.

My children. O, my children!

Cambridge Backs (King's College and Clare)

Connections

(a) The featured descendants of the brothers George and Philip Gilbard of Gloucestershire:

	George Gilbard = Lydia		Philip Gilbard = Mary
1	Oliver Gilbard = ? (Fiji)	Adelaide = Tomas Gerold	Laura = Jem Watson*
2	George Gilbard = ?	Ellen = a Harborough	?(daughter) = Finlay
3	Oliver Gilbard = Kelera	Winifred = Ned Ashcott	Bob 'Buttercup' Finlay = Mrs Finlay
4	Tela Gilbard	Jamie Ashcott	Fiona Finlay

*An illicit liaison. The descendants are unaware of this connection. The daughter born to Laura was 'adopted' by the Finlays, a couple from the Scottish Highlands, and she married a Finlay cousin.

(b) The true, but unrevealed, genealogy of Rowena Withey, and of Geordie Hicks:

1	Tomas Gerold = Ursula Withey*	Samuel Hicks m (1) Ursula Withey then = (2) Branwen Watson
2	Daniel Hicks (later Withey) = ?	? Hicks = ?
3	? Withey = ?	?Hicks = ?
4	? Withey = ?	Geordie Hicks
5	Rowena Withey	

*An illicit liaison. The descendants are apparently unaware of the connection.

(c) And of Maurice Wynne:

<pre>
1   Harold Wynne of Penrhyn = Jane Wynne (nee Butterworth) = Horatio Ellis*
                                                 |
2   Harold Wynne Jr = ?
                                                 |
3   ? Wynne = ?
                                                 |
4   Maurice Wynne
</pre>

*An illicit liaison. The true nature of Harold Wynne Jr's paternity remained a secret. He was raised as a Wynne, and as Harold Sr's heir. See The Youngest Son.

The Main Players

Adelaide Gilbard was the writer of the Journal. She was the daughter of George and Lydia Gilbard, the sister of Oliver Gilbard, the niece of Dr Philip and Mary Gilbard, and cousin to their daughter, Laura. She married Tomas Gerold of Tan-y-bwlch, and they emigrated to New Zealand (see Merely a Girl). They had a son, George, and two daughters, Inez and Ellen.

Winifred Ashcott is the granddaughter of Adelaide Gilbard/Gerold, and the daughter of Ellen Harborough (born Gerold). She married Ned Ashcott, and Jamie Ashcott is their youngest child.

Tela Gilbard is the great-granddaughter of Oliver Gilbard, Adelaide Gilbard's brother, who came to Fiji as Secretary to a Stipendiary Magistrate, and married a Fijian woman. Her father, the original Oliver's grandson, is also called Oliver (Ollie) Gilbard.

Fiona Finlay is descended from Adelaide Gilbard's cousin, Laura, who, at the age of sixteen, was seduced by the next-door neighbour's gardener. The resulting daughter was immediately given to a couple from the Scottish Highlands, the Finlays, who accepted her as their own. They emigrated to New Zealand via Nova Scotia (see Merely a Girl). Their daughter later married a 'cousin', also a Finlay.

Rowena Withey is (like Jamie Ashcott) a descendant of Tomas Gerold, who had a secret and passionate affair with Ursula Withey, the daughter of the man who acted as Agent for the Gerold family's estates in Wales. Tomas deserted the pregnant Ursula, who fled to Liverpool where she married Samuel Hicks and gave birth to Tomas's son. She died on the voyage to New Zealand. (See The Youngest Son). The son, Daniel, was later brought back to Wales by Ursula's father, who treated him as his heir.